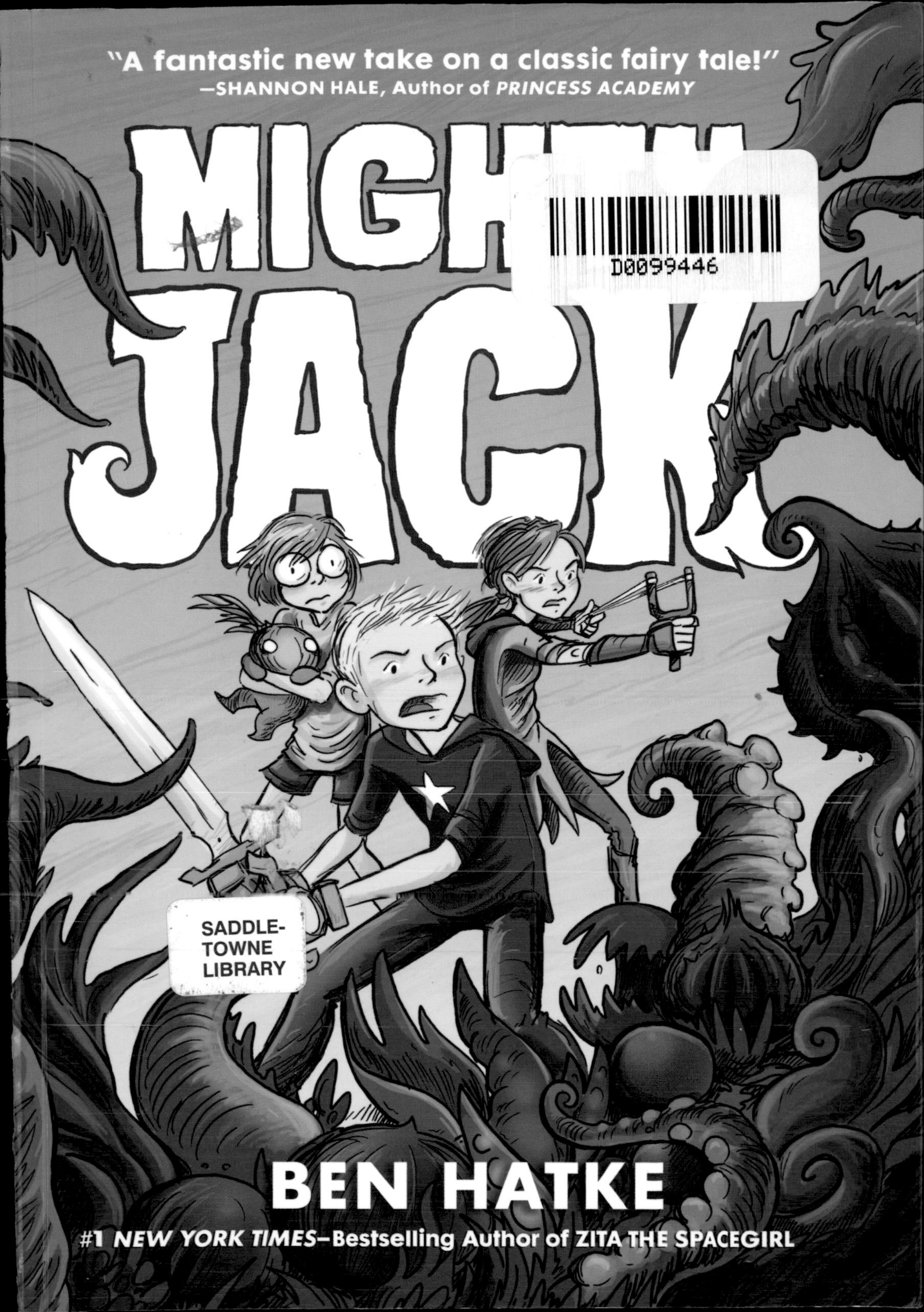
"A fantastic new take on a classic fairy tale!"
—SHANNON HALE, Author of *PRINCESS ACADEMY*
MIGH
JACK
BEN HATKE
#1 *NEW YORK TIMES*–Bestselling Author of ZITA THE SPACEGIRL

$14.99 US / $20.99 CAN

Jack might be the only kid in the world who is dreading the summer. But he's got a good reason: summer is when his single mom takes a second job and leaves him at home to watch his autistic kid sister, Maddy. It's a lot of responsibility, and it's boring, too, because Maddy doesn't talk. Ever. But then, one day at the flea market, Maddy *does* talk—and tells Jack to trade their mom's car for a box of mysterious seeds.

It's the best mistake Jack has ever made.

What starts as a normal garden behind the house quickly grows into a wild, magical jungle with tiny onion babies running amok, pink pumpkins that bite, and, on one moonlit night that changes everything . . . a dragon.

MIGHTY JACK

BOOK ONE

BEN HATKE

Color by Alex Campbell
and Hilary Sycamore

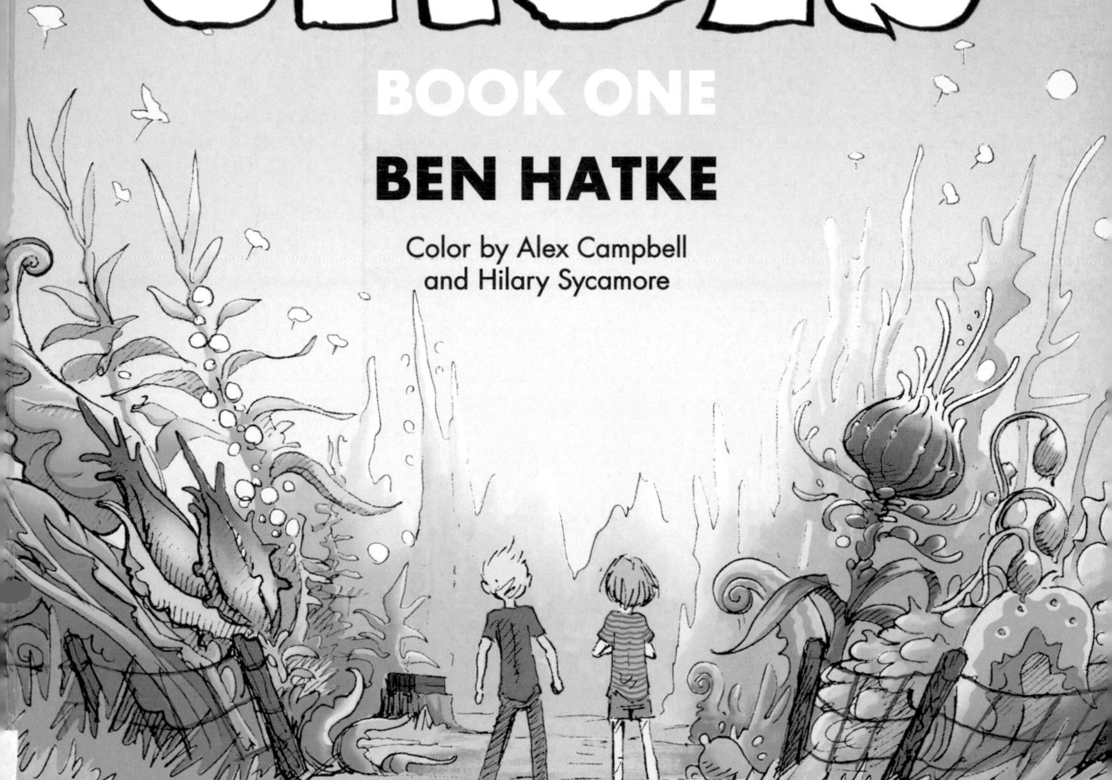

First Second
New York

This one's for my mom,
who taught me about the
magic of libraries

I started working on this story in 2006, so it's been a long road and there are plenty of people to thank.

First and foremost, great thanks and love go to my wife, Anna, who patiently listened to this story develop, and who believed in my voice. My gratitude also goes out to my friends who listened to me eagerly tell them early versions of this tale: Bill Powell, Andy O'Neill, Ryan Corrigan, Jaime Gorman, Regina Schmiedicke, Anna Formaggio, and Nick Marmalejo. To Sara Ricci, who listened to me tell this story in my terrible Italian and many other good people.

To the village of Gravagna Montale, where everyone was patient while I once again declined invitations to hike and instead drew all the pages of this book.

Huge thanks to my daughters, Angelica, Zita, Julia, Ronia, and Ida who all, individually and as a pack, keep me excited about my work. To Hilary Sycamore and Alex Campbell, my colorists for this book. This was my first time working with colorists for a whole book and you made it a pleasure.

And, of course, to the team at First Second: Mark, Gina, Danielle, and Joyana. And to Calista, editor and friend, who lets me ramble on at her about Marvel movies before we get to the good stuff. Big thanks to my agent, Judy Hansen, who works so tirelessly on my behalf. And special thanks to Kat Kopit, my very first editor, who is once again lending her sharp eyes to my stories. I'm ridiculously lucky to be surrounded by y'all.

“Pullin’ weeds and pickin’ stones,
Man is made of dreams and bones...”

—David Mallett,
from *The Garden Song*

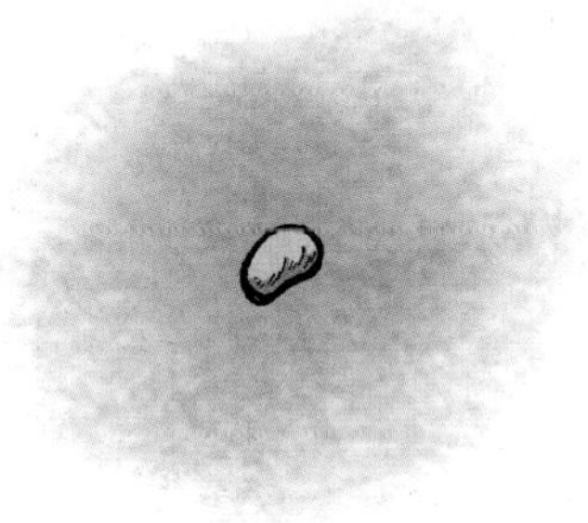

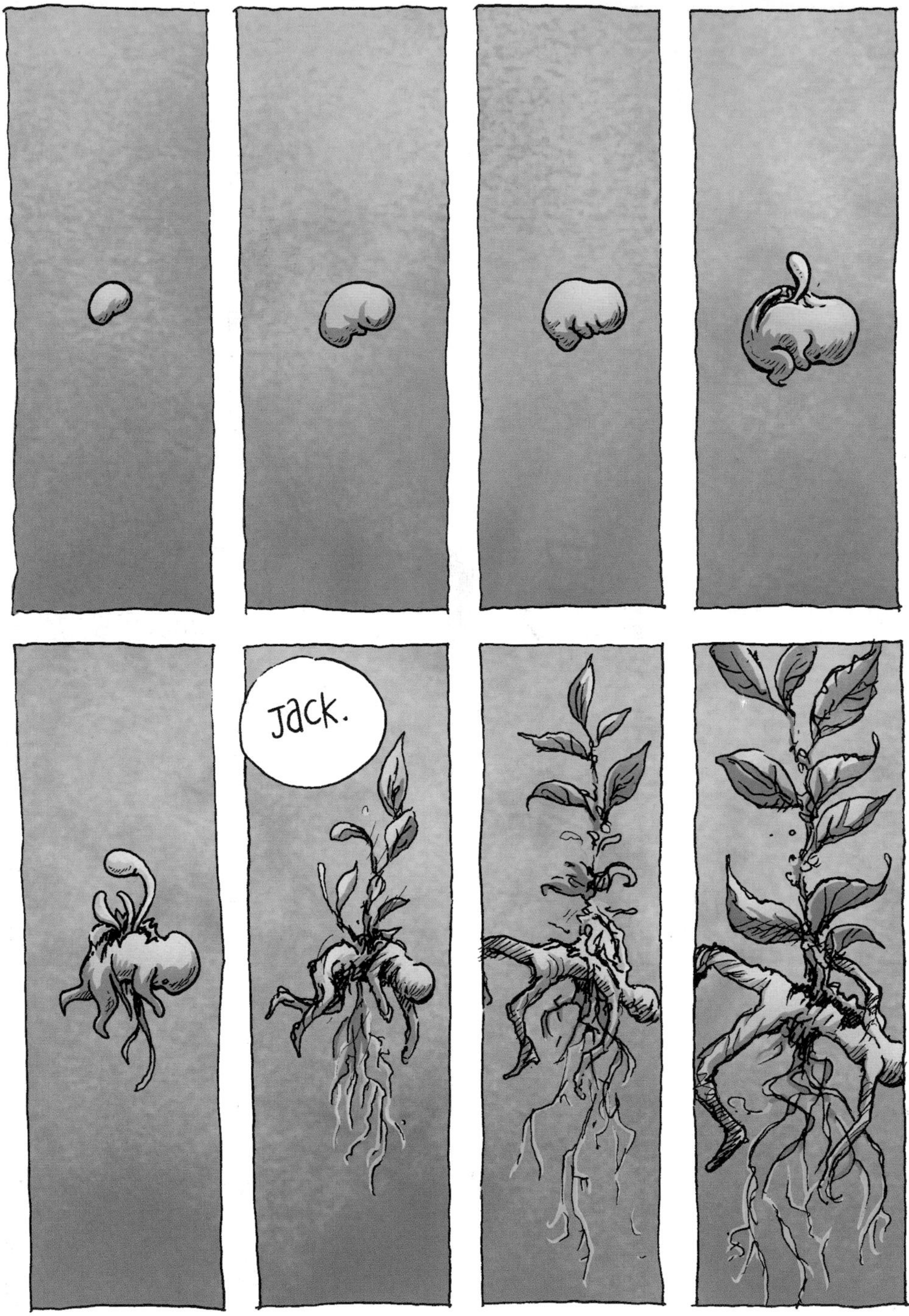
JACK.

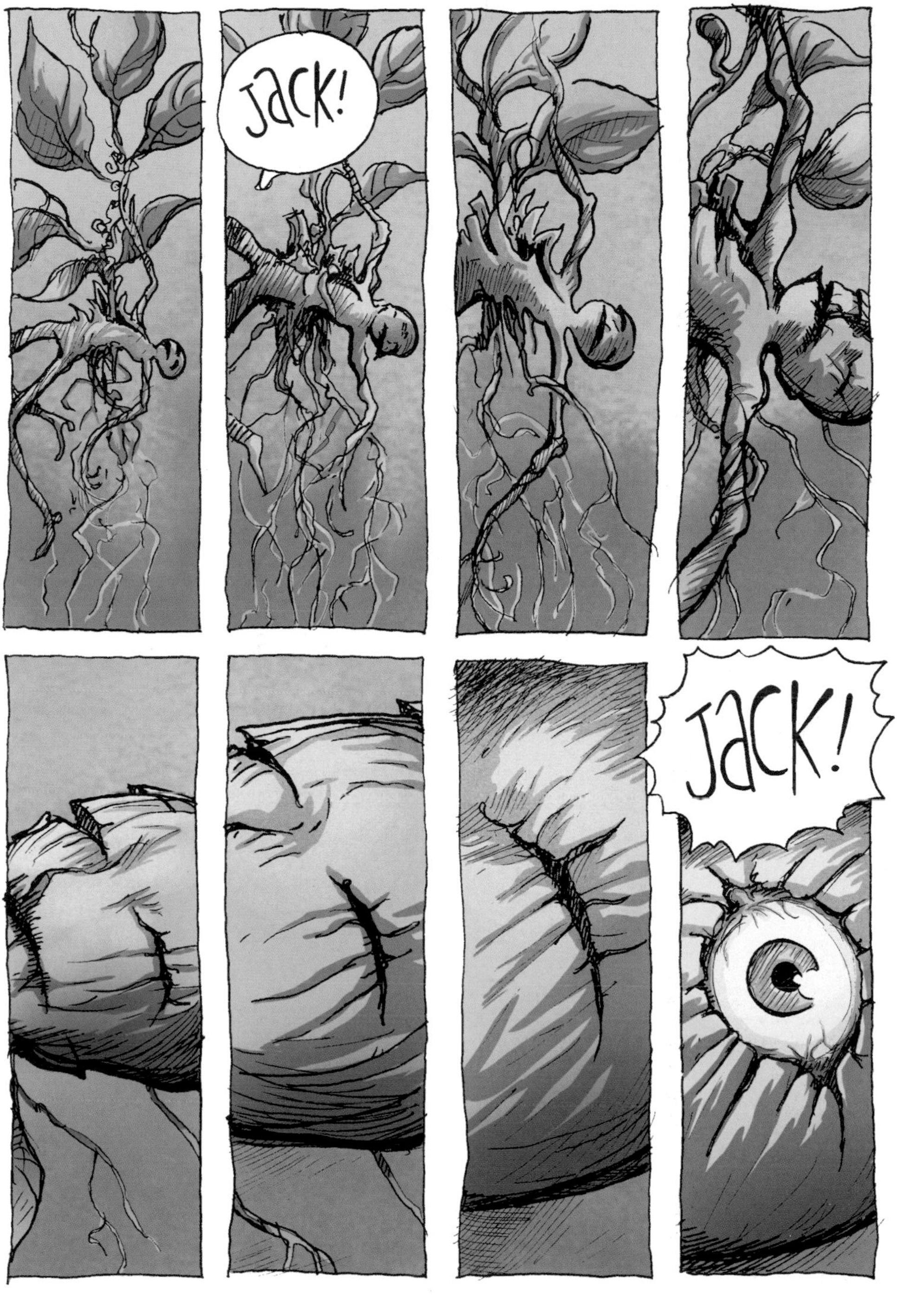
JACK!
JACK!

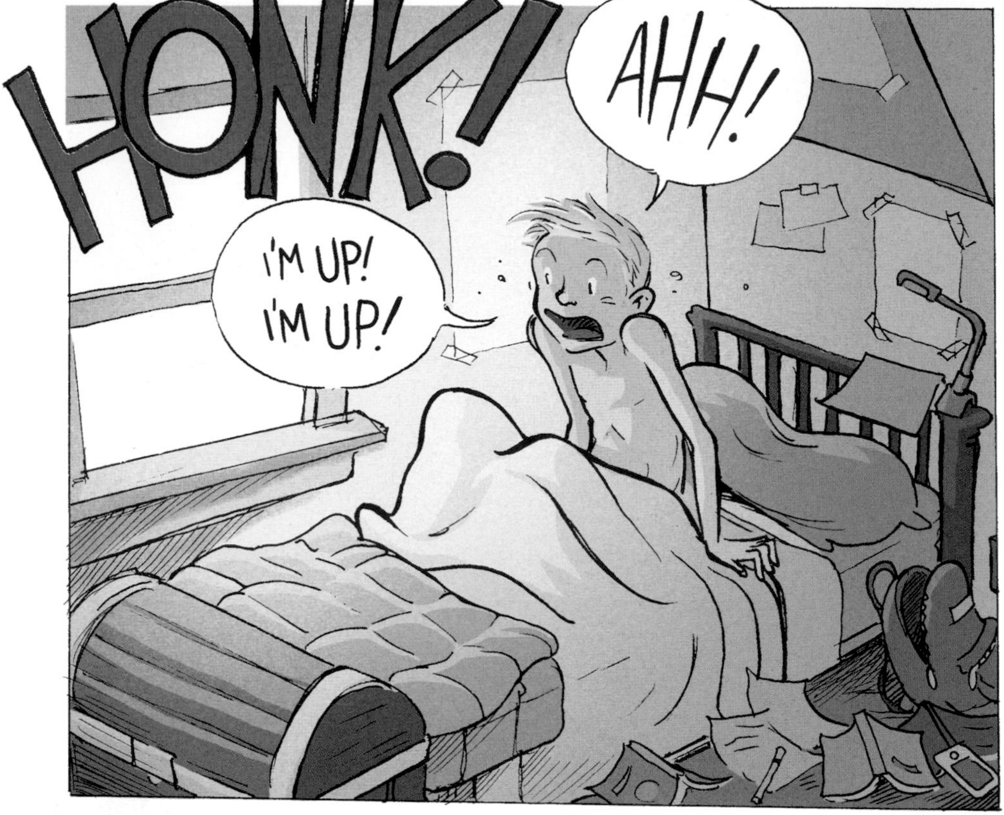
HONK!
AHH!
I'M UP! I'M UP!

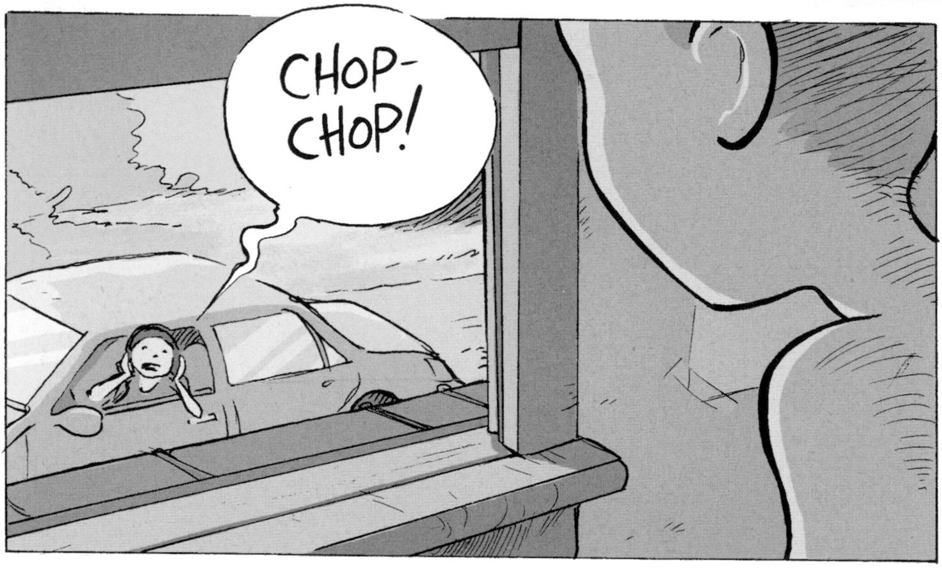
CHOP-CHOP!

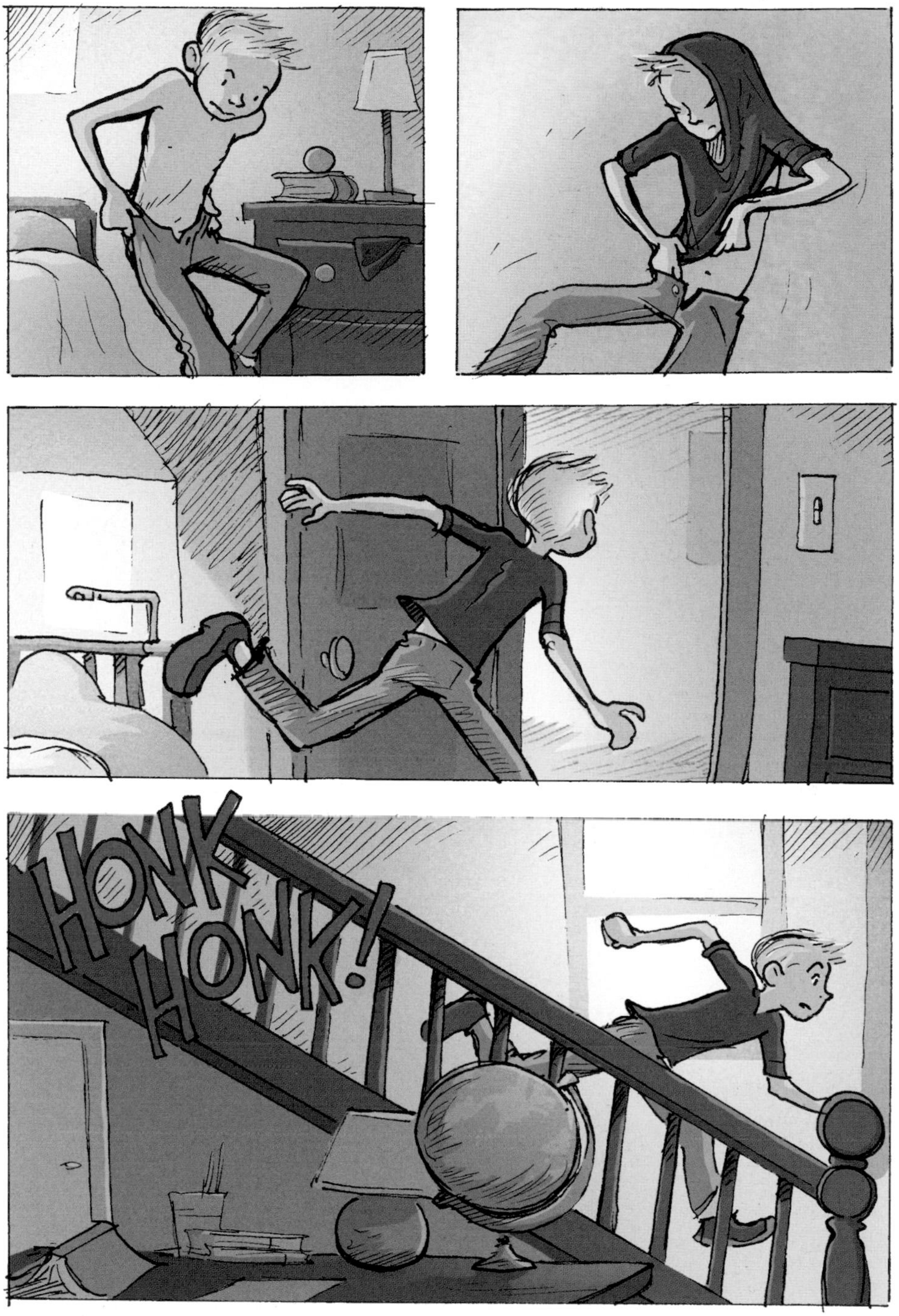
HONK HONK!

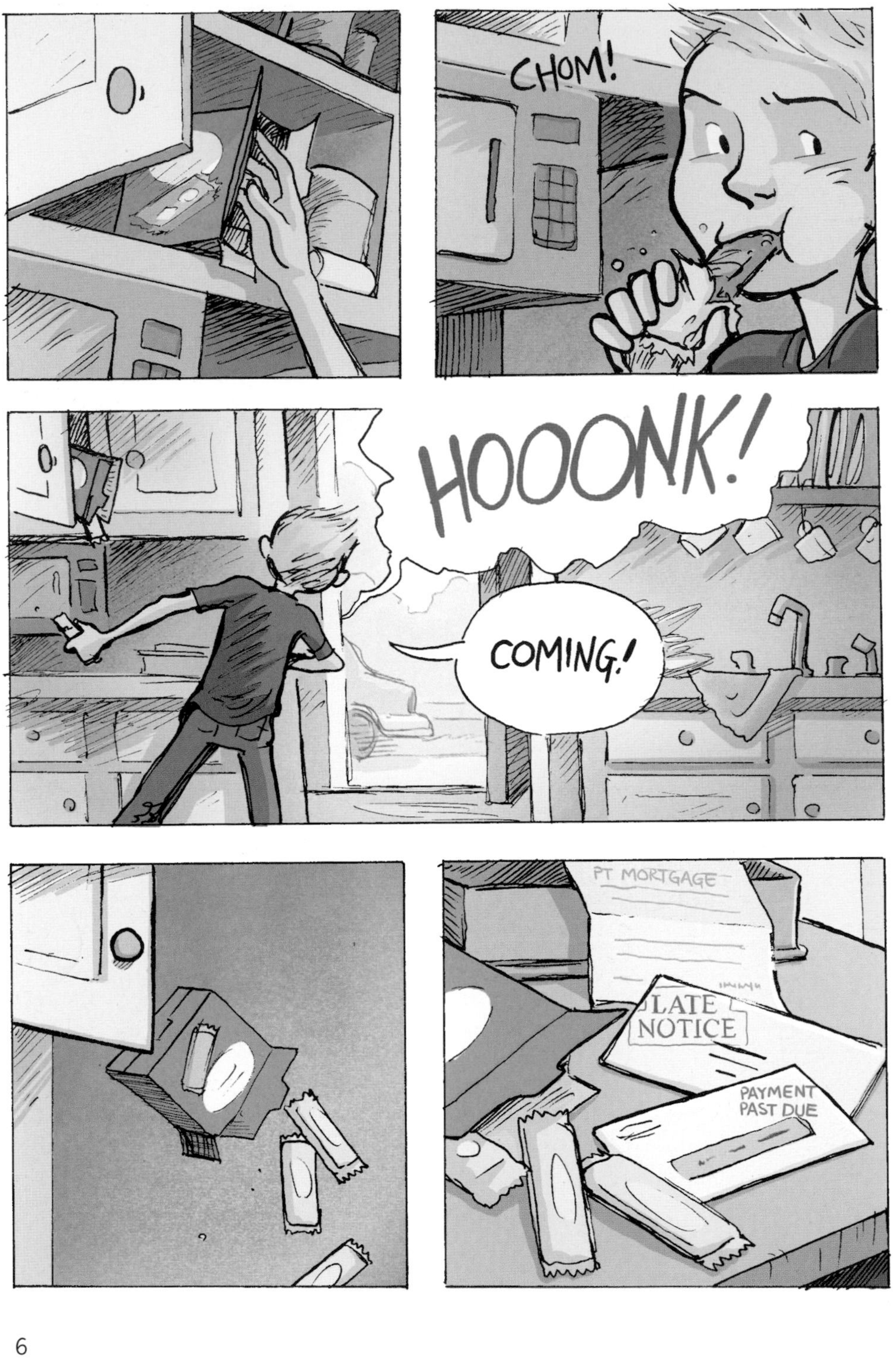
CHOM!
HOOONK!
COMING!
PT MORTGAGE
LATE NOTICE
PAYMENT PAST DUE

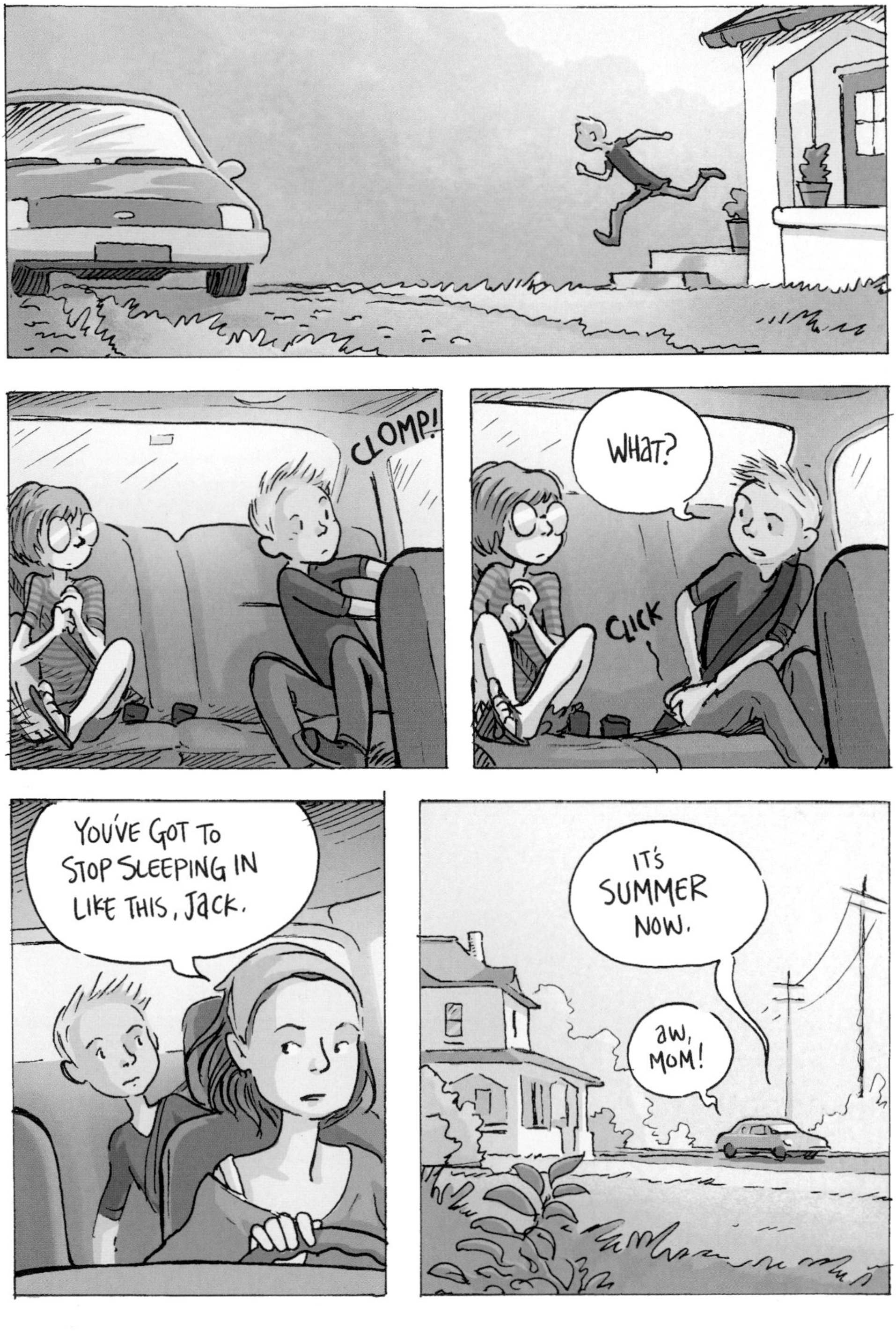
CLOMP!
WHAT?
CLICK
YOU'VE GOT TO STOP SLEEPING IN LIKE THIS, JACK.
IT'S SUMMER NOW.
AW, MOM!

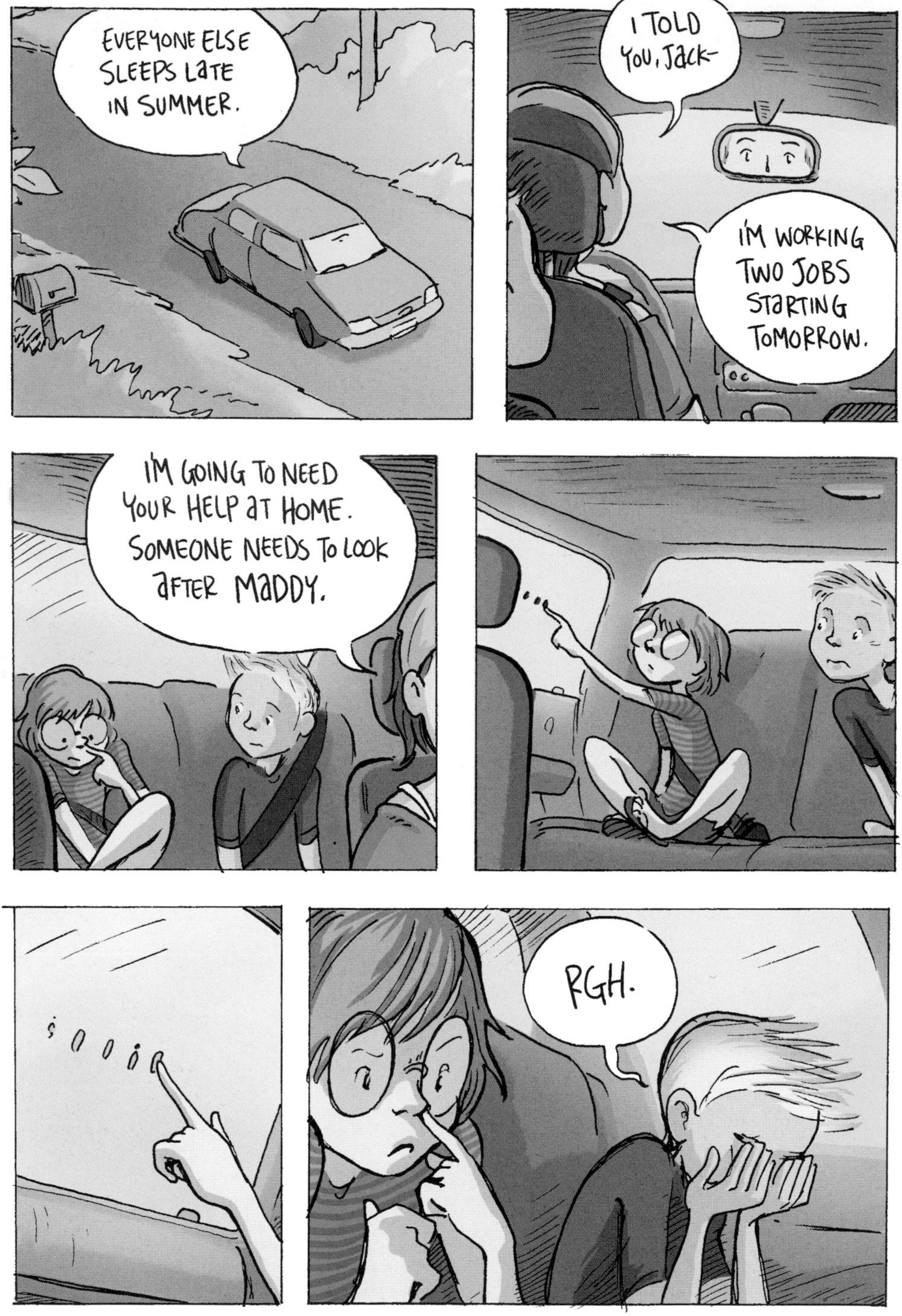
EVERYONE ELSE SLEEPS LATE IN SUMMER.
I TOLD YOU, JACK-
I'M WORKING TWO JOBS STARTING TOMORROW.
I'M GOING TO NEED YOUR HELP AT HOME. SOMEONE NEEDS TO LOOK AFTER MADDY.
RGH.

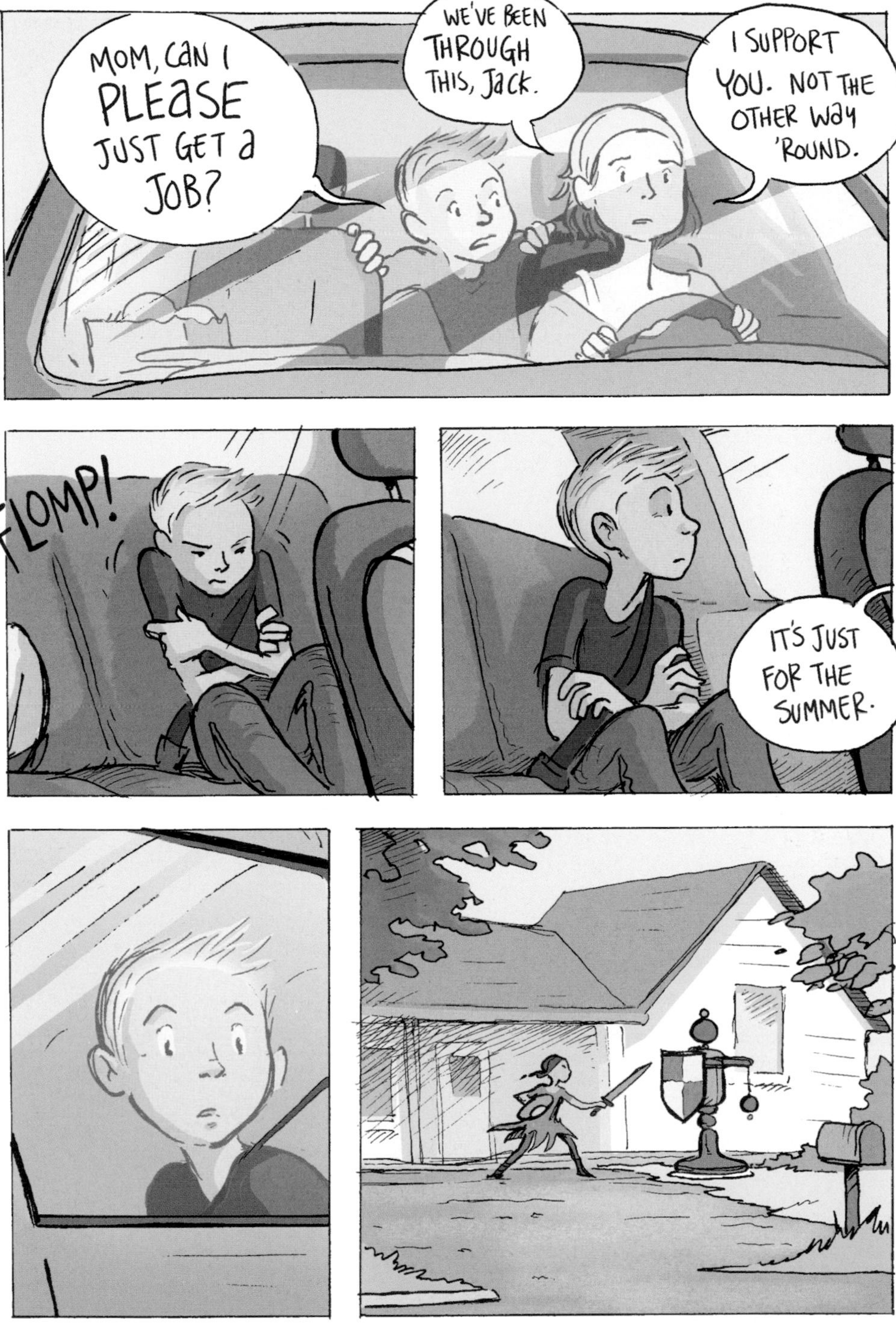
MOM, CAN I PLEASE JUST GET A JOB?
WE'VE BEEN THROUGH THIS, JACK.
I SUPPORT YOU. NOT THE OTHER WAY 'ROUND.
FLOMP!
IT'S JUST FOR THE SUMMER.

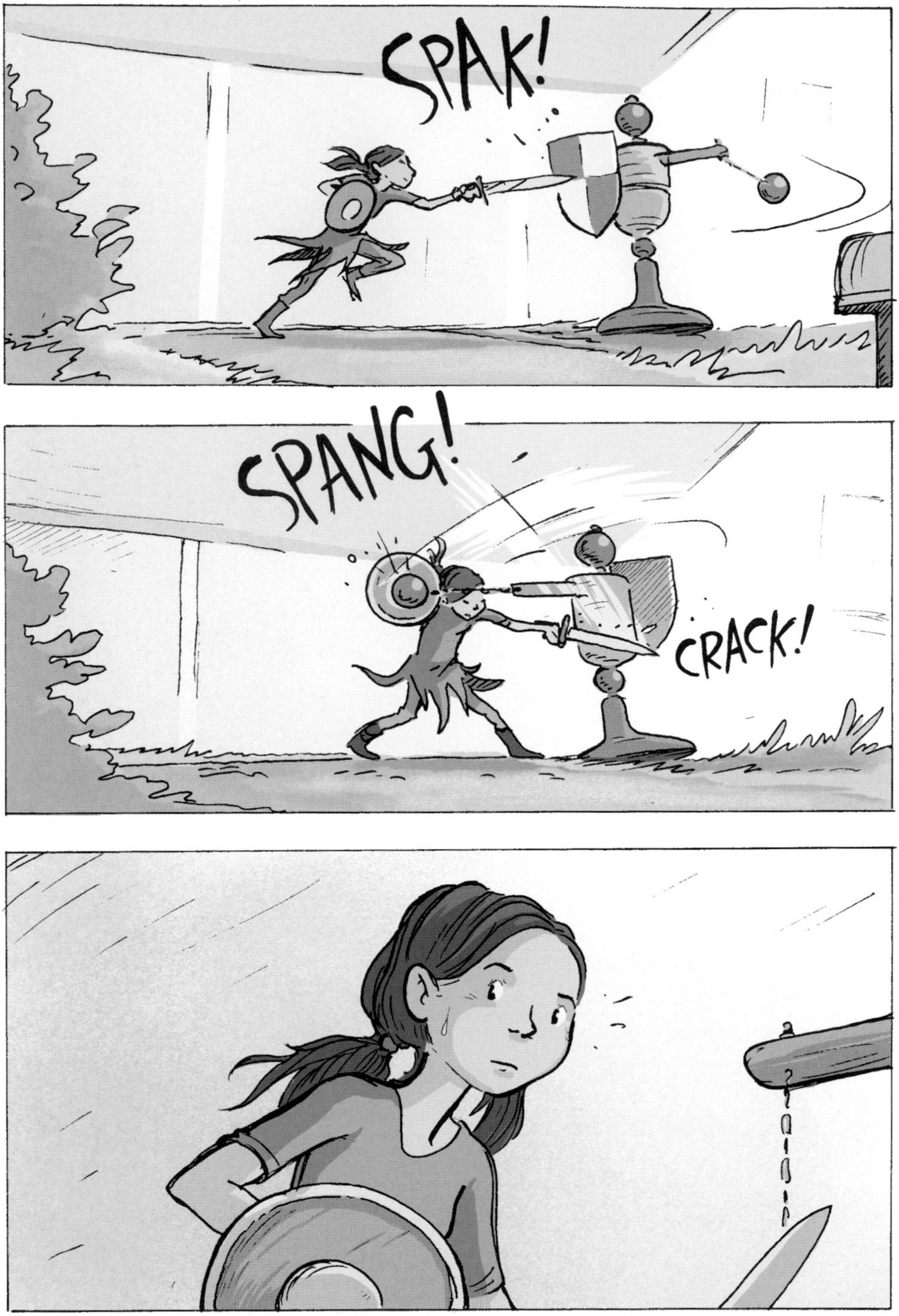
SPAK!
SPANG!
CRACK!

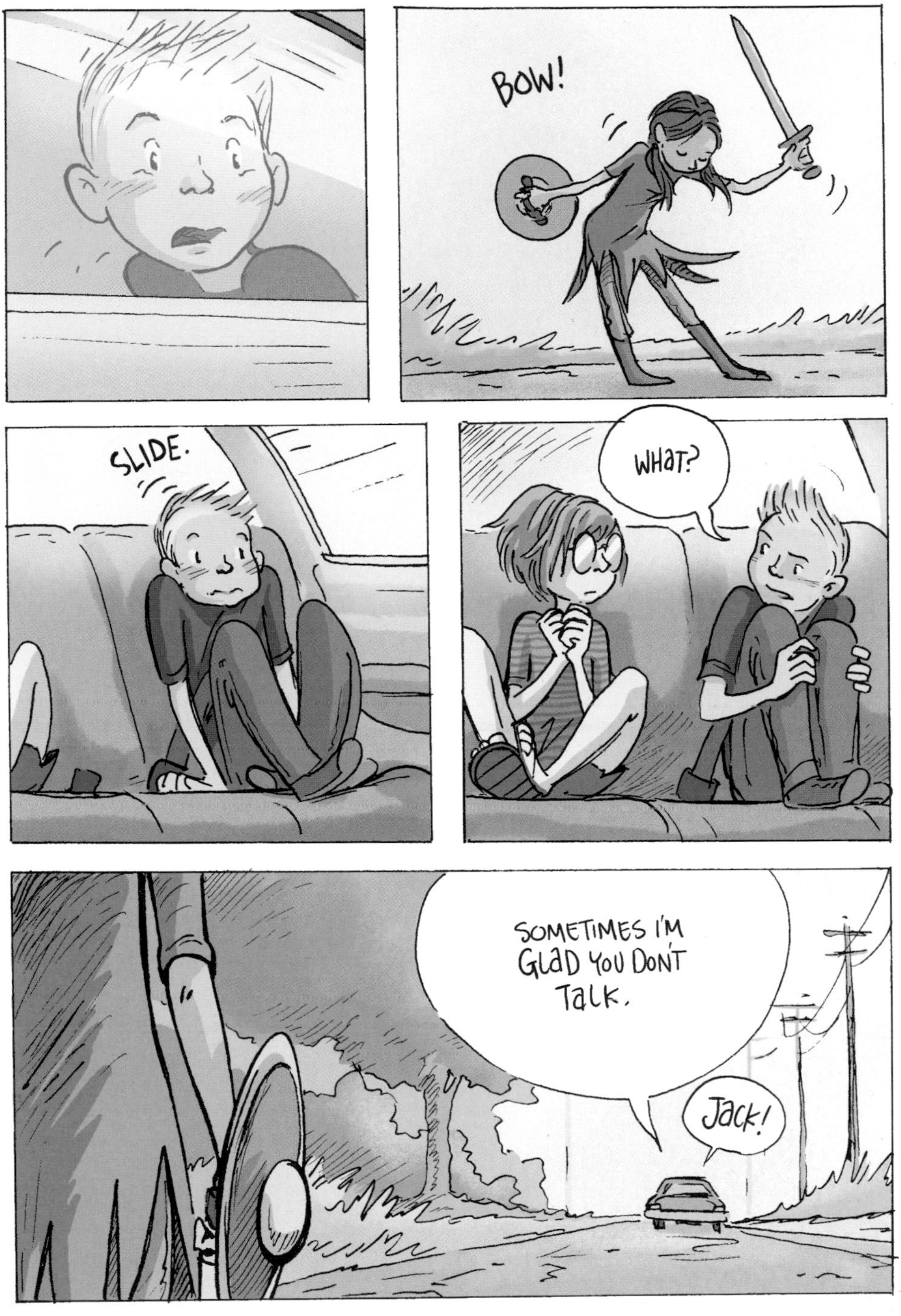
BOW!
SLIDE.
WHAT?
SOMETIMES I'M GLAD YOU DON'T TALK.
JACK!

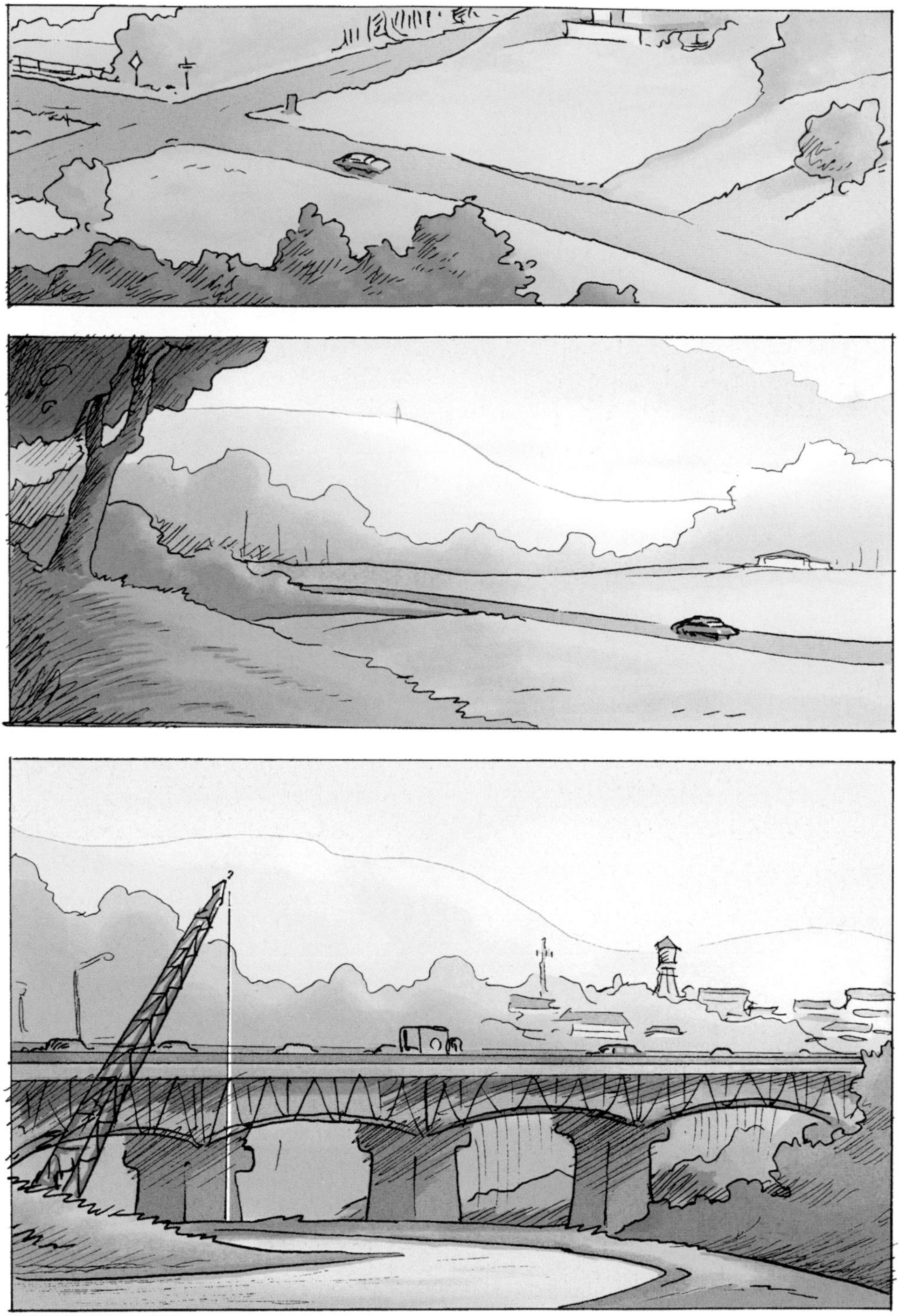

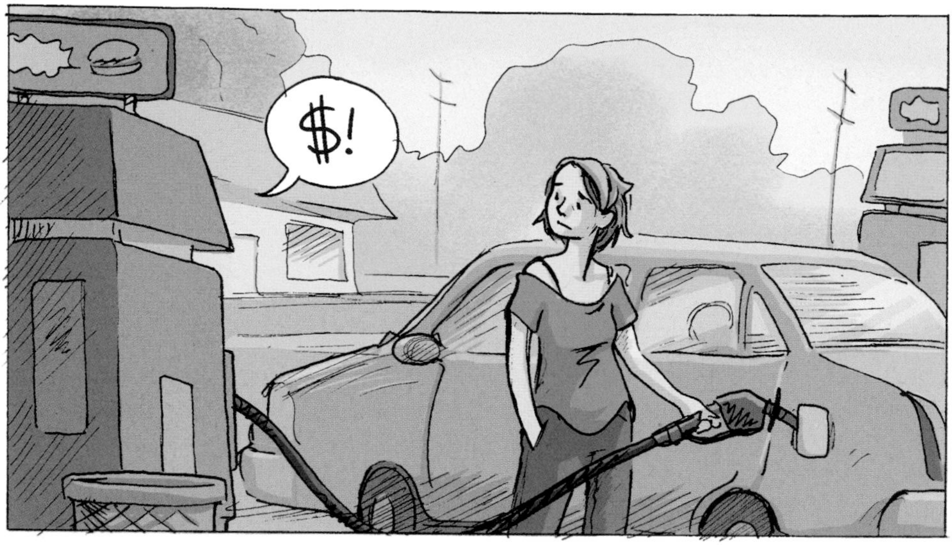
$!

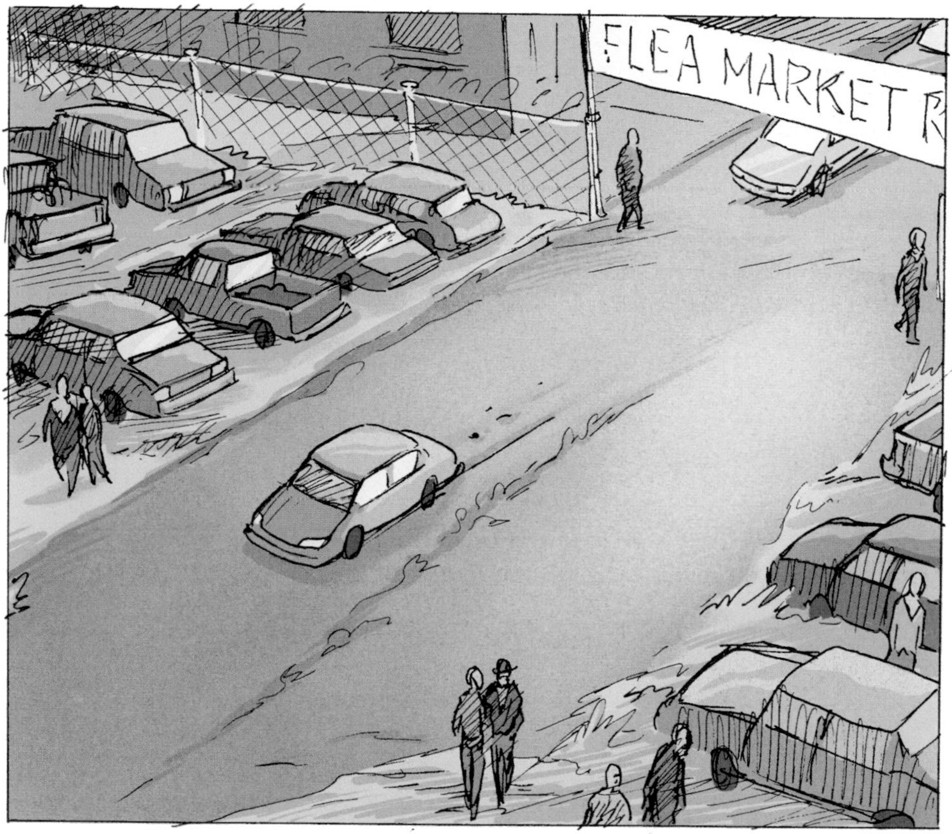
FLEA MARKET R

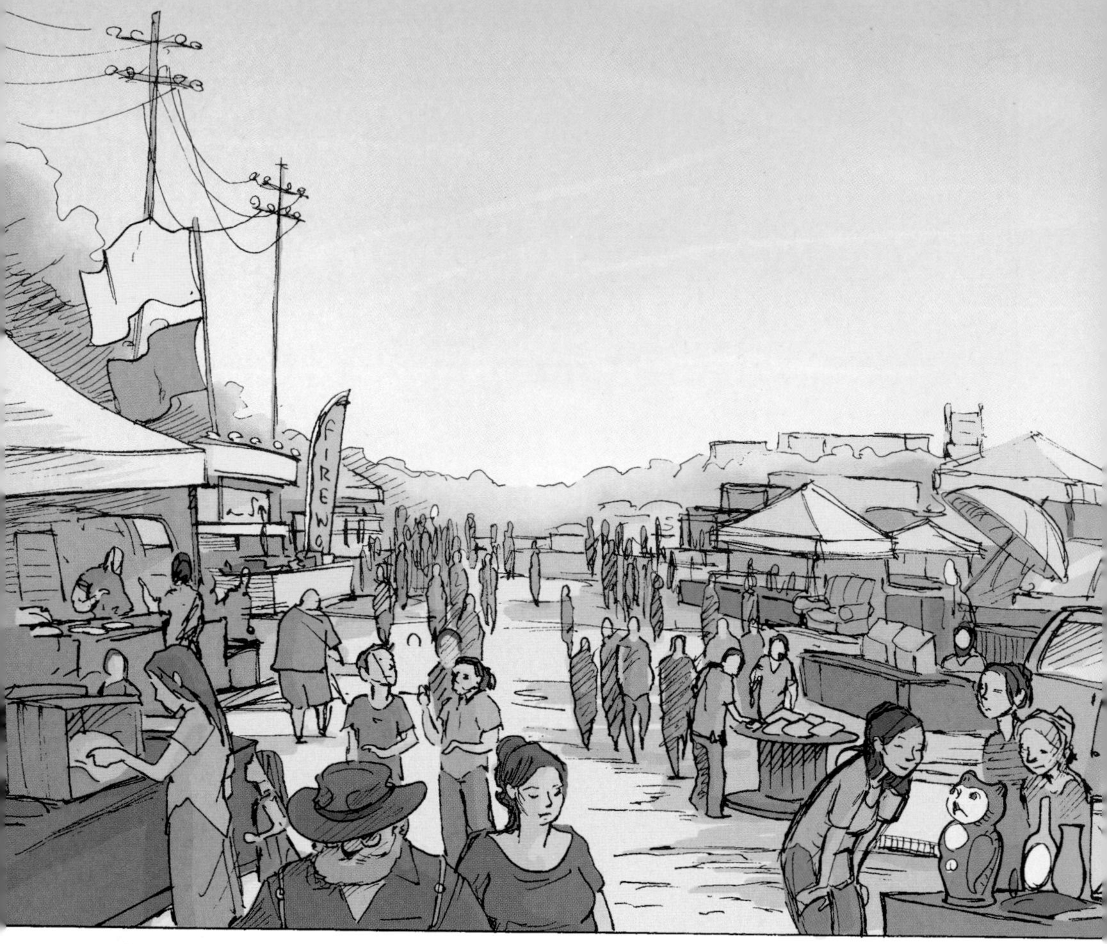
FIREWO

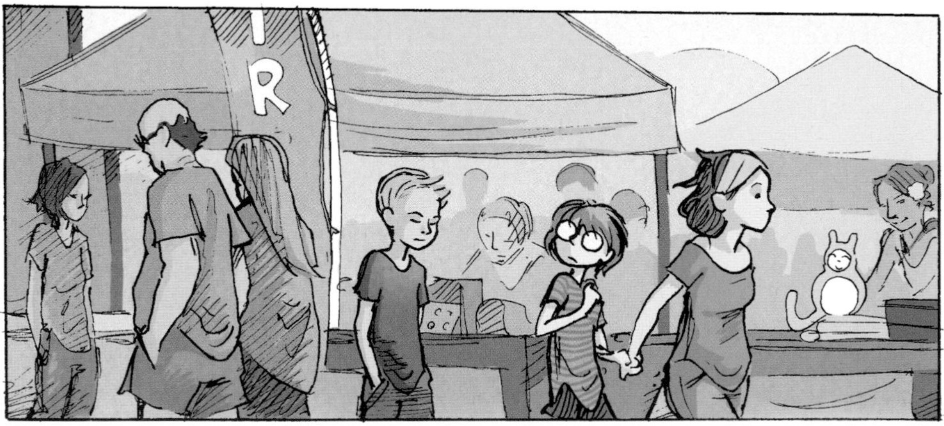
R

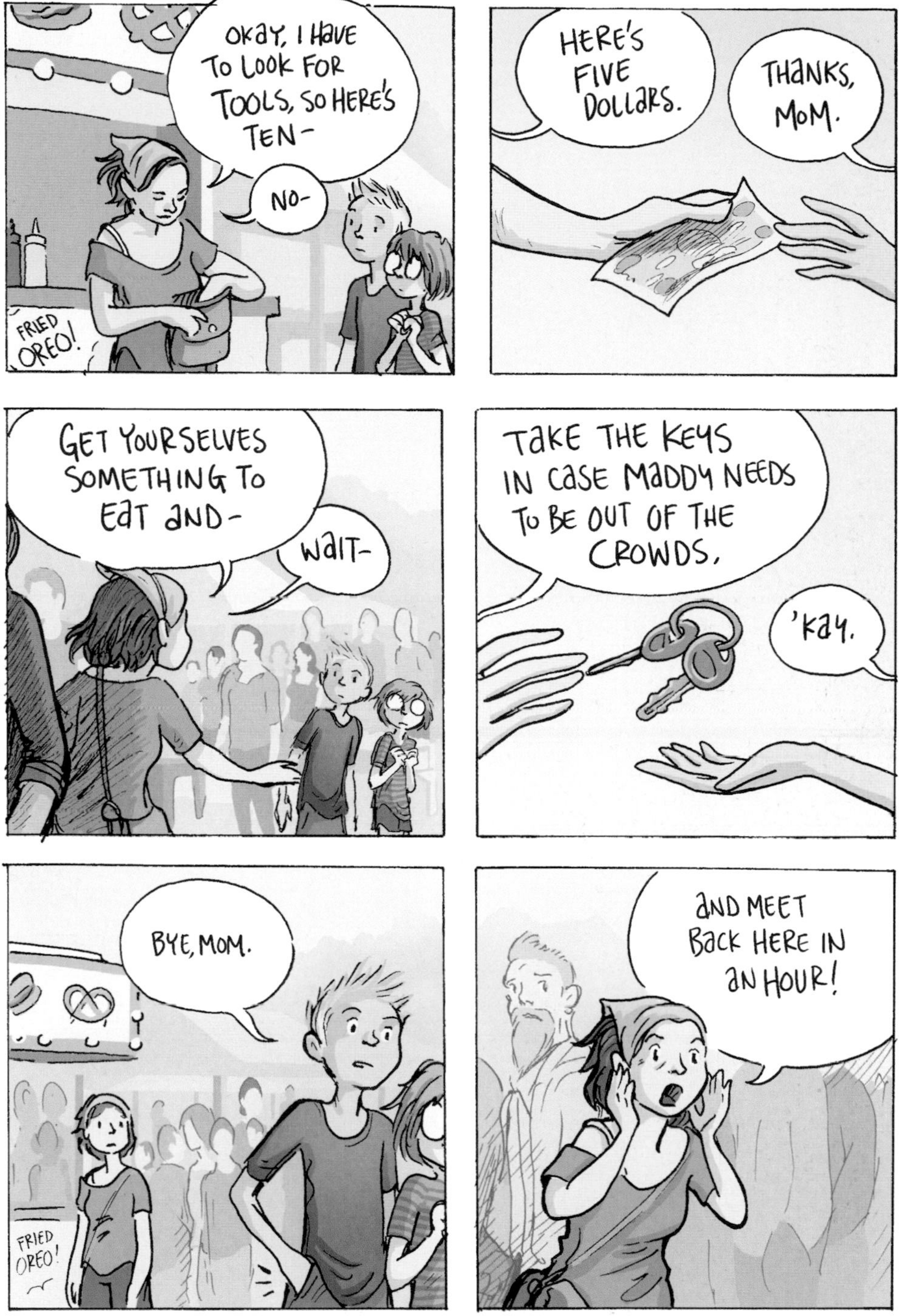
Okay, I have to look for tools, so here's ten-
No-
Fried Oreo!
Here's five dollars.
Thanks, Mom.
Get yourselves something to eat and-
Wait-
Take the keys in case Maddy needs to be out of the crowds.
'Kay.
Bye, Mom.
Fried Oreo!
And meet back here in an hour!

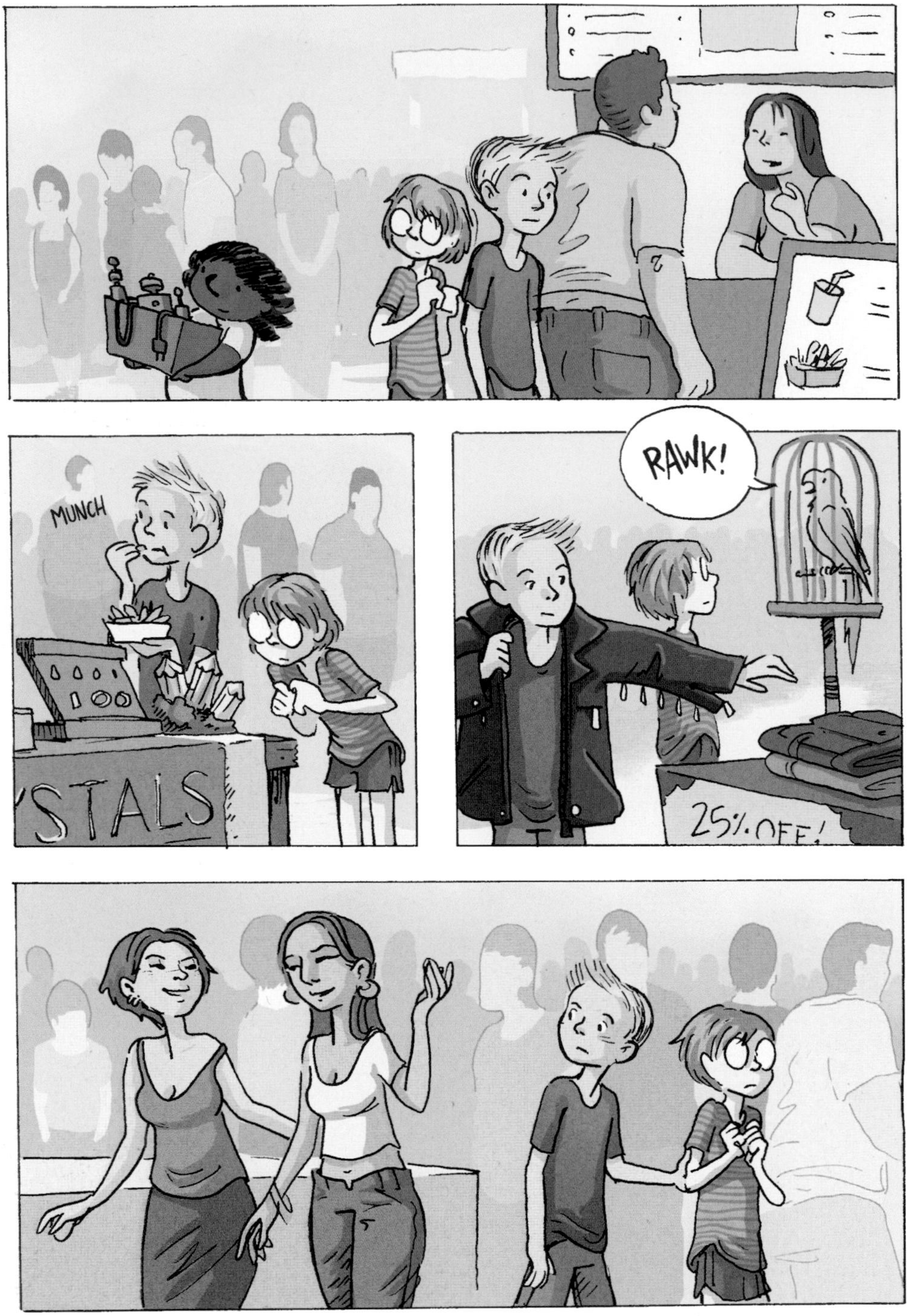
MUNCH
STALS
RAWK!
25% OFF!

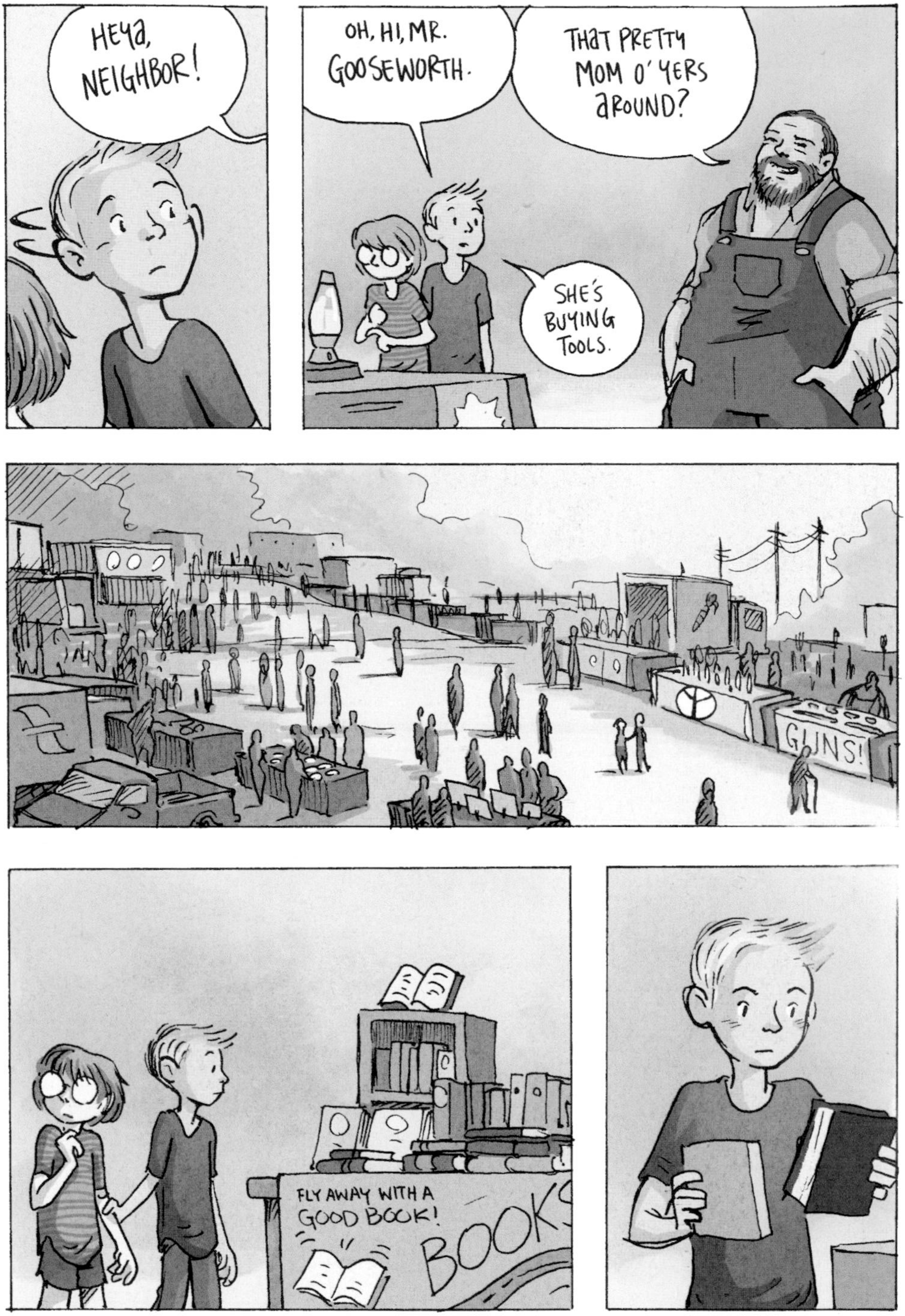
HEYA, NEIGHBOR!
OH, HI, MR. GOOSEWORTH.
THAT PRETTY MOM O' YERS AROUND?
SHE'S BUYING TOOLS.
GUNS!
FLY AWAY WITH A GOOD BOOK!
BOOKS

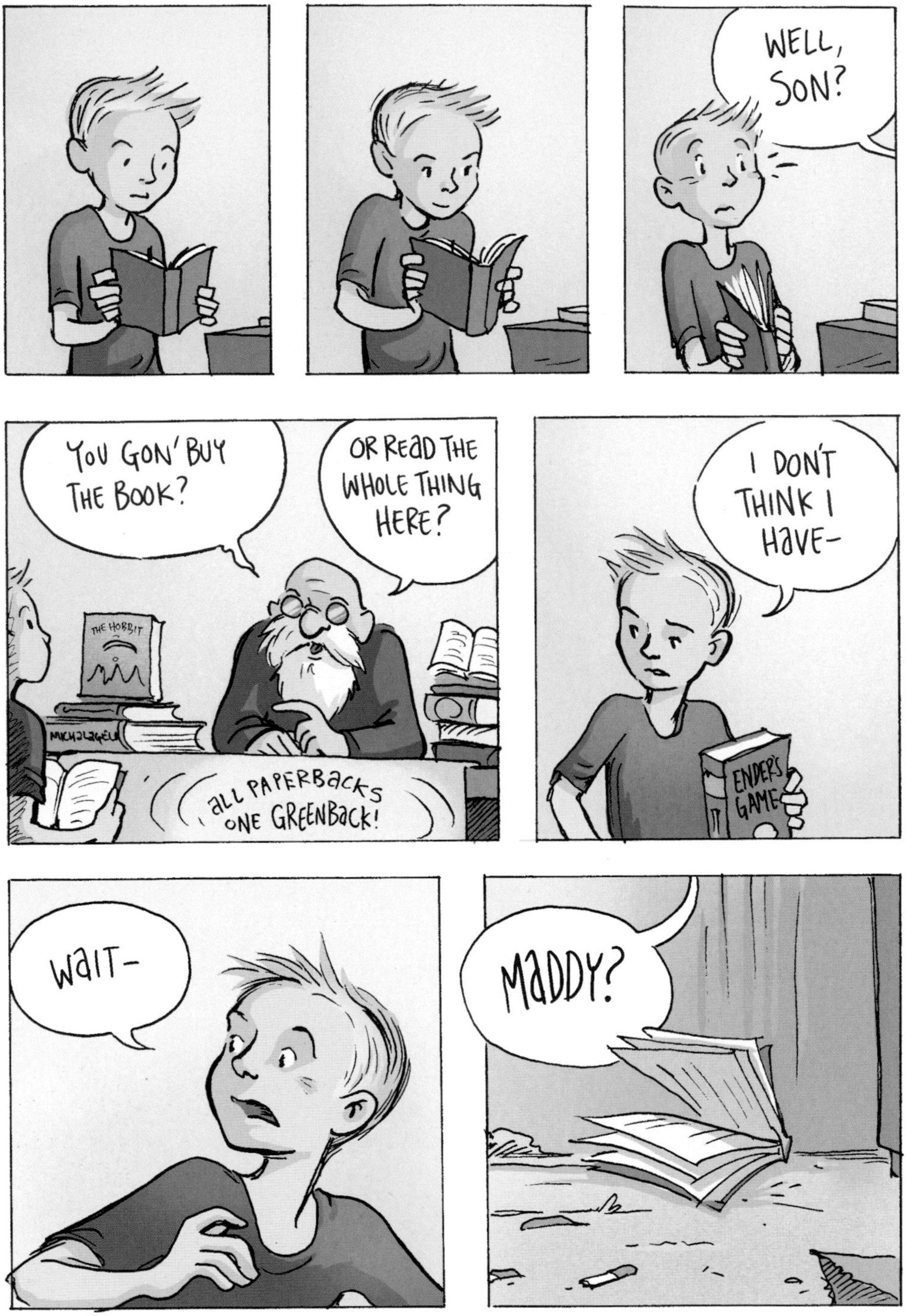
WELL, SON?
YOU GON' BUY THE BOOK?
OR READ THE WHOLE THING HERE?
THE HOBBIT
MICHELANGELO
ALL PAPERBACKS ONE GREENBACK!
I DON'T THINK I HAVE-
ENDER'S GAME
WAIT-
MADDY?

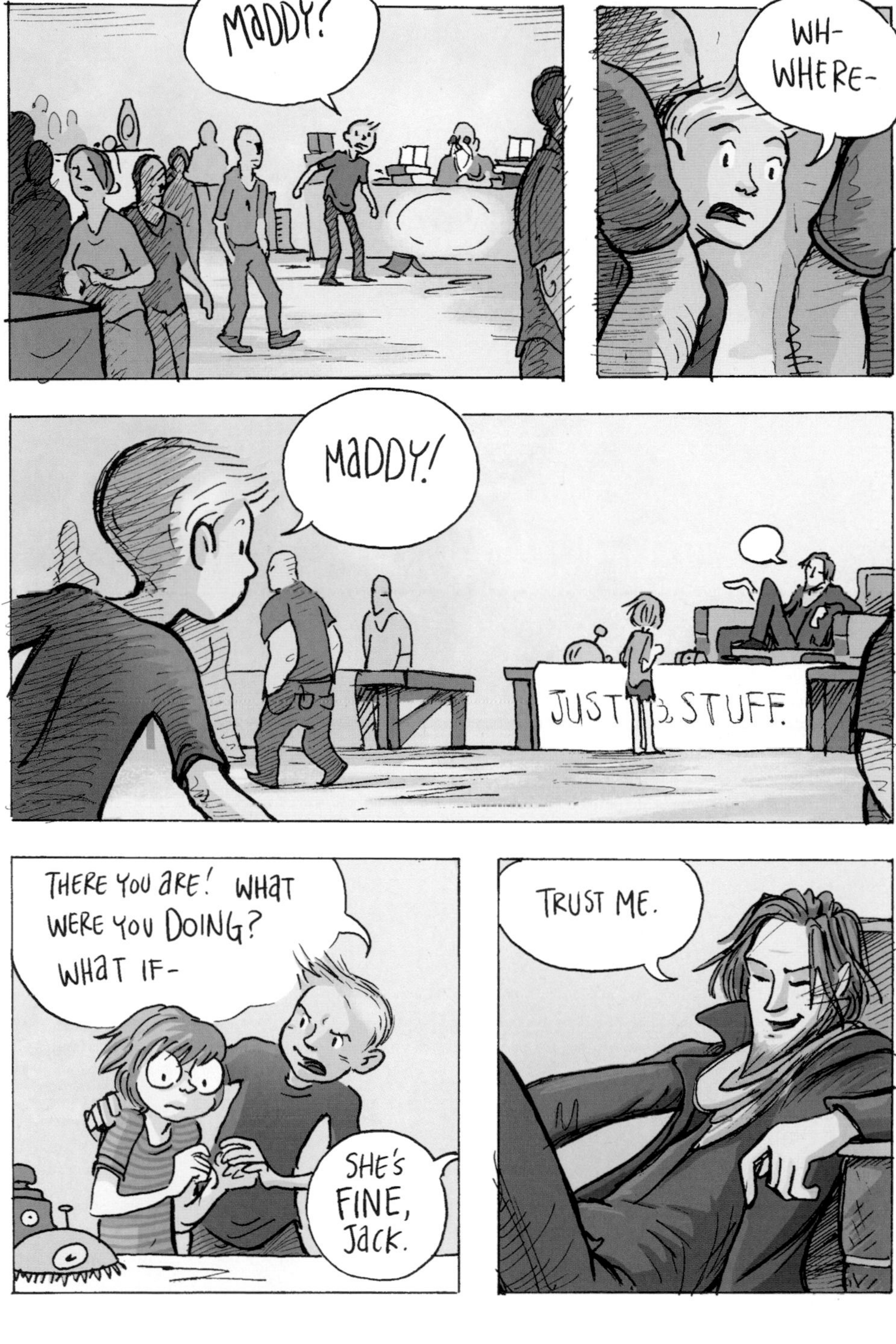
MADDY?
WH-
WHERE-
MADDY!
JUST STUFF.
THERE YOU ARE! WHAT WERE YOU DOING? WHAT IF-
SHE'S FINE, JACK.
TRUST ME.

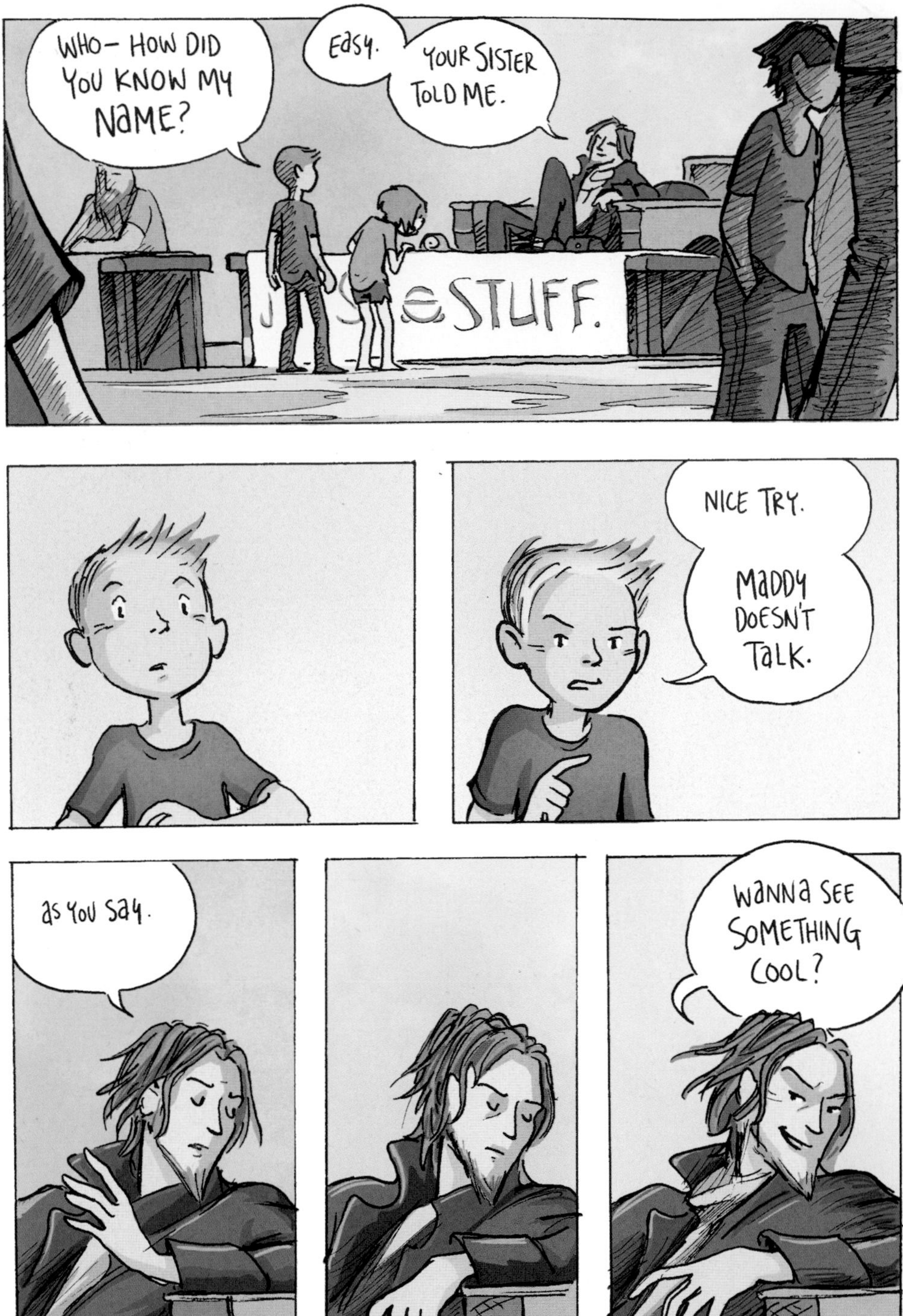
WHO– HOW DID YOU KNOW MY NAME?
Easy.
YOUR SISTER TOLD ME.
JUST STUFF.
NICE TRY.
MADDY DOESN'T TALK.
as YOU SaY.
WaNNa SEE SOMETHING COOL?

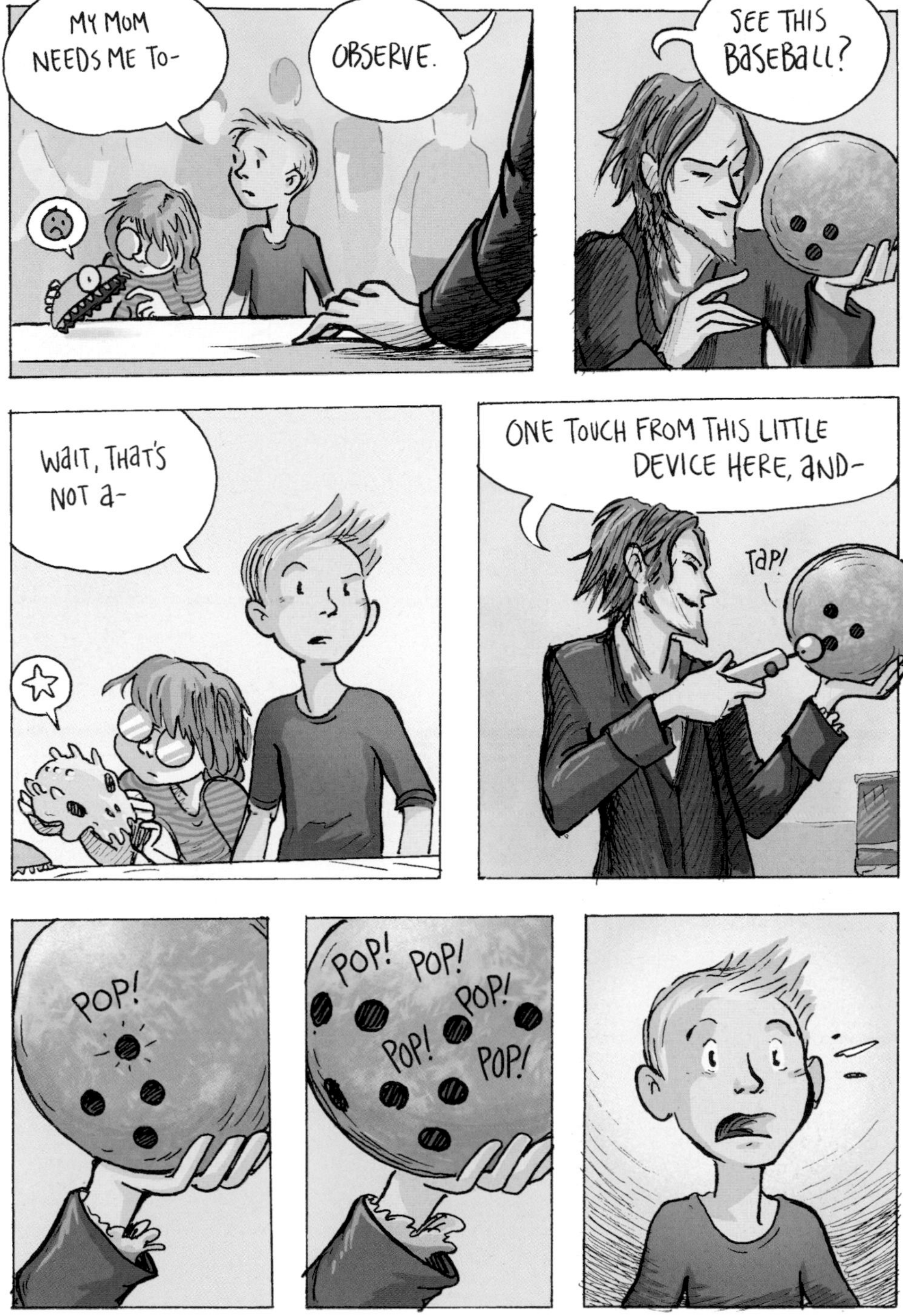
MY MOM NEEDS ME TO-
OBSERVE.
SEE THIS BASEBALL?
WAIT, THAT'S NOT A-
ONE TOUCH FROM THIS LITTLE DEVICE HERE, AND-
TAP!
POP!
POP! POP! POP! POP! POP!

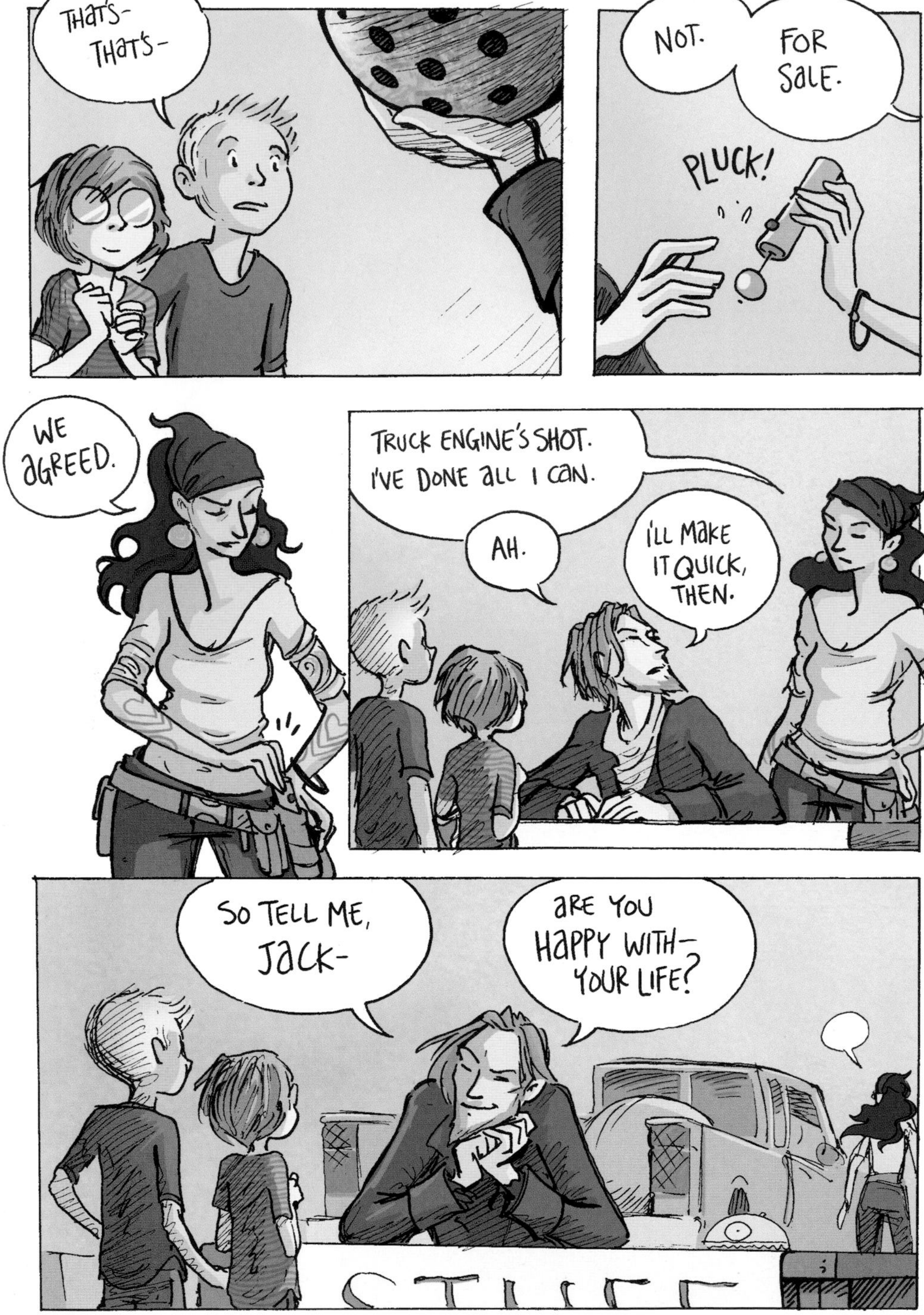
THAT'S-
THAT'S-
NOT.
FOR SALE.
PLUCK!
WE AGREED.
TRUCK ENGINE'S SHOT. I'VE DONE ALL I CAN.
AH.
I'LL MAKE IT QUICK, THEN.
SO TELL ME, JACK-
ARE YOU HAPPY WITH-
YOUR LIFE?

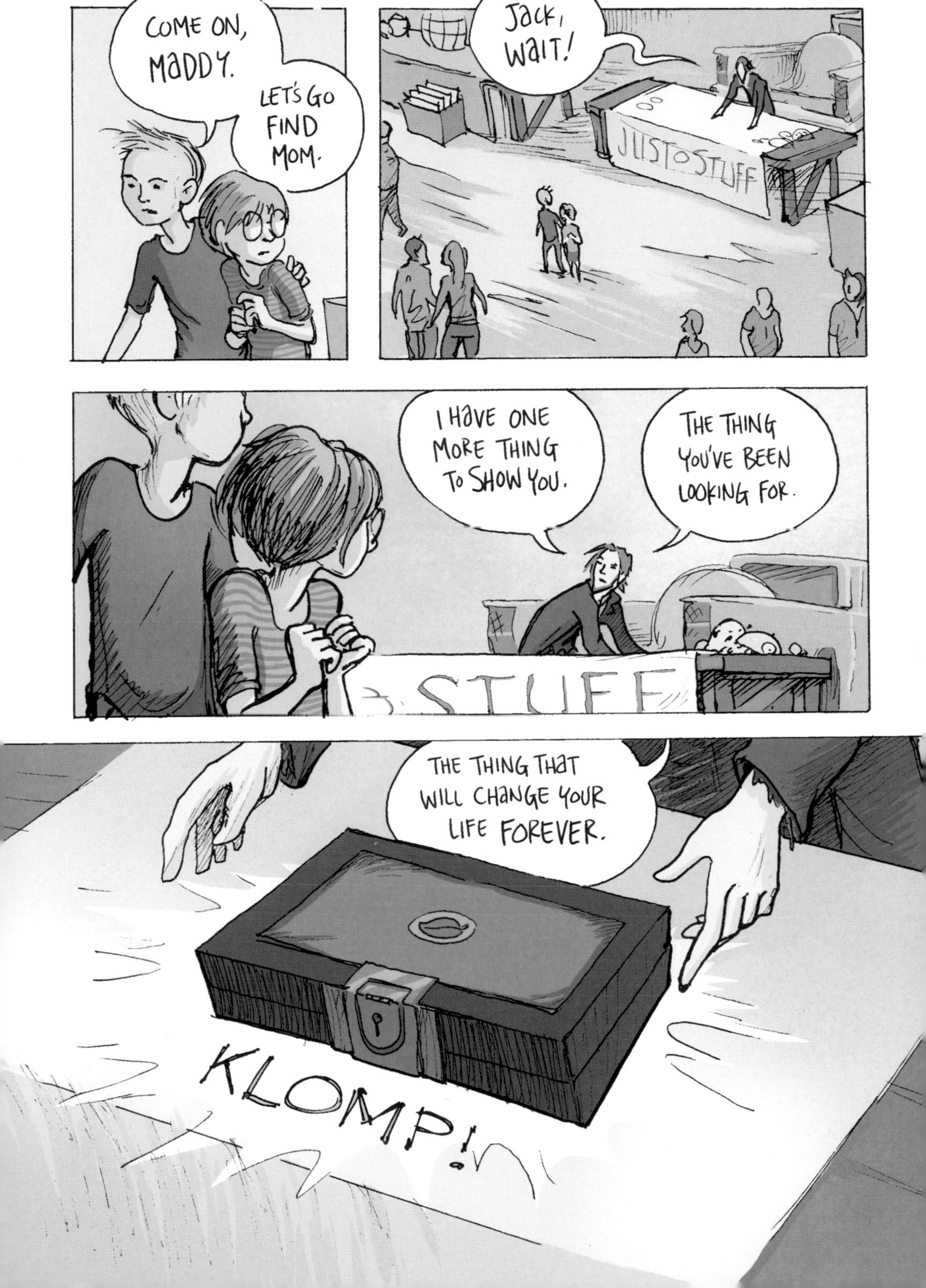
COME ON, MADDY.
LET'S GO FIND MOM.
Jack, wait!
JUST STUFF
I have ONE MORE THING TO SHOW YOU.
THE THING YOU'VE BEEN LOOKING FOR.
STUFF
THE THING THAT WILL CHANGE YOUR LIFE FOREVER.
KLOMP!

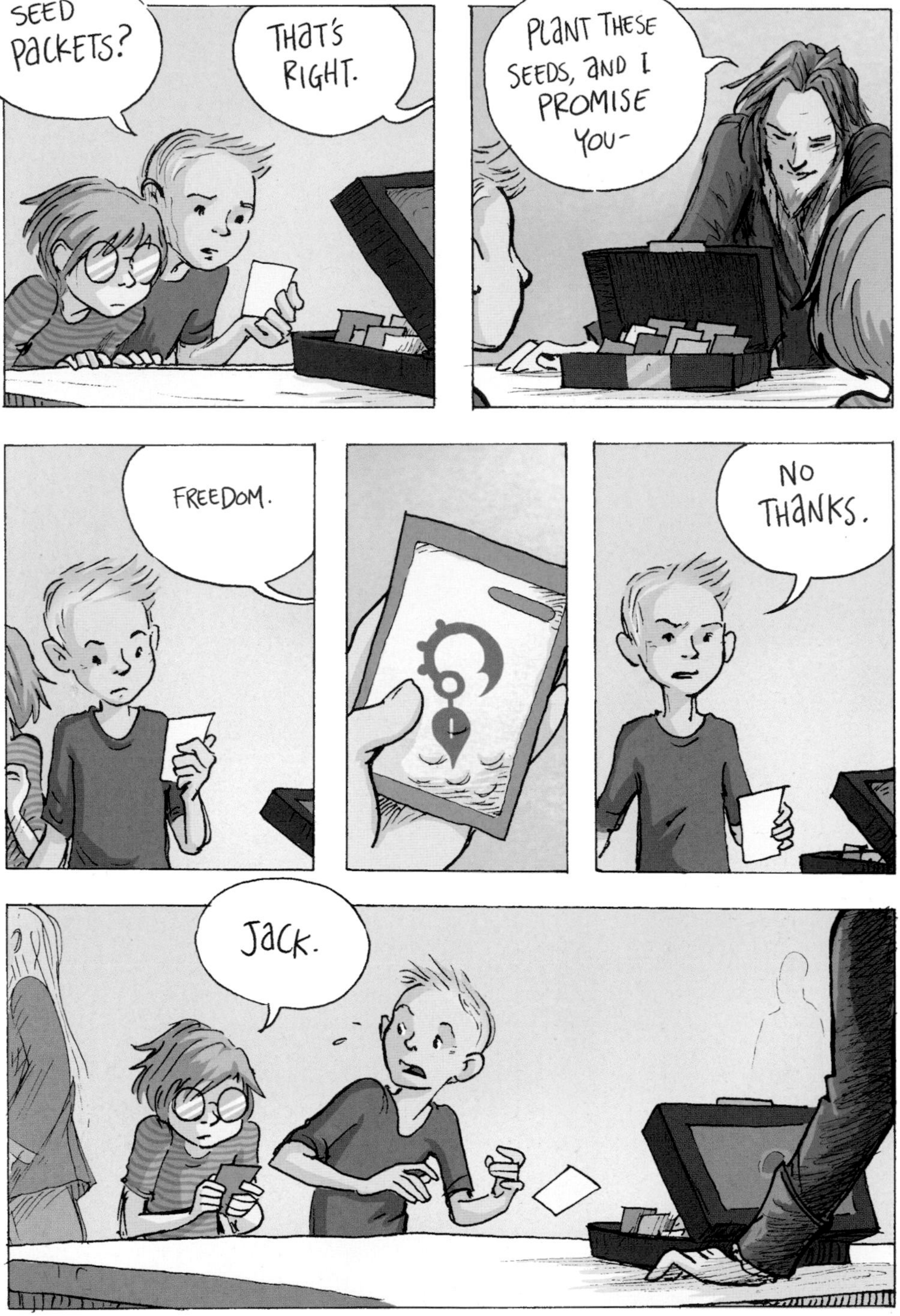
SEED PACKETS?
THAT'S RIGHT.
PLANT THESE SEEDS, AND I PROMISE YOU-
FREEDOM.
NO THANKS.
JACK.

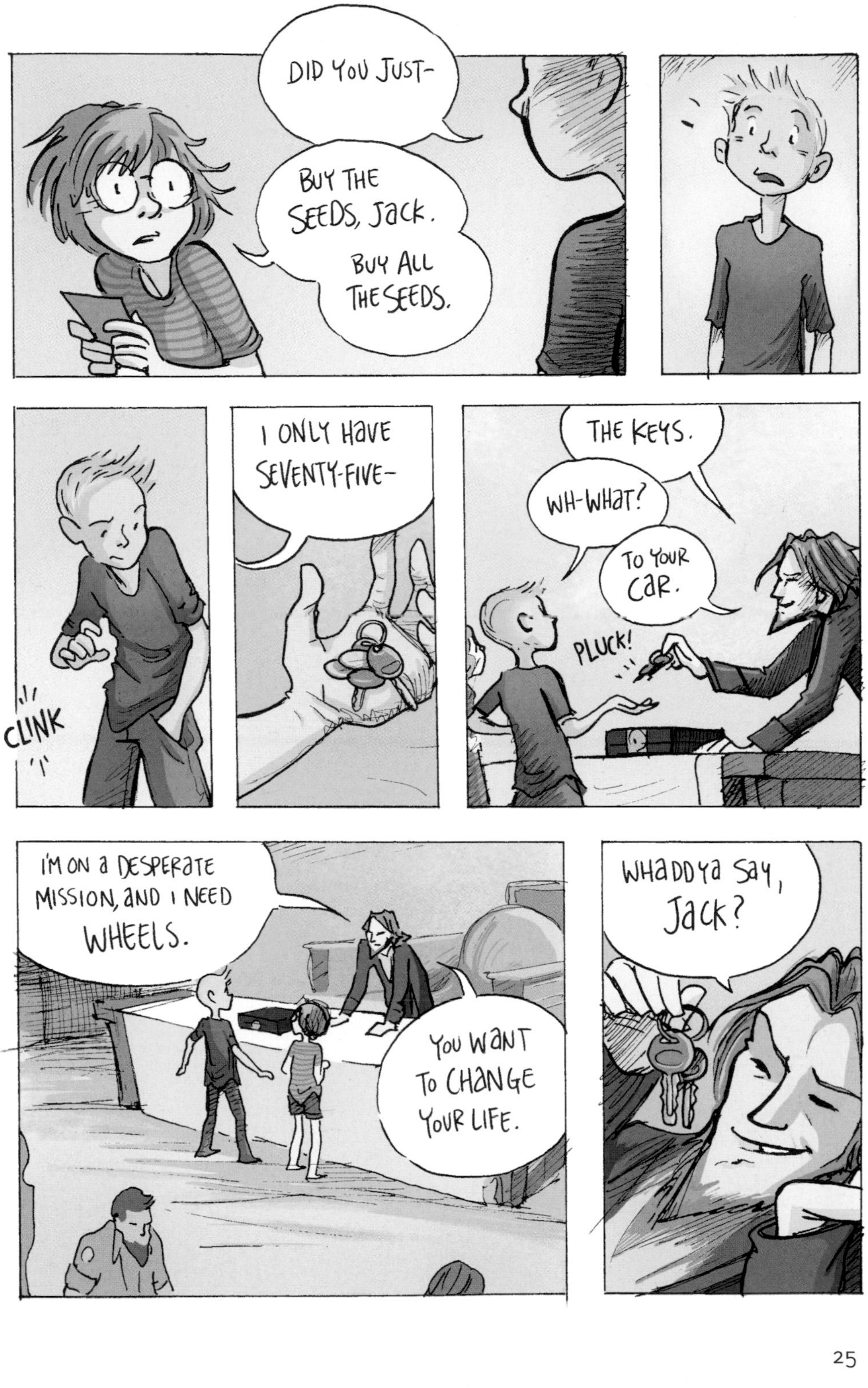
DID YOU JUST-
BUY THE SEEDS, JACK.
BUY ALL THE SEEDS.
CLINK
I ONLY HAVE SEVENTY-FIVE-
THE KEYS.
WH-WHAT?
TO YOUR CAR.
PLUCK!
I'M ON A DESPERATE MISSION, AND I NEED WHEELS.
YOU WANT TO CHANGE YOUR LIFE.
WHADDYA SAY, JACK?

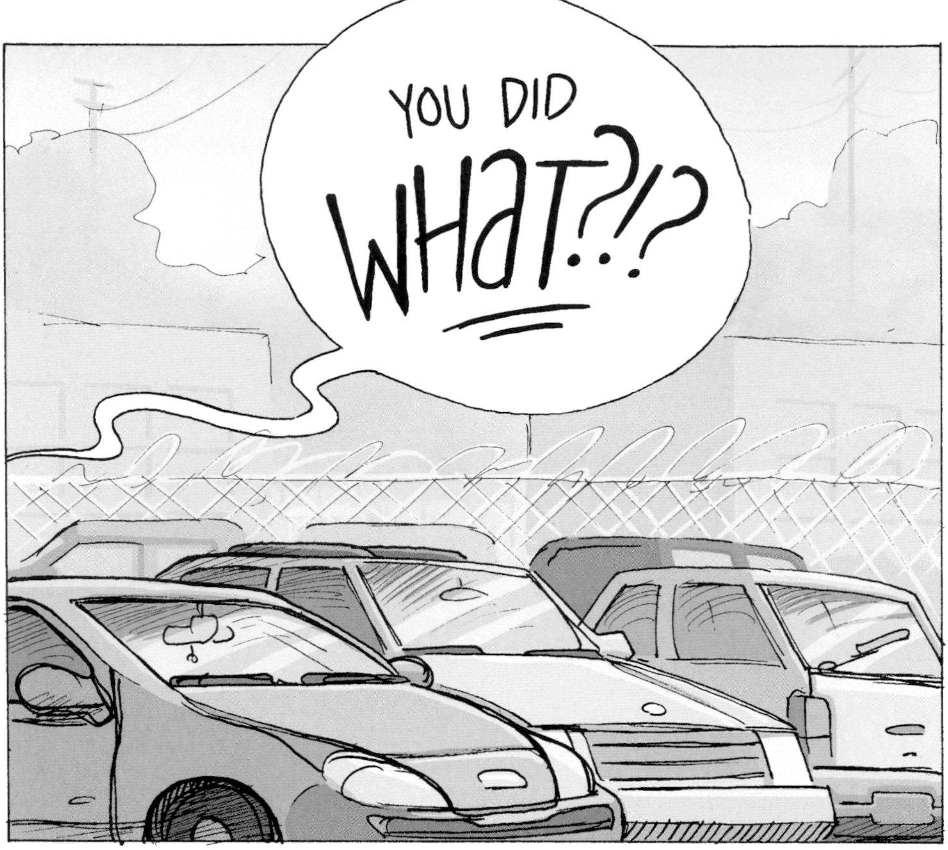
YOU DID WHAT?!?

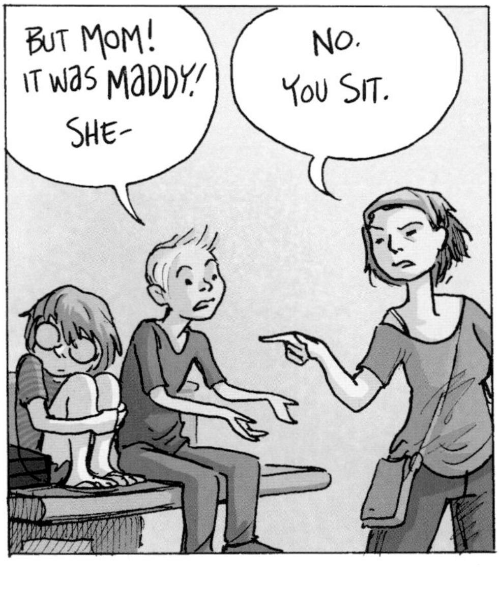
BUT MOM! IT WAS MADDY! SHE-
NO. YOU SIT.

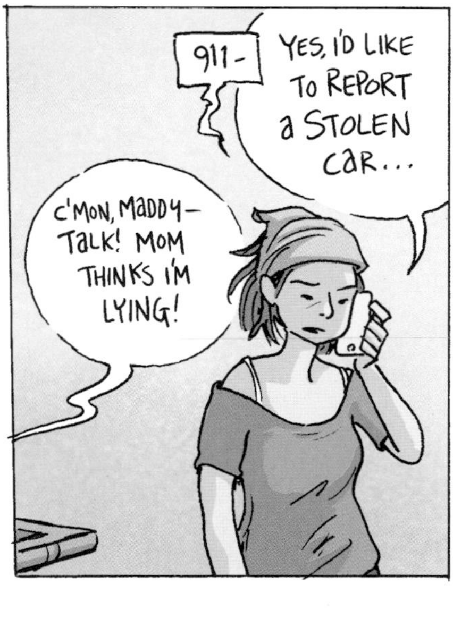
911-
YES, I'D LIKE TO REPORT A STOLEN CAR...
C'MON, MADDY- TALK! MOM THINKS I'M LYING!

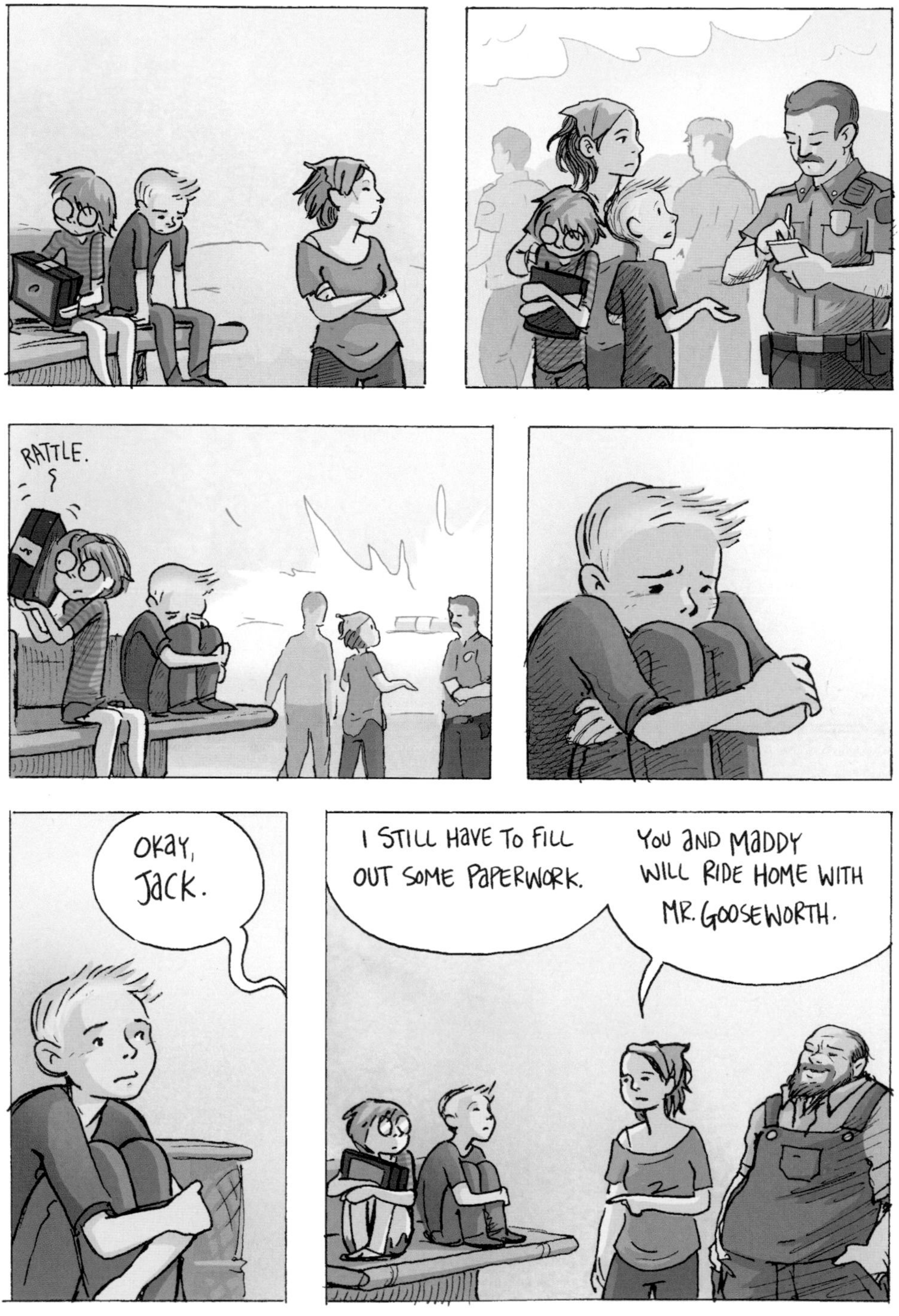
RATTLE.
OKAY, JACK.
I STILL HAVE TO FILL OUT SOME PAPERWORK.
YOU AND MADDY WILL RIDE HOME WITH MR. GOOSEWORTH.

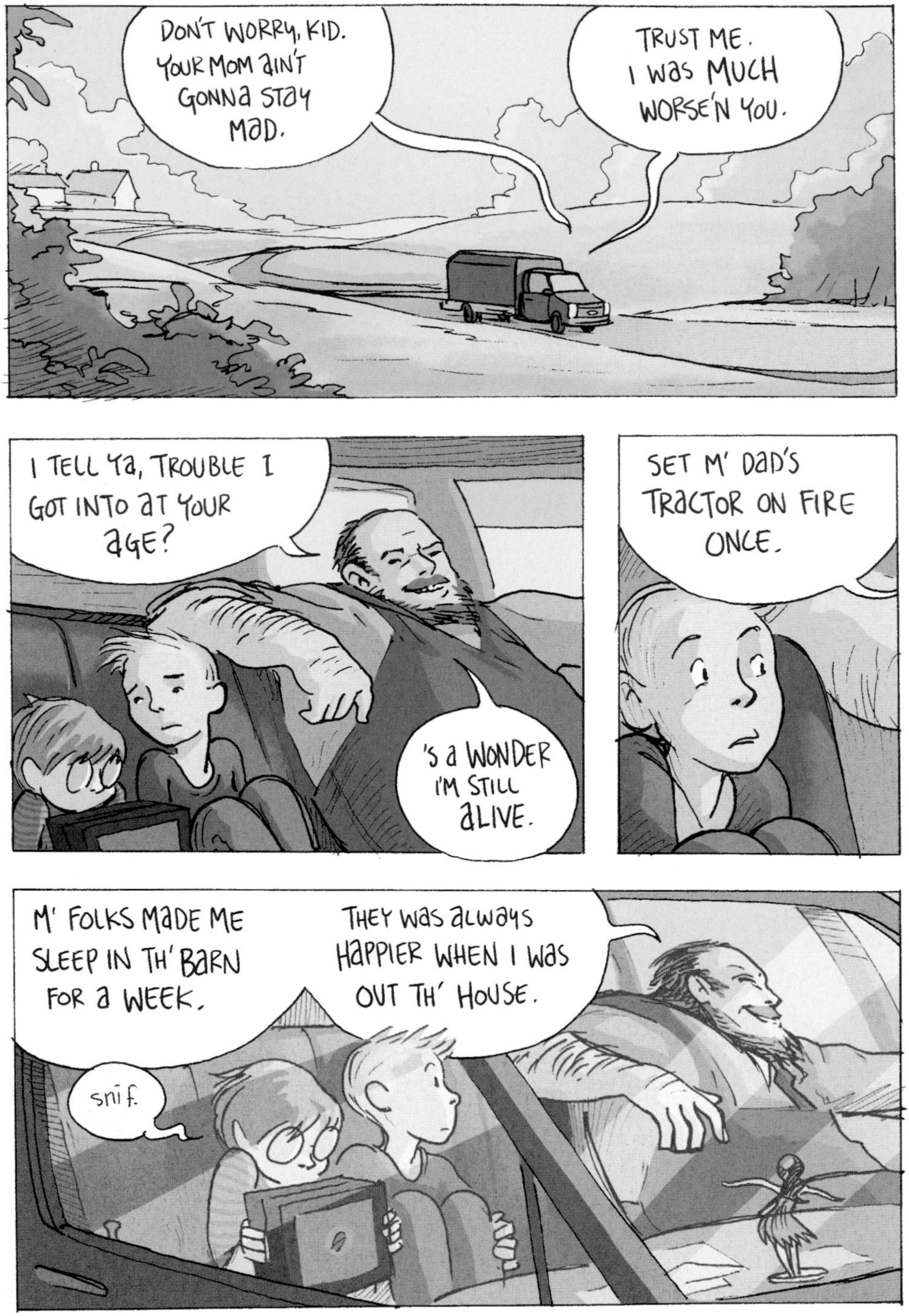
DON'T WORRY, KID. YOUR MOM AIN'T GONNA STAY MAD.
TRUST ME. I WAS MUCH WORSE'N YOU.
I TELL YA, TROUBLE I GOT INTO AT YOUR AGE?
'S A WONDER I'M STILL ALIVE.
SET M' DAD'S TRACTOR ON FIRE ONCE.
M' FOLKS MADE ME SLEEP IN TH' BARN FOR A WEEK.
THEY WAS ALWAYS HAPPIER WHEN I WAS OUT TH' HOUSE.
snif.

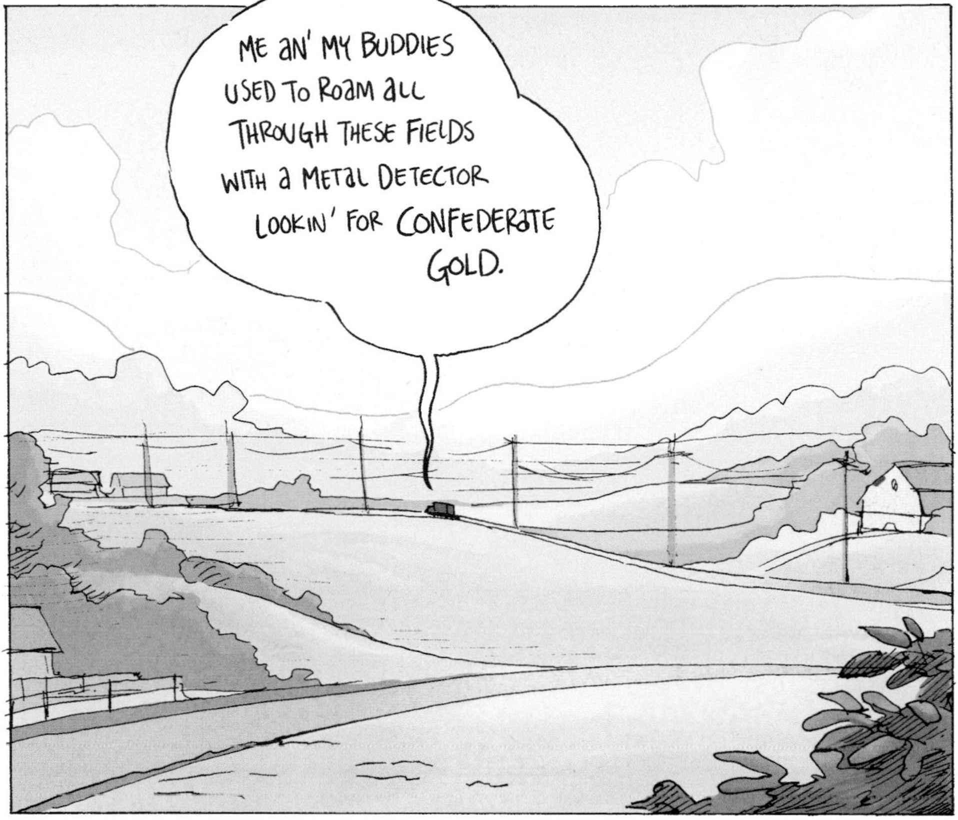
ME AN' MY BUDDIES USED TO ROAM ALL THROUGH THESE FIELDS WITH A METAL DETECTOR LOOKIN' FOR CONFEDERATE GOLD.

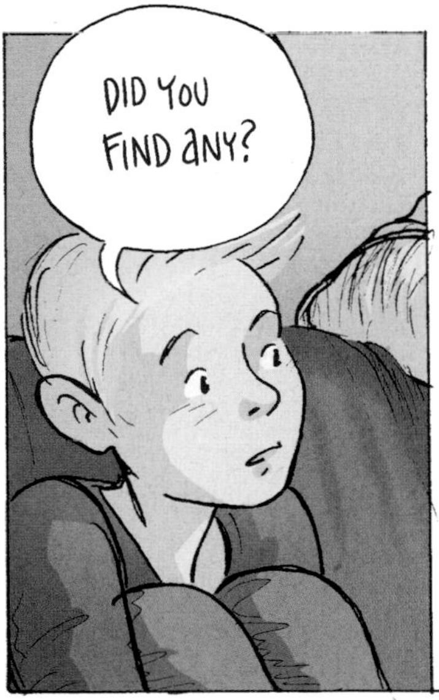
DID YOU FIND ANY?

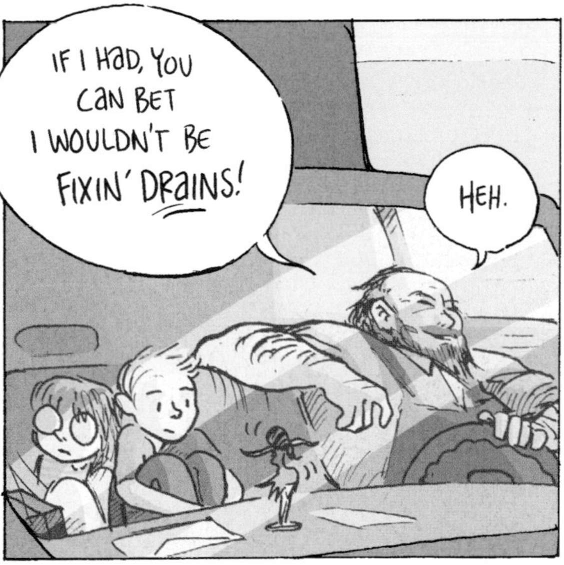
IF I HAD, YOU CAN BET I WOULDN'T BE FIXIN' DRAINS!
HEH.

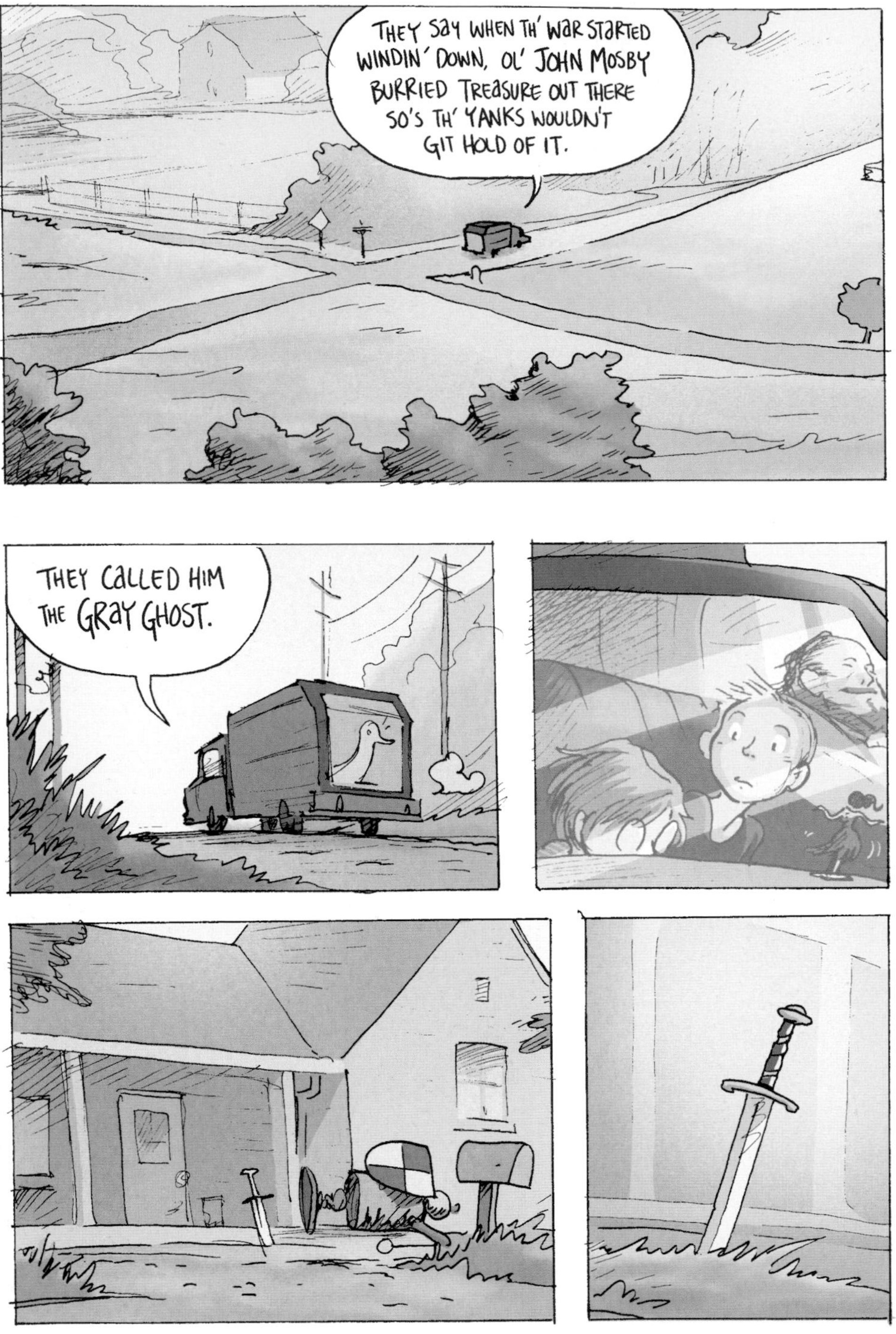
THEY SAY WHEN TH' WAR STARTED WINDIN' DOWN, OL' JOHN MOSBY BURRIED TREASURE OUT THERE SO'S TH' YANKS WOULDN'T GIT HOLD OF IT.
THEY CALLED HIM THE GRAY GHOST.

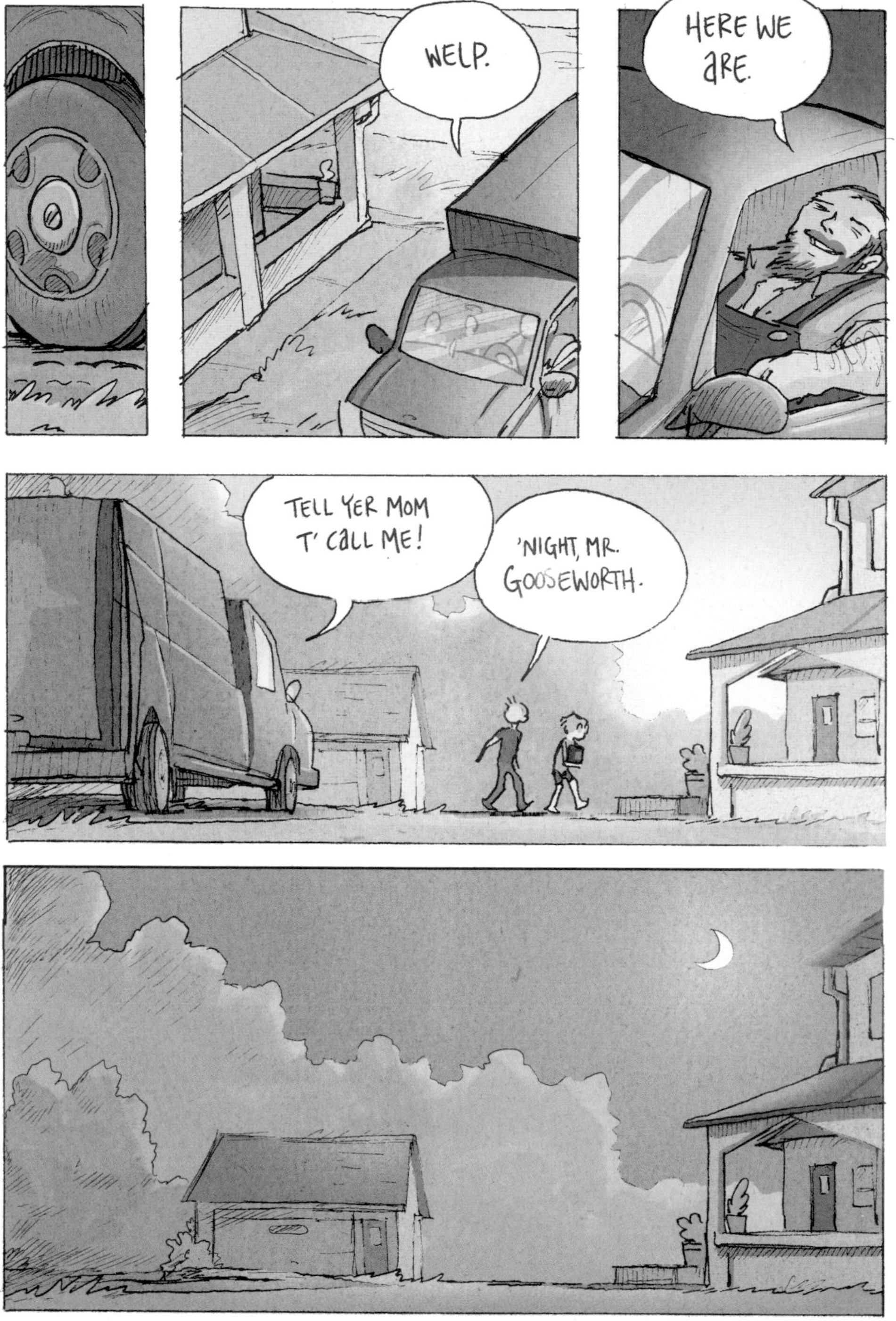
WELP.
HERE WE ARE.
TELL YER MOM T' CALL ME!
'NIGHT, MR. GOOSEWORTH.

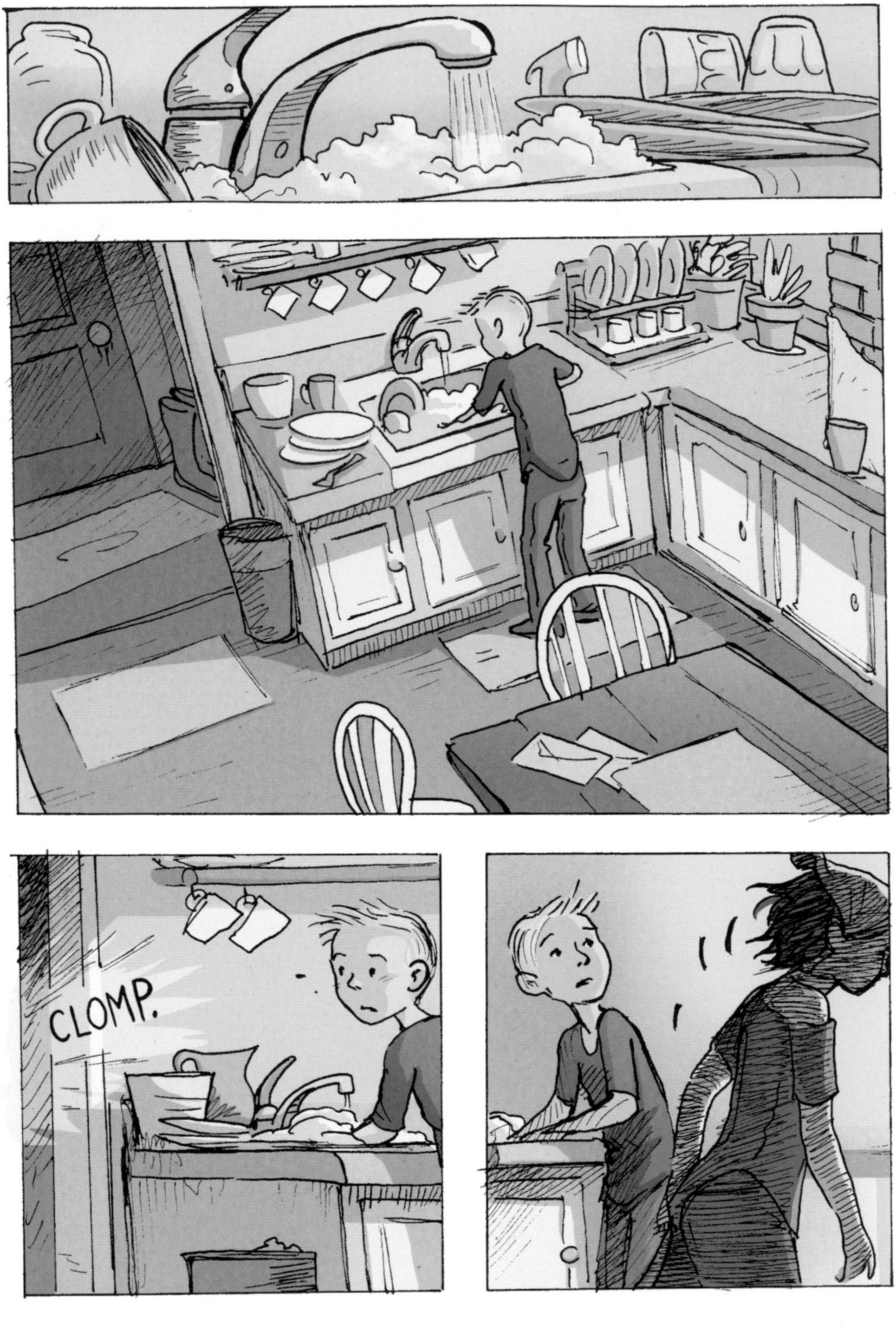
CLOMP.

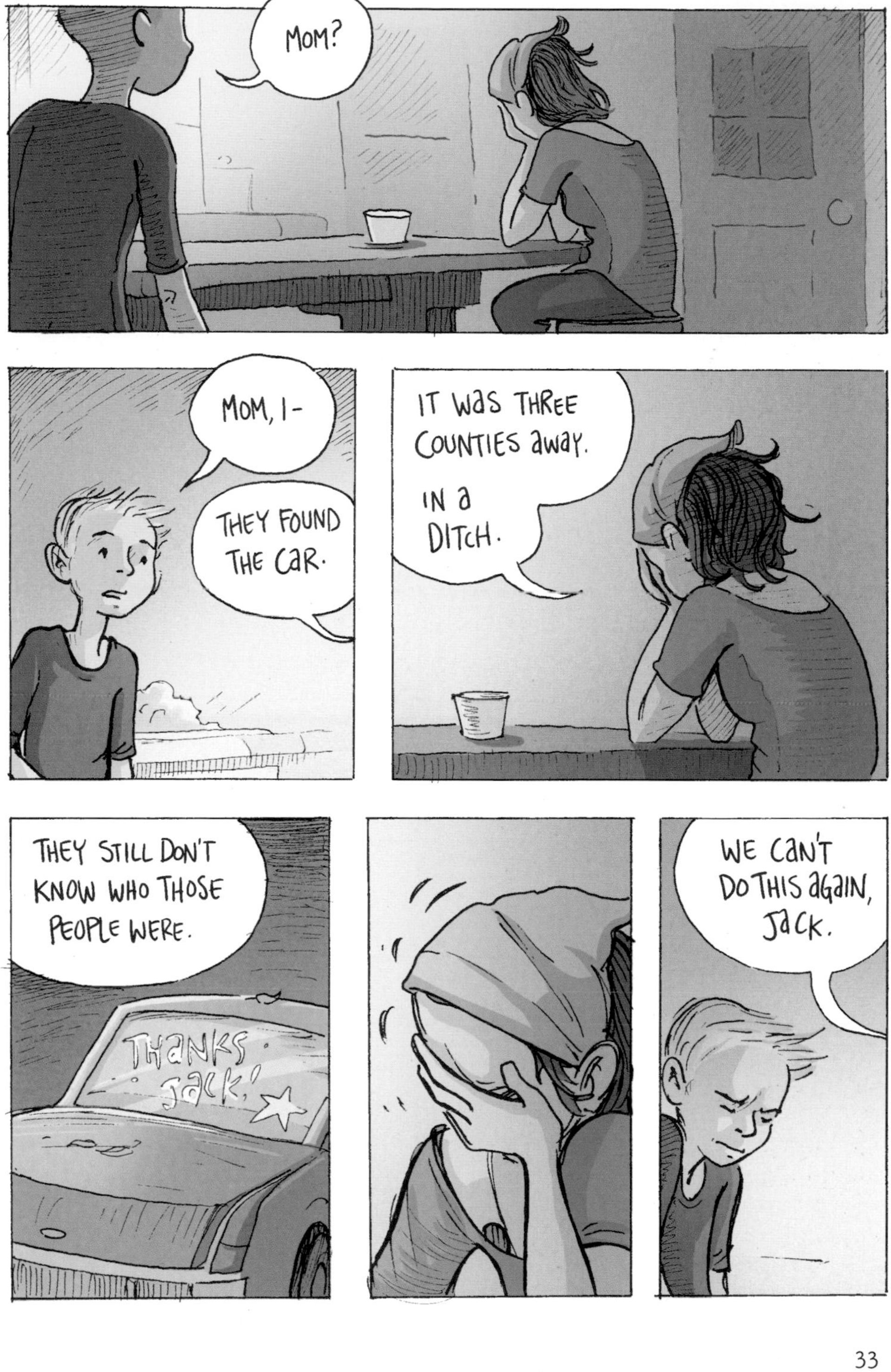
MOM?
MOM, I-
THEY FOUND THE CAR.
IT WAS THREE COUNTIES AWAY.
IN A DITCH.
THEY STILL DON'T KNOW WHO THOSE PEOPLE WERE.
THANKS JACK!
WE CAN'T DO THIS AGAIN, JACK.

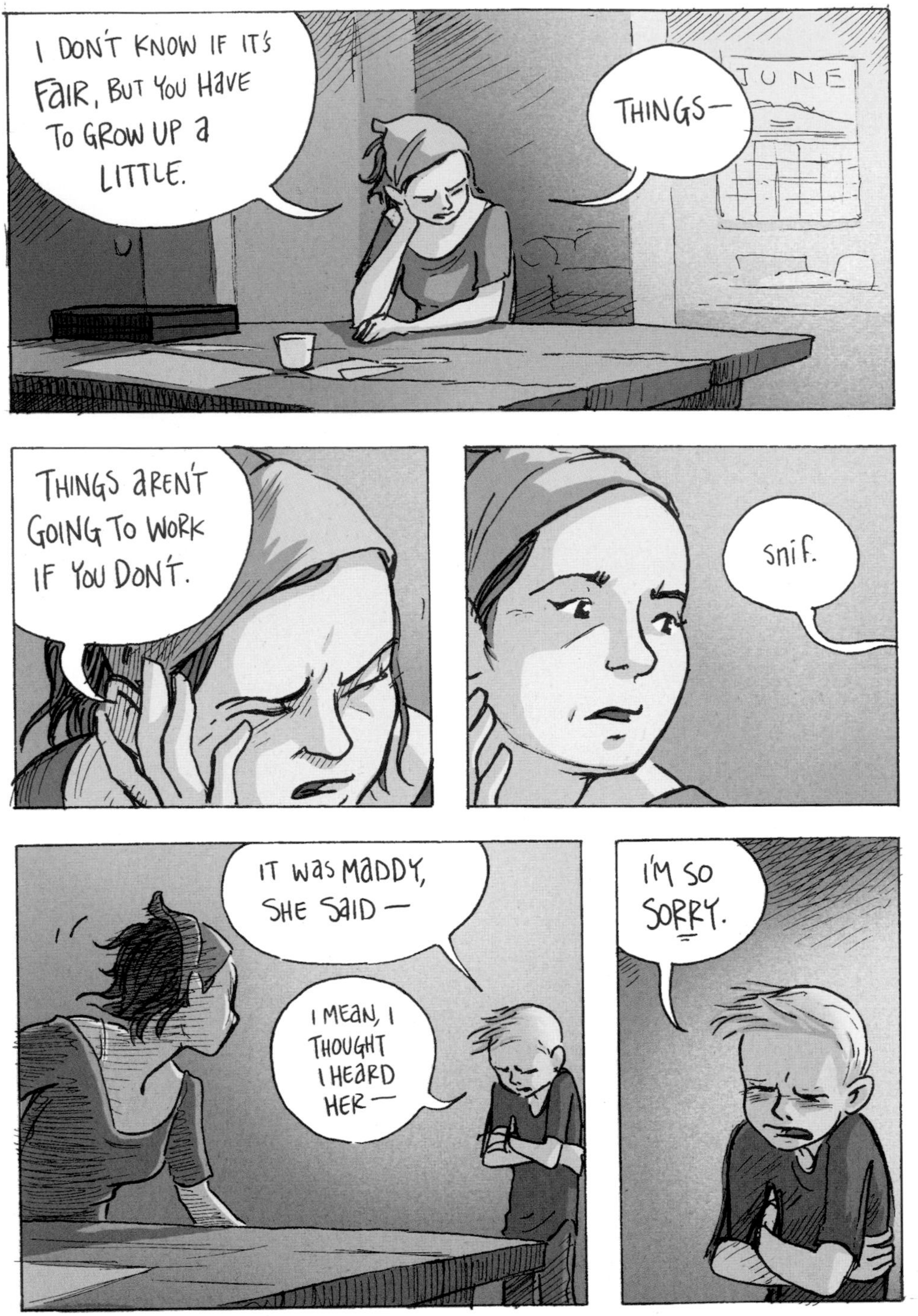
I DON'T KNOW IF IT'S FAIR, BUT YOU HAVE TO GROW UP A LITTLE.
THINGS—
JUNE
THINGS AREN'T GOING TO WORK IF YOU DON'T.
SNIF.
IT WAS MADDY, SHE SAID —
I MEAN, I THOUGHT I HEARD HER —
I'M SO SORRY.

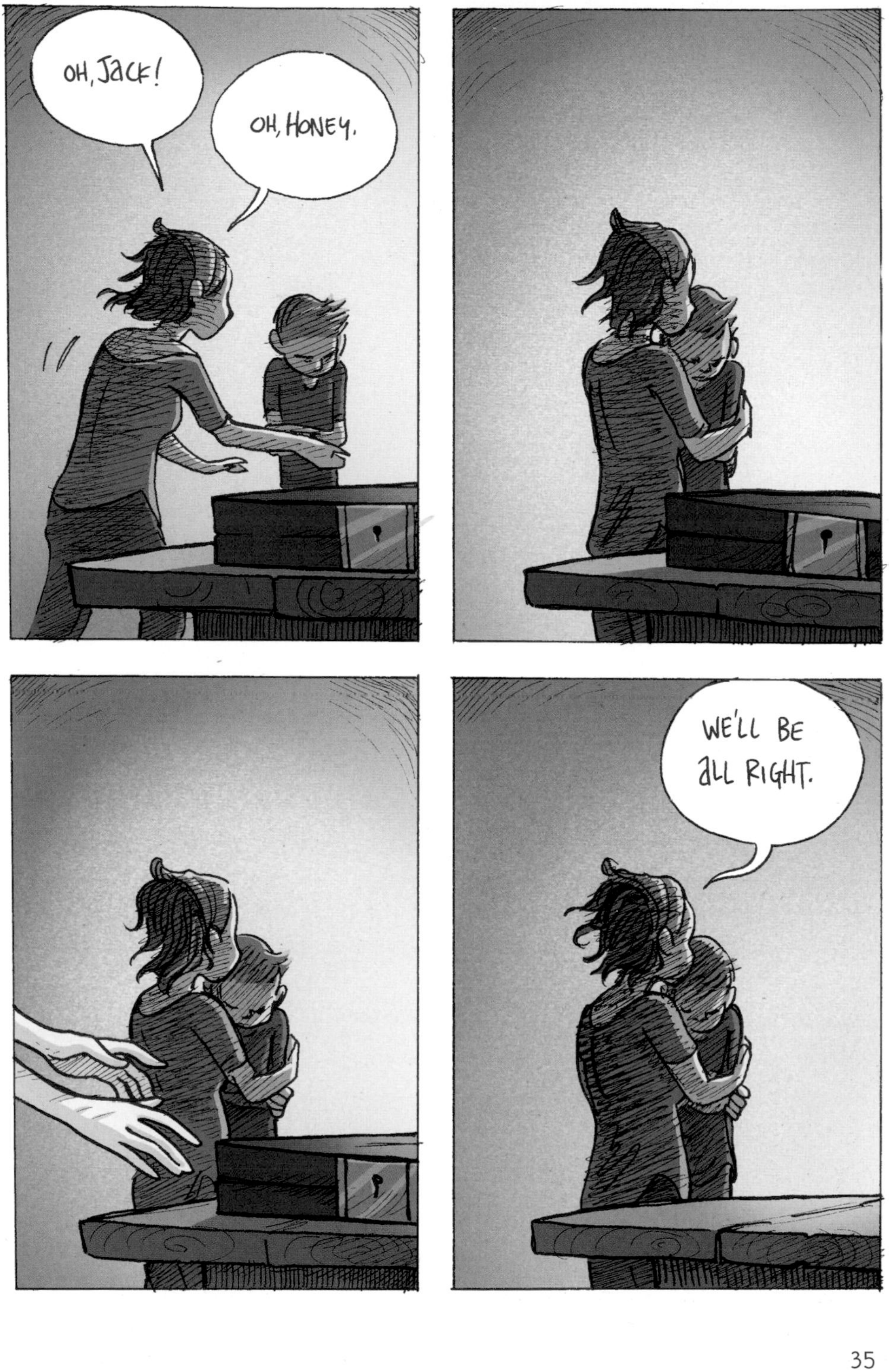
OH, JACK!
OH, HONEY.
WE'LL BE ALL RIGHT.

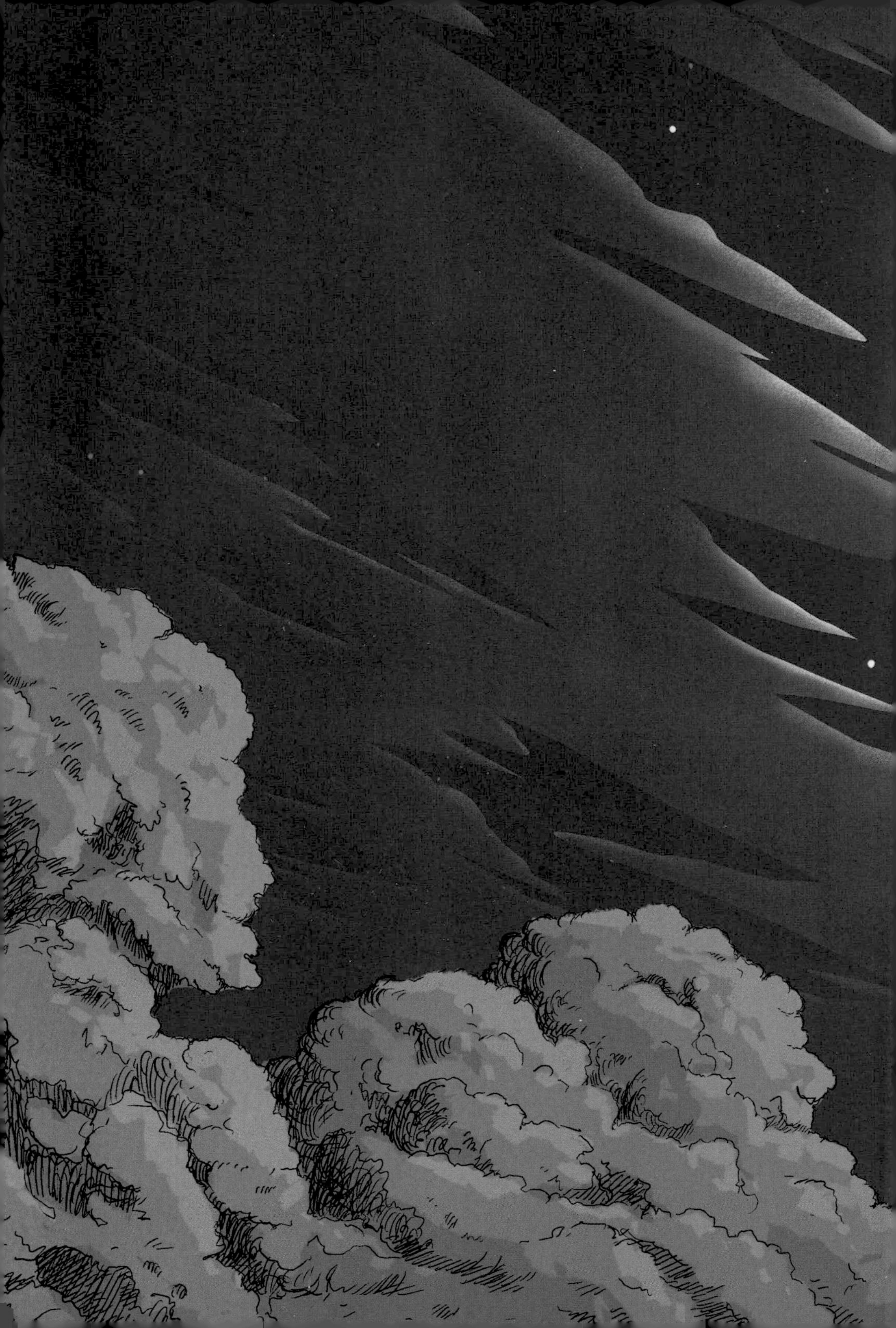

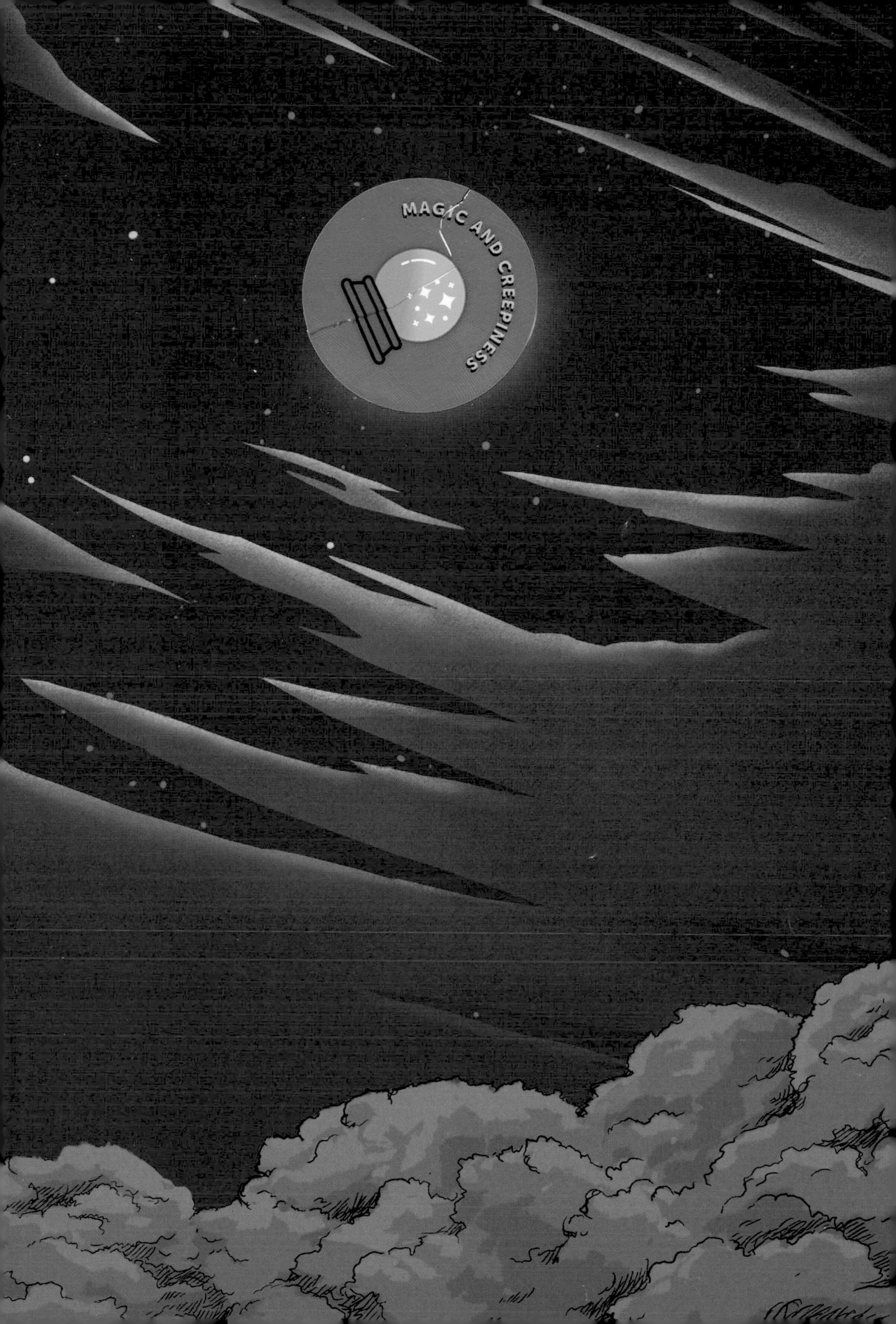
MAGIC AND CREEPINESS

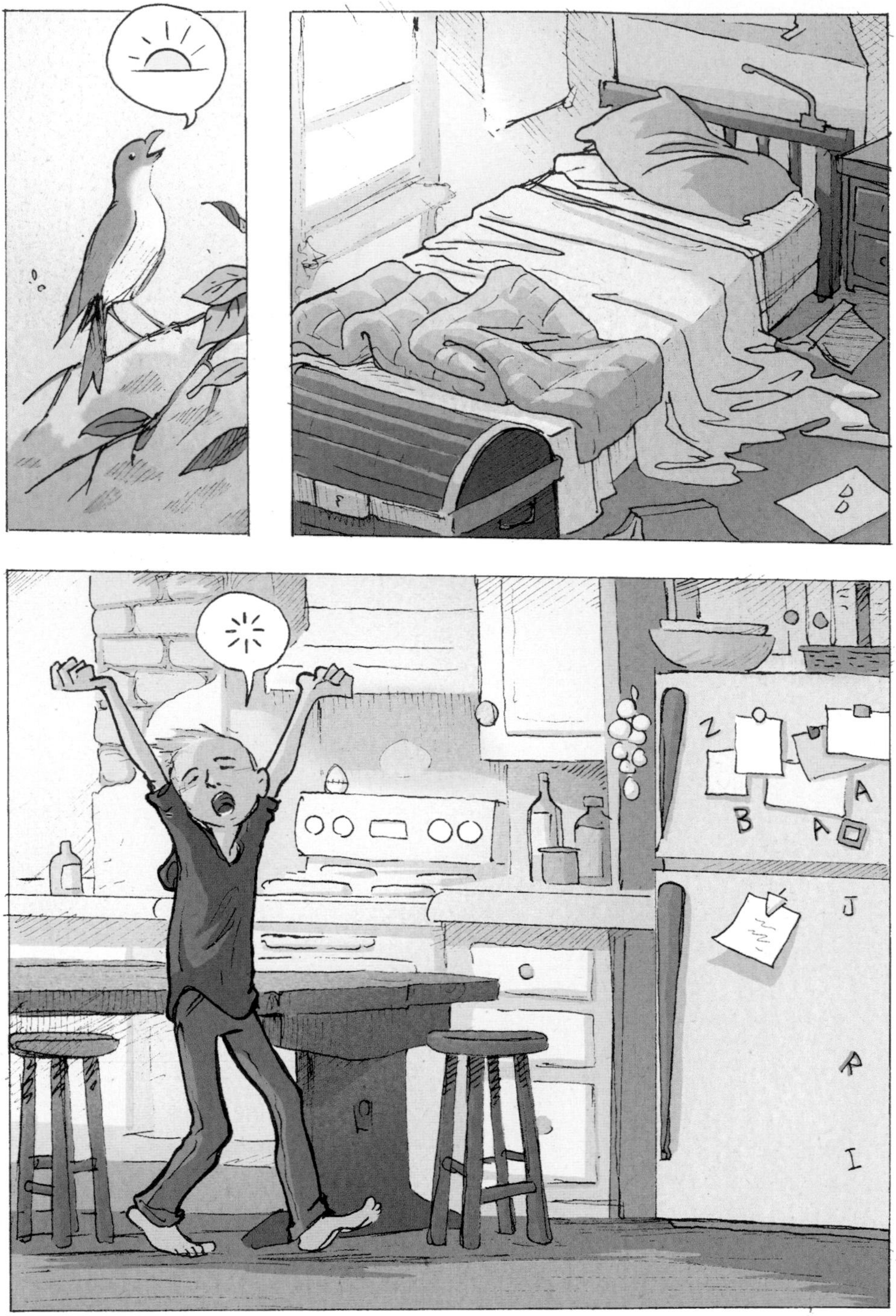

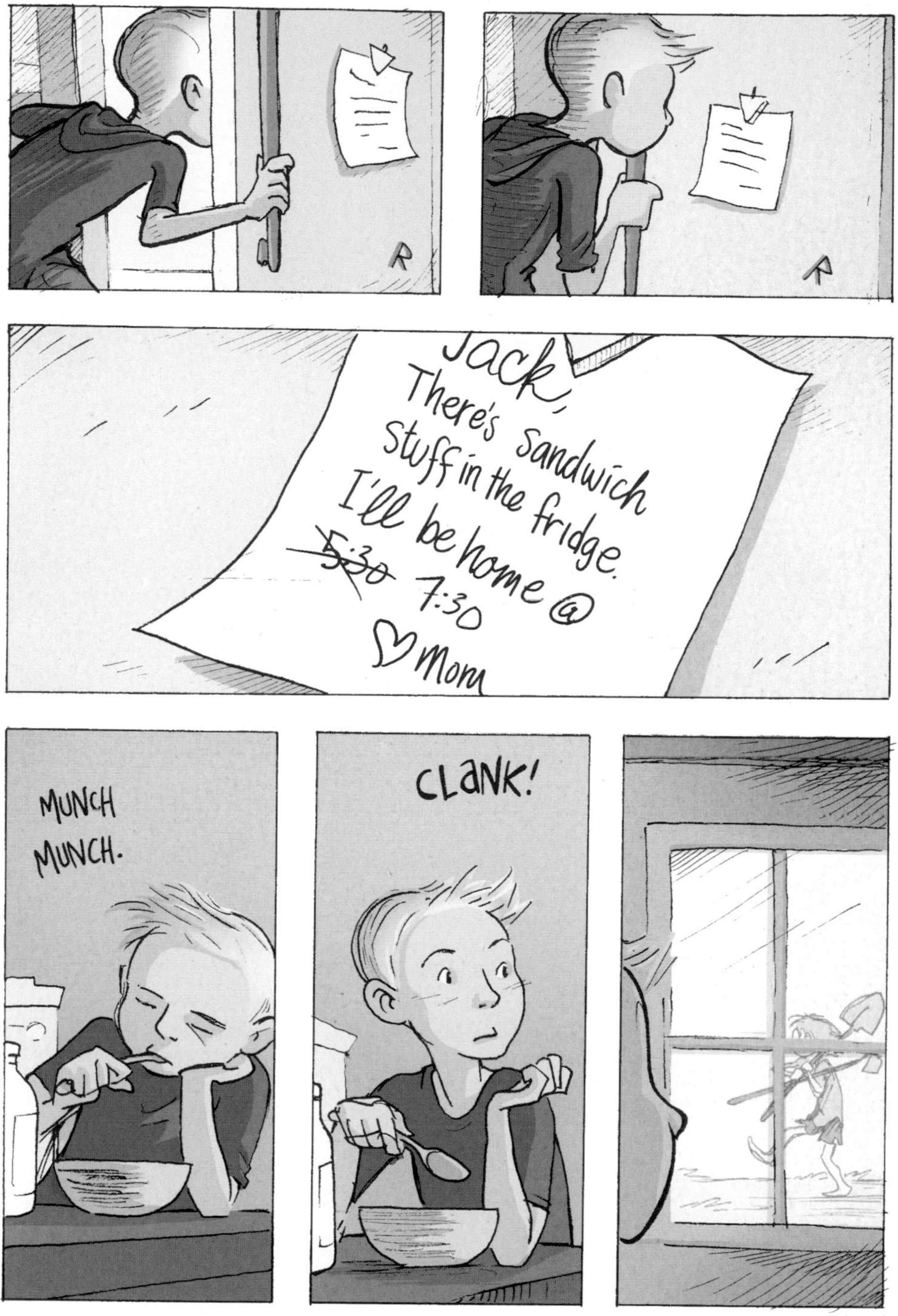
R
R
Jack,
There's sandwich stuff in the fridge.
I'll be home @ 5:30 7:30
♥ Mom
MUNCH MUNCH.
CLANK!

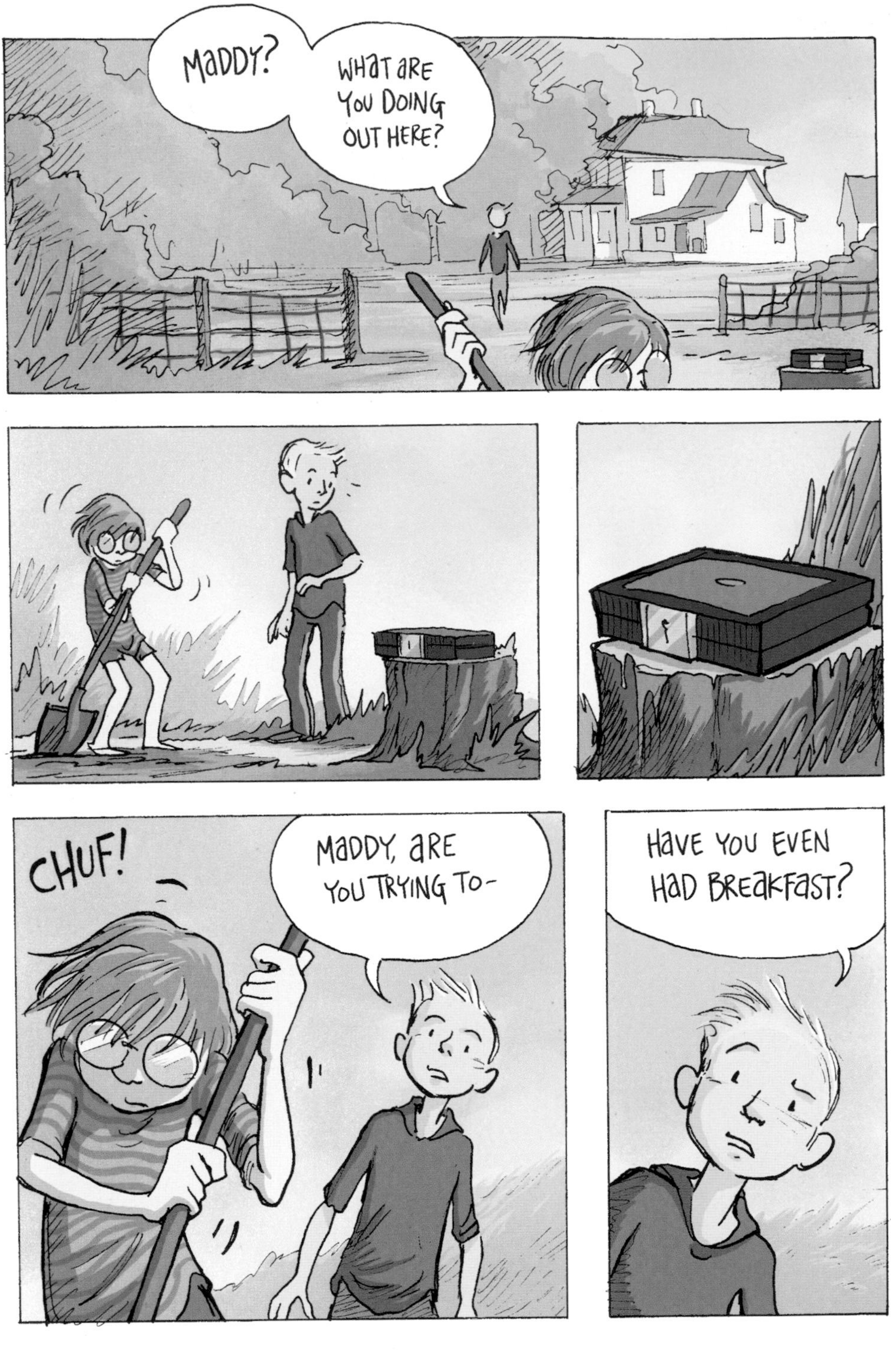
MADDY?
WHAT ARE YOU DOING OUT HERE?
CHUF!
MADDY, ARE YOU TRYING TO-
HAVE YOU EVEN HAD BREAKFAST?

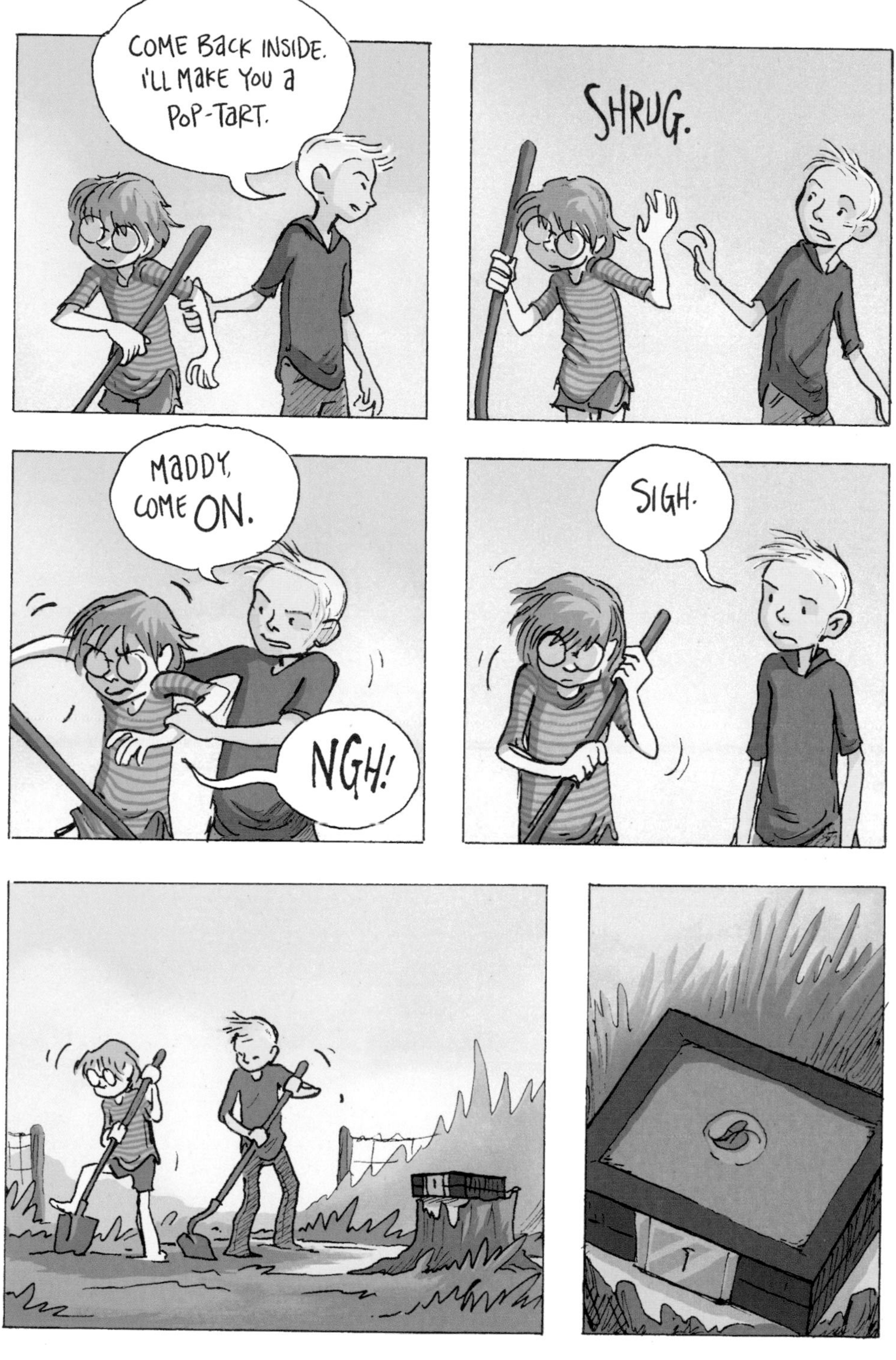
COME BACK INSIDE. I'LL MAKE YOU A POP-TART.
SHRUG.
MADDY, COME ON.
NGH!
SIGH.

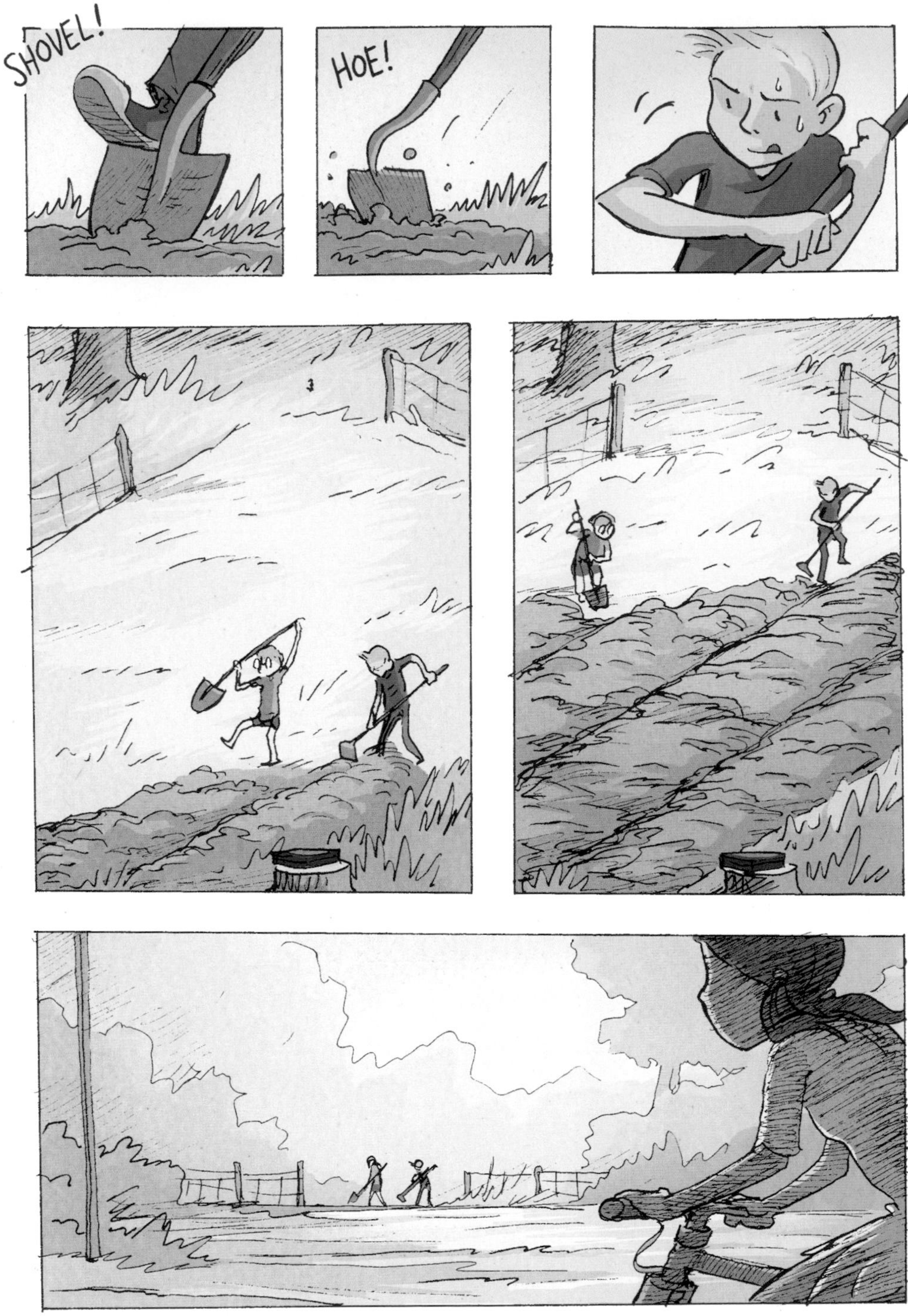
SHOVEL!
HOE!

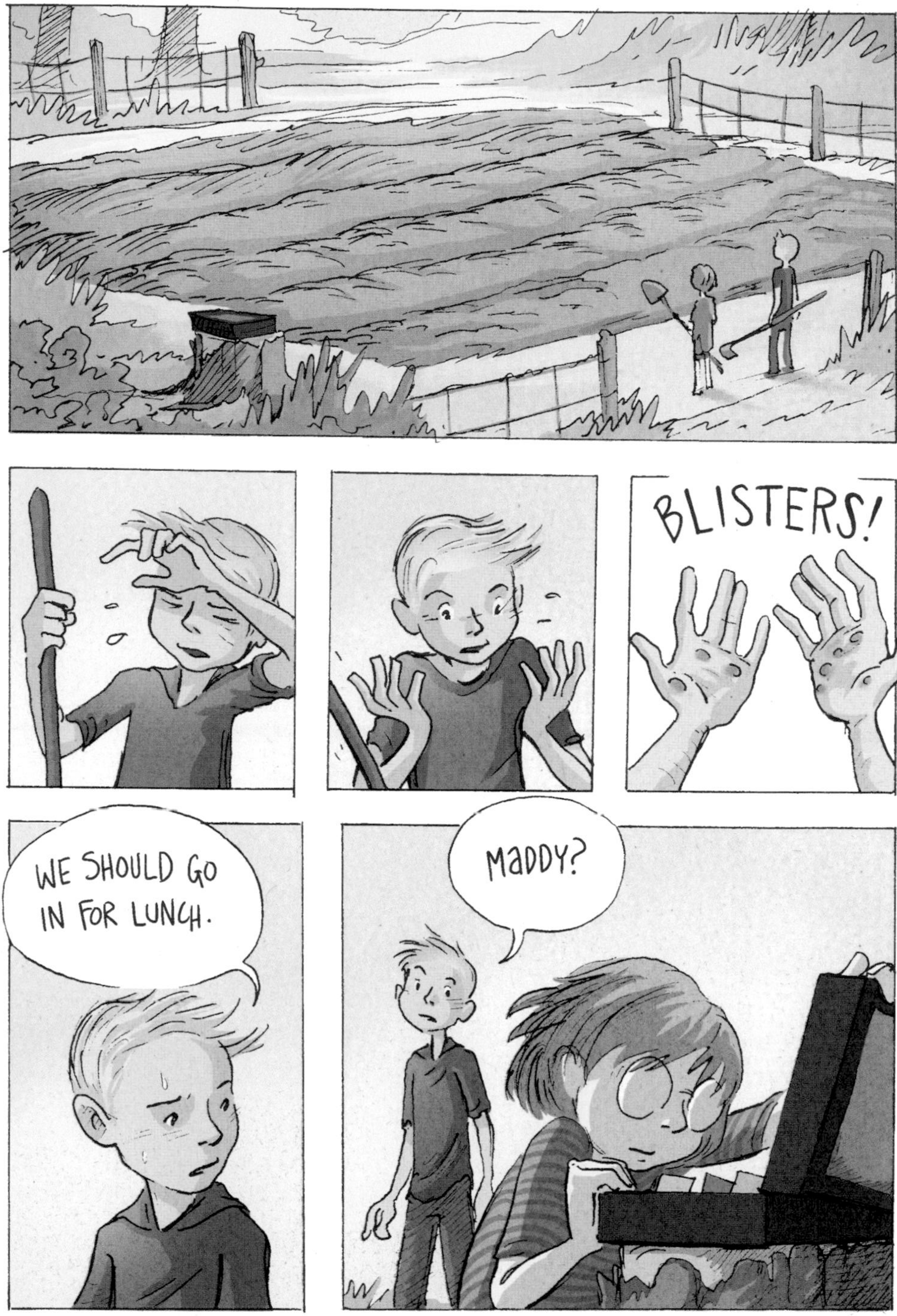
BLISTERS!
WE SHOULD GO IN FOR LUNCH.
MADDY?

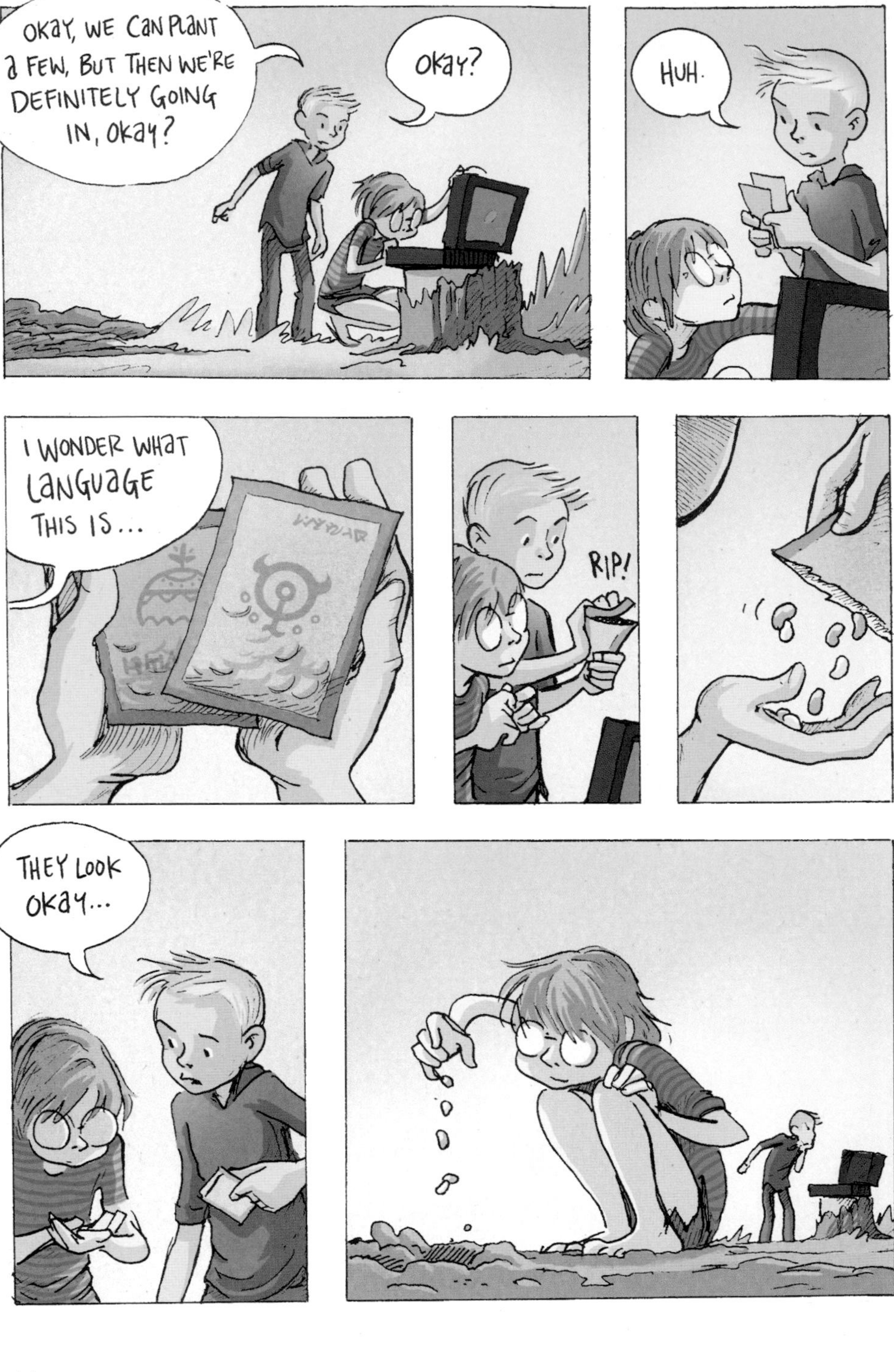
OKAY, WE CAN PLANT A FEW, BUT THEN WE'RE DEFINITELY GOING IN, OKAY?
OKAY?
HUH.
I WONDER WHAT LANGUAGE THIS IS...
RIP!
THEY LOOK OKAY...

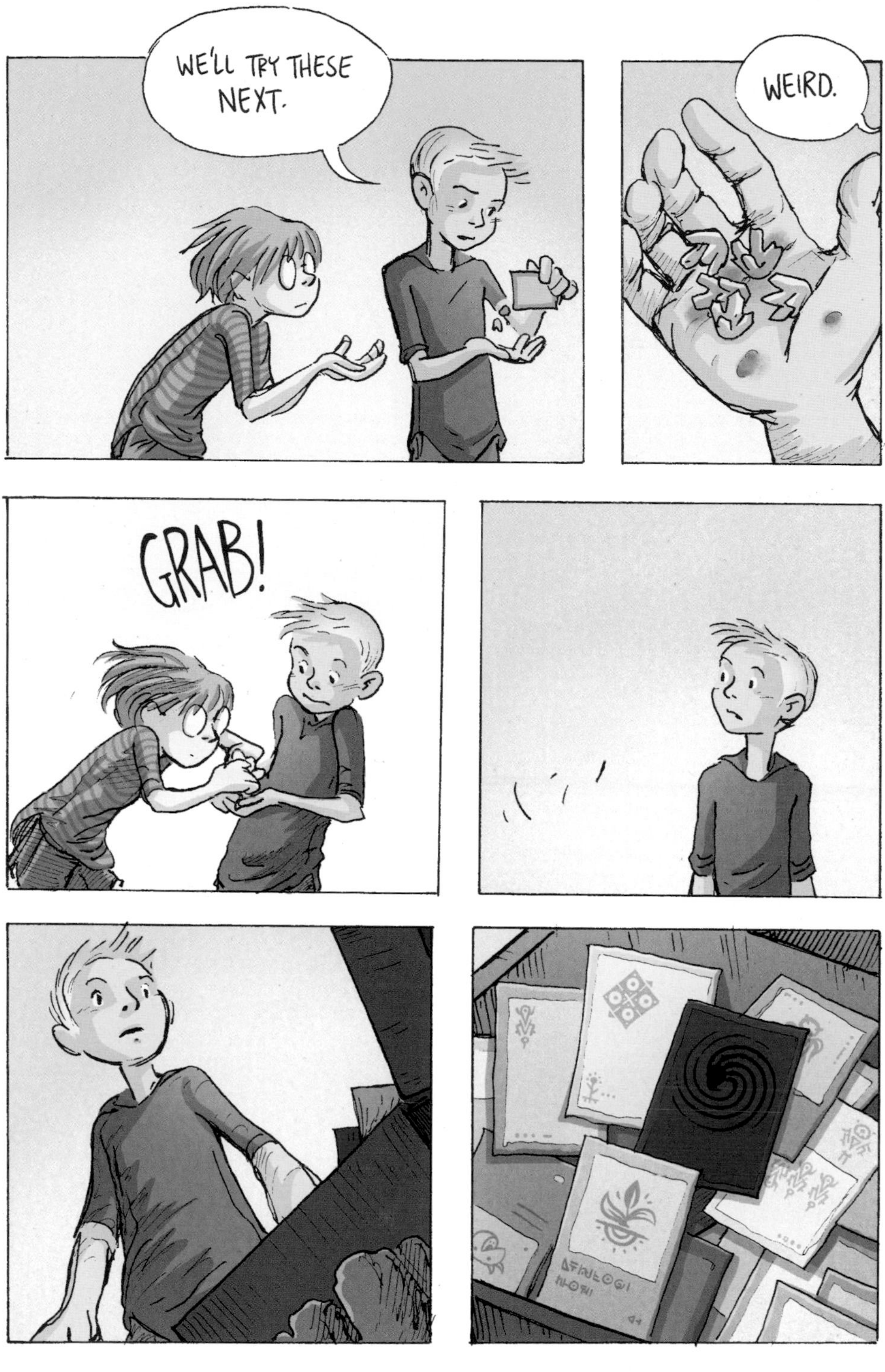
WE'LL TRY THESE NEXT.
WEIRD.
GRAB!

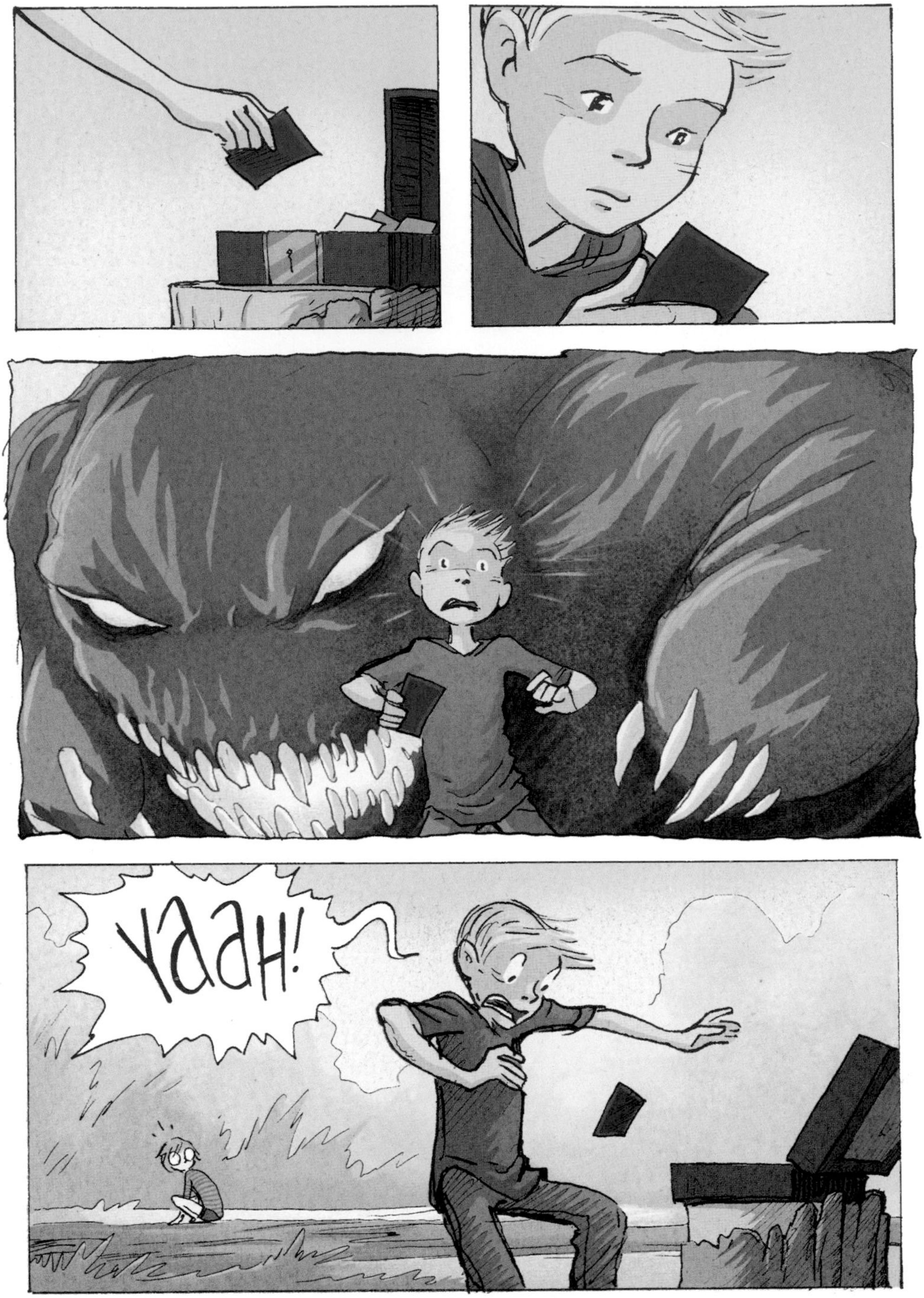
YAAH!

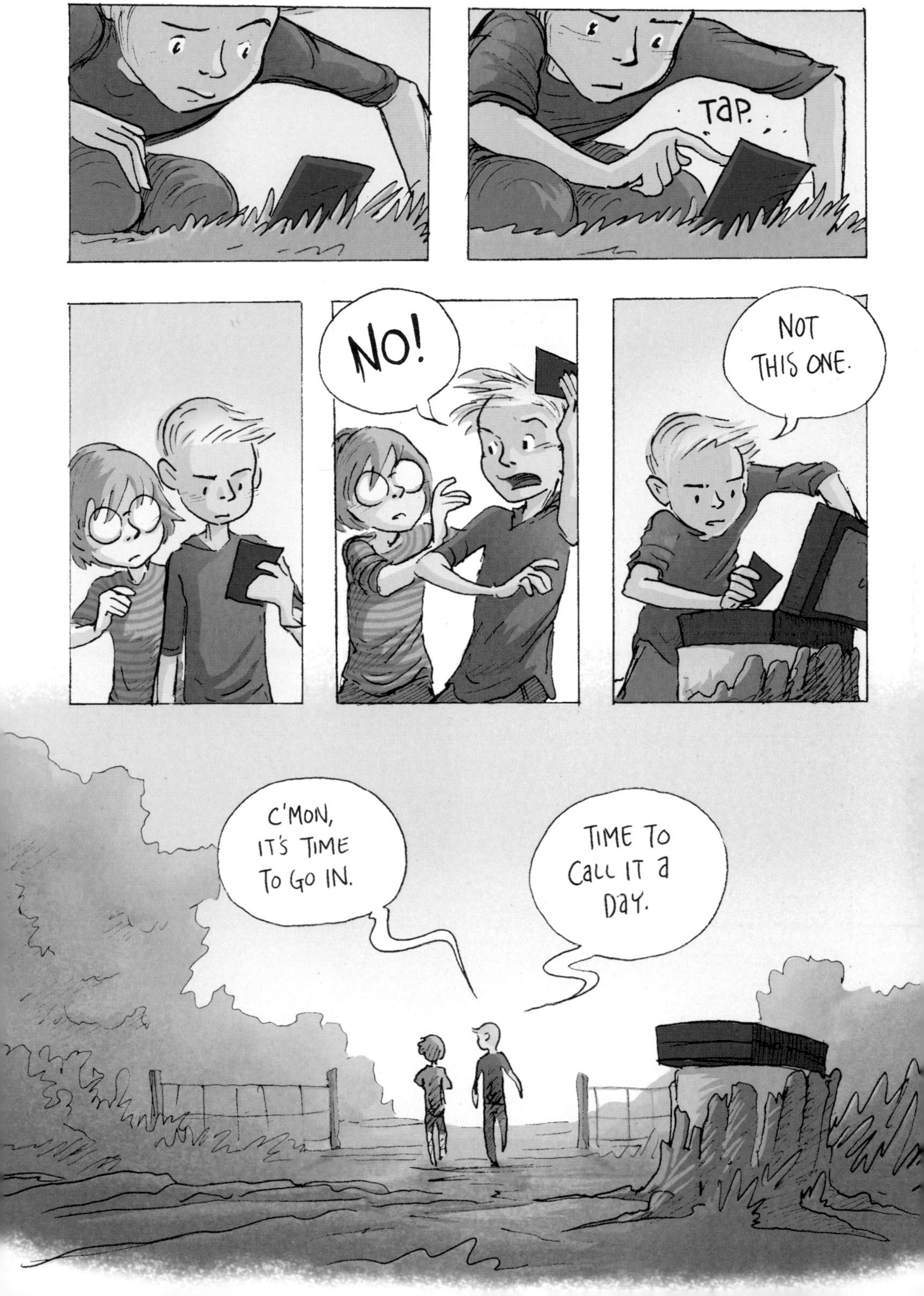

TAP.
NO!
NOT THIS ONE.
C'MON, IT'S TIME TO GO IN.
TIME TO CALL IT A DAY.

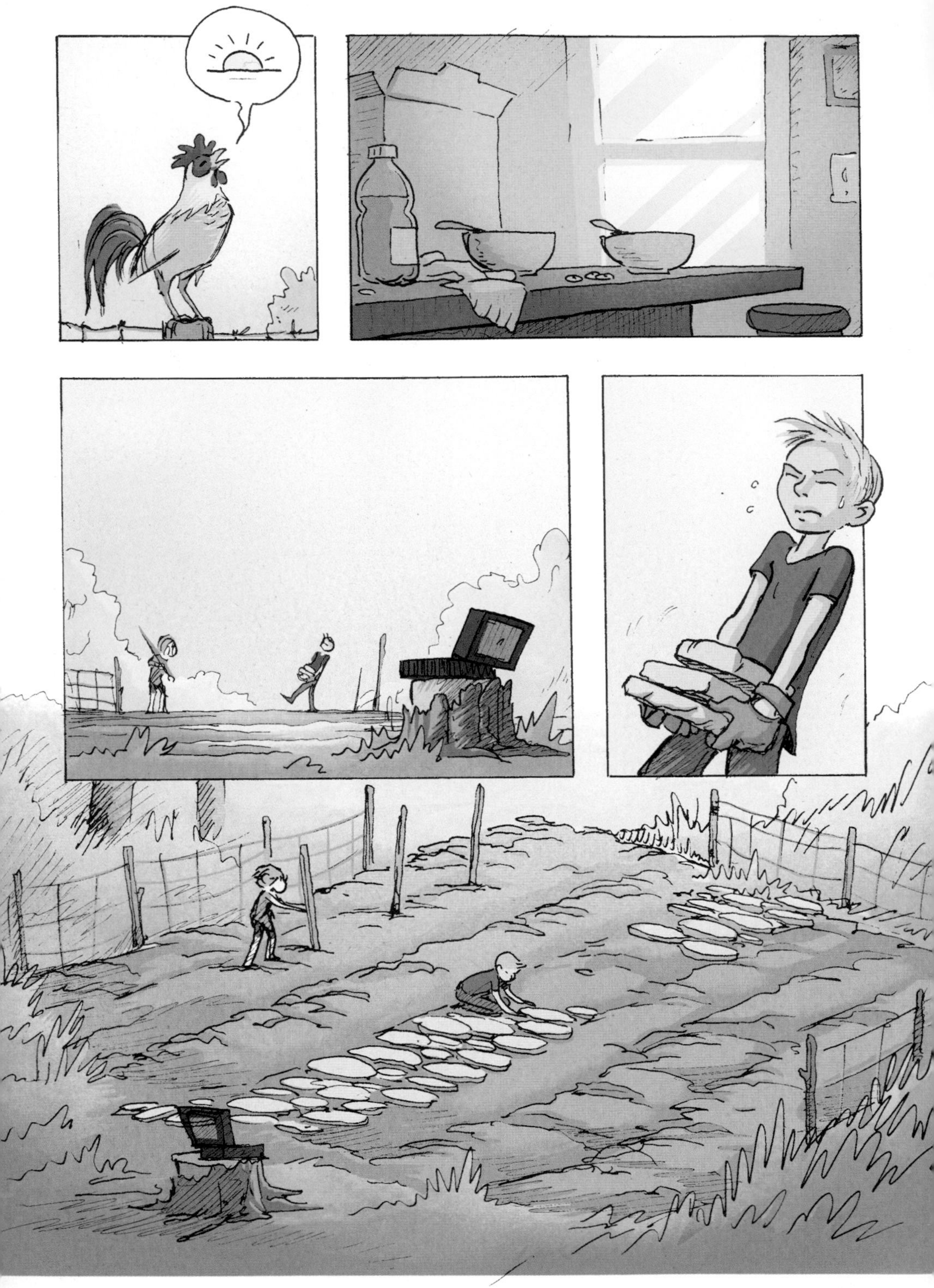

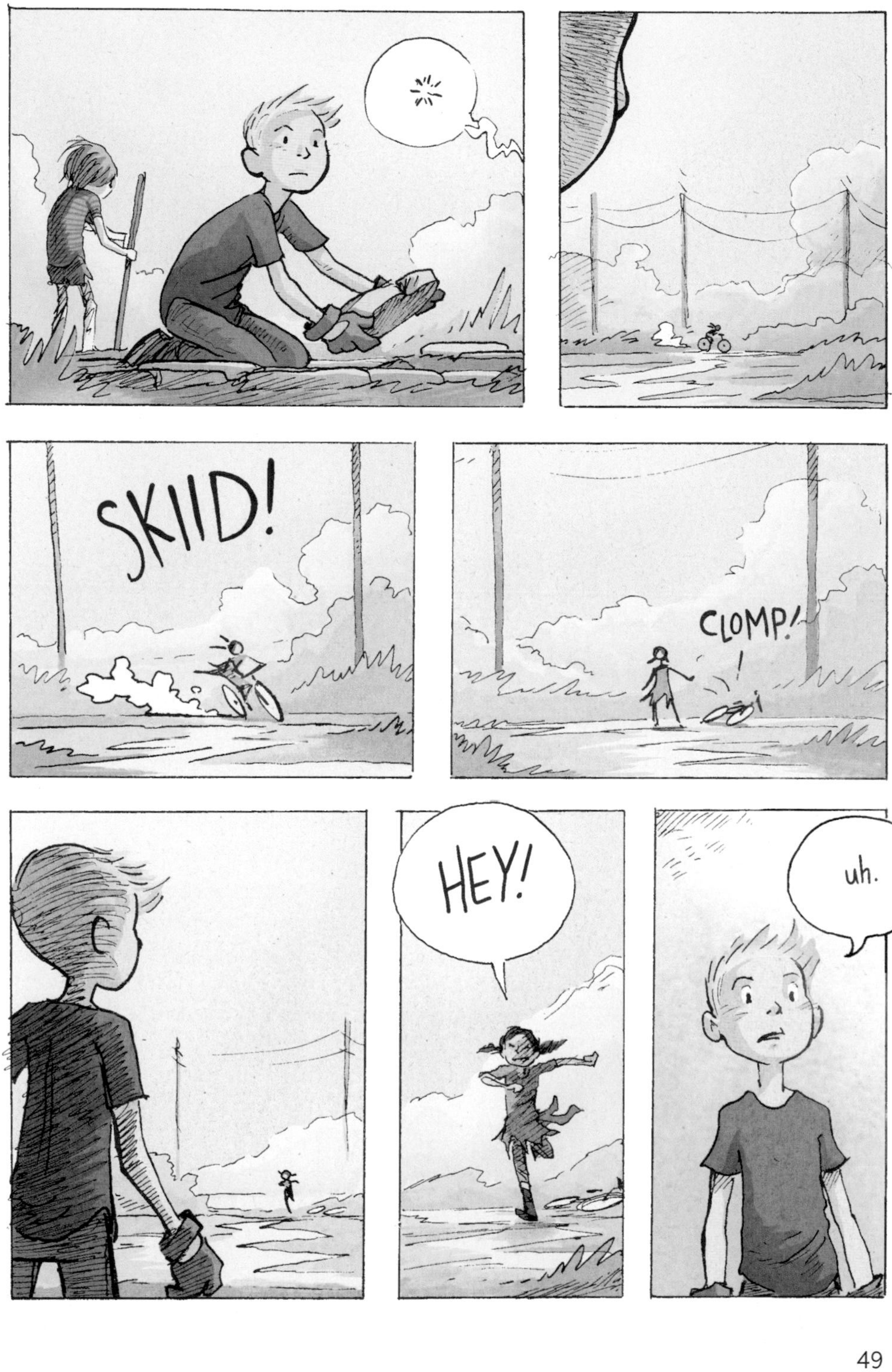
SKIID!
CLOMP!
HEY!
uh.

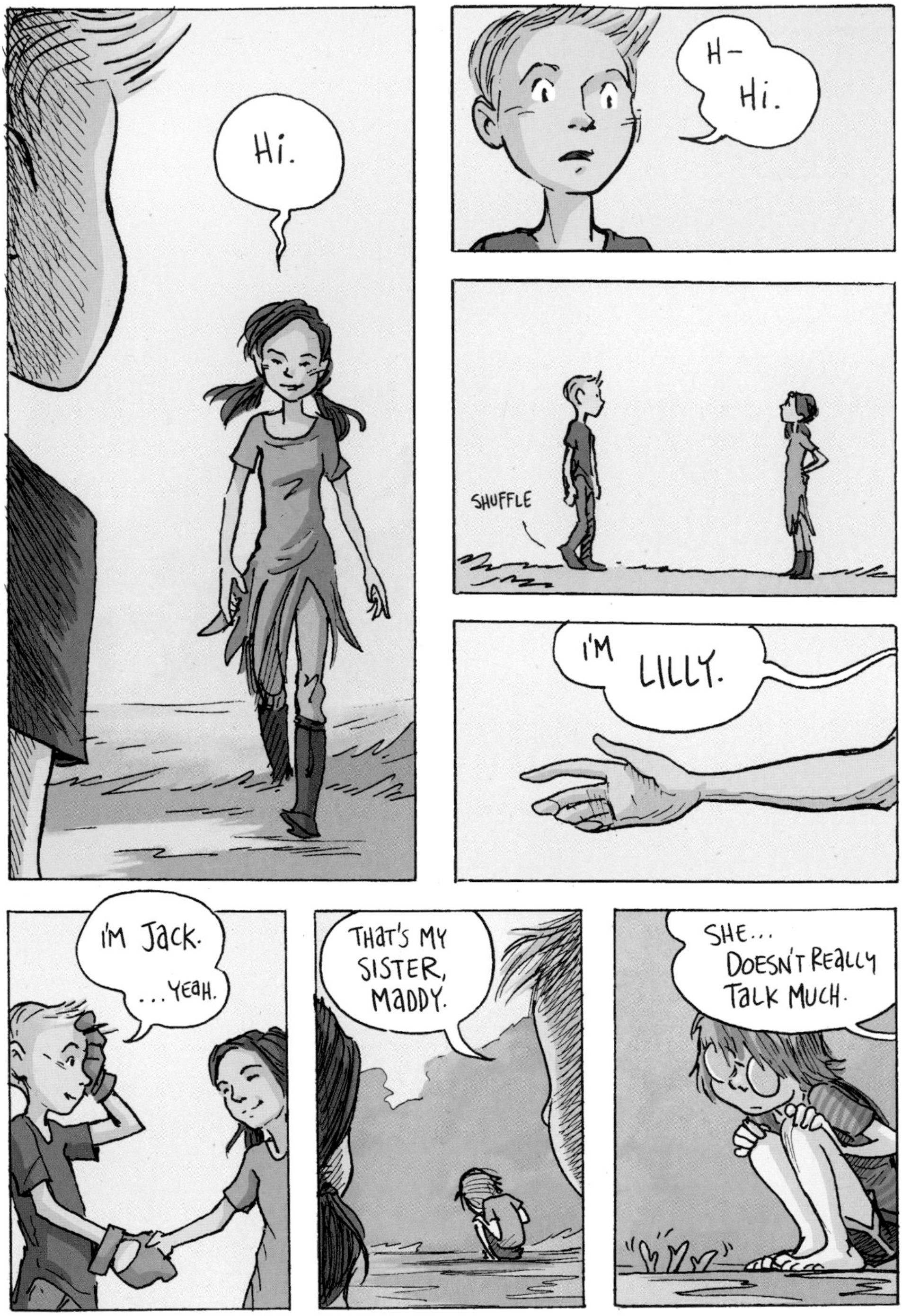
Hi.
H– Hi.
SHUFFLE
I'M LILLY.
I'M Jack.
...Yeah.
THAT'S MY SISTER, MADDY.
SHE... DOESN'T REALLY TALK MUCH.

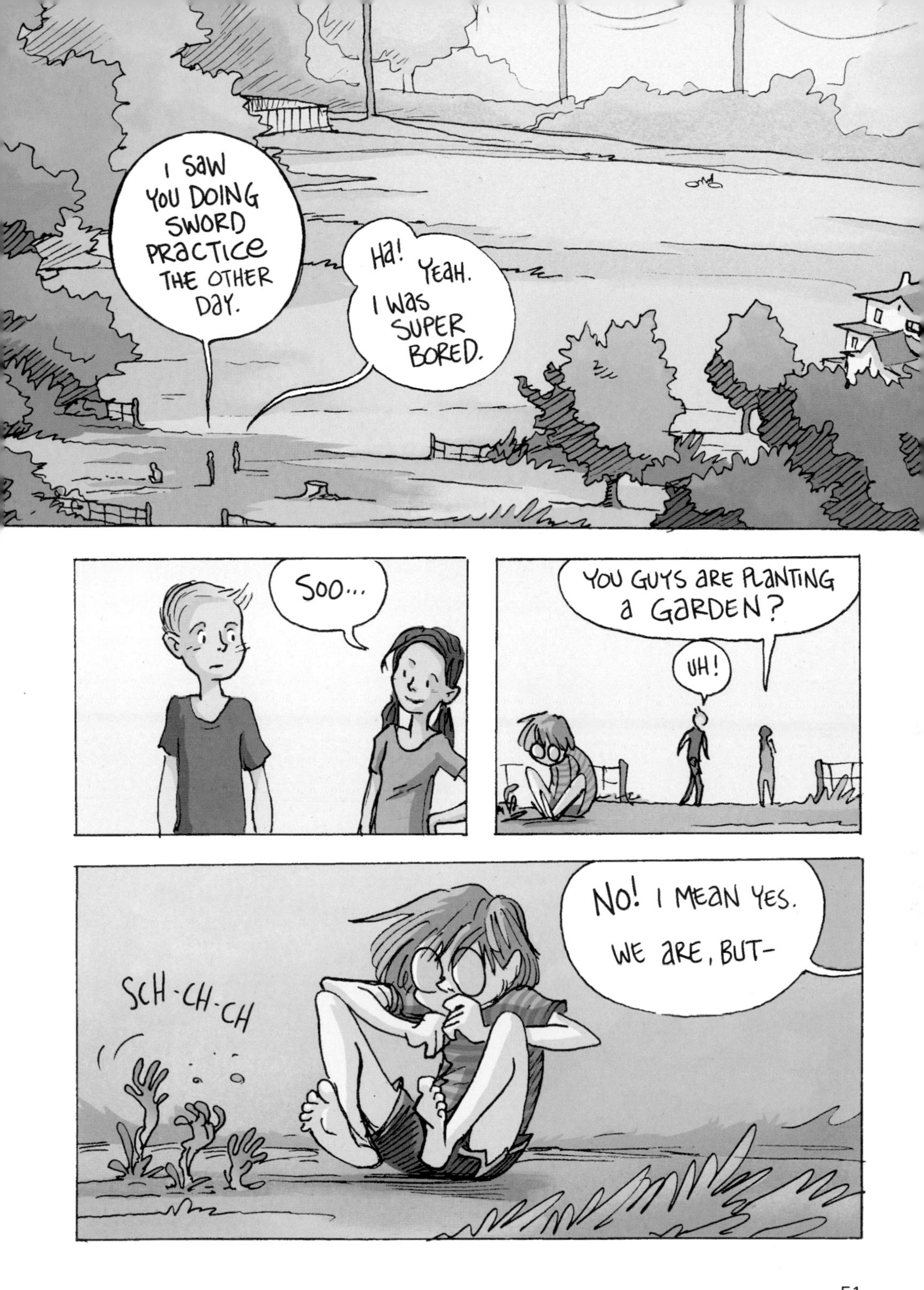
I SAW YOU DOING SWORD PRACTICE THE OTHER DAY.
HA! YEAH. I WAS SUPER BORED.
SOO...
YOU GUYS ARE PLANTING A GARDEN?
UH!
SCH-CH-CH
NO! I MEAN YES. WE ARE, BUT-

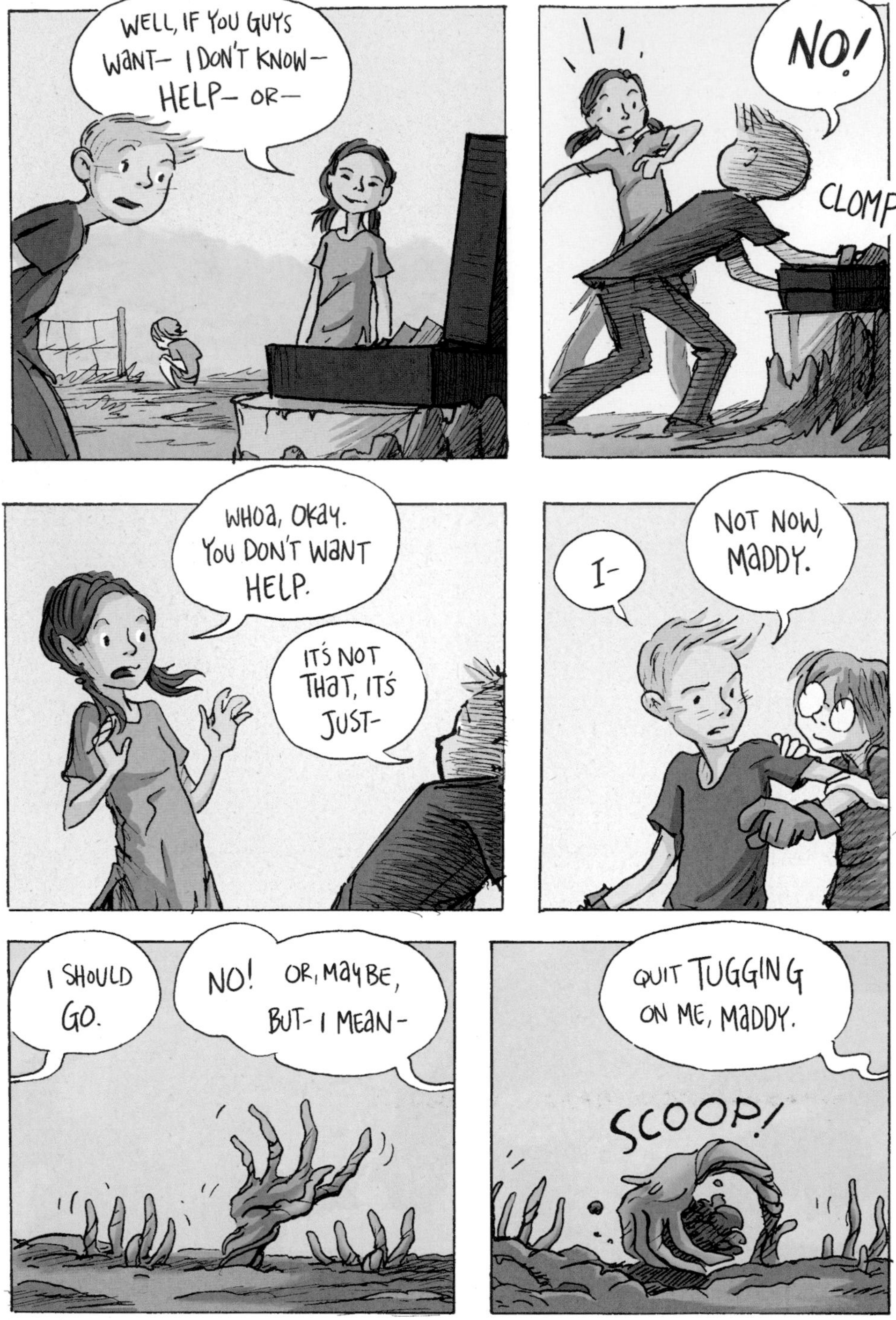

WELL, IF YOU GUYS WANT– I DON'T KNOW– HELP– OR–
NO!
CLOMP!
WHOA, OKAY. YOU DON'T WANT HELP.
IT'S NOT THAT, IT'S JUST-
I-
NOT NOW, MADDY.
I SHOULD GO.
NO! OR, MAYBE, BUT- I MEAN-
QUIT TUGGING ON ME, MADDY.
SCOOP!

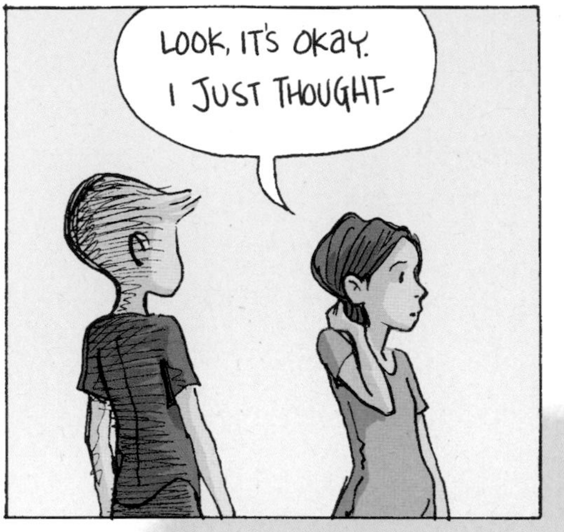
LOOK, IT'S OKAY.
I JUST THOUGHT-

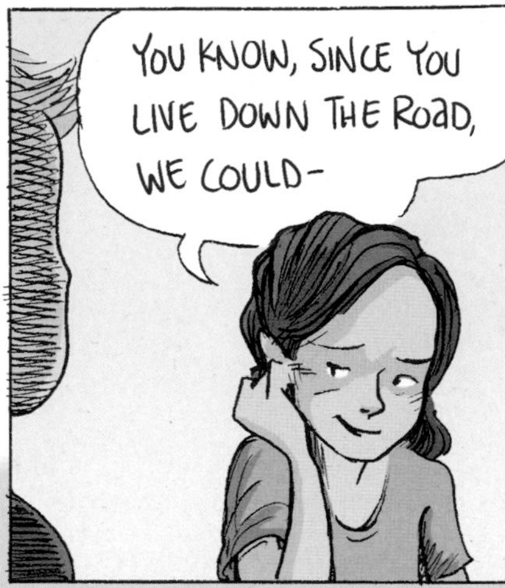
YOU KNOW, SINCE YOU LIVE DOWN THE ROAD, WE COULD-

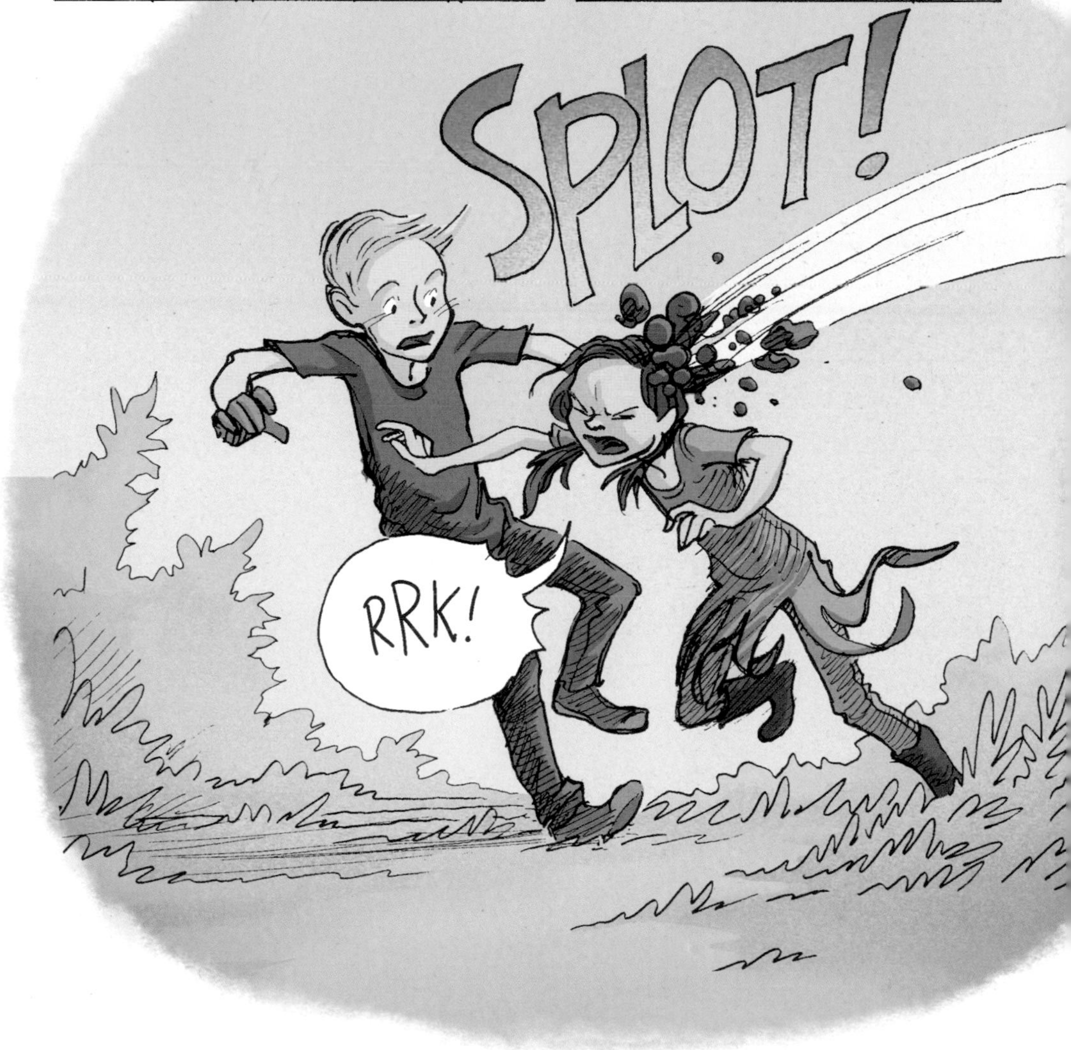
SPLOT!
RRK!

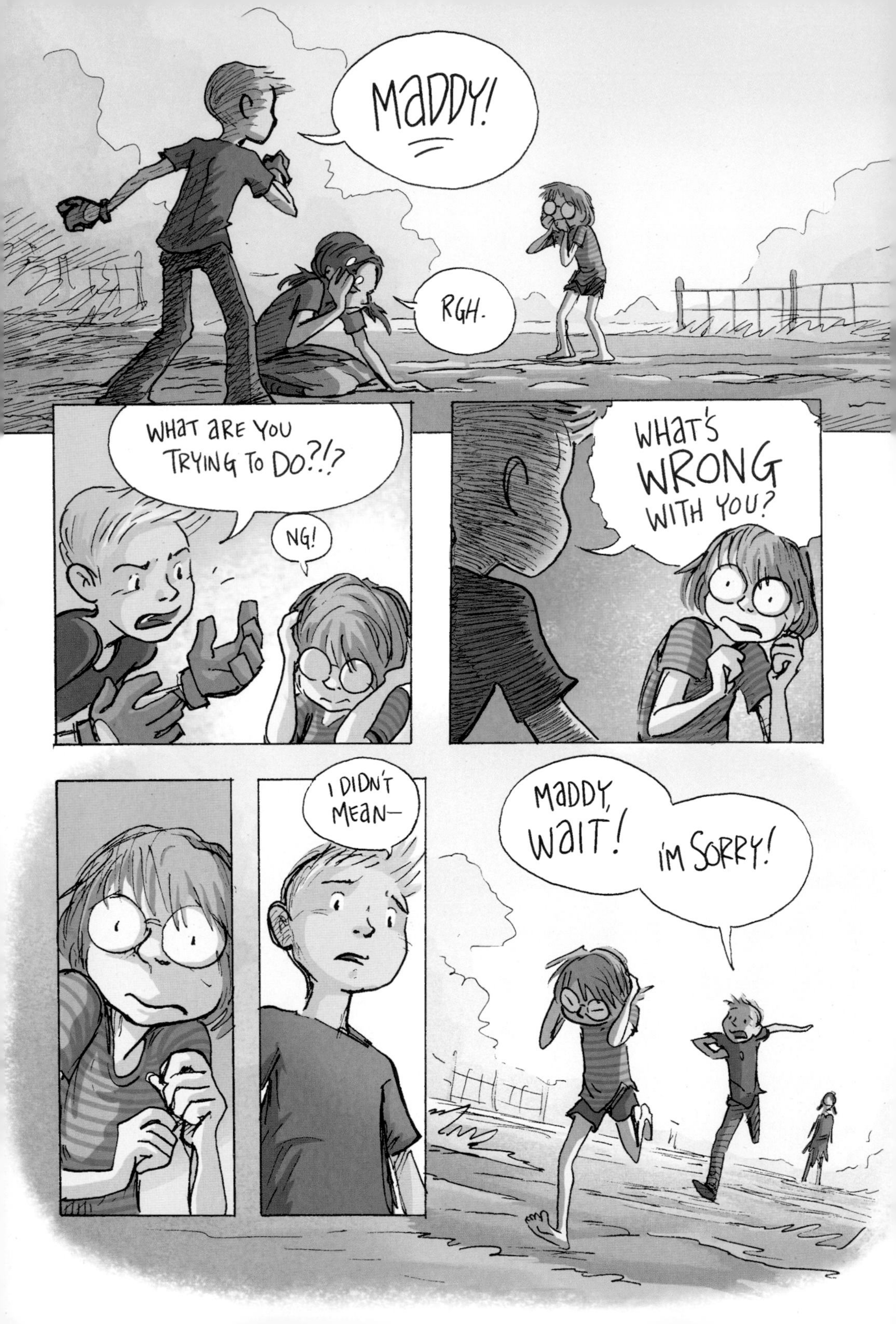
MADDY!
RGH.
WHAT ARE YOU TRYING TO DO?!?
NG!
WHAT'S WRONG WITH YOU?
I DIDN'T MEAN—
MADDY, WAIT!
I'M SORRY!

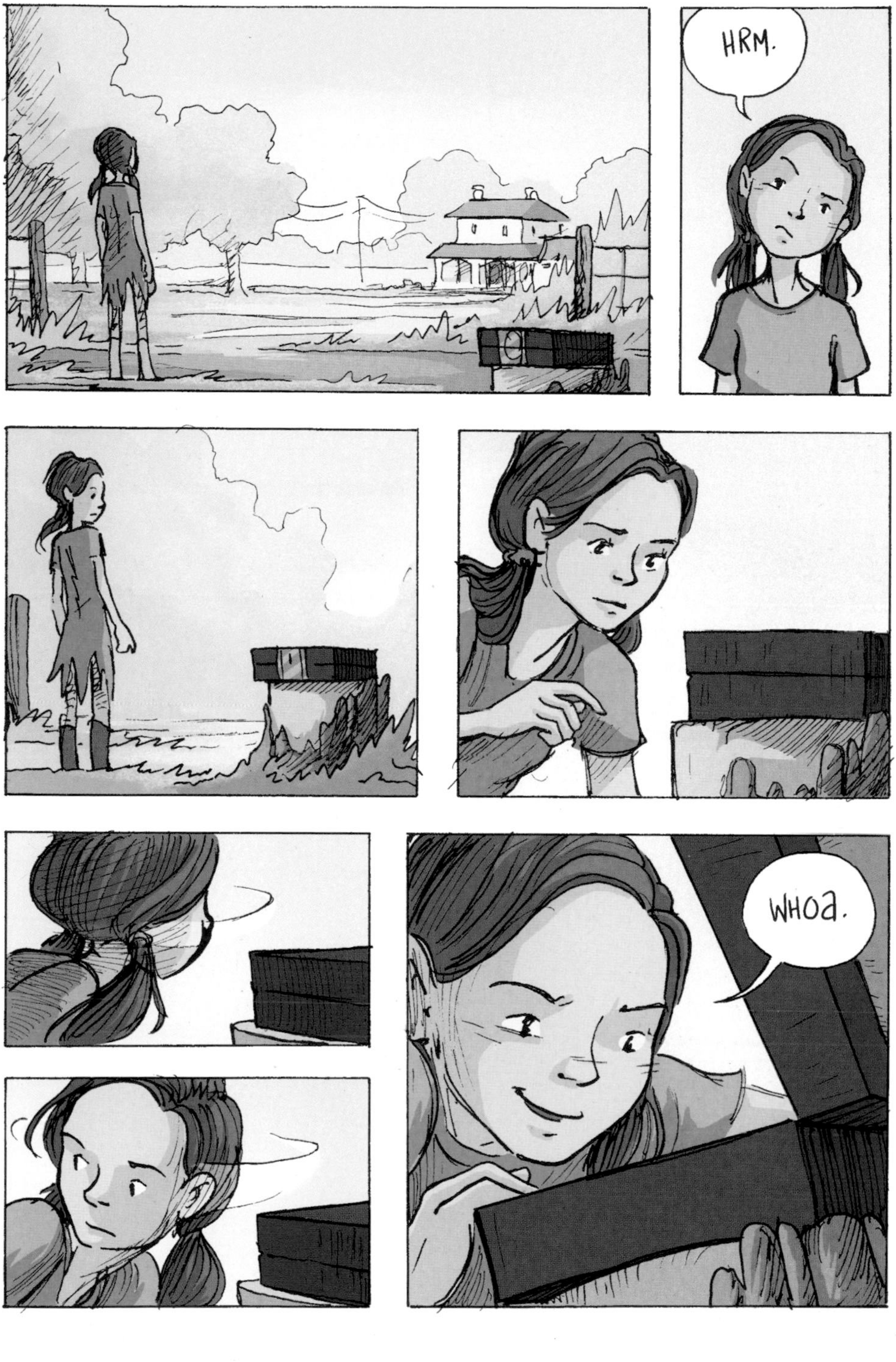
HRM.
WHOA.

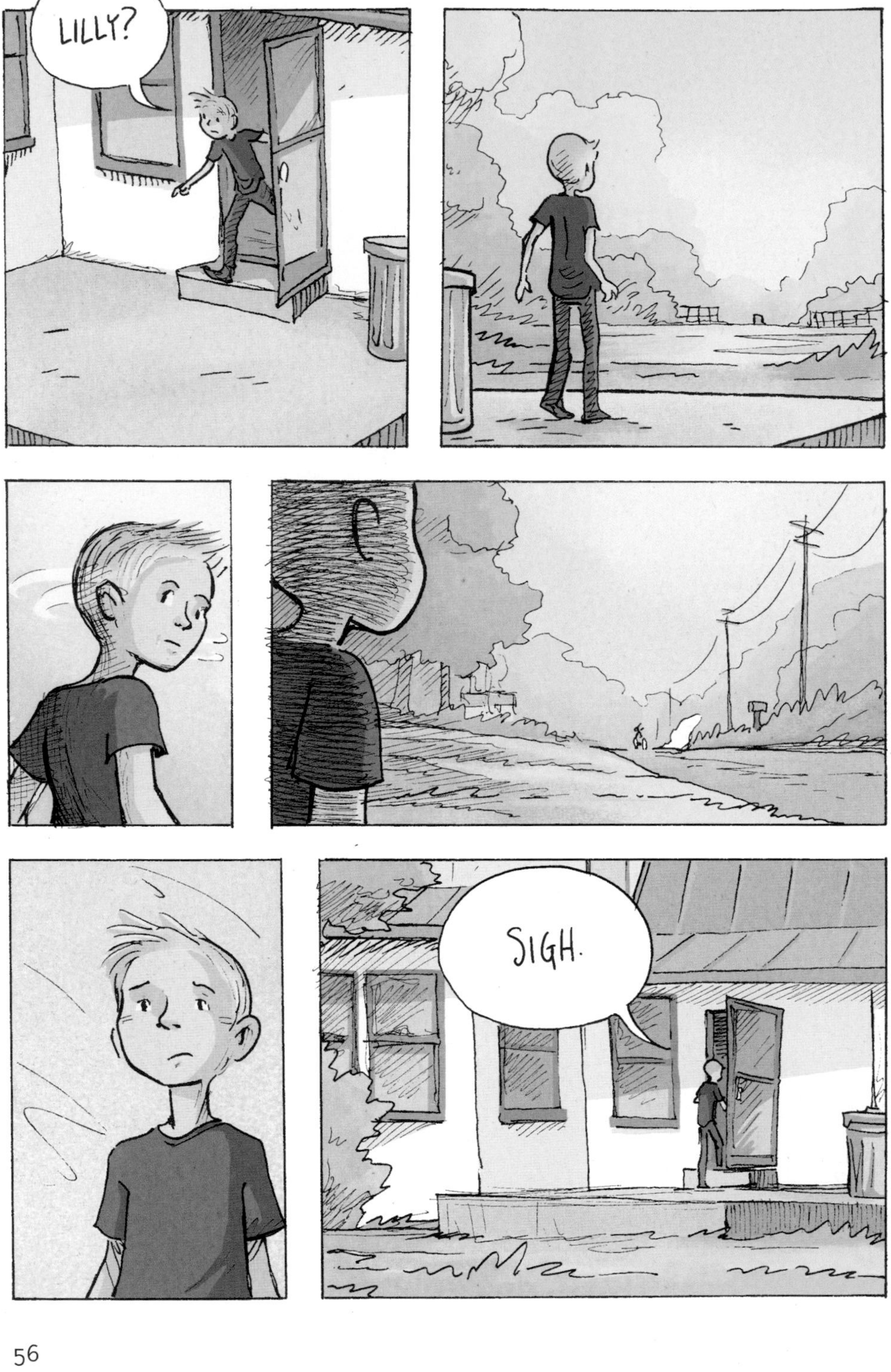
LILLY?
SIGH.

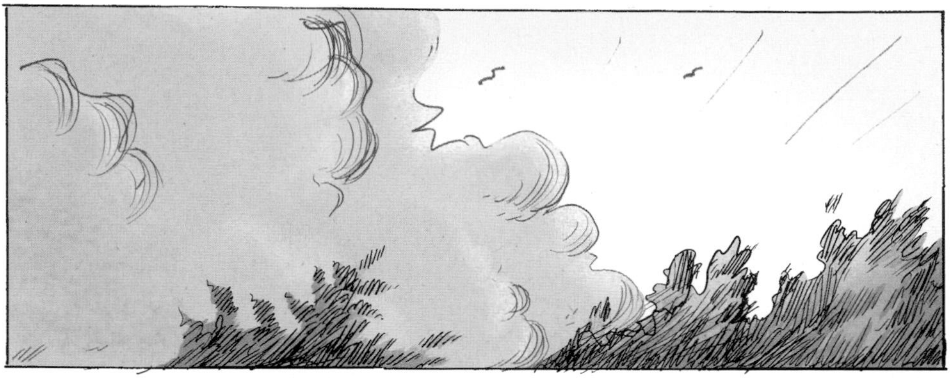
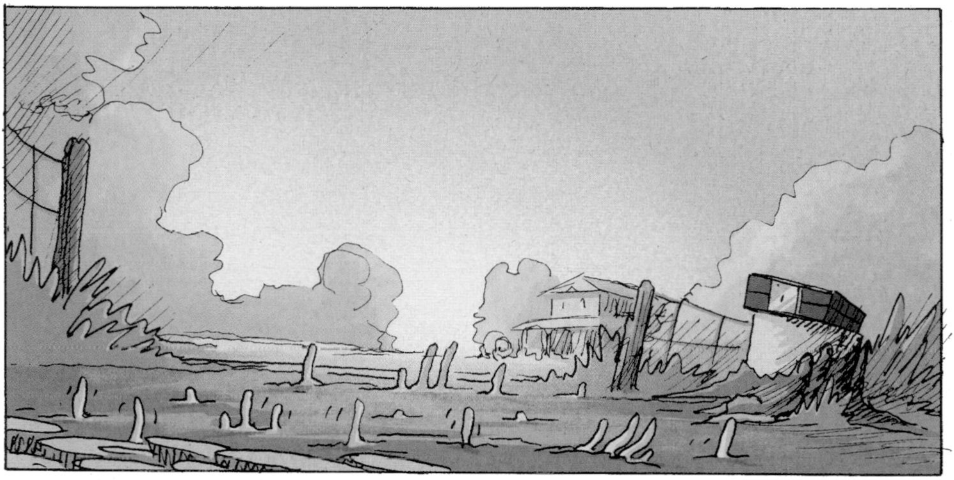
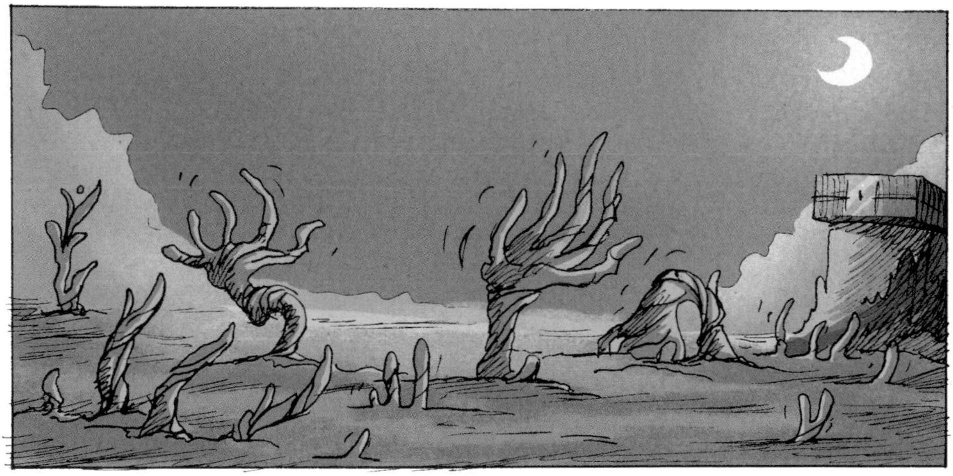

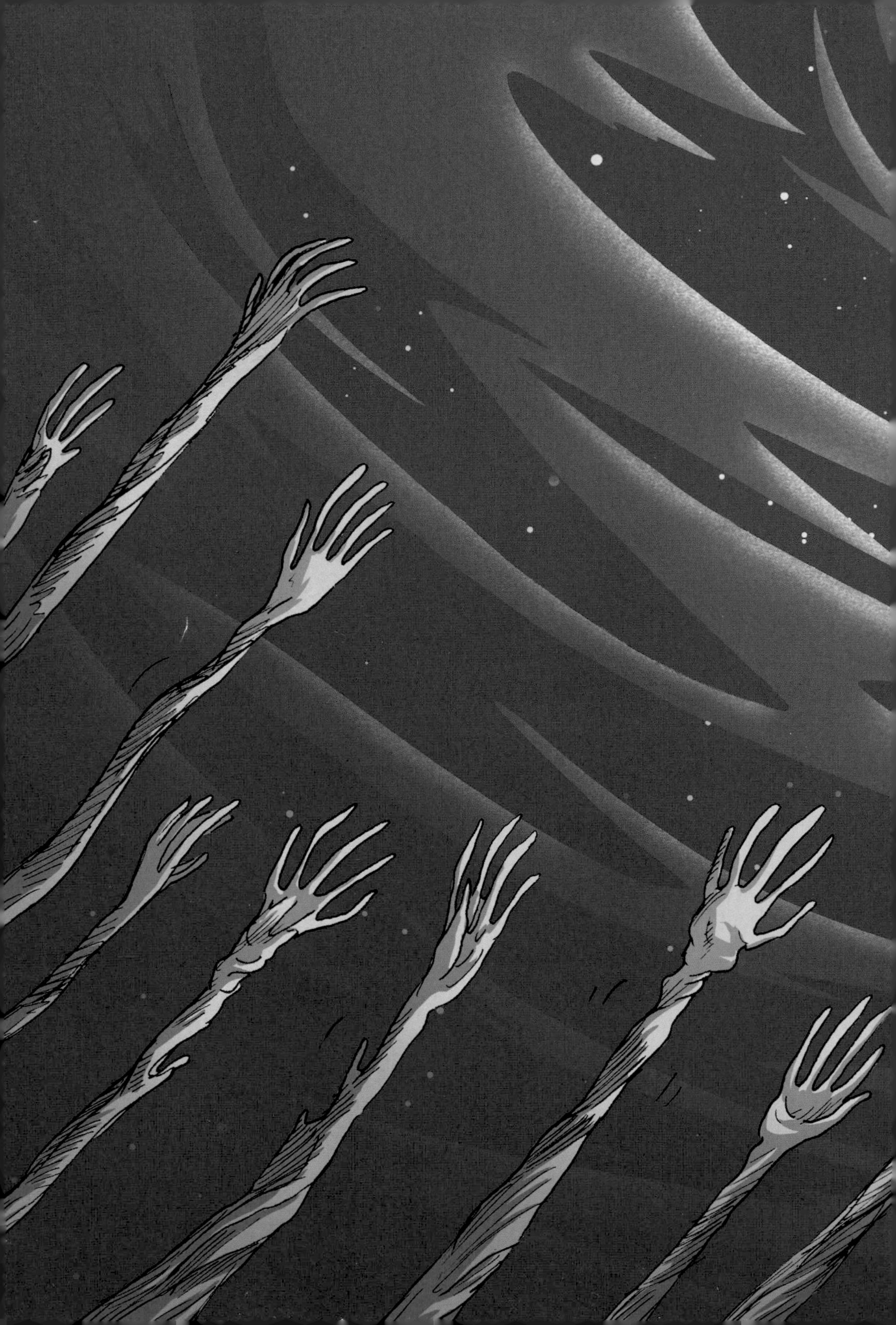

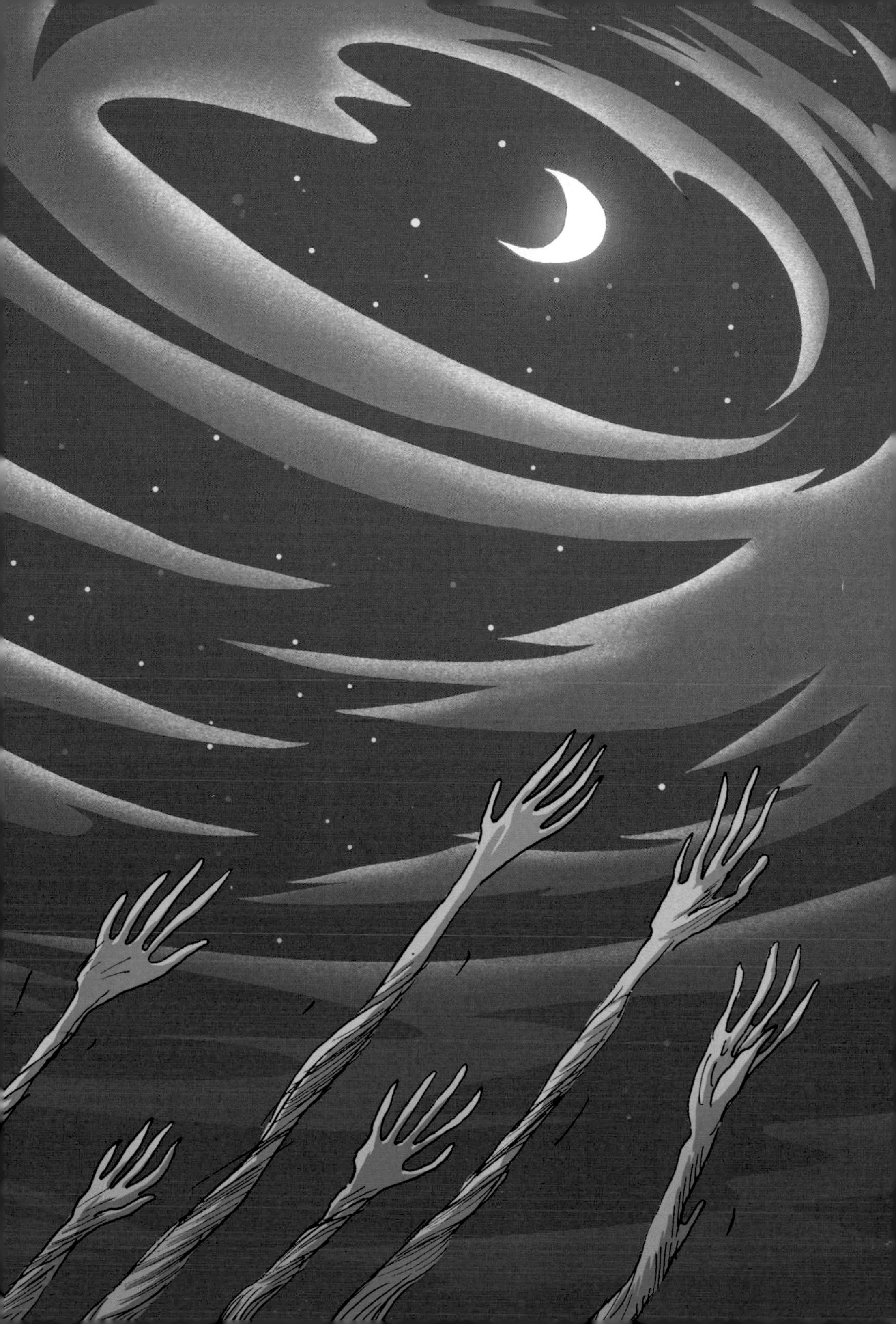

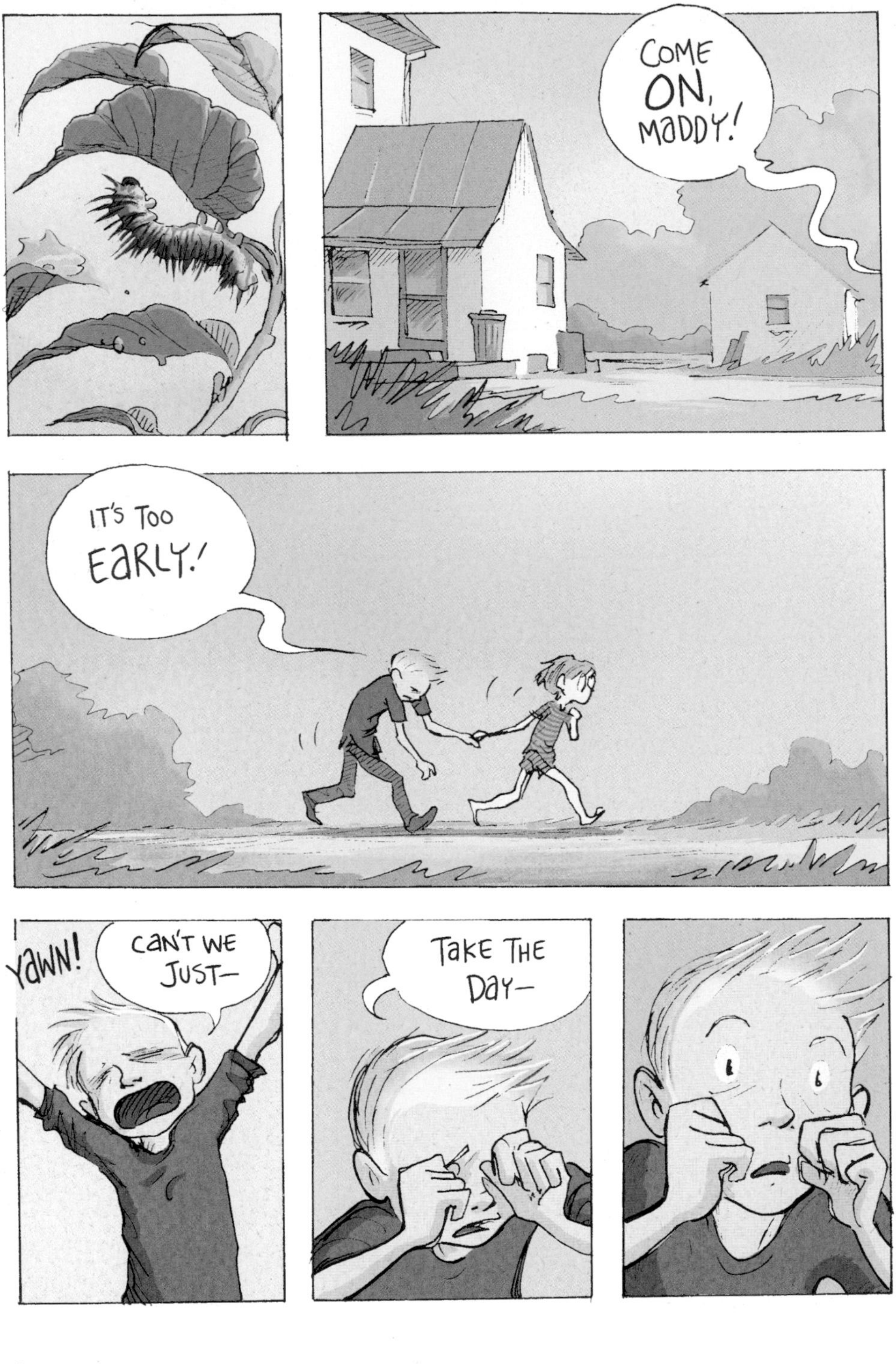
COME ON, MADDY!
IT'S TOO EARLY!
YAWN!
CAN'T WE JUST—
TAKE THE DAY—

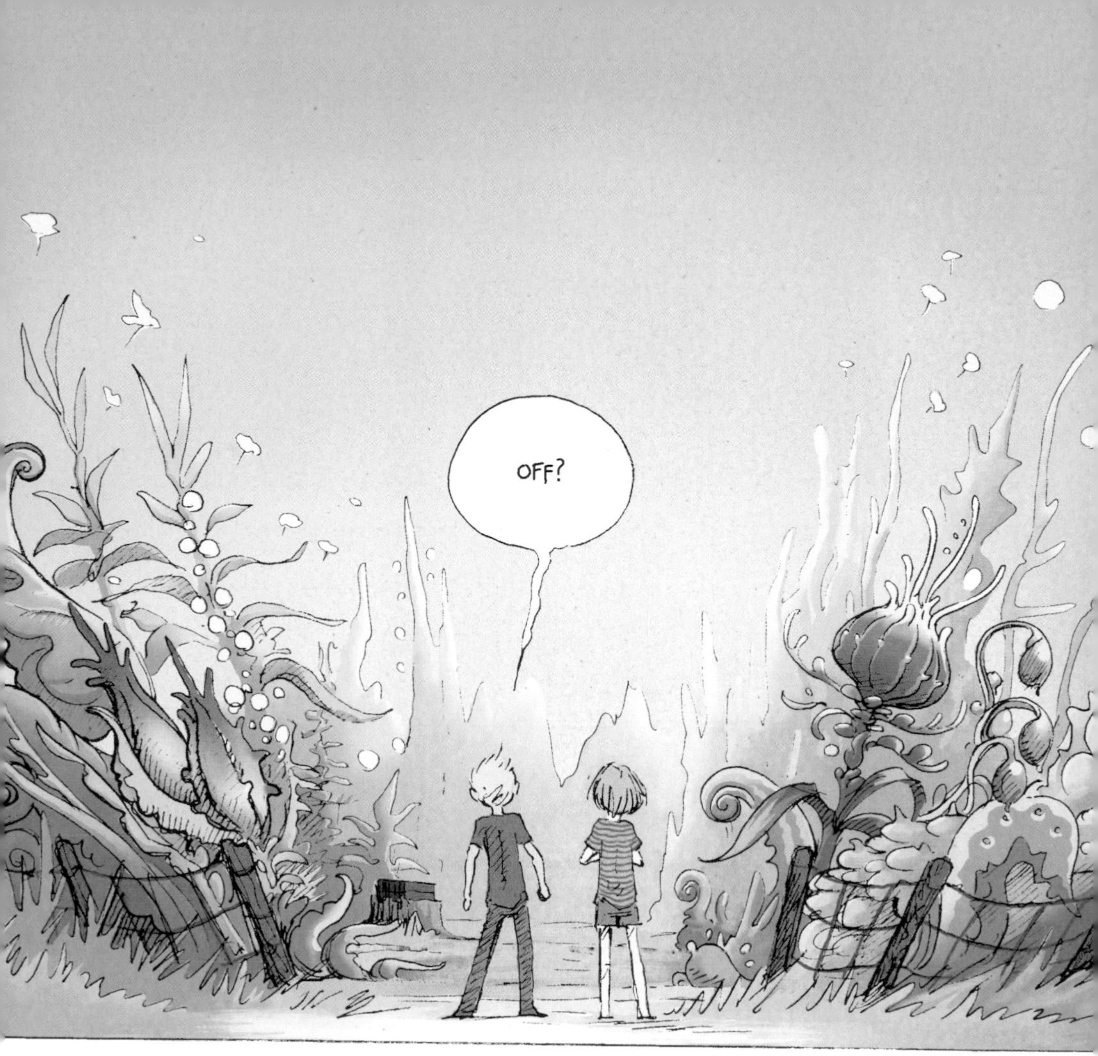
OFF?

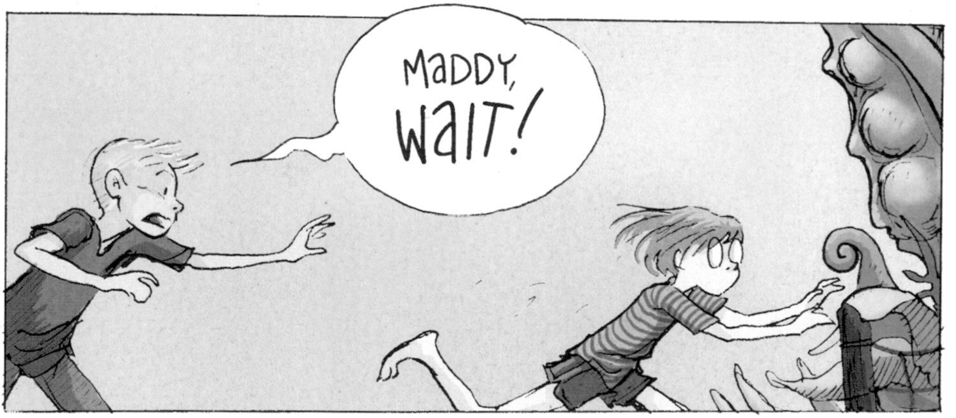
MADDY, WAIT!

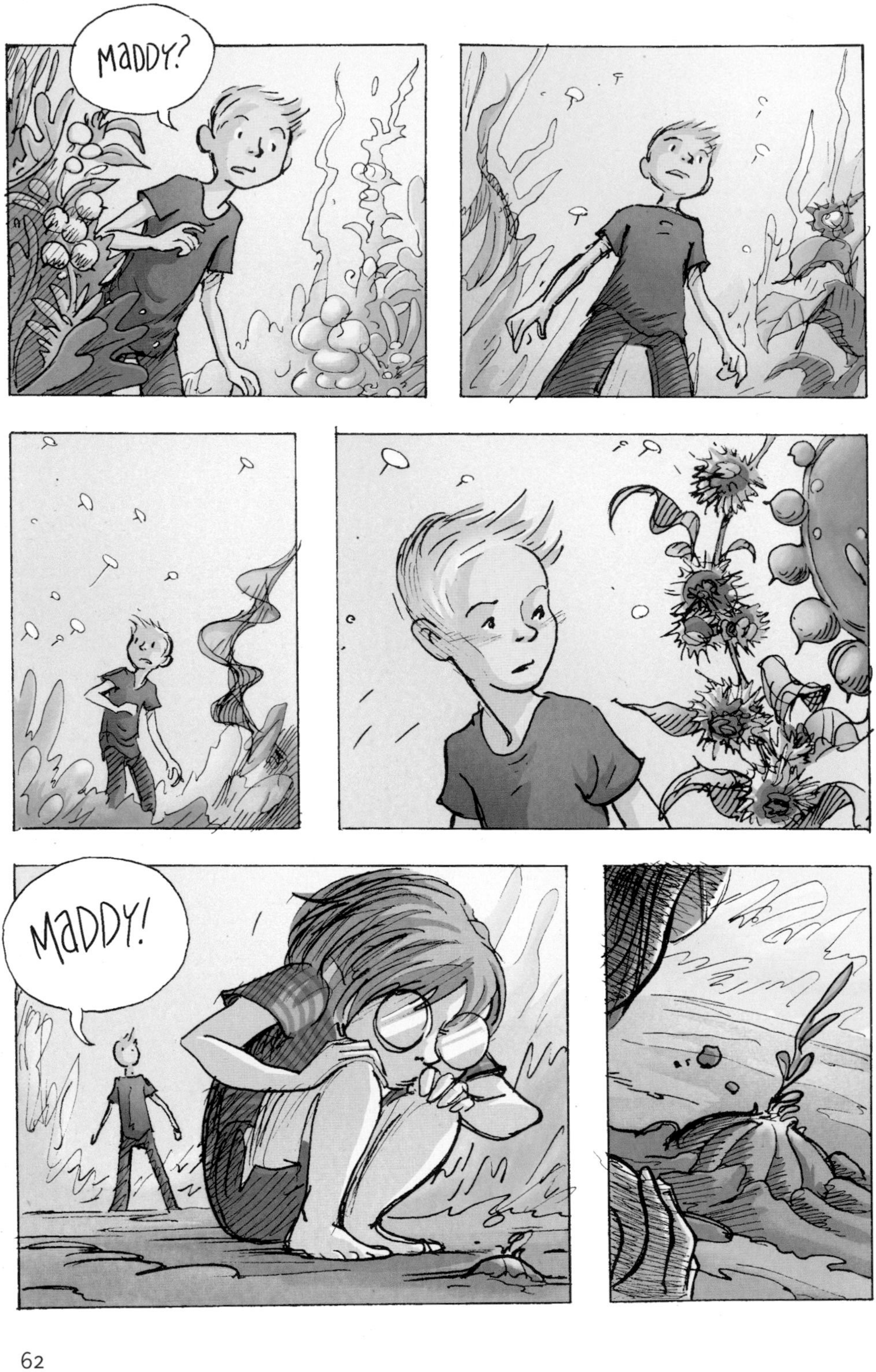
MADDY?
MADDY!

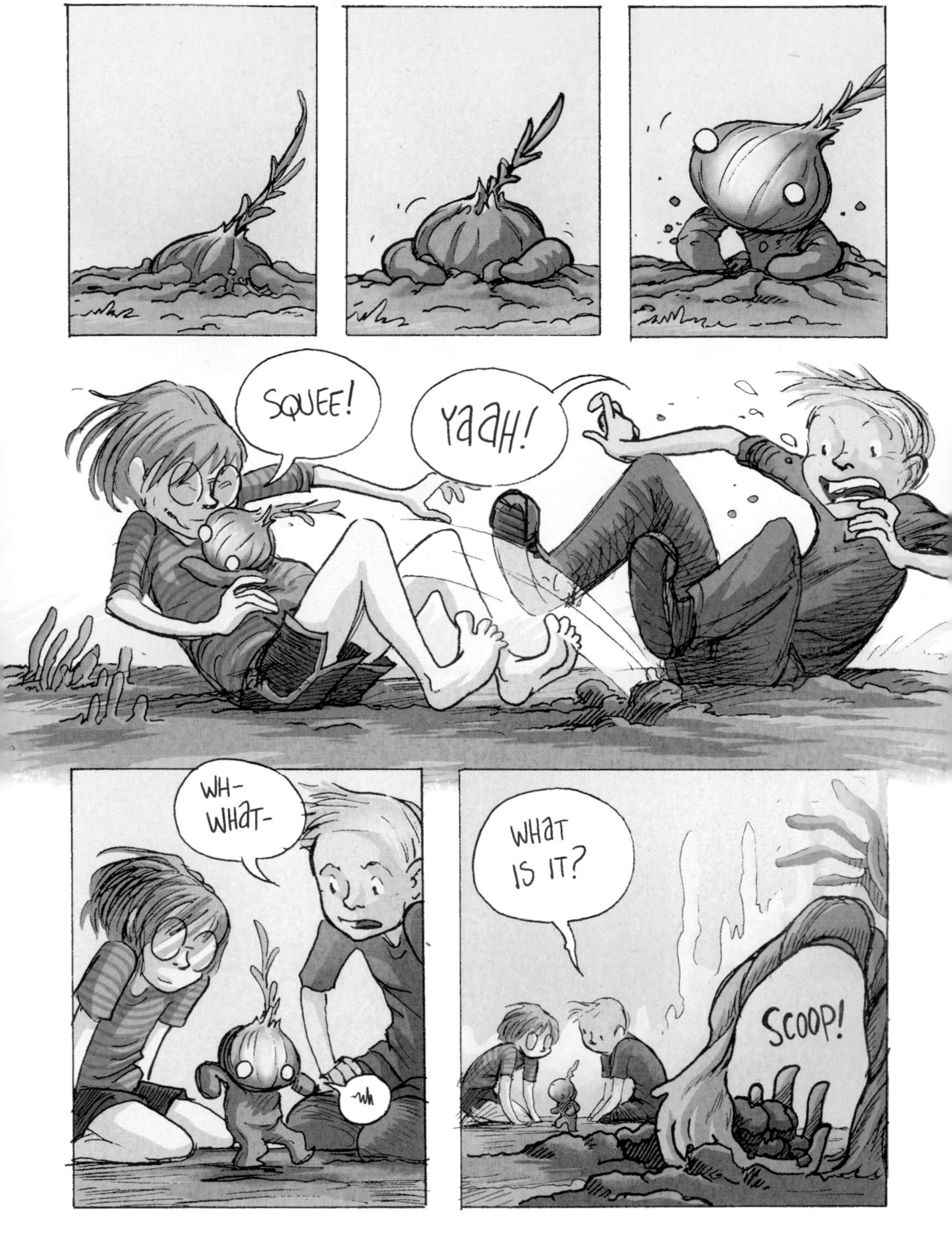
SQUEE!
YAAH!
WH-
WHAT-
WHAT
IS IT?
SCOOP!

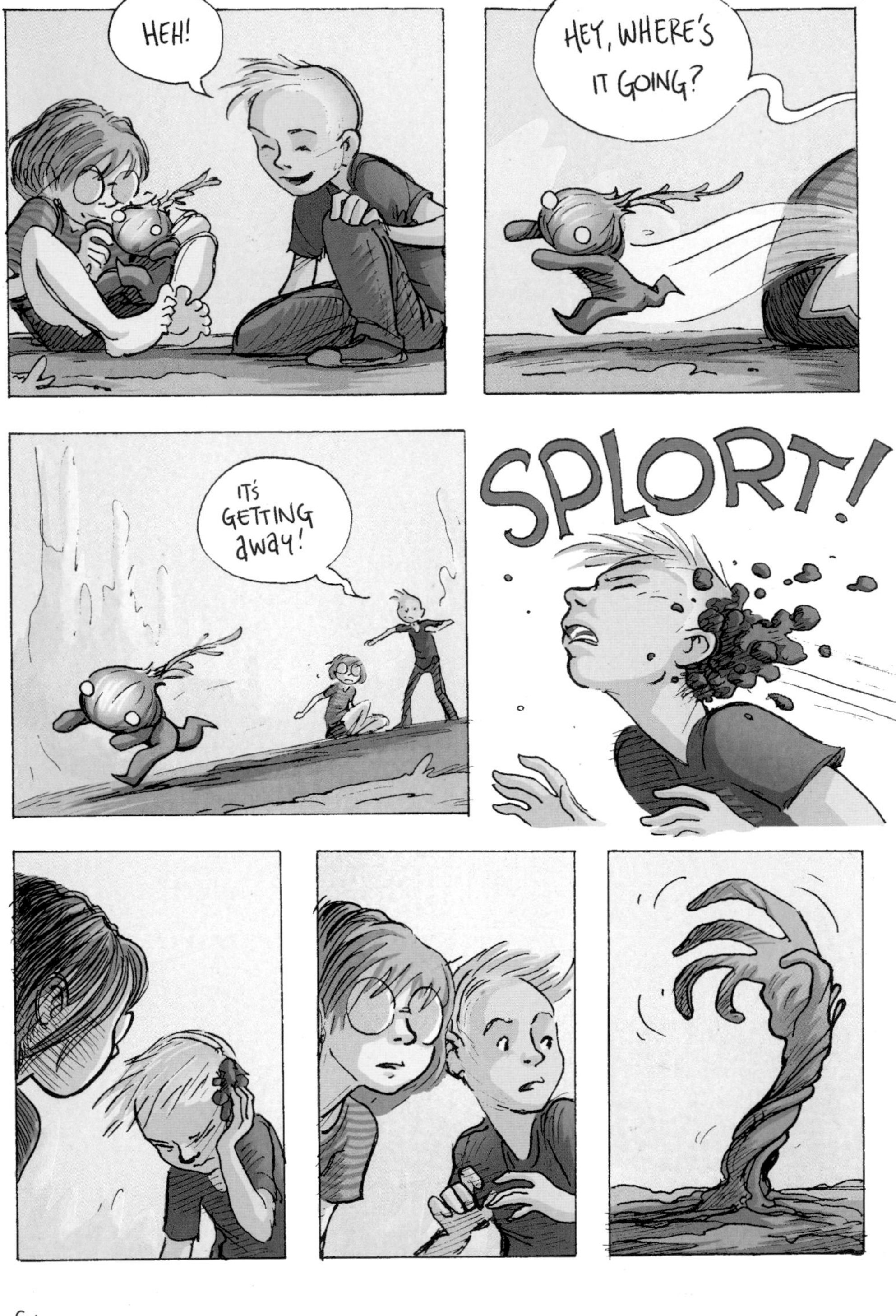
HEH!
HEY, WHERE'S IT GOING?
IT'S GETTING away!
SPLORT!

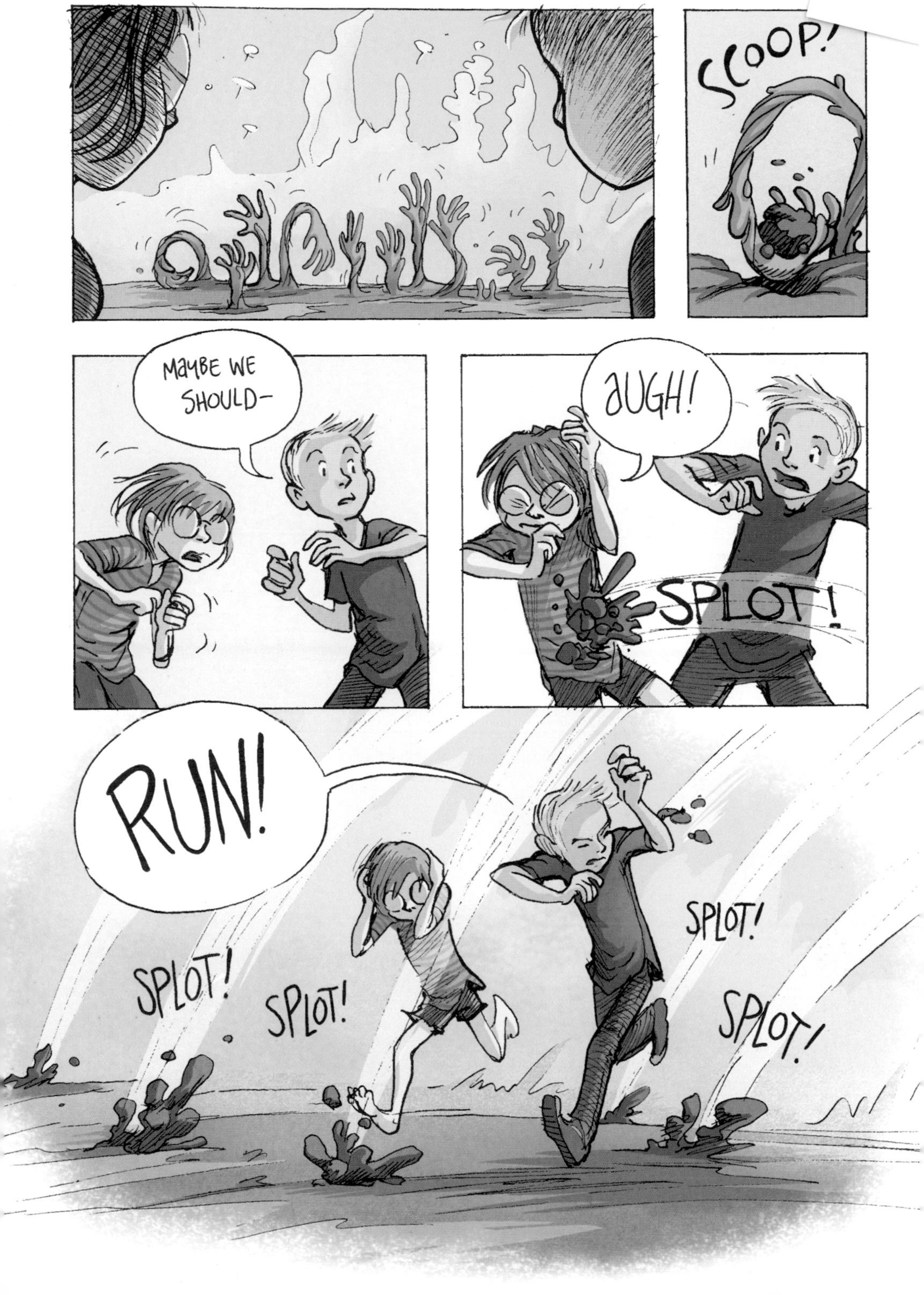
SCOOP!
MAYBE WE SHOULD-
AUGH!
SPLOT!
RUN!
SPLOT!
SPLOT!
SPLOT!
SPLOT!

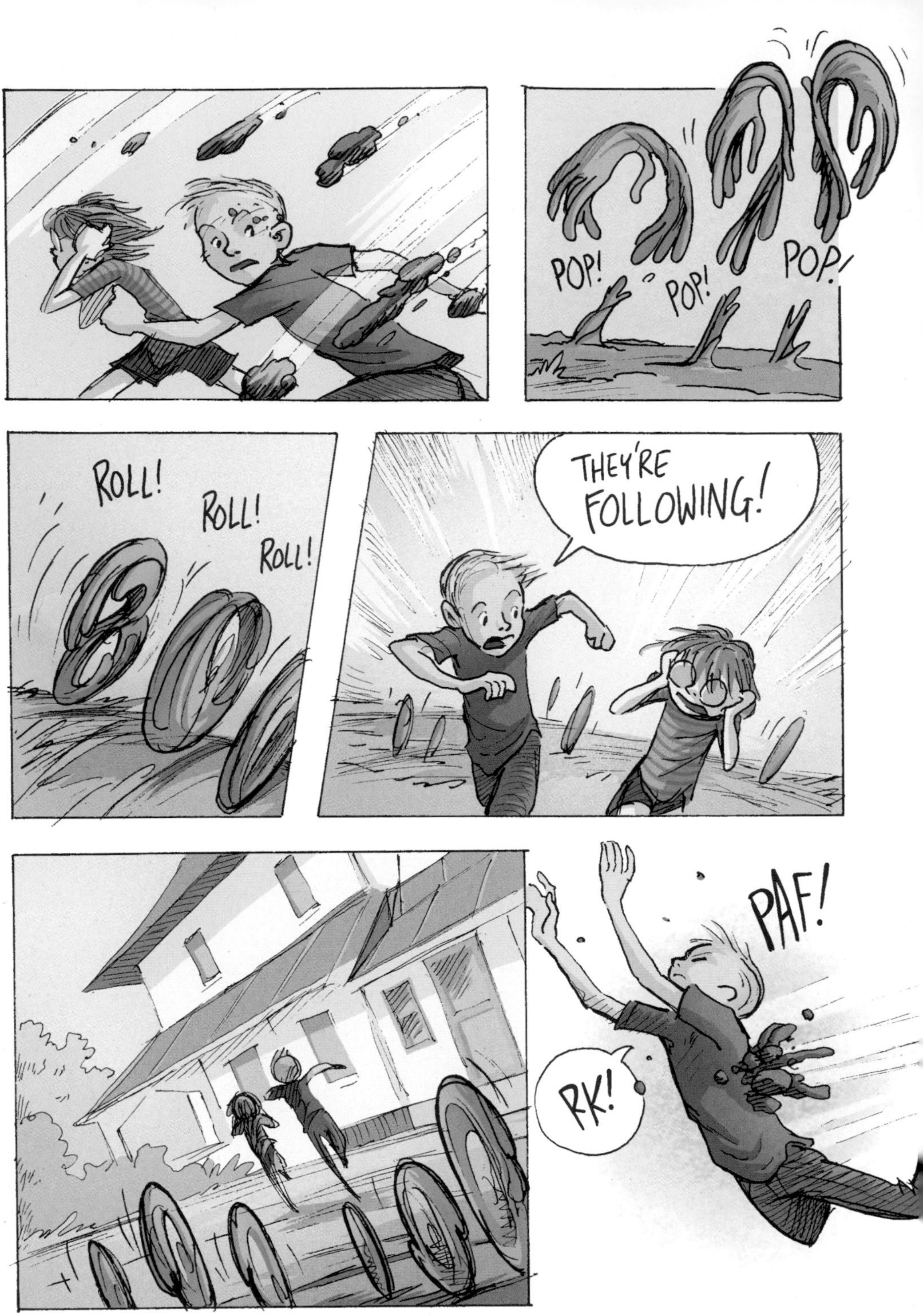
POP!
POP!
POP!
ROLL!
ROLL!
ROLL!
THEY'RE FOLLOWING!
PAF!
RK!

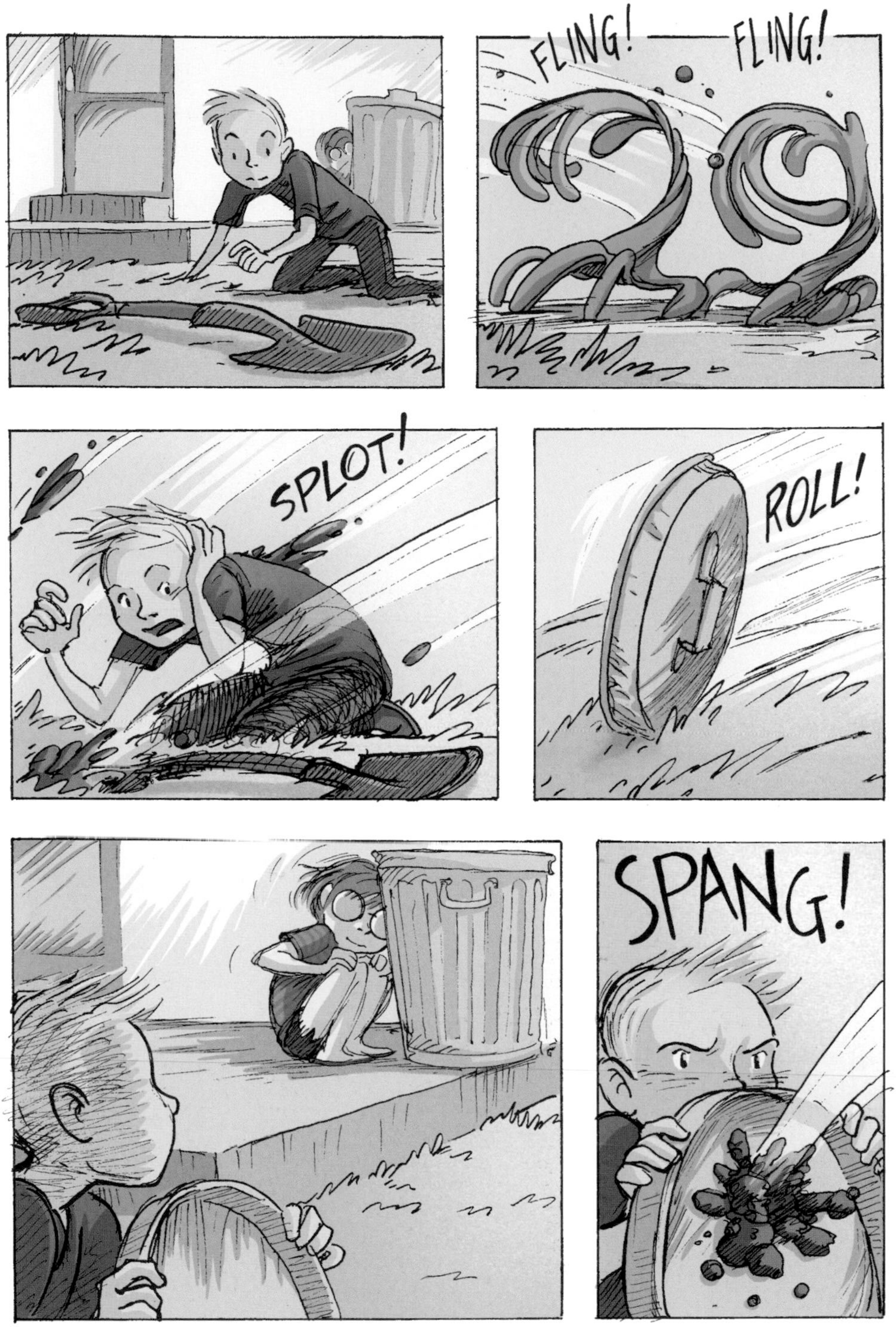
FLING!
FLING!
SPLOT!
ROLL!
SPANG!

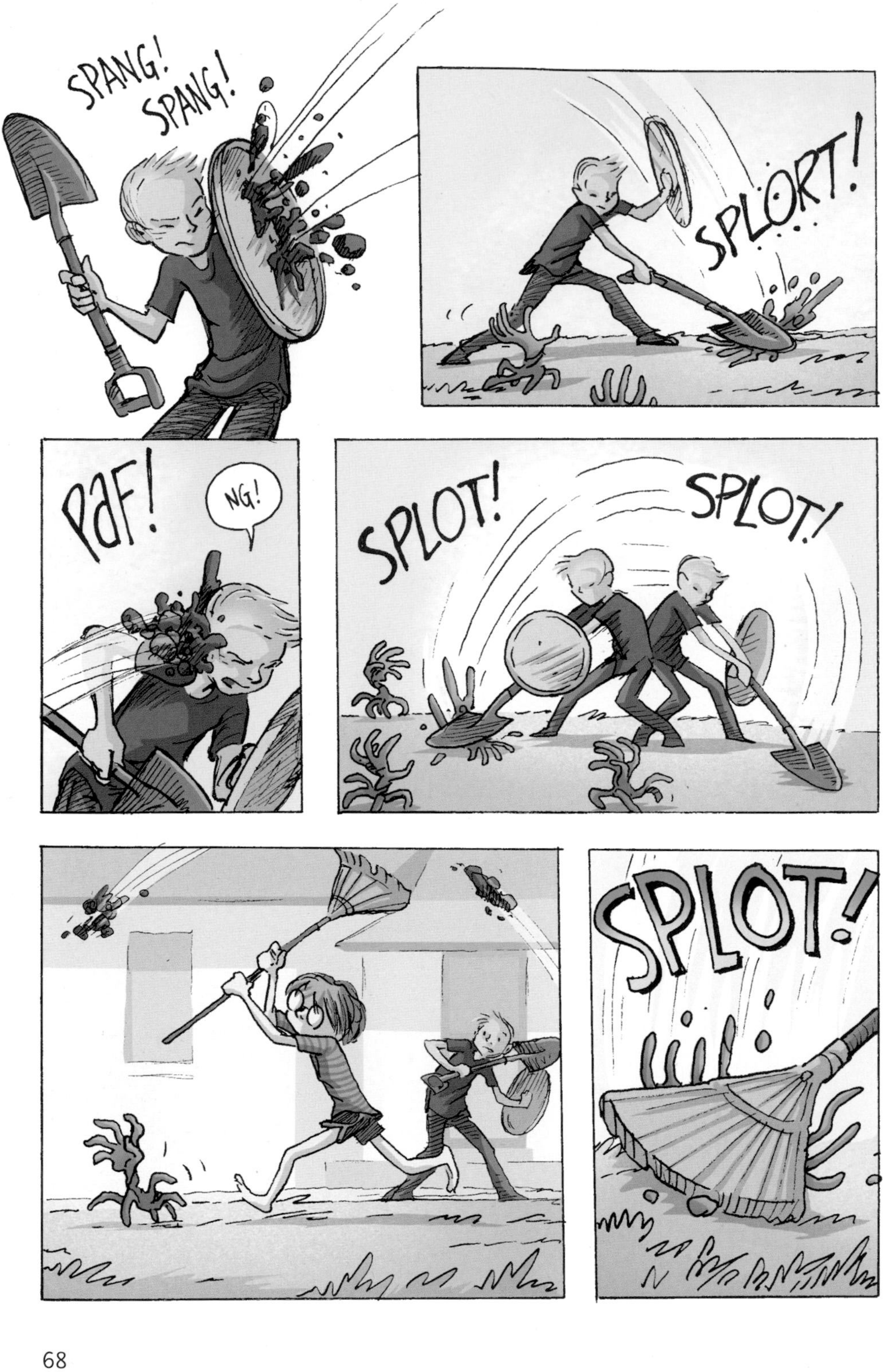
SPANG! SPANG!
SPLORT!
PAF!
NG!
SPLOT!
SPLOT!
SPLOT!

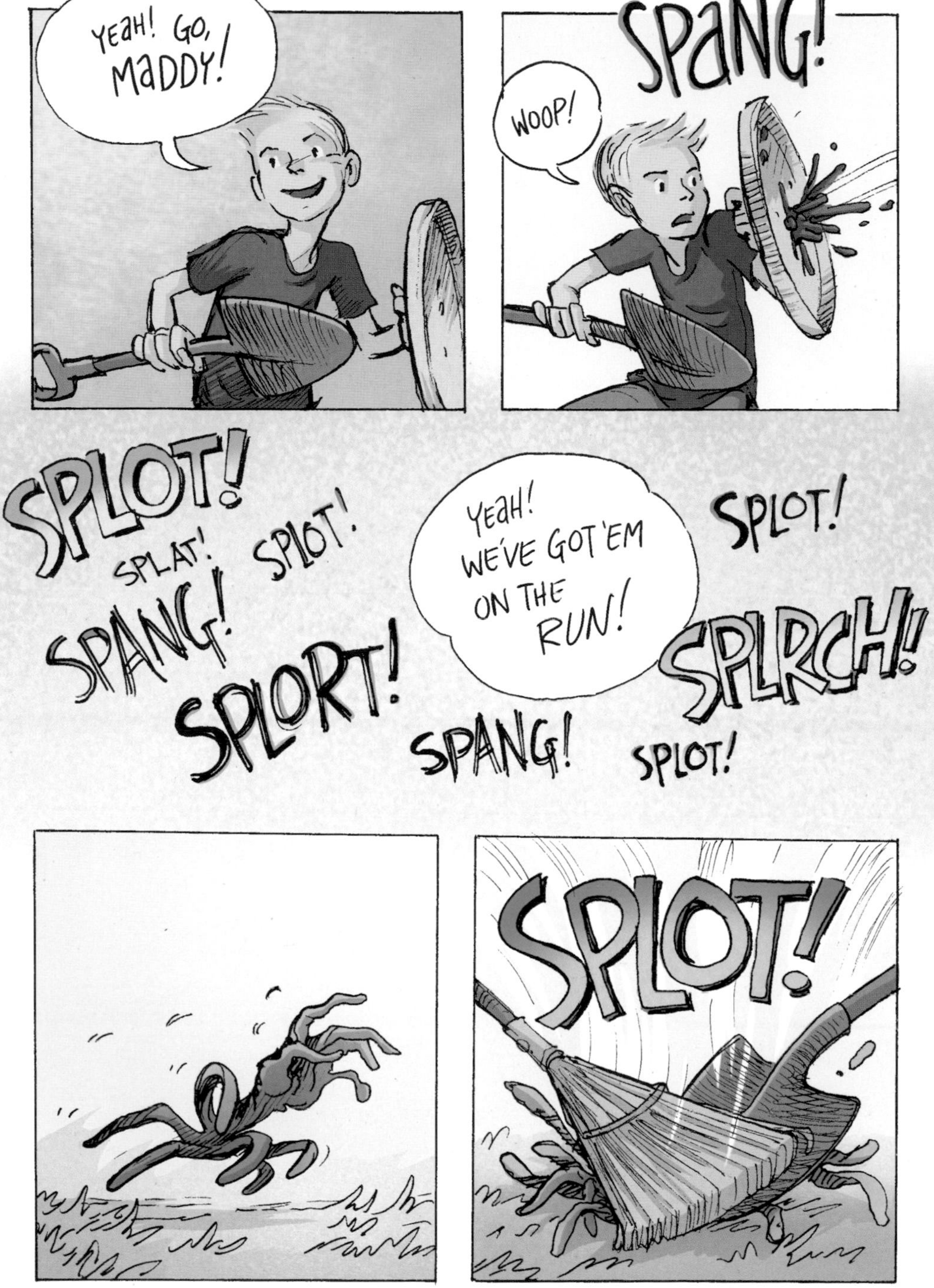
YEAH! GO, MADDY!
SPANG!
WOOP!
SPLOT!
SPLAT!
SPLOT!
SPANG!
SPLORT!
YEAH! WE'VE GOT 'EM ON THE RUN!
SPLOT!
SPLRCH!
SPANG!
SPLOT!
SPLOT!

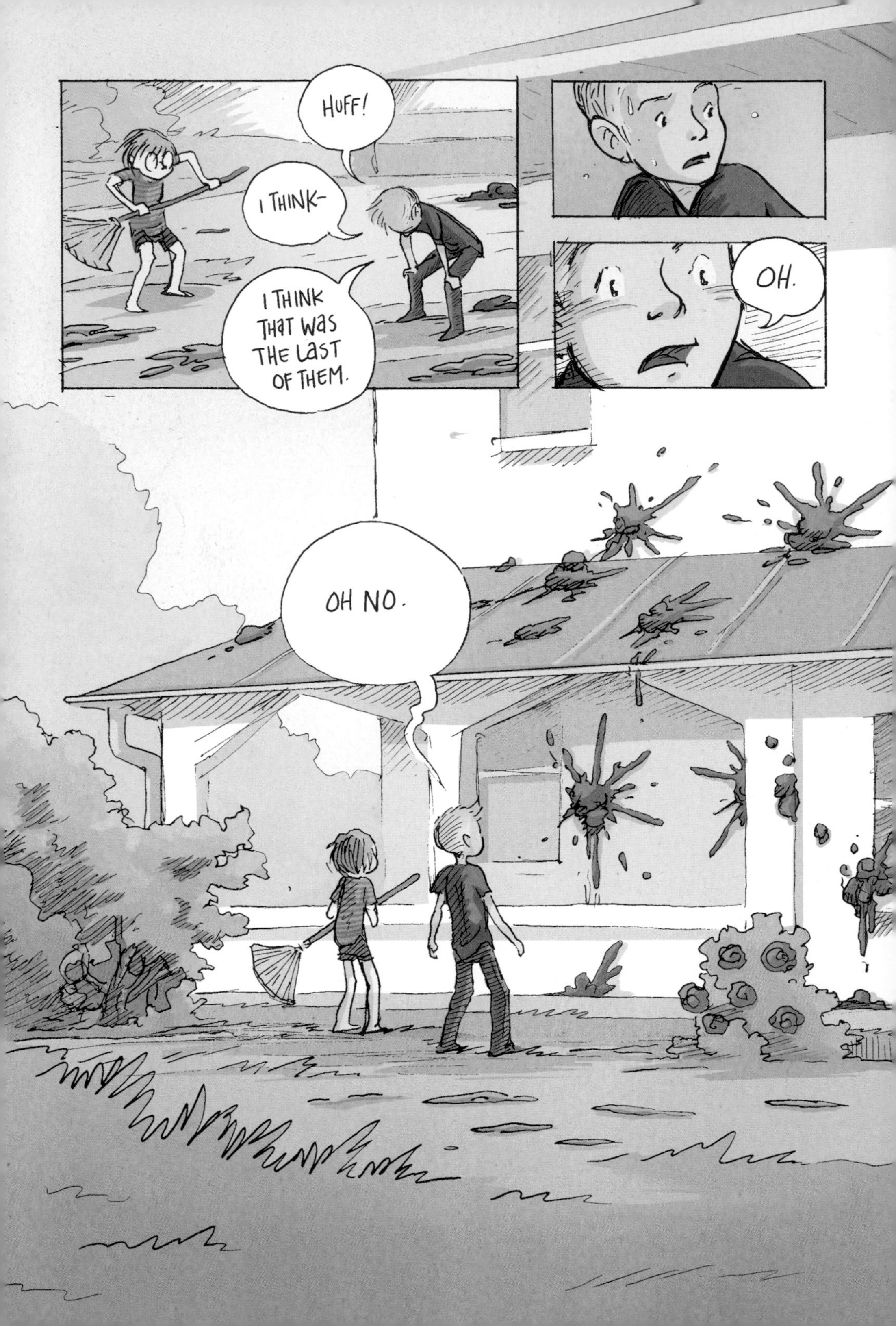
HUFF!
I THINK-
I THINK THAT WAS THE LAST OF THEM.
OH.
OH NO.

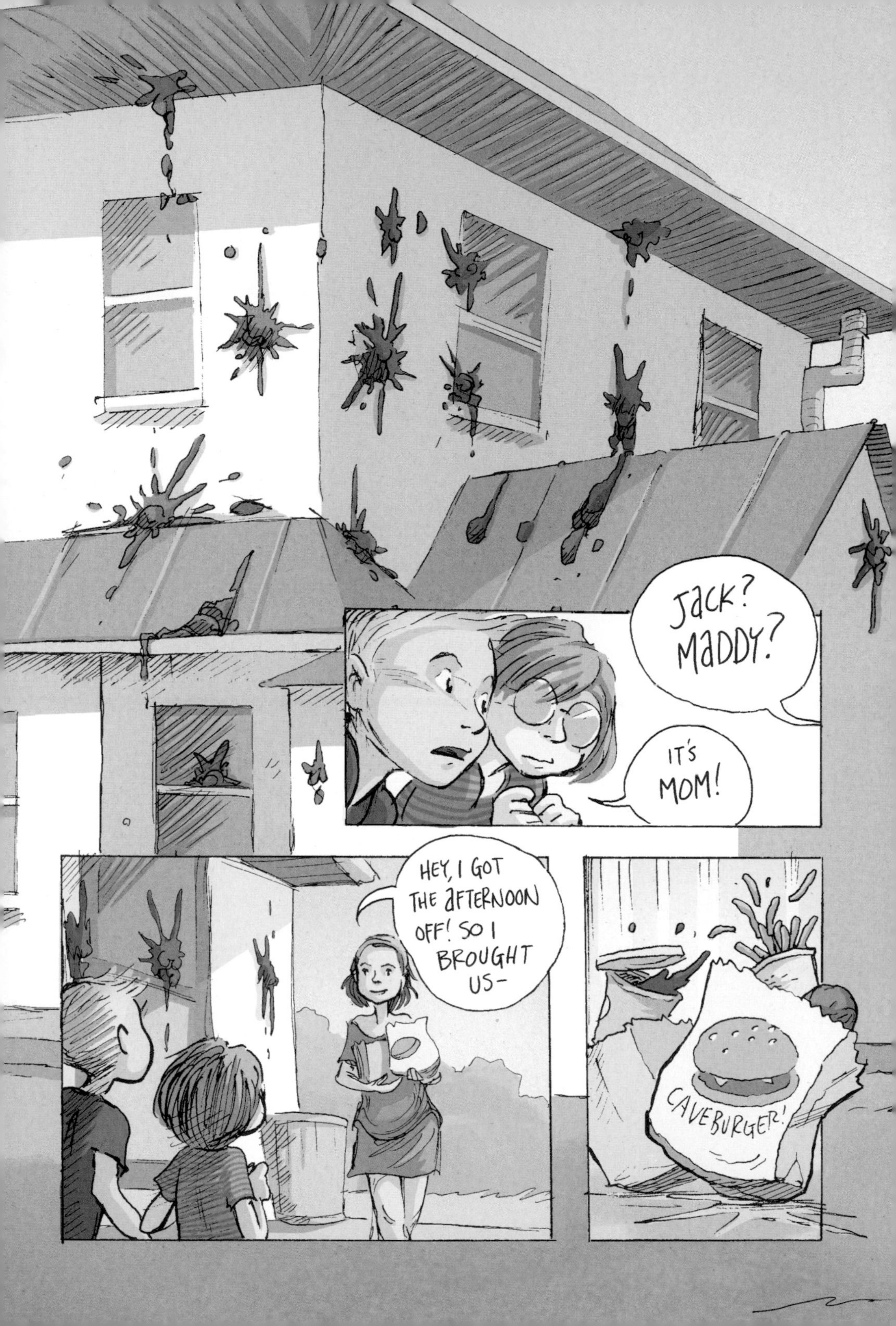

JACK? MADDY?
IT'S MOM!
HEY, I GOT THE AFTERNOON OFF! SO I BROUGHT US-
CAVEBURGER!

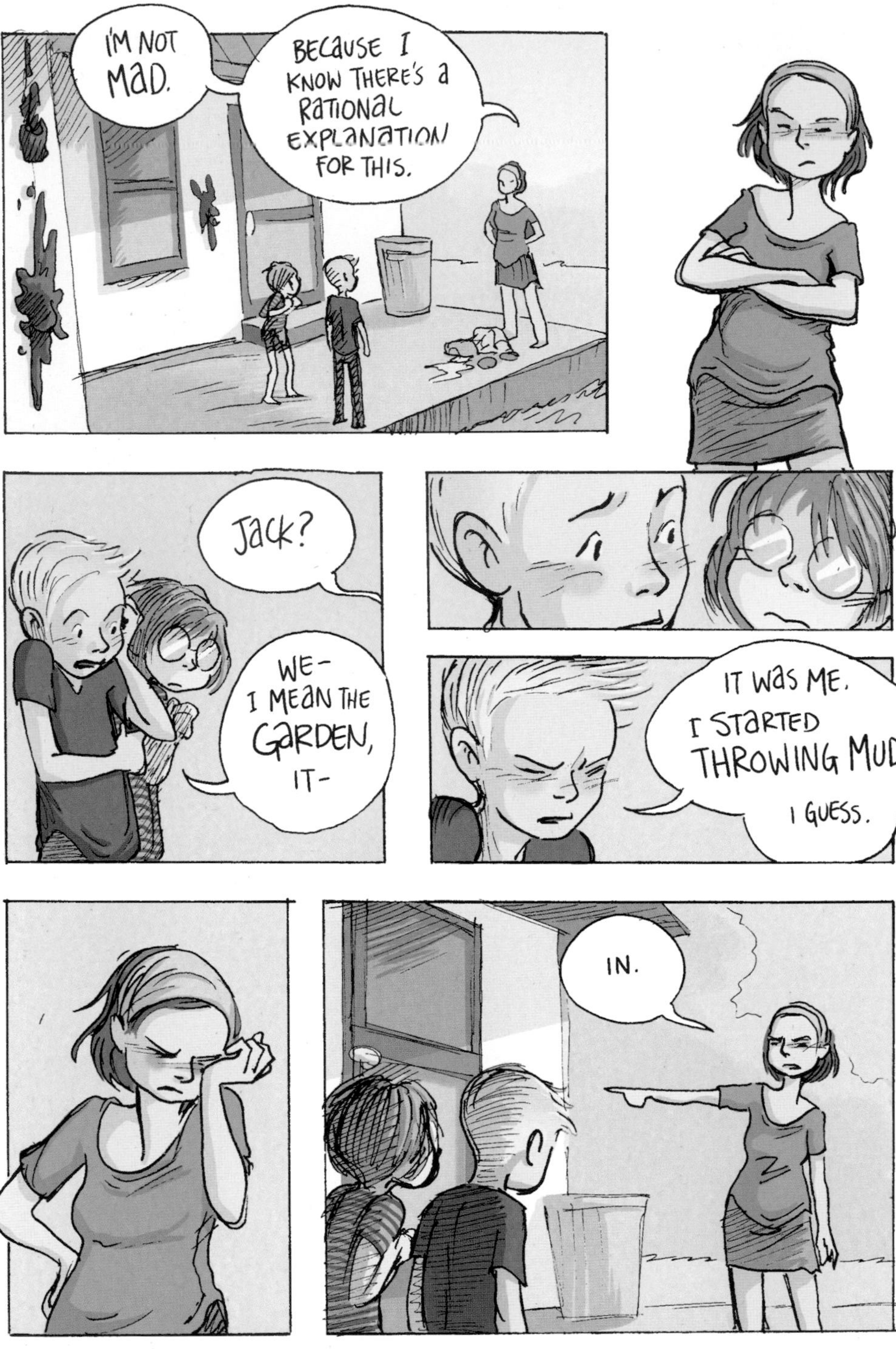
I'M NOT MAD.
BECAUSE I KNOW THERE'S A RATIONAL EXPLANATION FOR THIS.
JACK?
WE- I MEAN THE GARDEN, IT-
IT WAS ME. I STARTED THROWING MUD.
I GUESS.
IN.

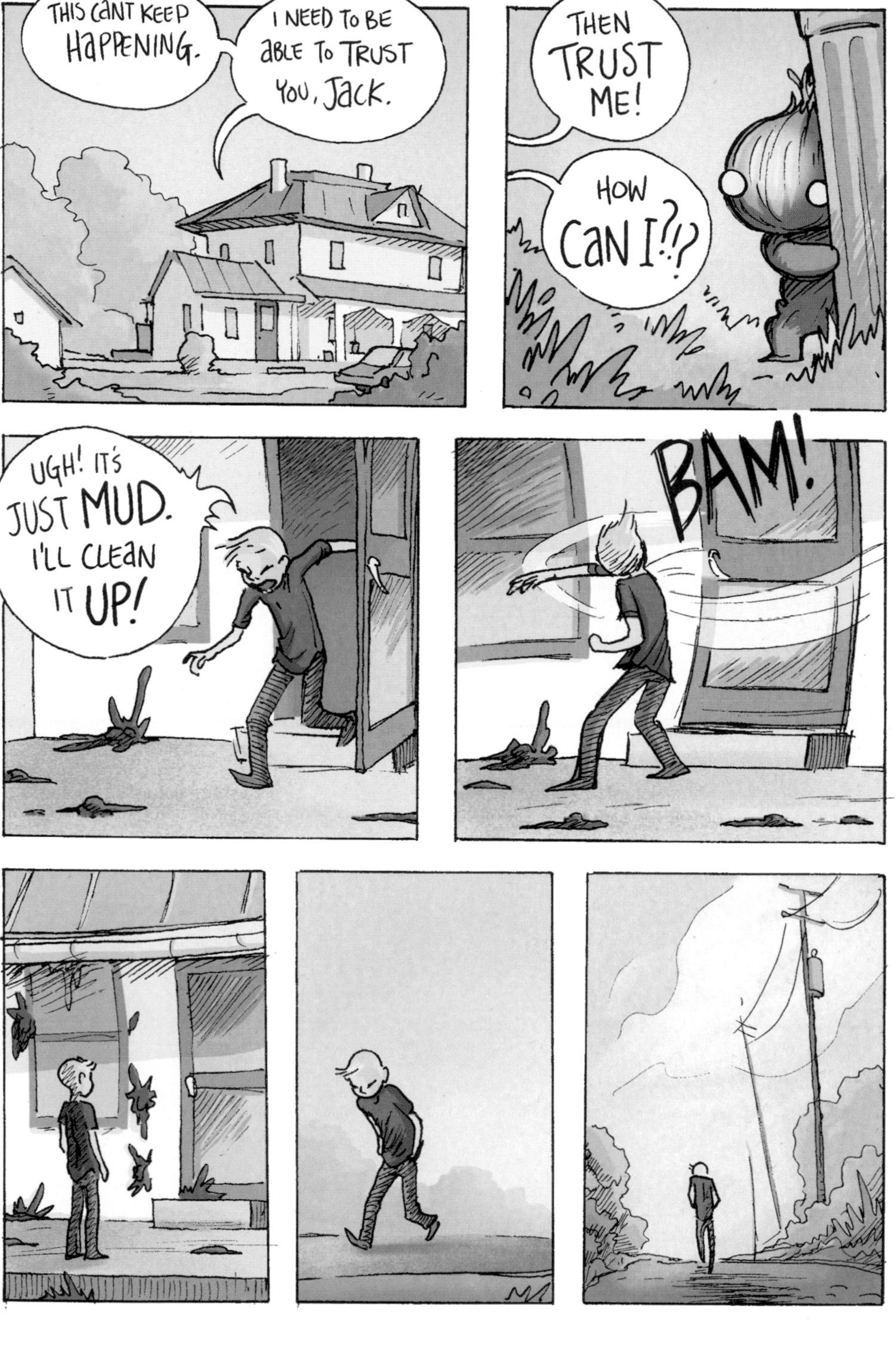
THIS CAN'T KEEP HAPPENING.
I NEED TO BE ABLE TO TRUST YOU, JACK.
THEN TRUST ME!
HOW CAN I?!?
UGH! IT'S JUST MUD. I'LL CLEAN IT UP!
BAM!

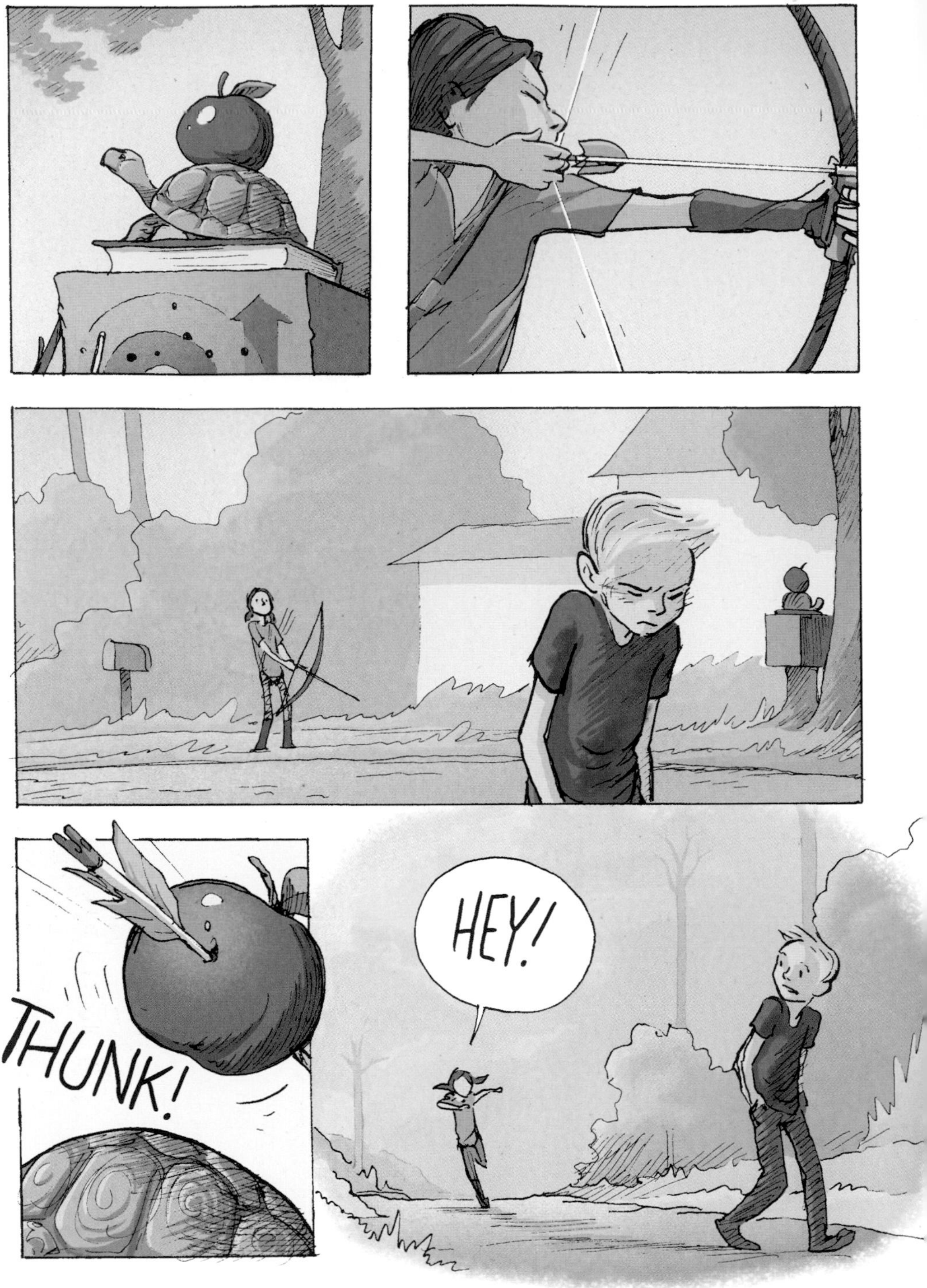
THUNK!
HEY!

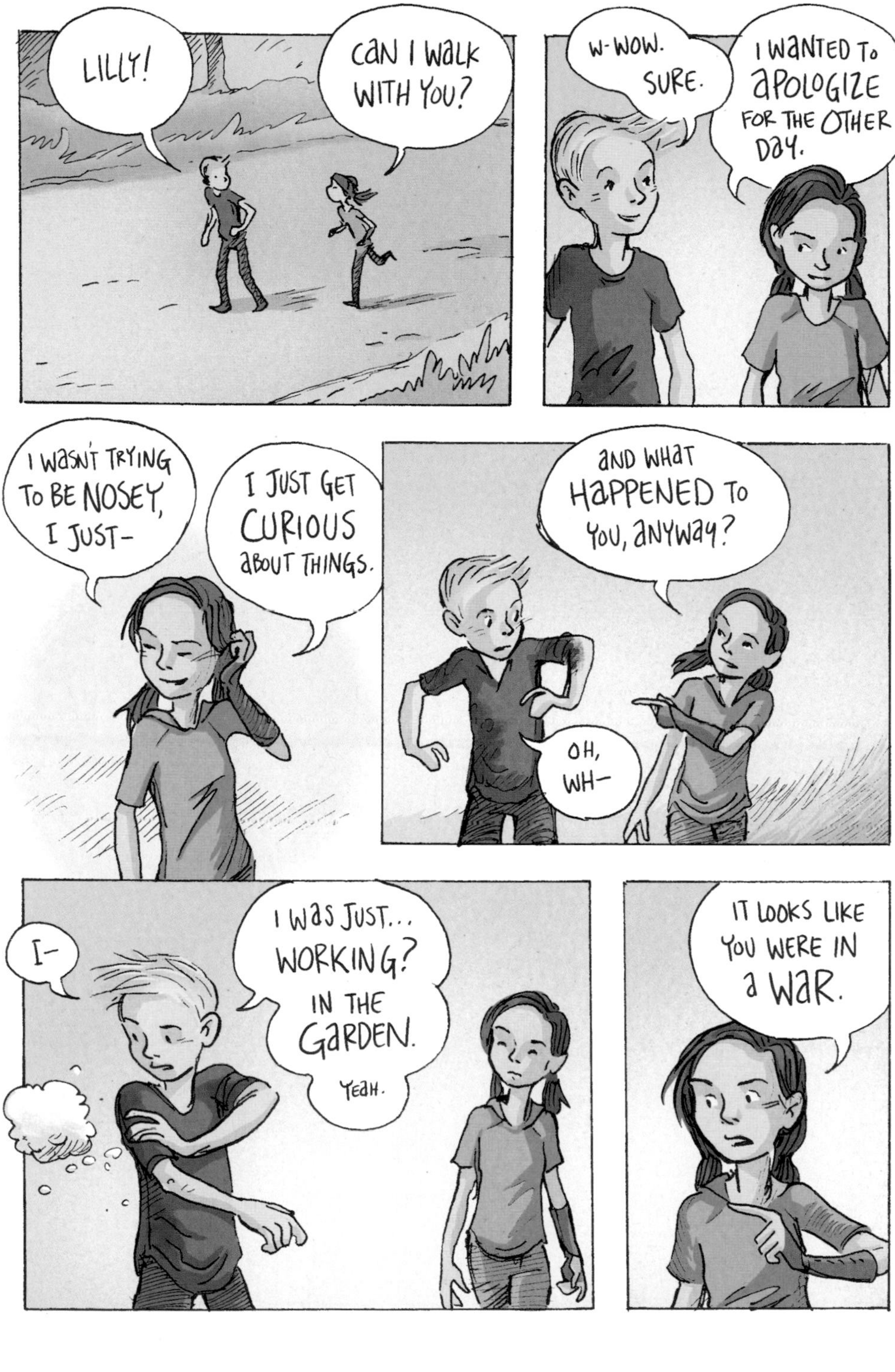
LILLY!
CAN I WALK WITH YOU?
W-WOW. SURE.
I WANTED TO APOLOGIZE FOR THE OTHER DAY.
I WASN'T TRYING TO BE NOSEY, I JUST-
I JUST GET CURIOUS ABOUT THINGS.
AND WHAT HAPPENED TO YOU, ANYWAY?
OH, WH-
I-
I WAS JUST... WORKING? IN THE GARDEN.
YEAH.
IT LOOKS LIKE YOU WERE IN A WAR.

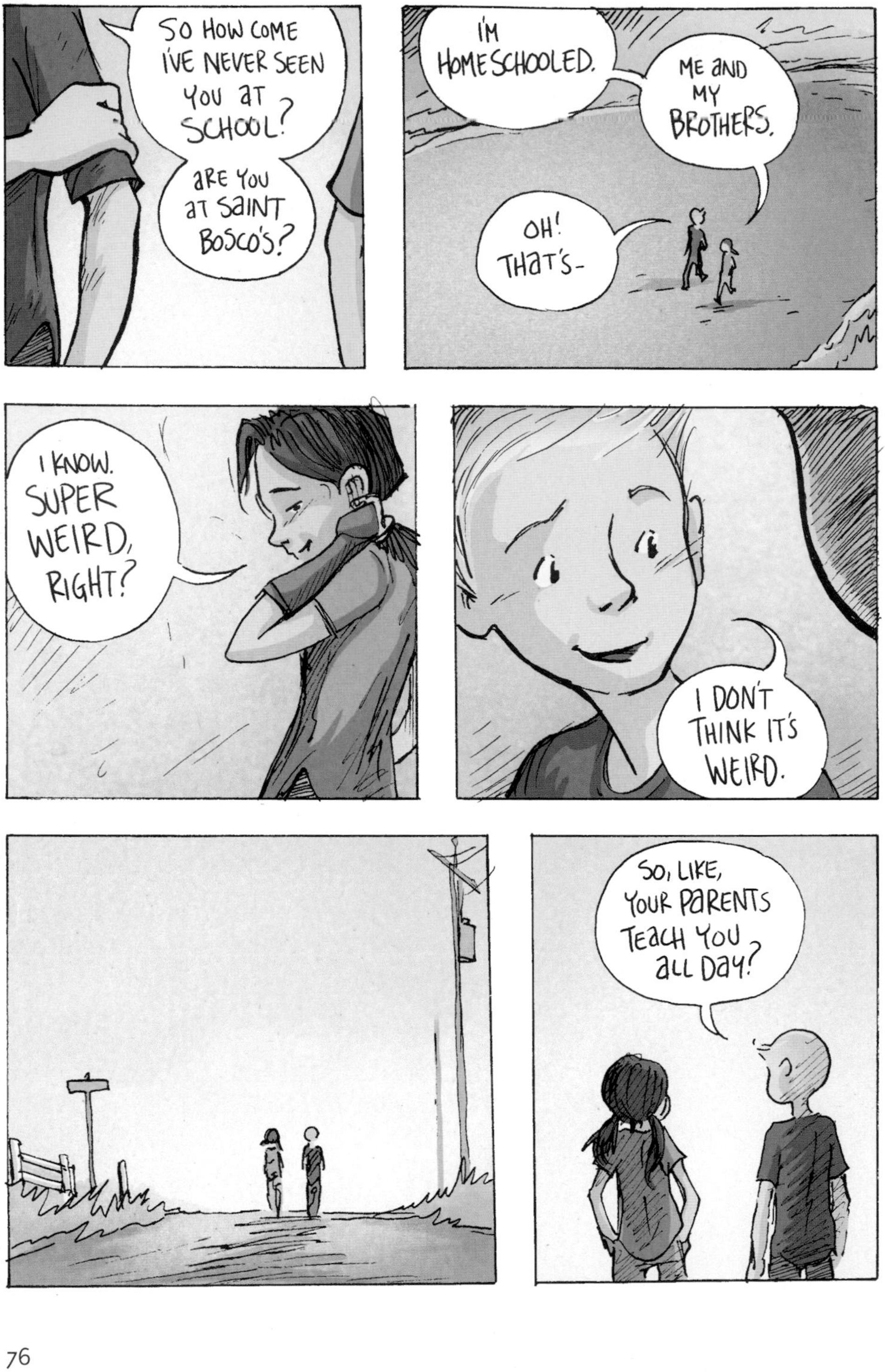

SO HOW COME I'VE NEVER SEEN YOU AT SCHOOL?
ARE YOU AT SAINT BOSCO'S?
I'M HOMESCHOOLED.
ME AND MY BROTHERS.
OH! THAT'S-
I KNOW. SUPER WEIRD, RIGHT?
I DON'T THINK IT'S WEIRD.
SO, LIKE, YOUR PARENTS TEACH YOU ALL DAY?

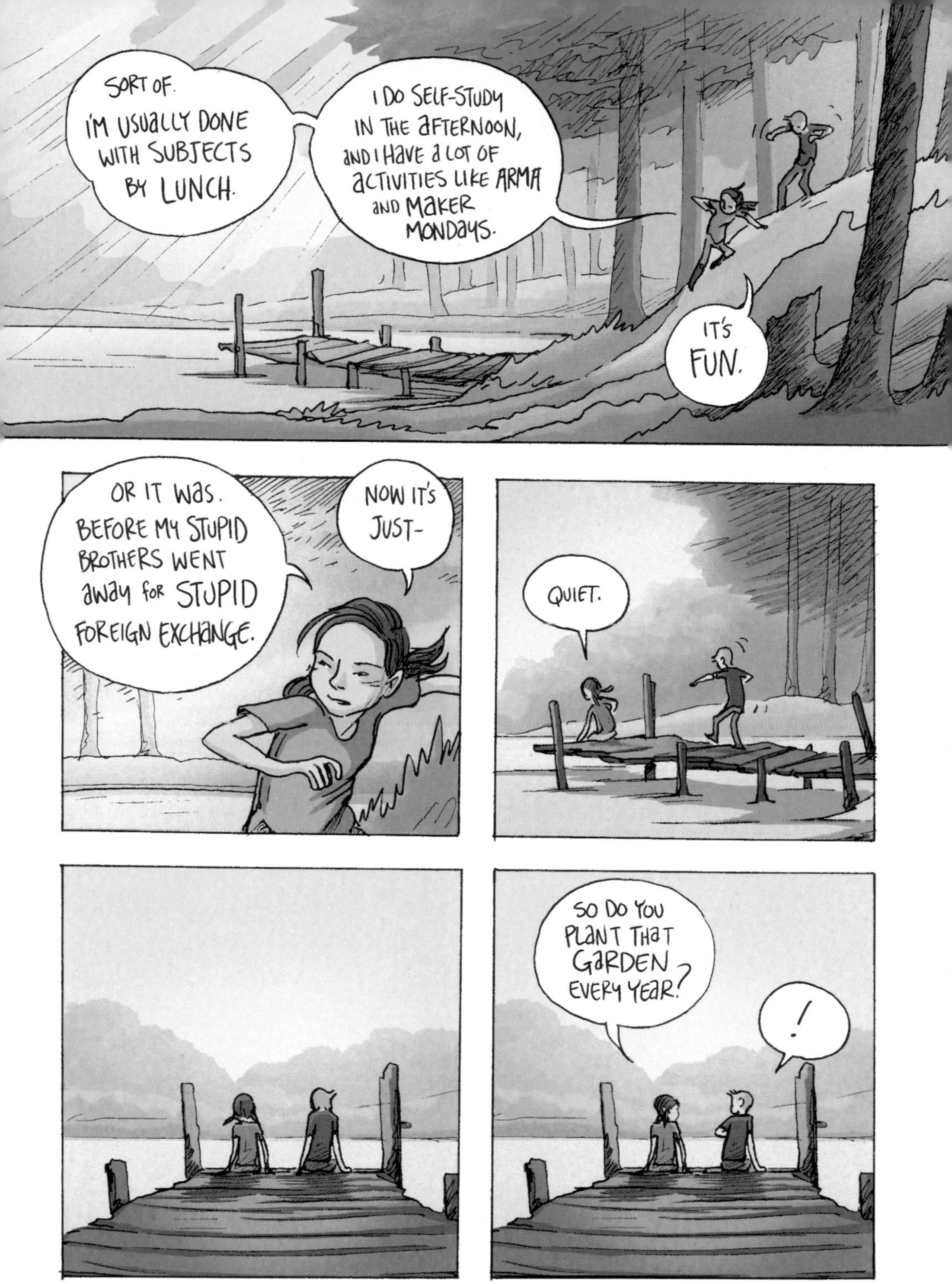
SORT OF.
I'M USUALLY DONE WITH SUBJECTS BY LUNCH.
I DO SELF-STUDY IN THE AFTERNOON, AND I HAVE A LOT OF ACTIVITIES LIKE ARMA AND MAKER MONDAYS.
IT'S FUN.
OR IT WAS. BEFORE MY STUPID BROTHERS WENT AWAY FOR STUPID FOREIGN EXCHANGE.
NOW IT'S JUST-
QUIET.
SO DO YOU PLANT THAT GARDEN EVERY YEAR?
!

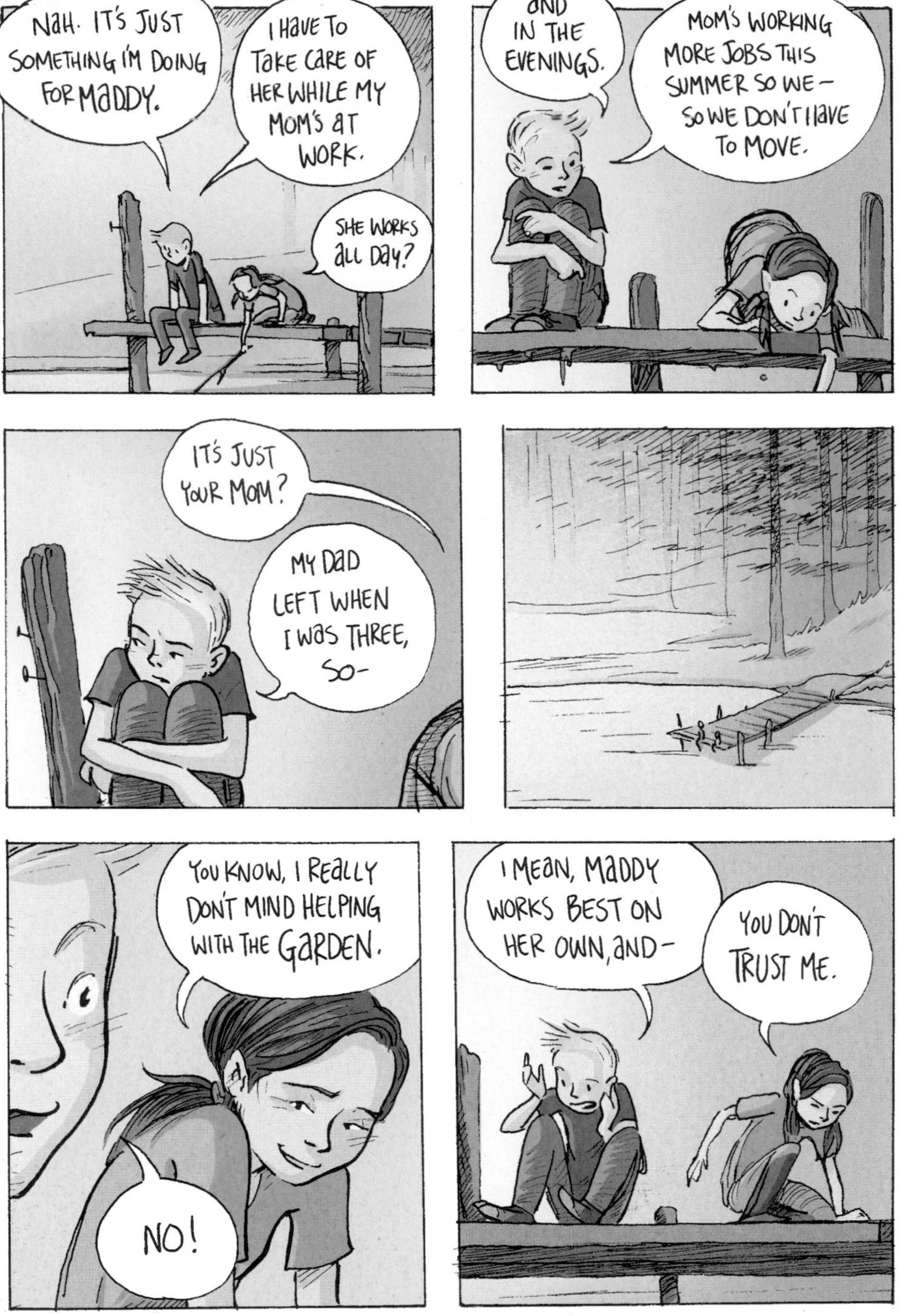
NAH. IT'S JUST SOMETHING I'M DOING FOR MADDY.
I HAVE TO TAKE CARE OF HER WHILE MY MOM'S AT WORK.
SHE WORKS ALL DAY?
AND IN THE EVENINGS.
MOM'S WORKING MORE JOBS THIS SUMMER SO WE- SO WE DON'T HAVE TO MOVE.
IT'S JUST YOUR MOM?
MY DAD LEFT WHEN I WAS THREE, SO-
YOU KNOW, I REALLY DON'T MIND HELPING WITH THE GARDEN.
NO!
I MEAN, MADDY WORKS BEST ON HER OWN, AND-
YOU DON'T TRUST ME.

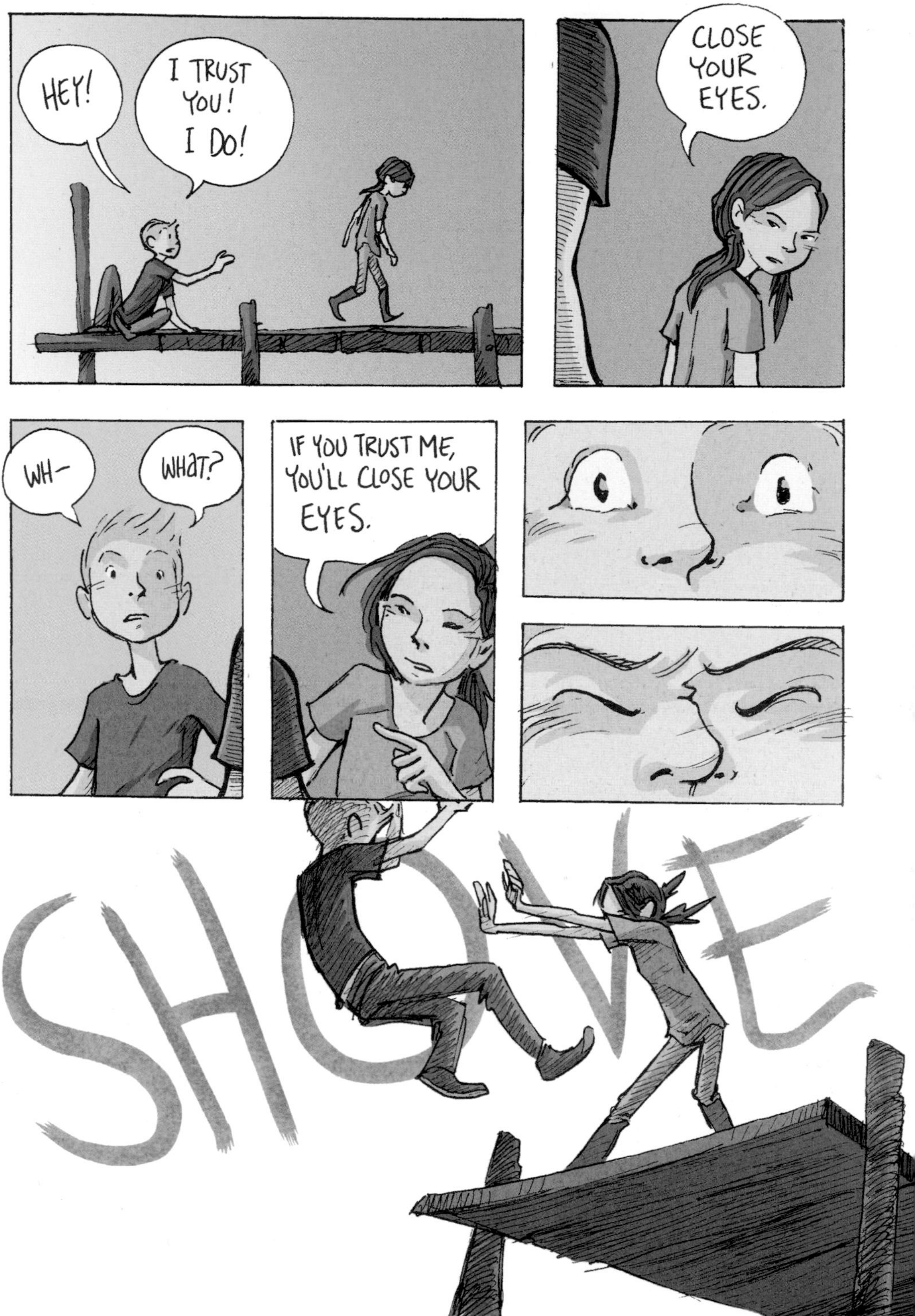
HEY!
I TRUST YOU! I DO!
CLOSE YOUR EYES.
WH-
WHAT?
IF YOU TRUST ME, YOU'LL CLOSE YOUR EYES.
SHOVE

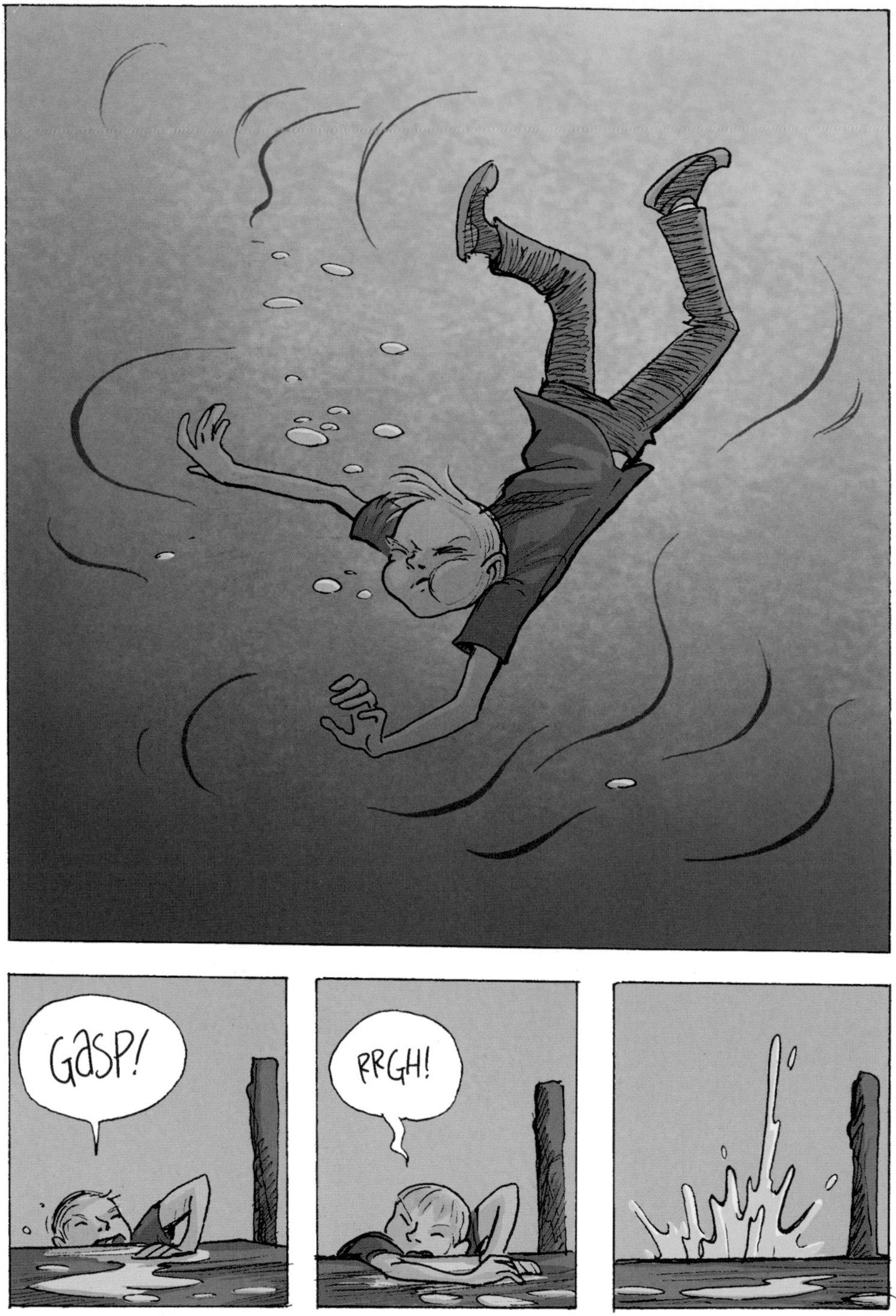
GASP!
RRGH!

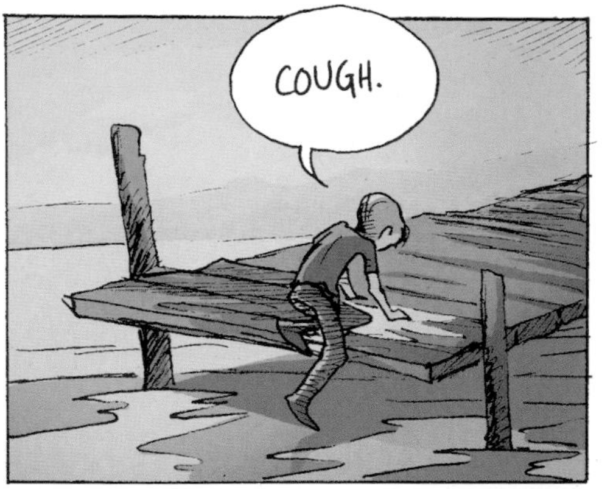
COUGH.
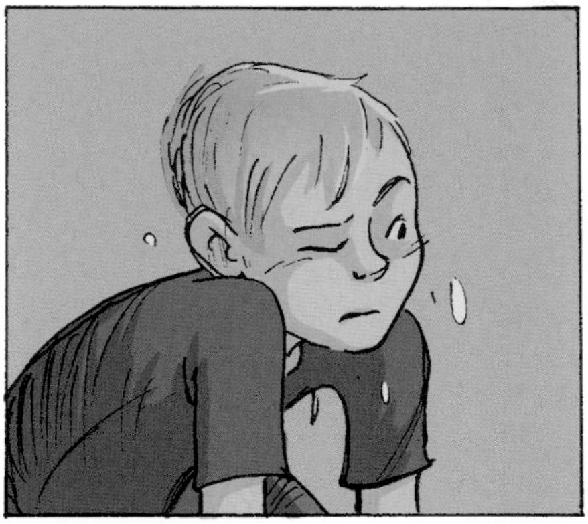
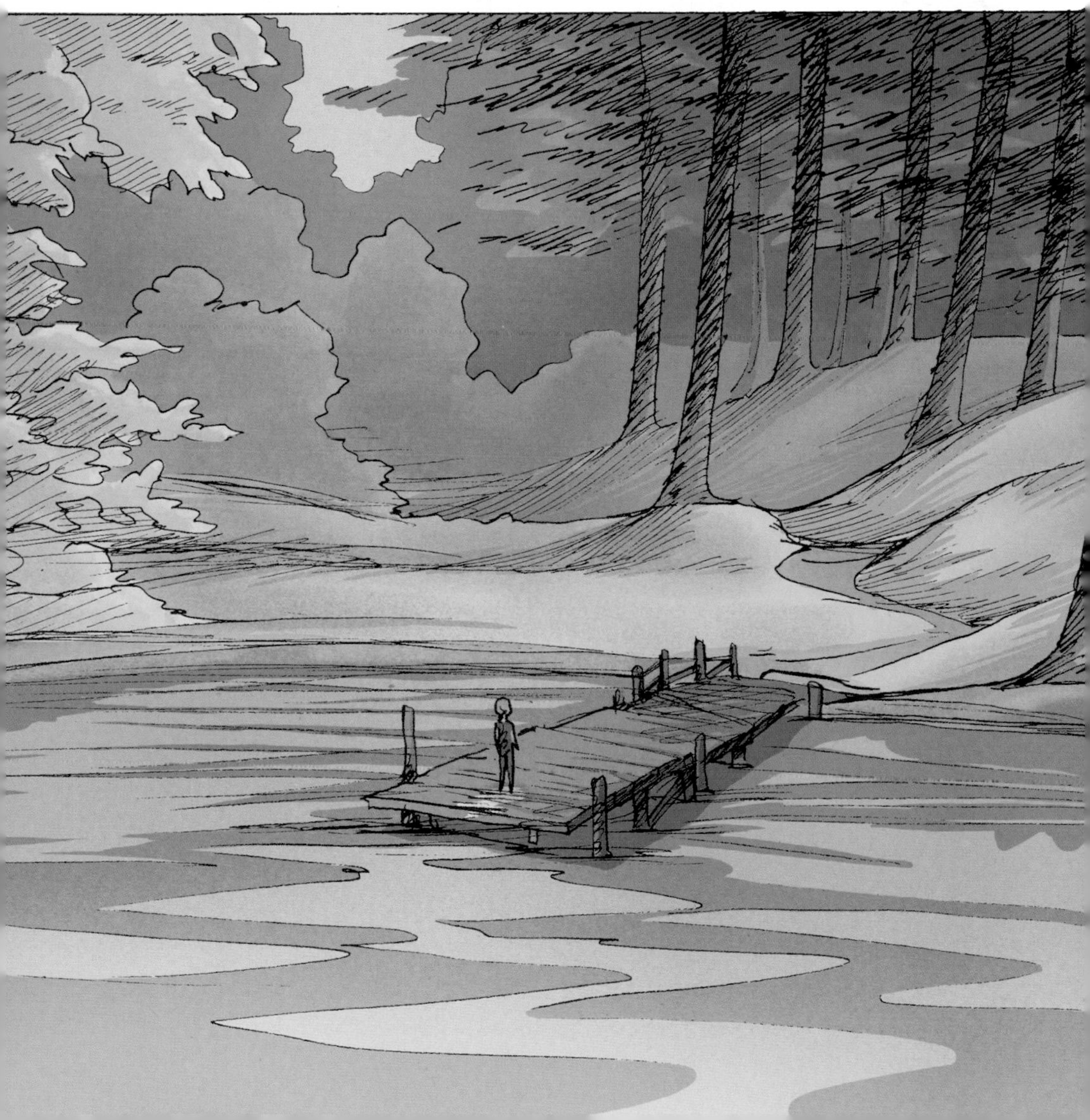

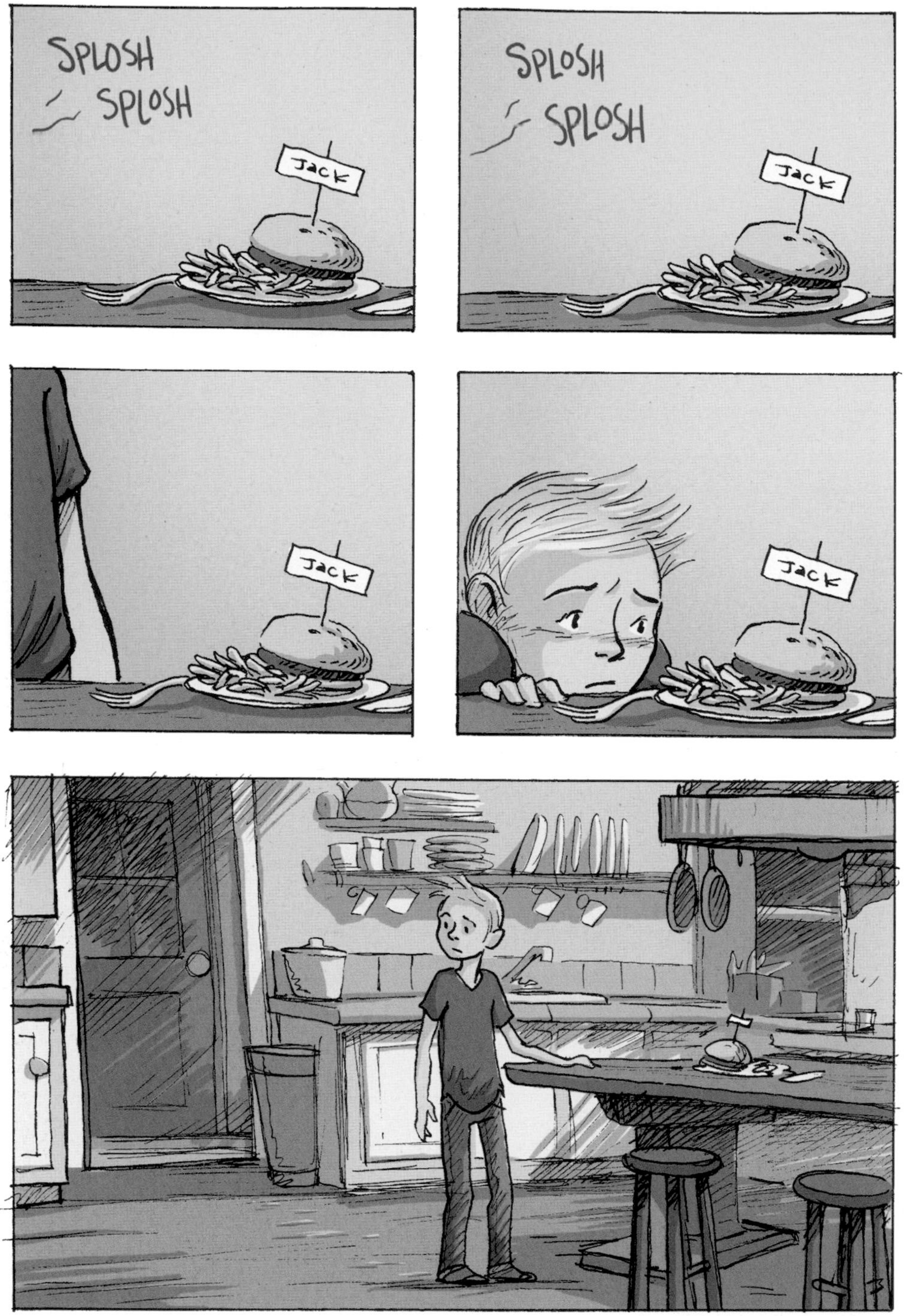
SPLOSH
SPLOSH
JACK
SPLOSH
SPLOSH
JACK
JACK
JACK

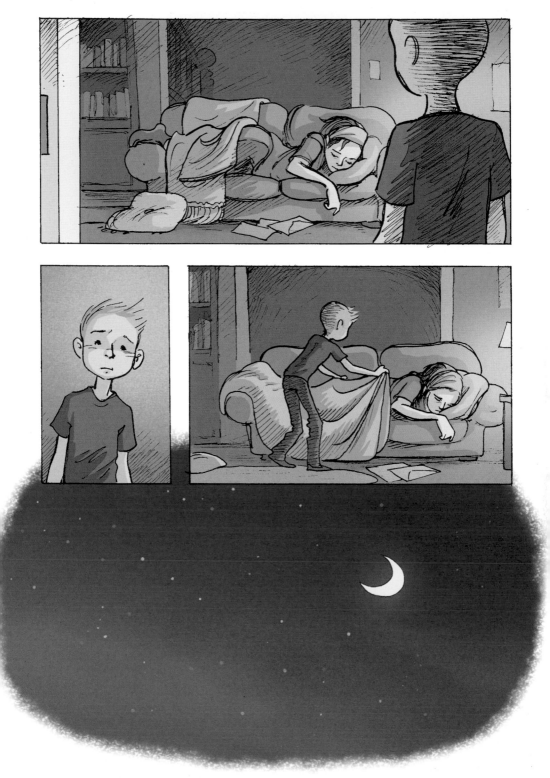

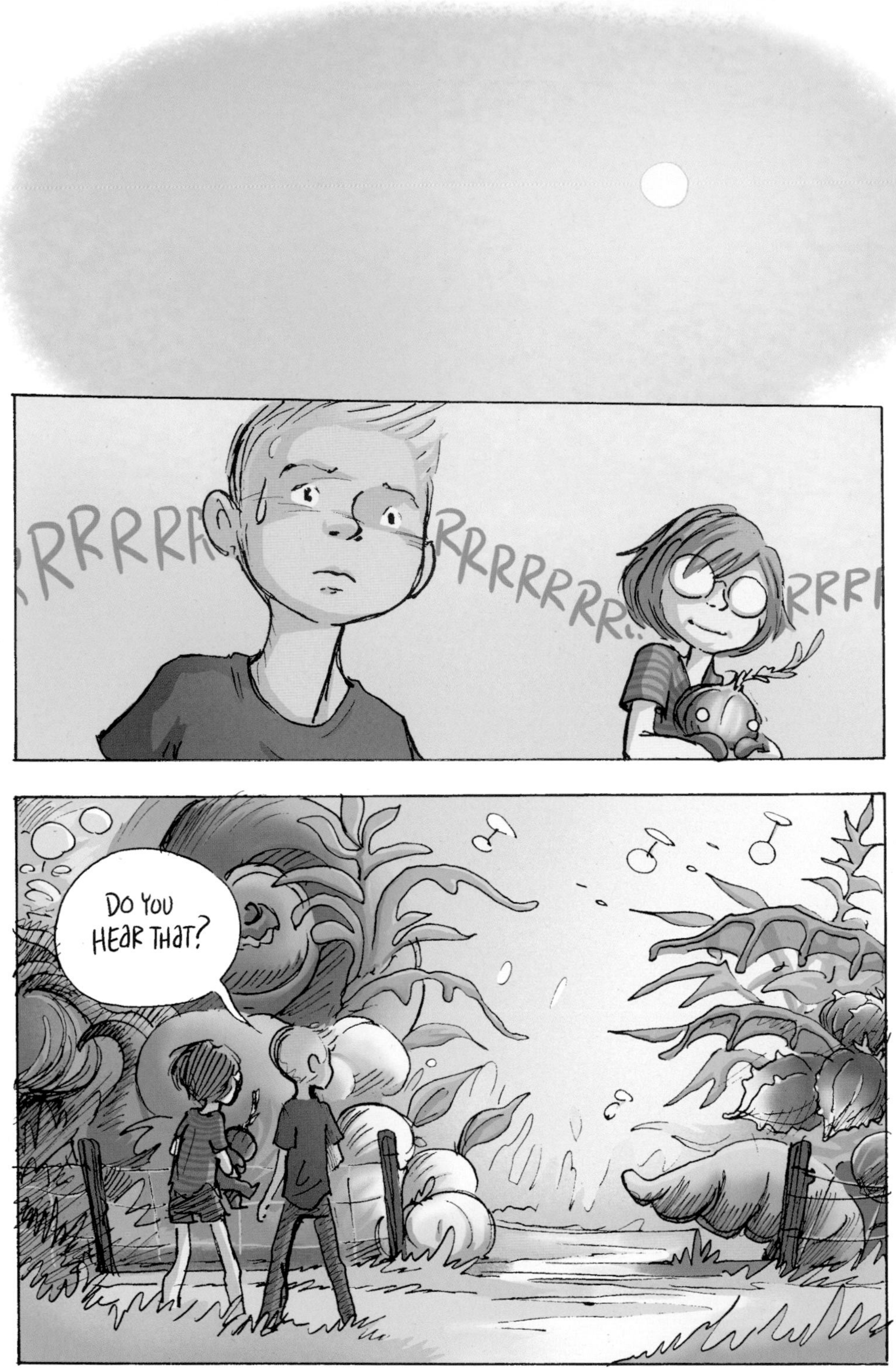
RRRRR
RRRRRRR
RRRR
DO YOU HEAR THAT?

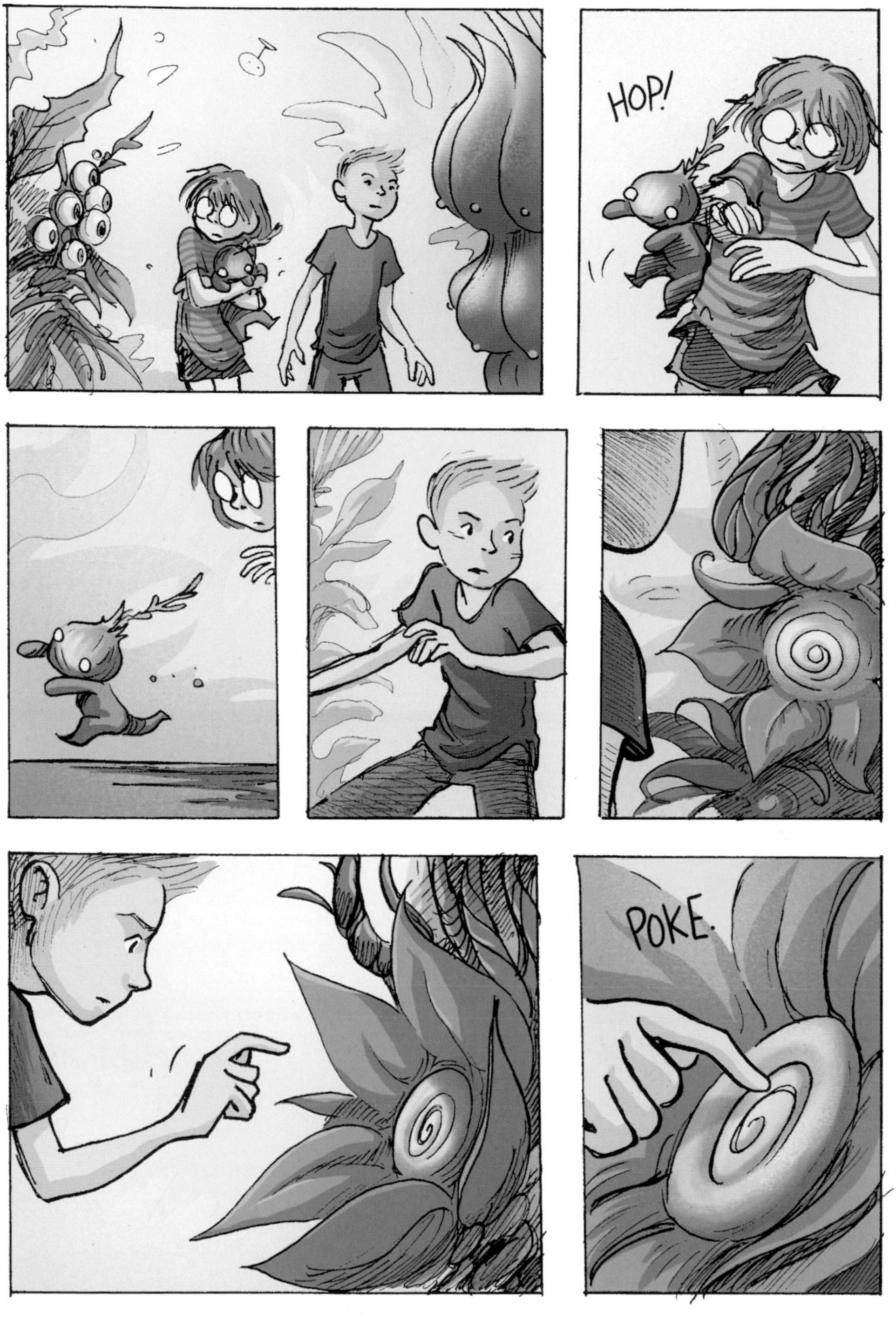
HOP!
POKE.

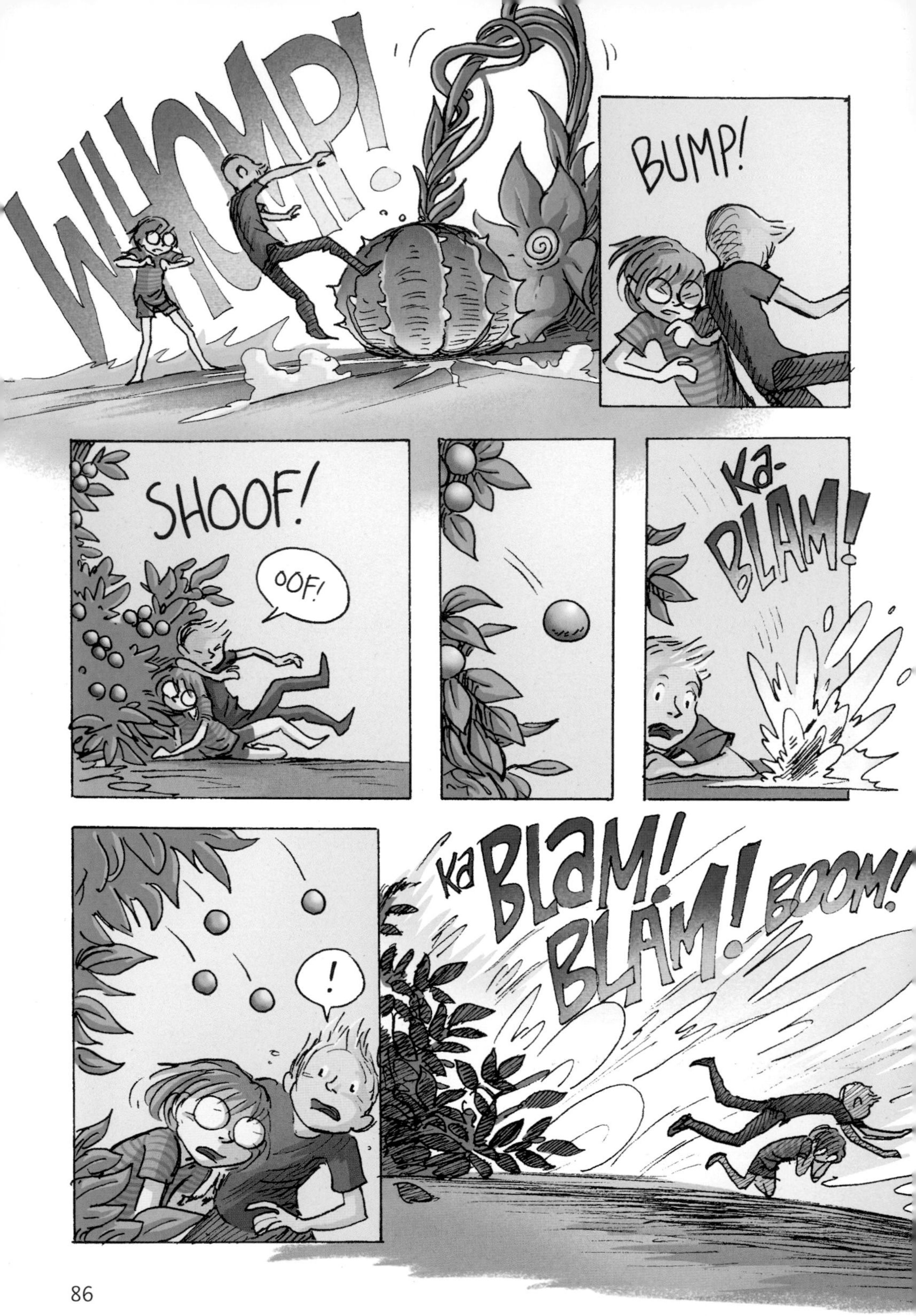
WHOMP!
BUMP!
SHOOF!
OOF!
Ka-BLAM!
!
KaBLAM!
BLAM!
BOOM!

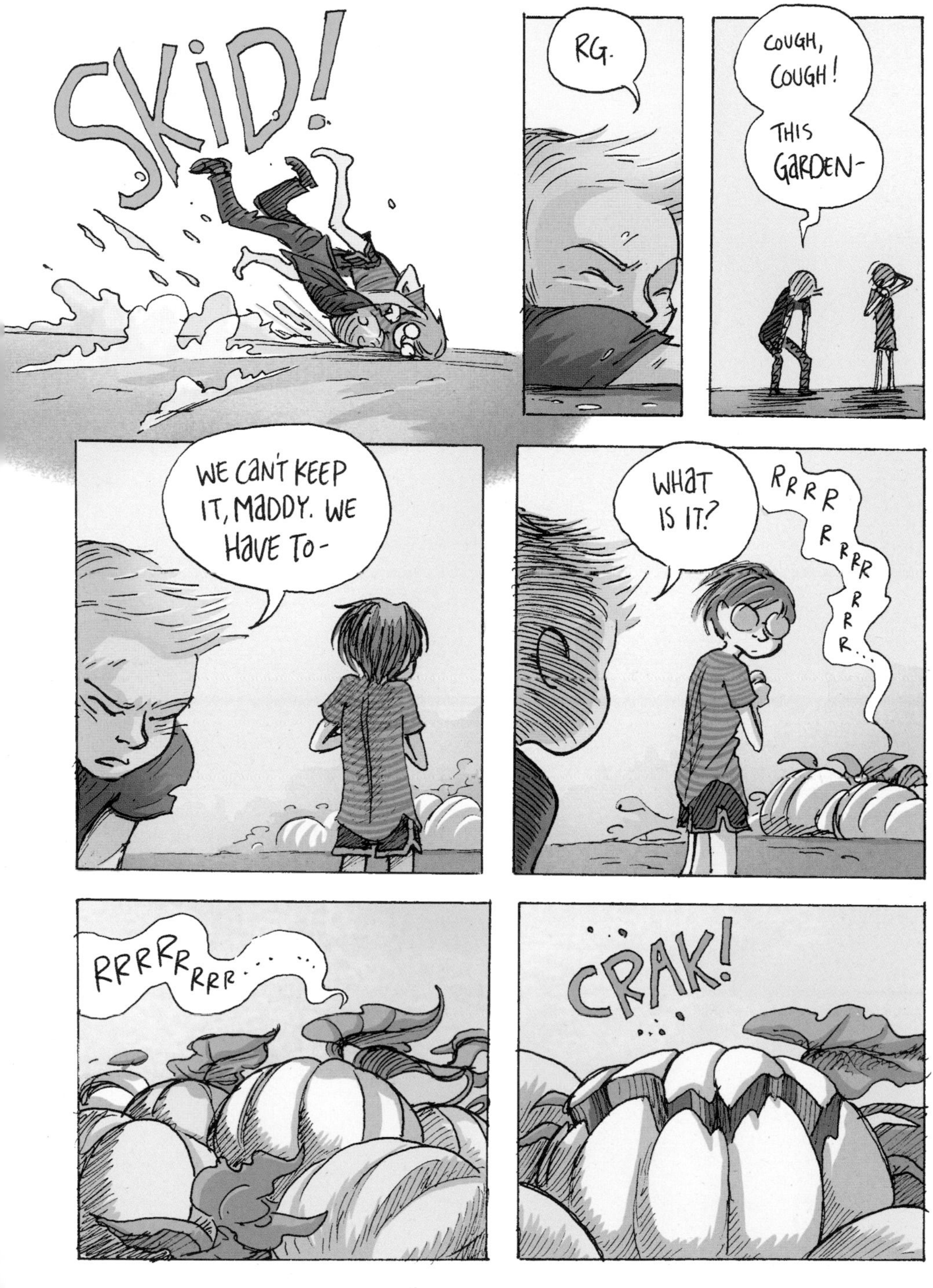
SKID!
RG.
COUGH, COUGH!
THIS GARDEN-
WE CAN'T KEEP IT, MADDY. WE HAVE TO-
WHAT IS IT?
RRRRRRRRRRR...
RRRRRRRR...
CRAK!

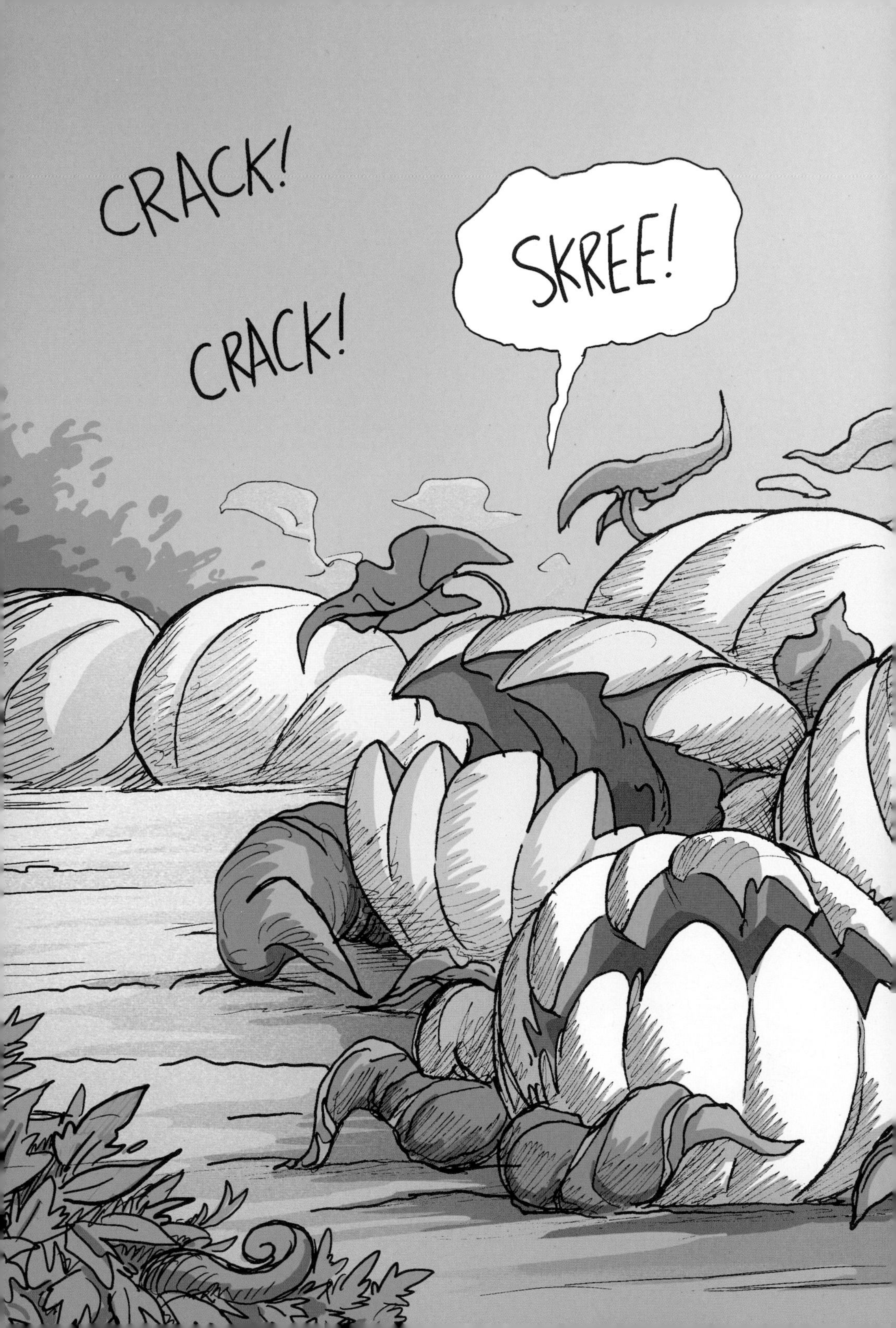
CRACK!
CRACK!
SKREE!

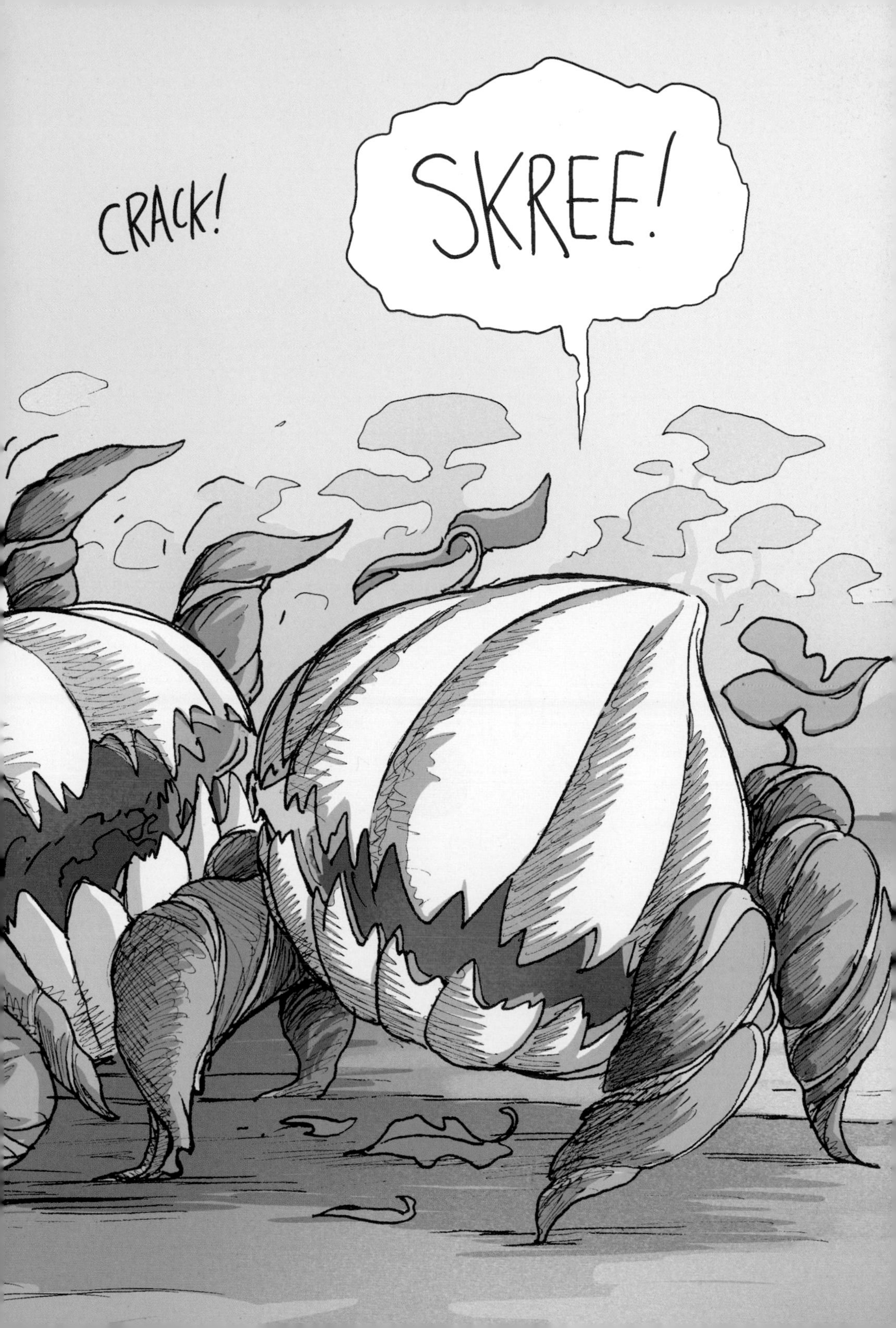
CRACK!
SKREE!

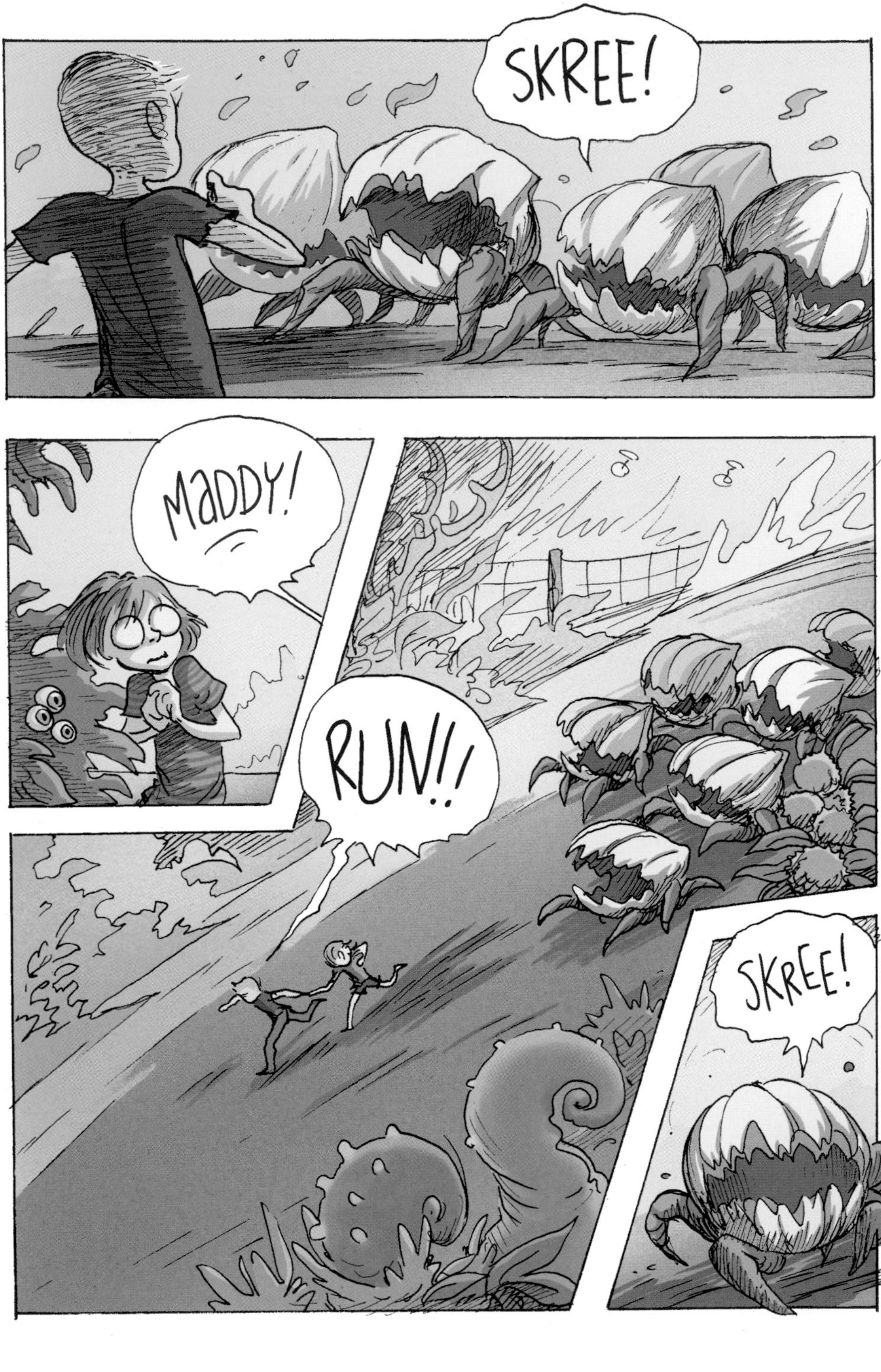

SKREE!
MADDY!
RUN!!
SKREE!

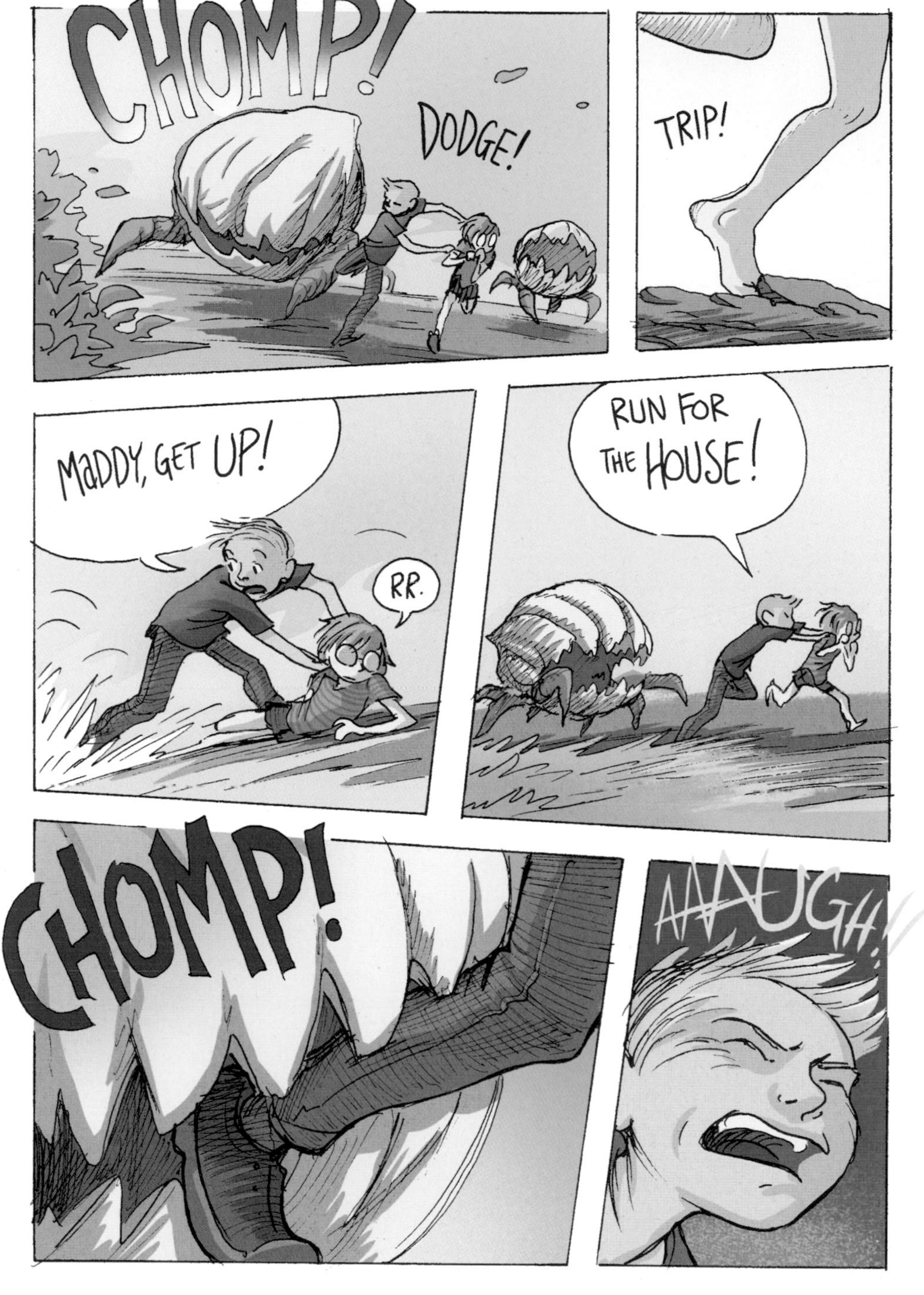
CHOMP!
DODGE!
TRIP!
MADDY, GET UP!
RR.
RUN FOR THE HOUSE!
CHOMP!
AAAUGH!

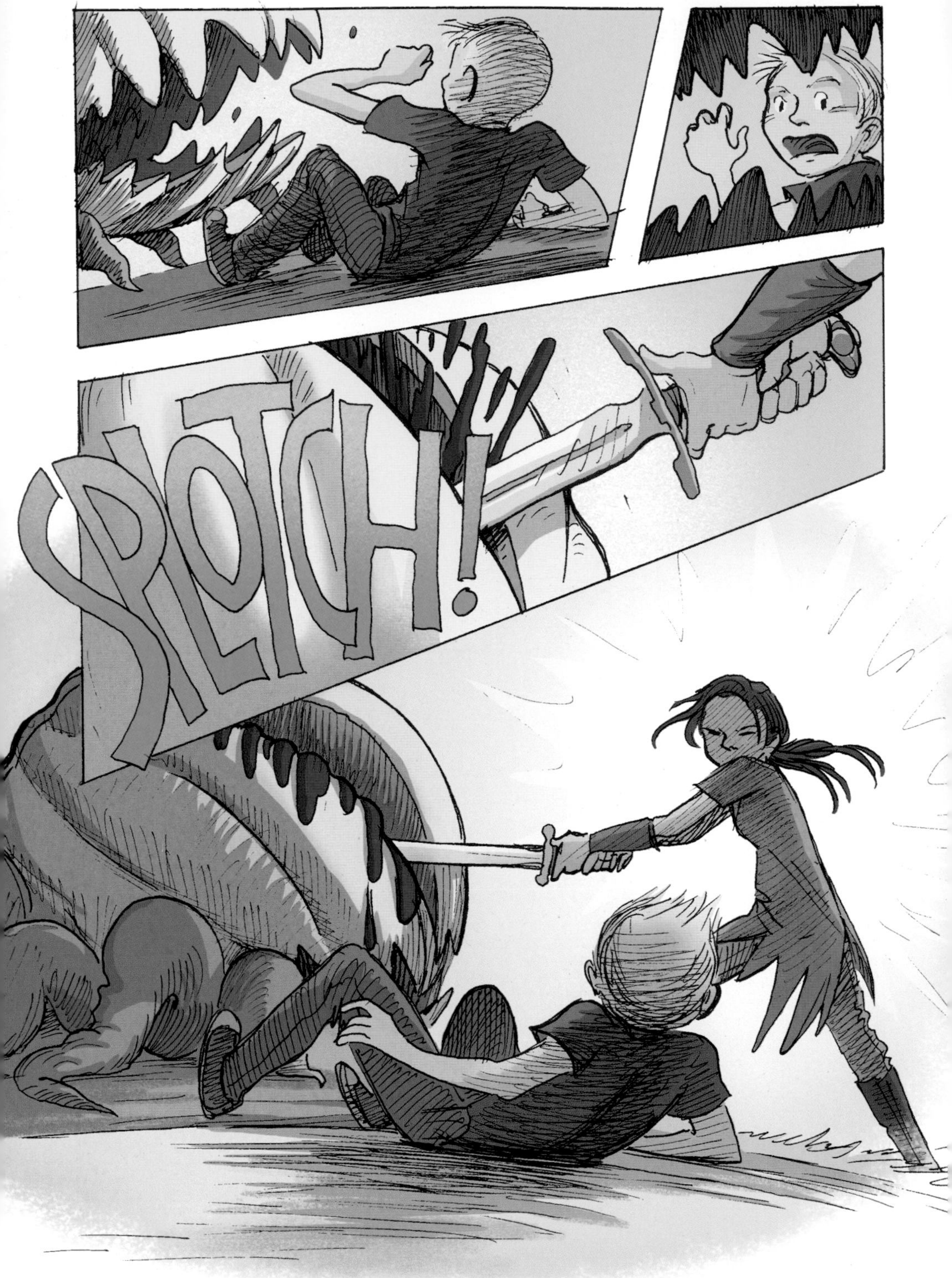
SPLOTCH!

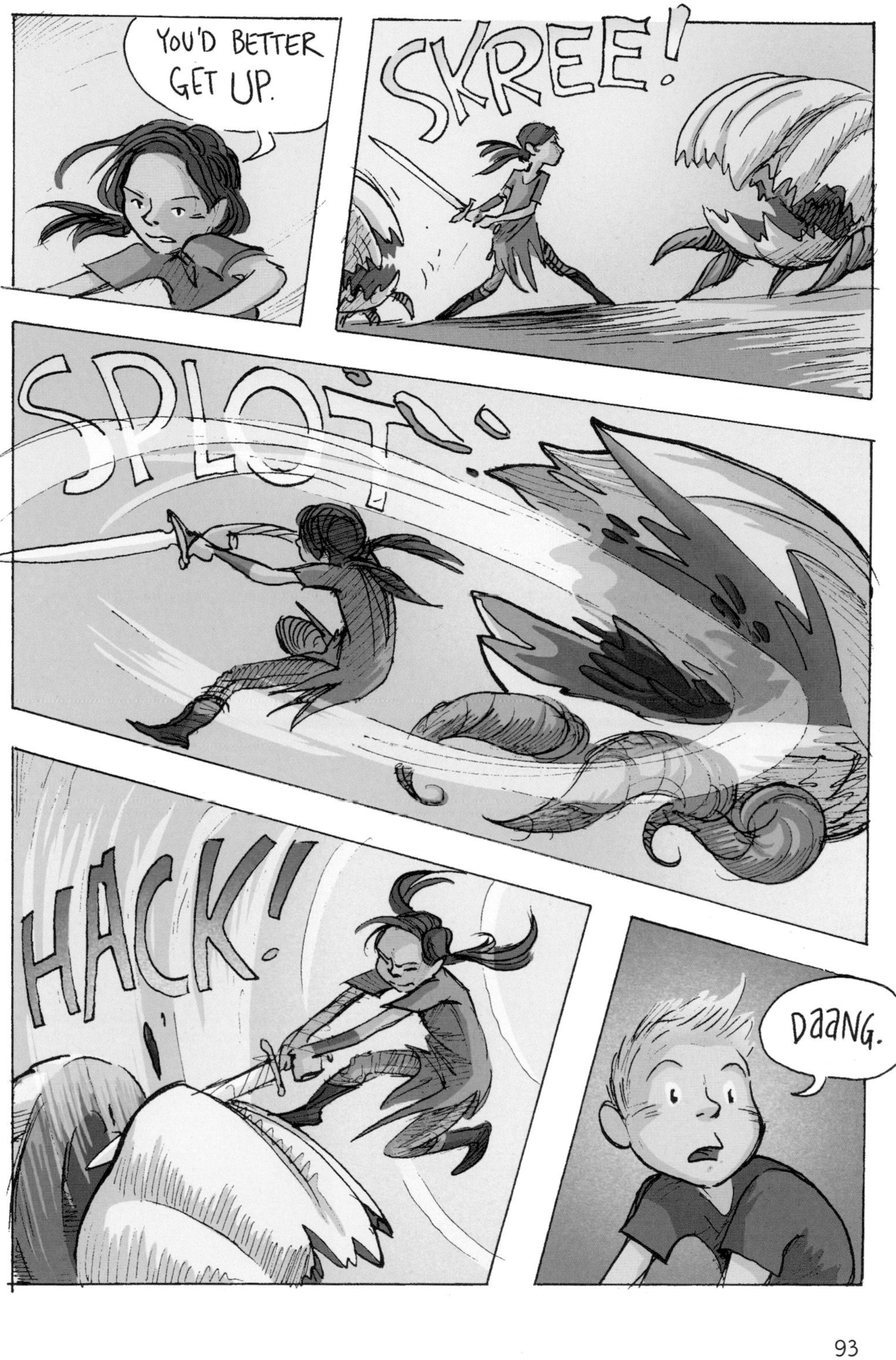
YOU'D BETTER GET UP.
SKREE!
SPLOT
HACK!
DaaNG.

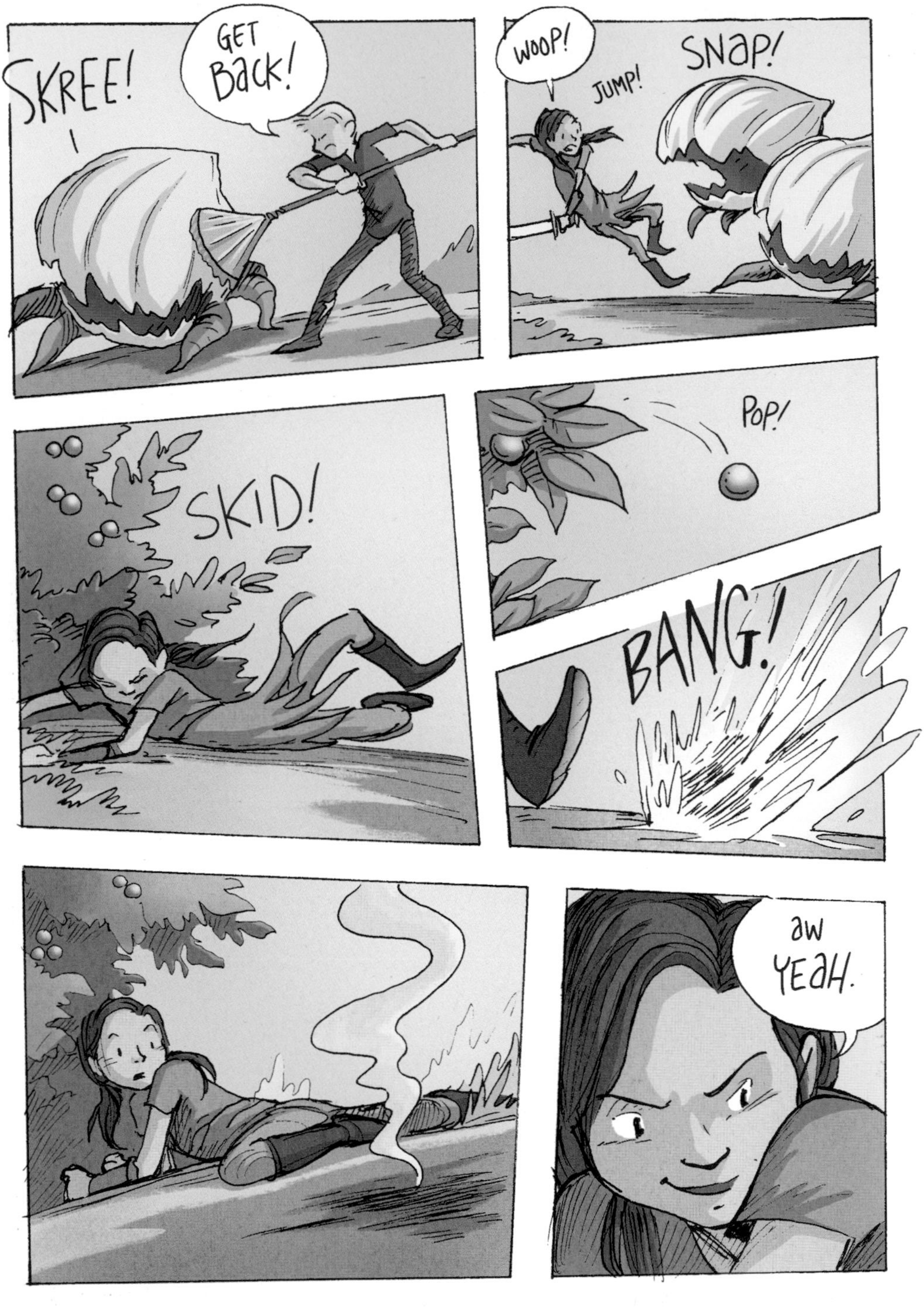
SKREE!
GET BACK!
WOOP!
JUMP!
SNAP!
SKID!
POP!
BANG!
aw YEAH.

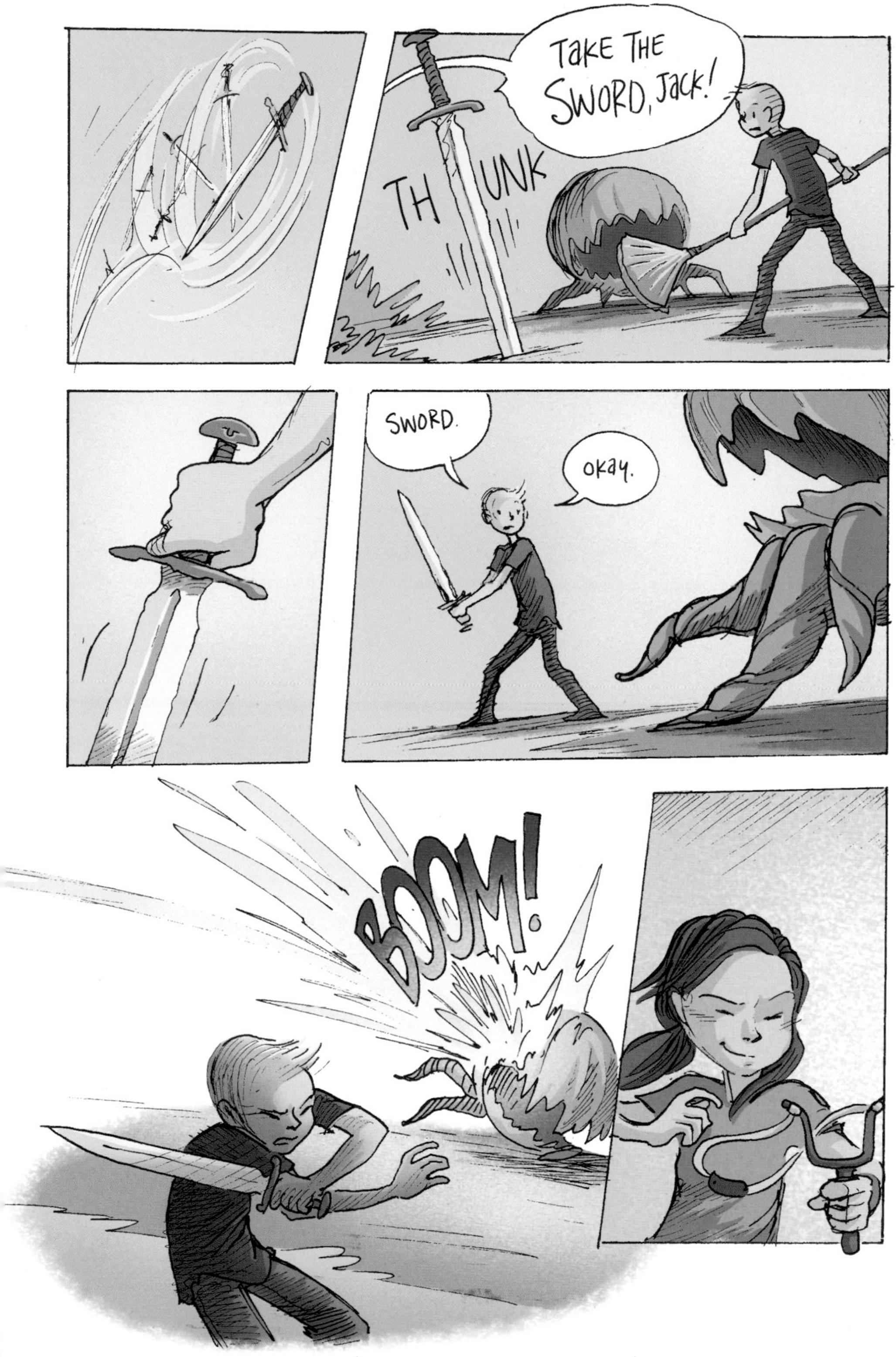
THUNK
TAKE THE SWORD, JACK!
SWORD.
OKAY.
BOOM!

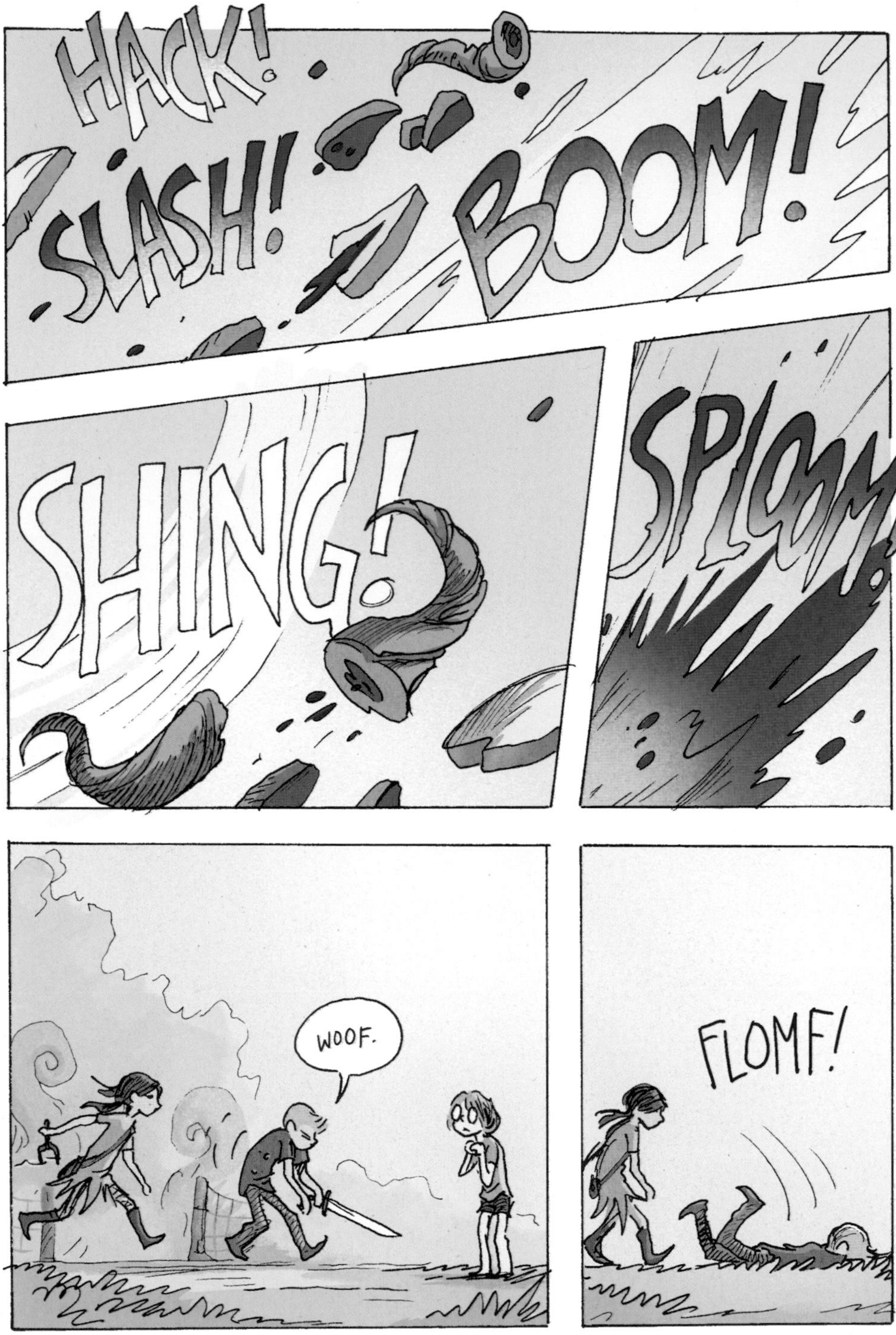
HACK!
SLASH!
BOOM!
SHING!
SPLOOM!
WOOF.
FLOMF!

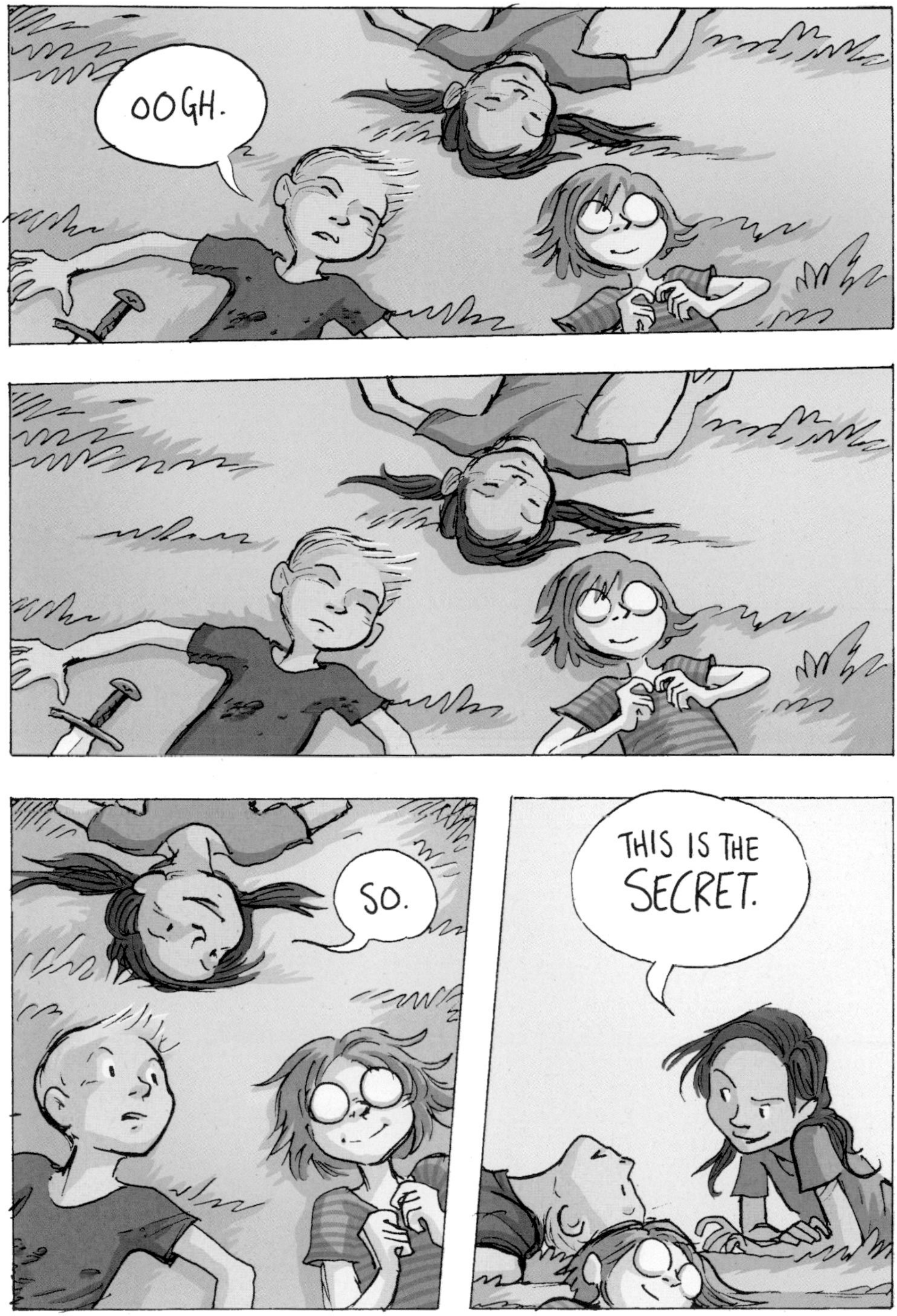
OOGH.
SO.
THIS IS THE SECRET.

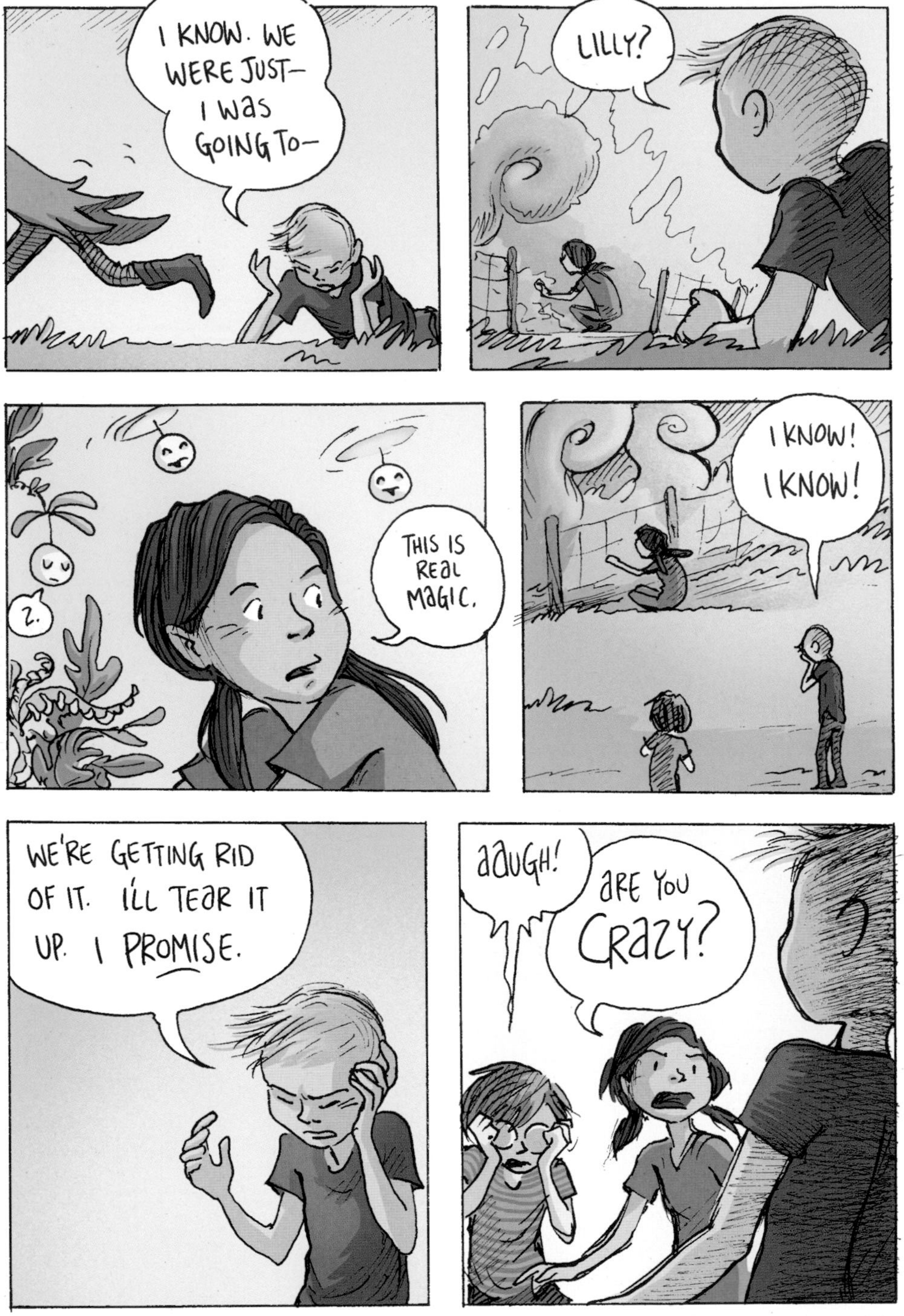
I KNOW. WE WERE JUST— I WAS GOING TO—
LILLY?
2.
THIS IS REAL MAGIC.
I KNOW! I KNOW!
WE'RE GETTING RID OF IT. I'LL TEAR IT UP. I PROMISE.
AAUGH!
ARE YOU CRAZY?

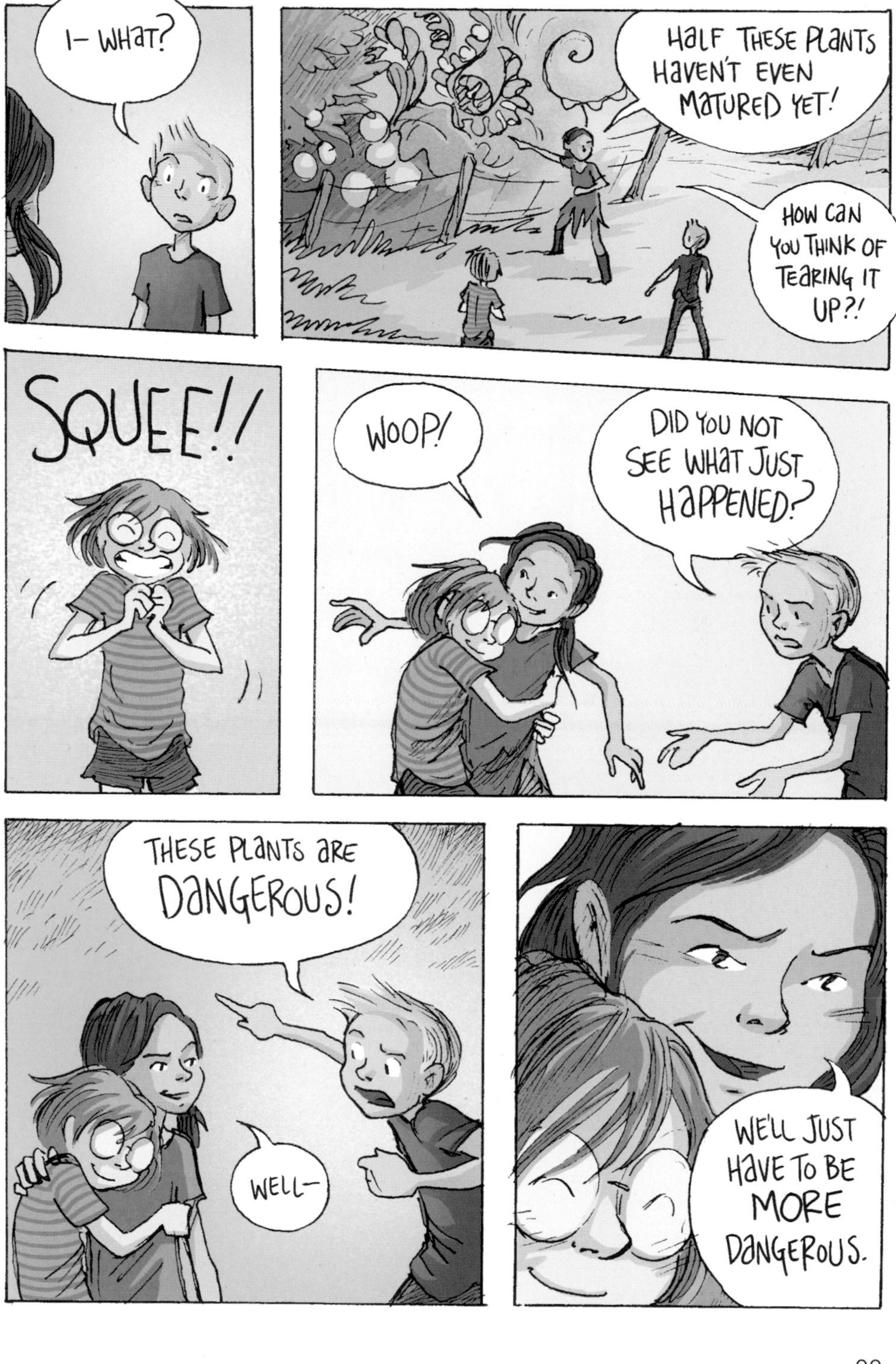
I- WHAT?
HALF THESE PLANTS HAVEN'T EVEN MATURED YET!
HOW CAN YOU THINK OF TEARING IT UP?!
SQUEE!!
WOOP!
DID YOU NOT SEE WHAT JUST HAPPENED?
THESE PLANTS ARE DANGEROUS!
WELL-
WE'LL JUST HAVE TO BE MORE DANGEROUS.

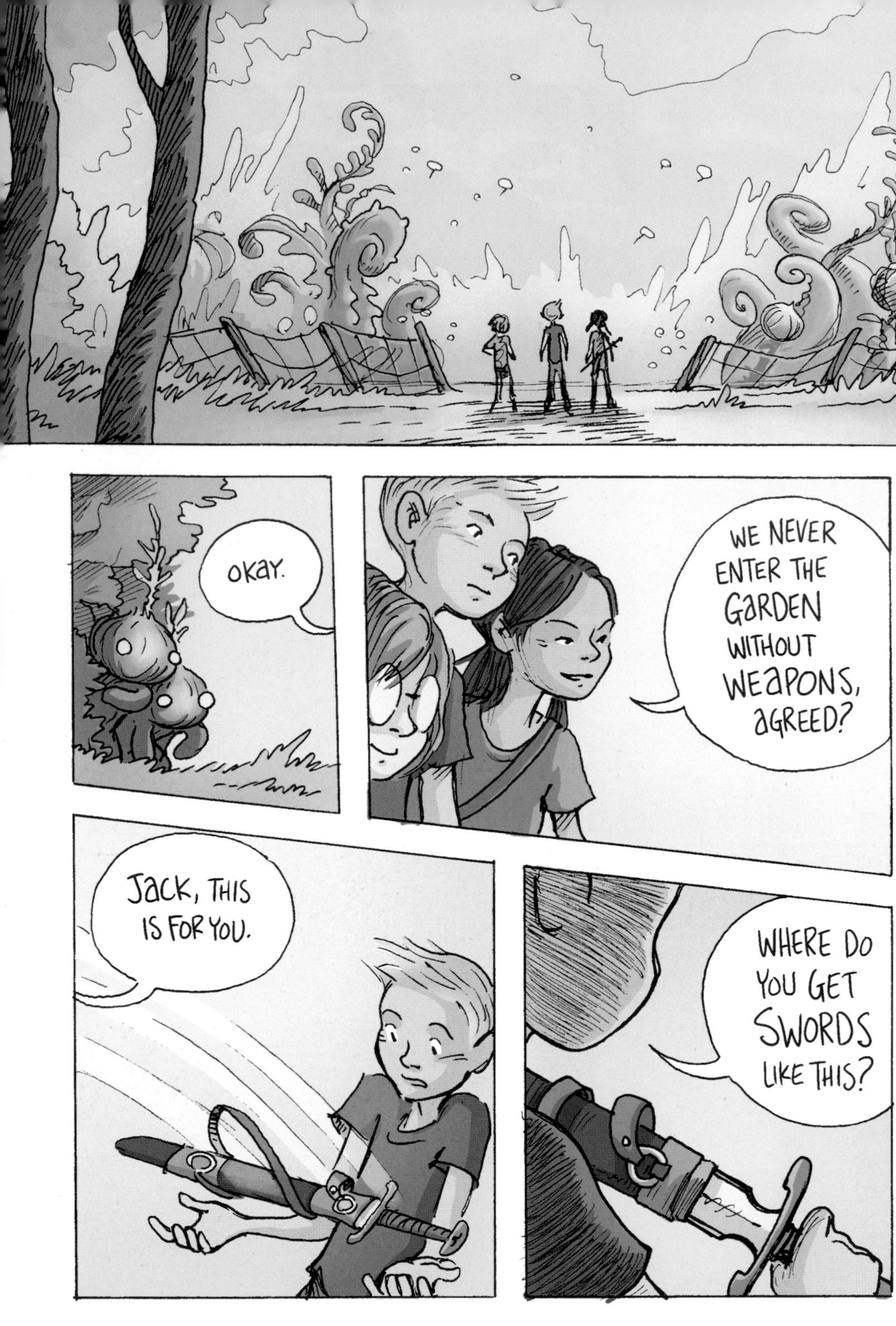
OKAY.
WE NEVER ENTER THE GARDEN WITHOUT WEAPONS, AGREED?
JACK, THIS IS FOR YOU.
WHERE DO YOU GET SWORDS LIKE THIS?

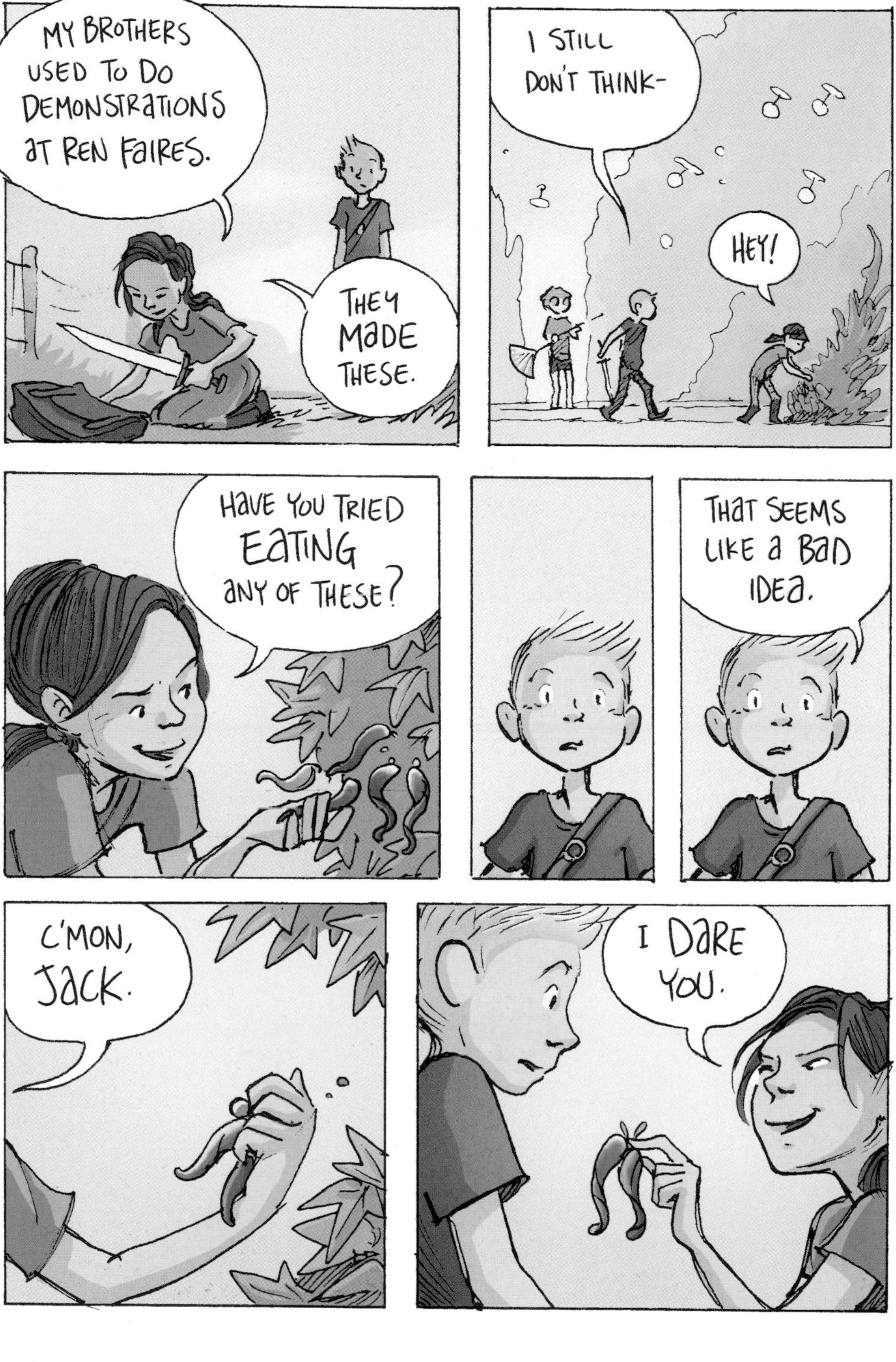
MY BROTHERS USED TO DO DEMONSTRATIONS AT REN FAIRES.
THEY MADE THESE.
I STILL DON'T THINK-
HEY!
HAVE YOU TRIED EATING ANY OF THESE?
THAT SEEMS LIKE A BAD IDEA.
C'MON, JACK.
I DARE YOU.

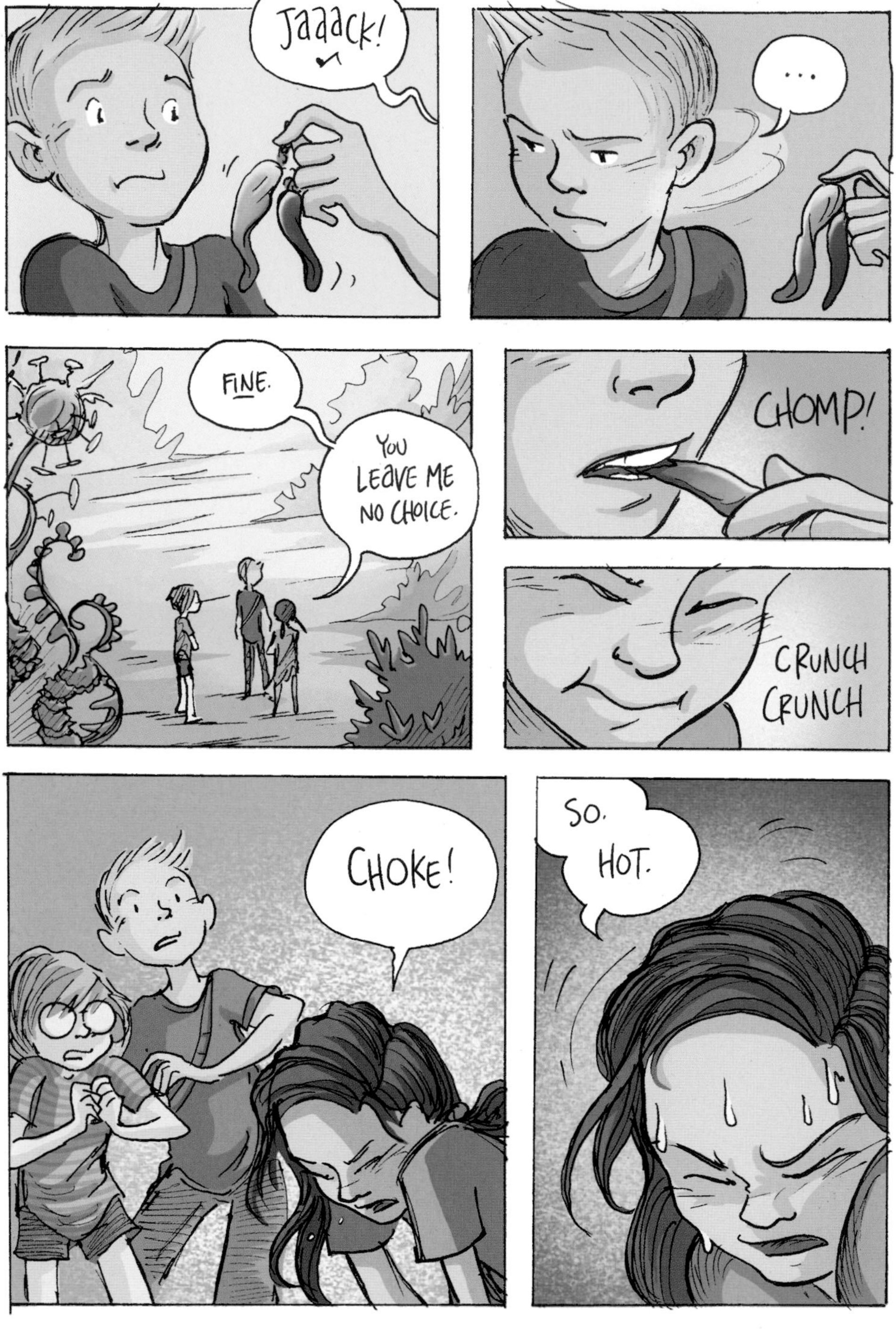

Jaaack!
...
FINE.
YOU LEAVE ME NO CHOICE.
CHOMP!
CRUNCH CRUNCH
CHOKE!
SO. HOT.

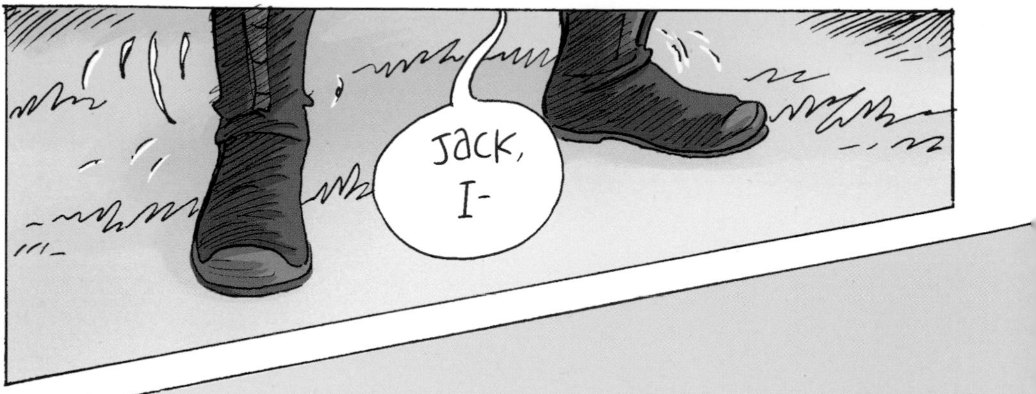
Jack,
I-

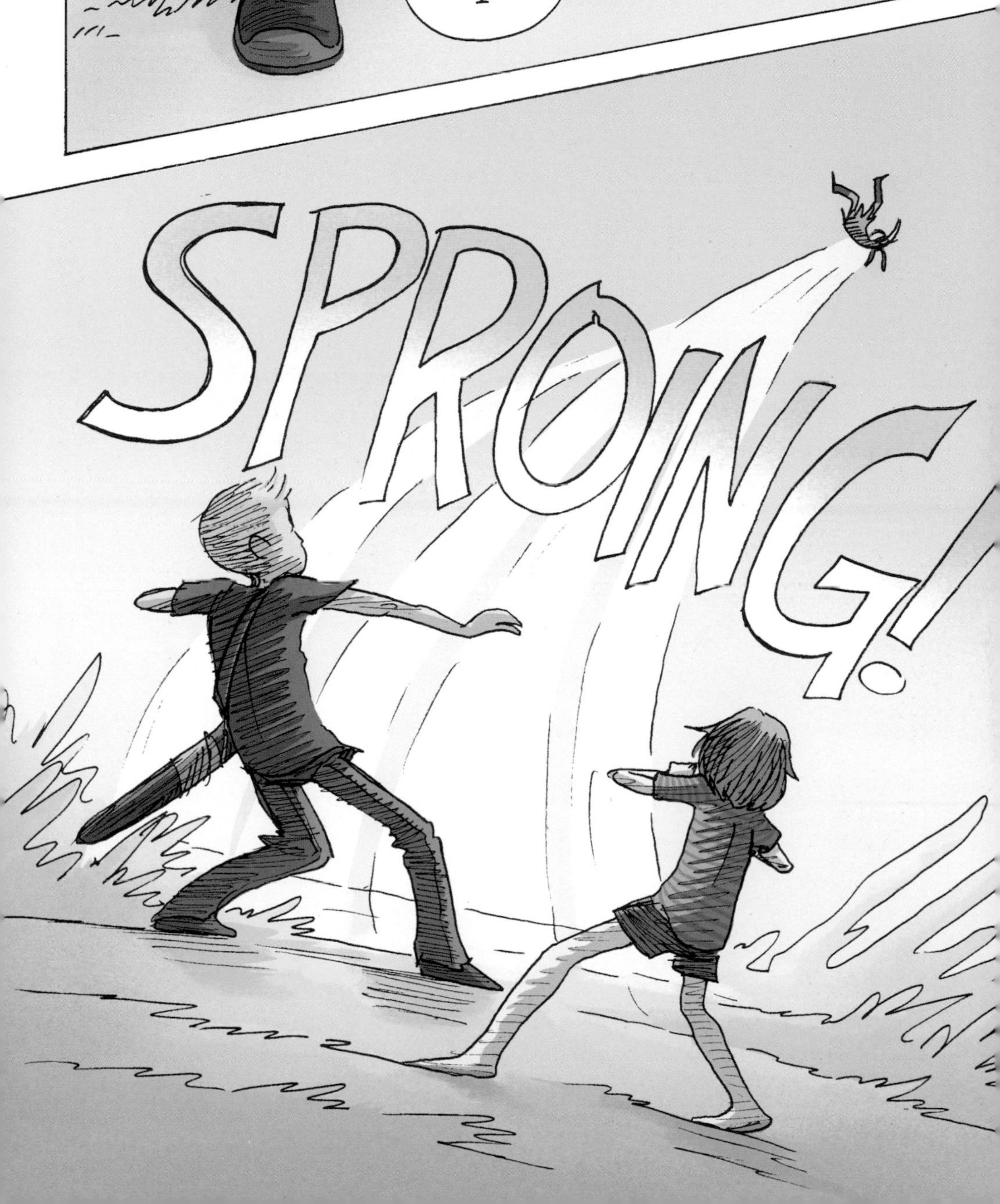
SPRONG!

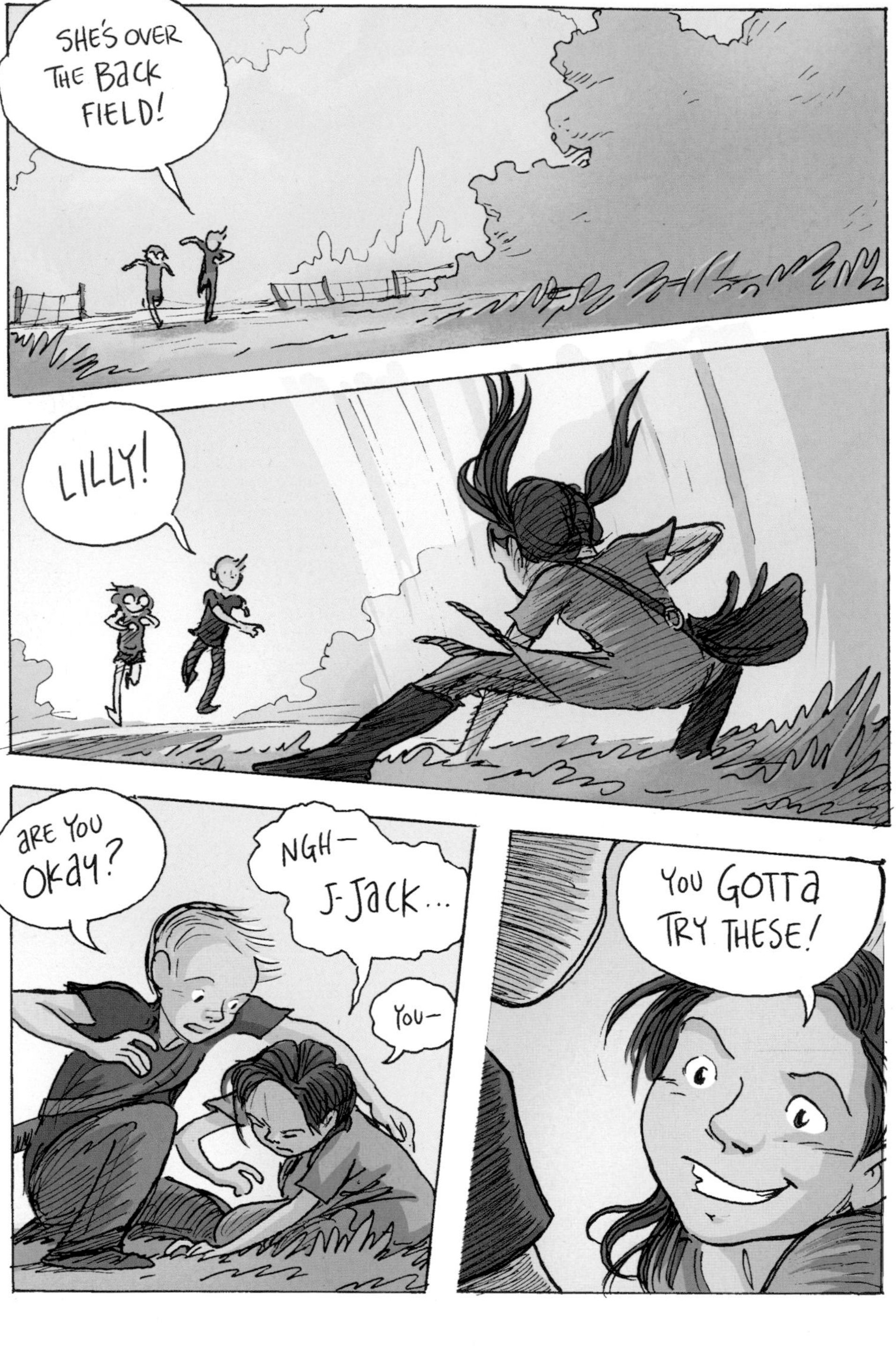
SHE'S OVER THE BACK FIELD!
LILLY!
are YOU Okay?
NGH— J-Jack...
YOU—
YOU GOTTA TRY THESE!

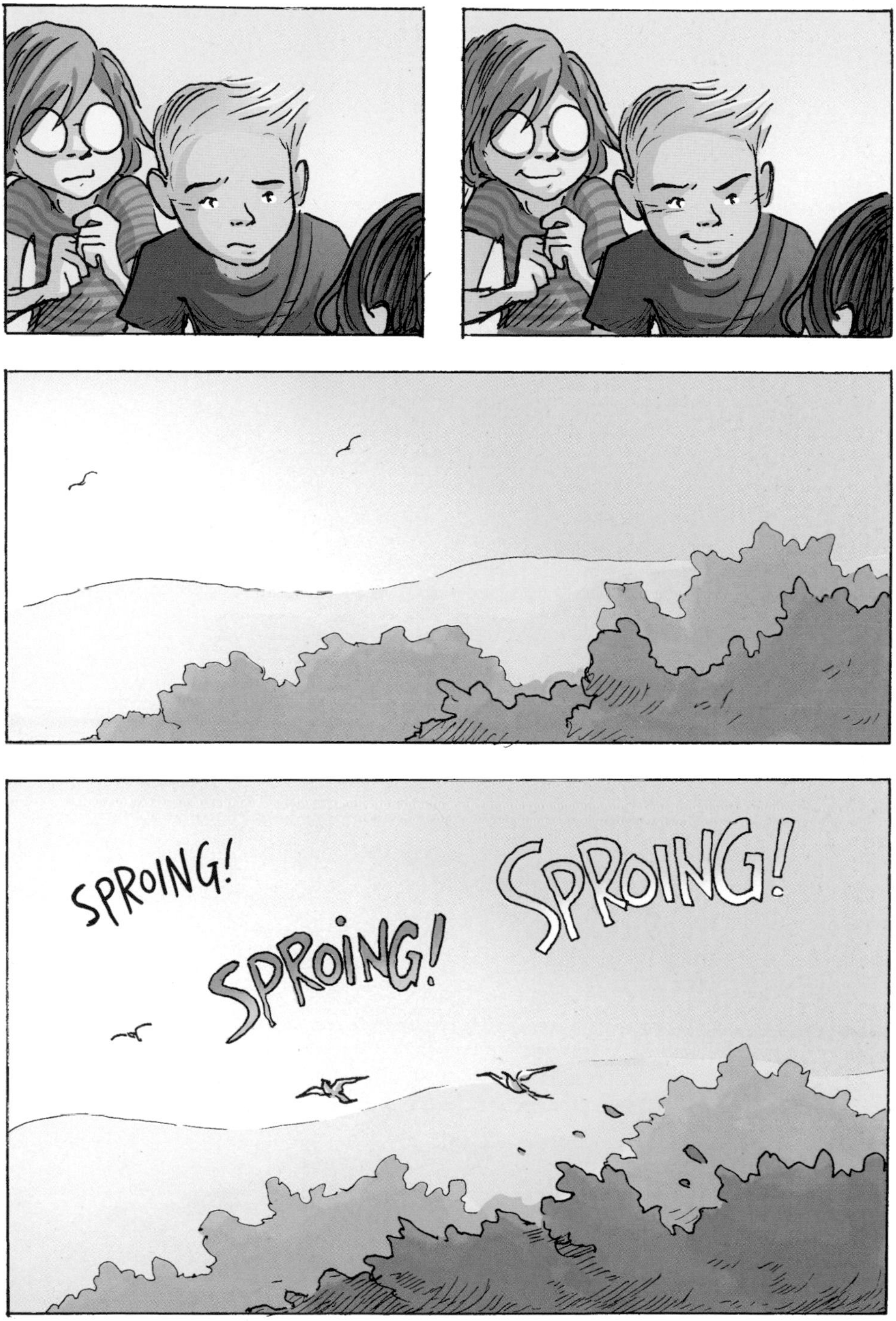
SPROING!
SPROING!
SPROING!

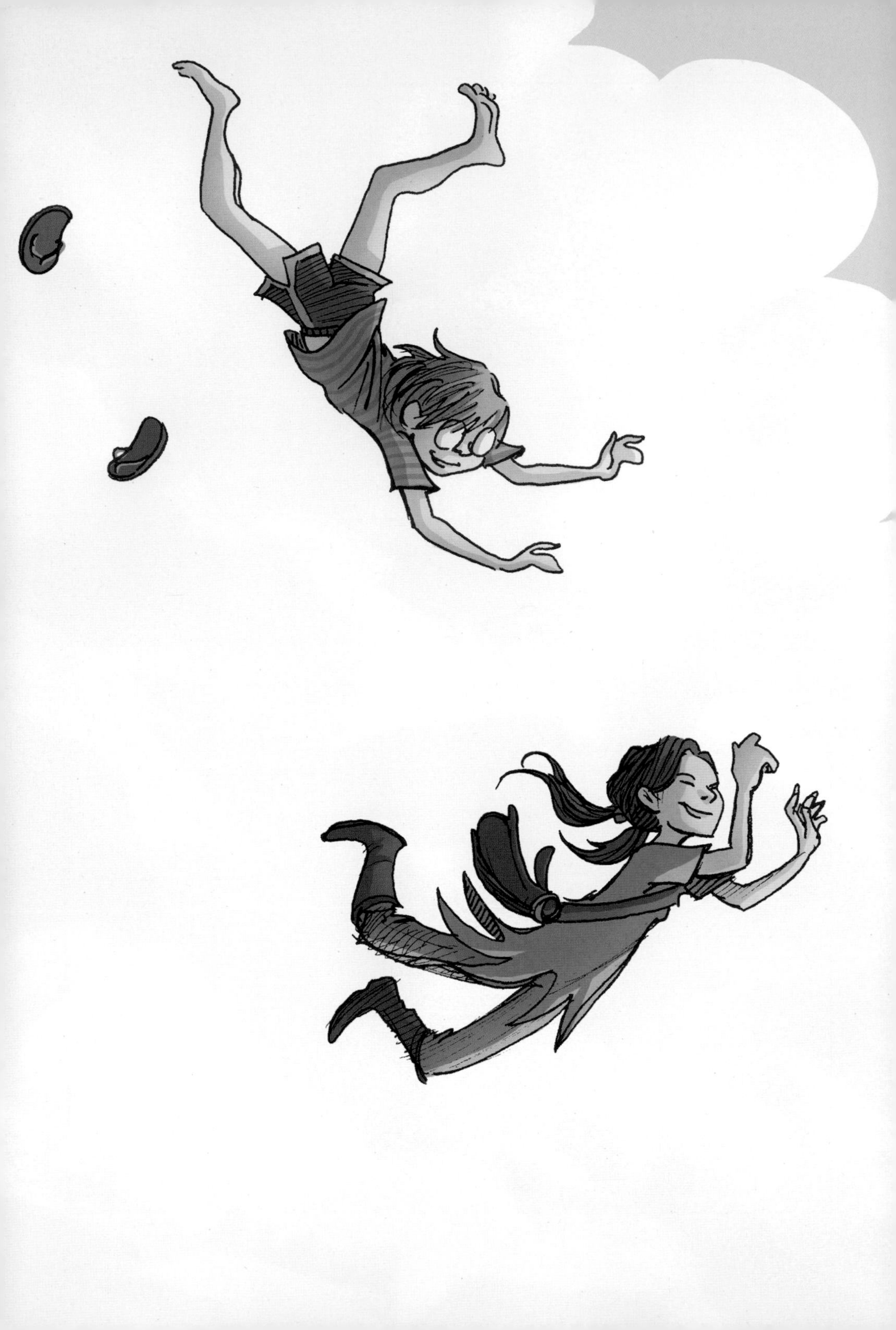

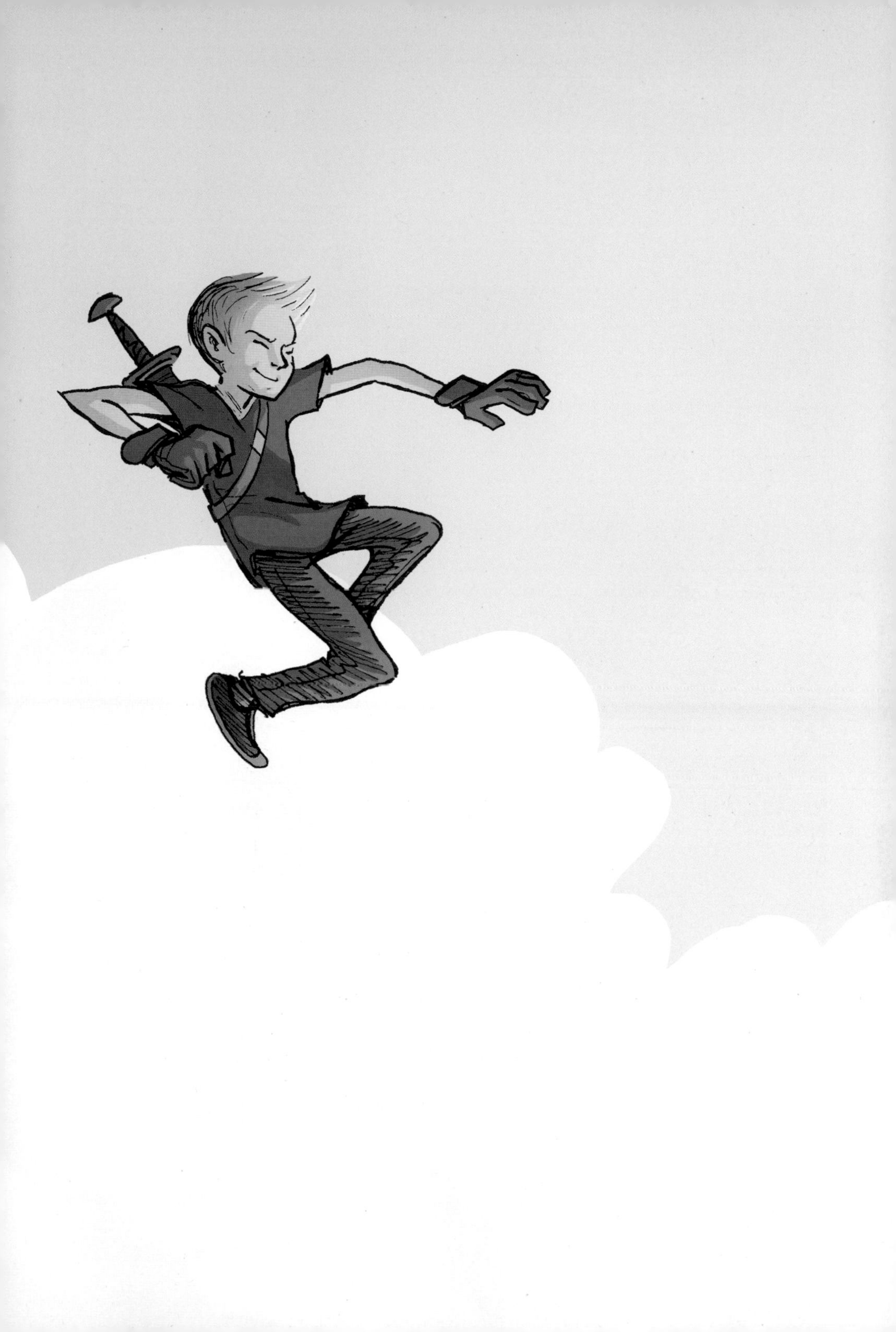

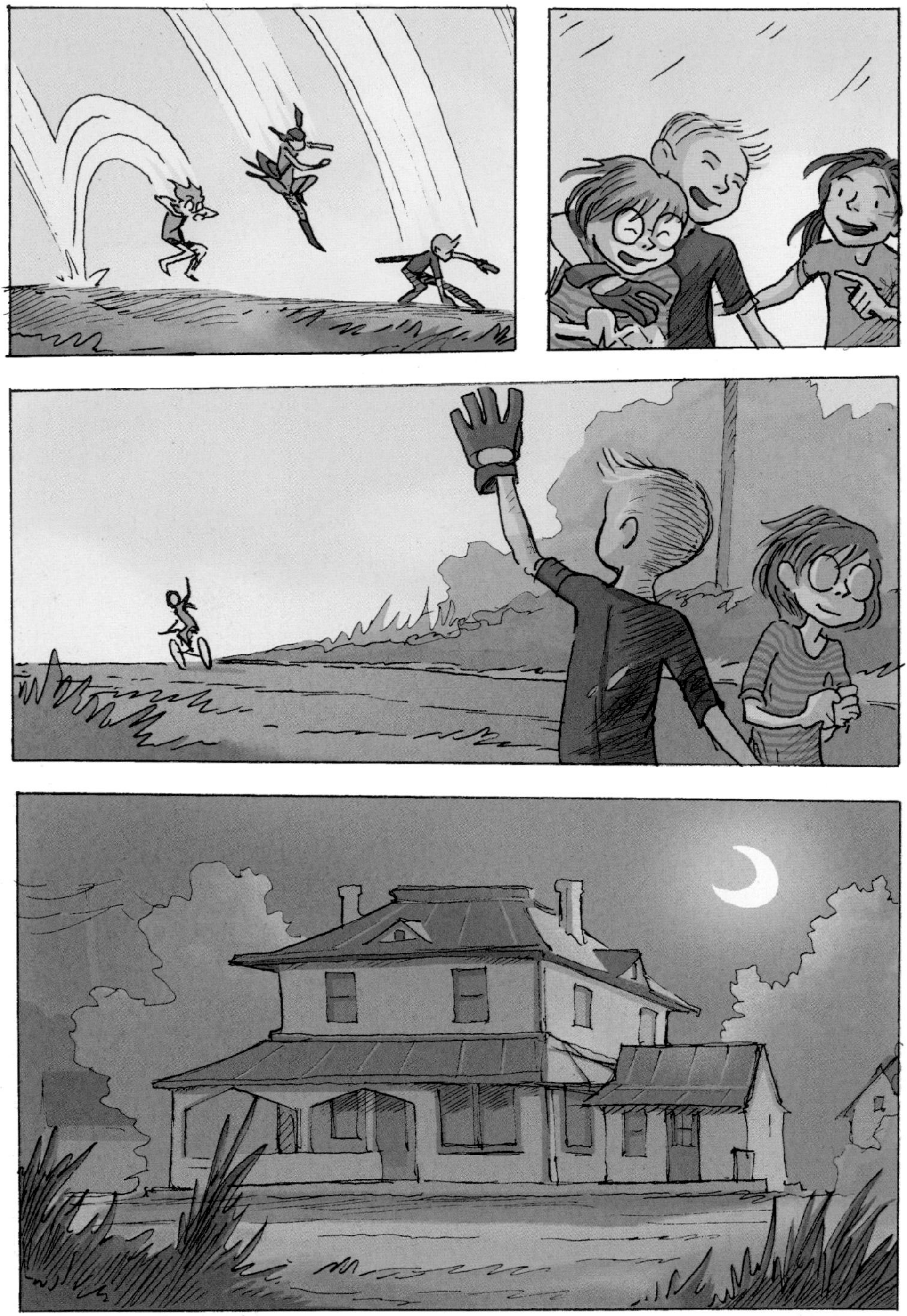

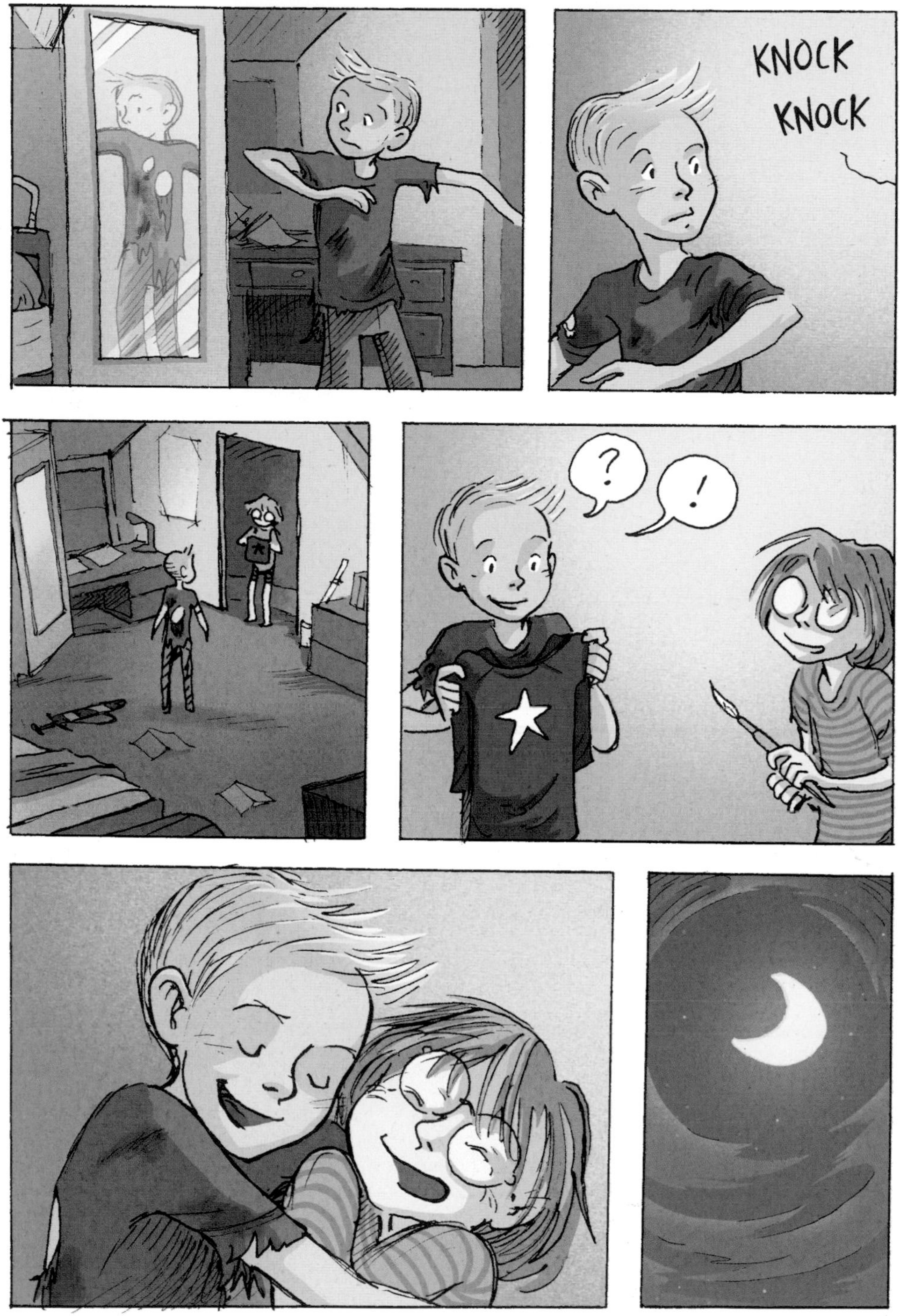
KNOCK
KNOCK
?
!

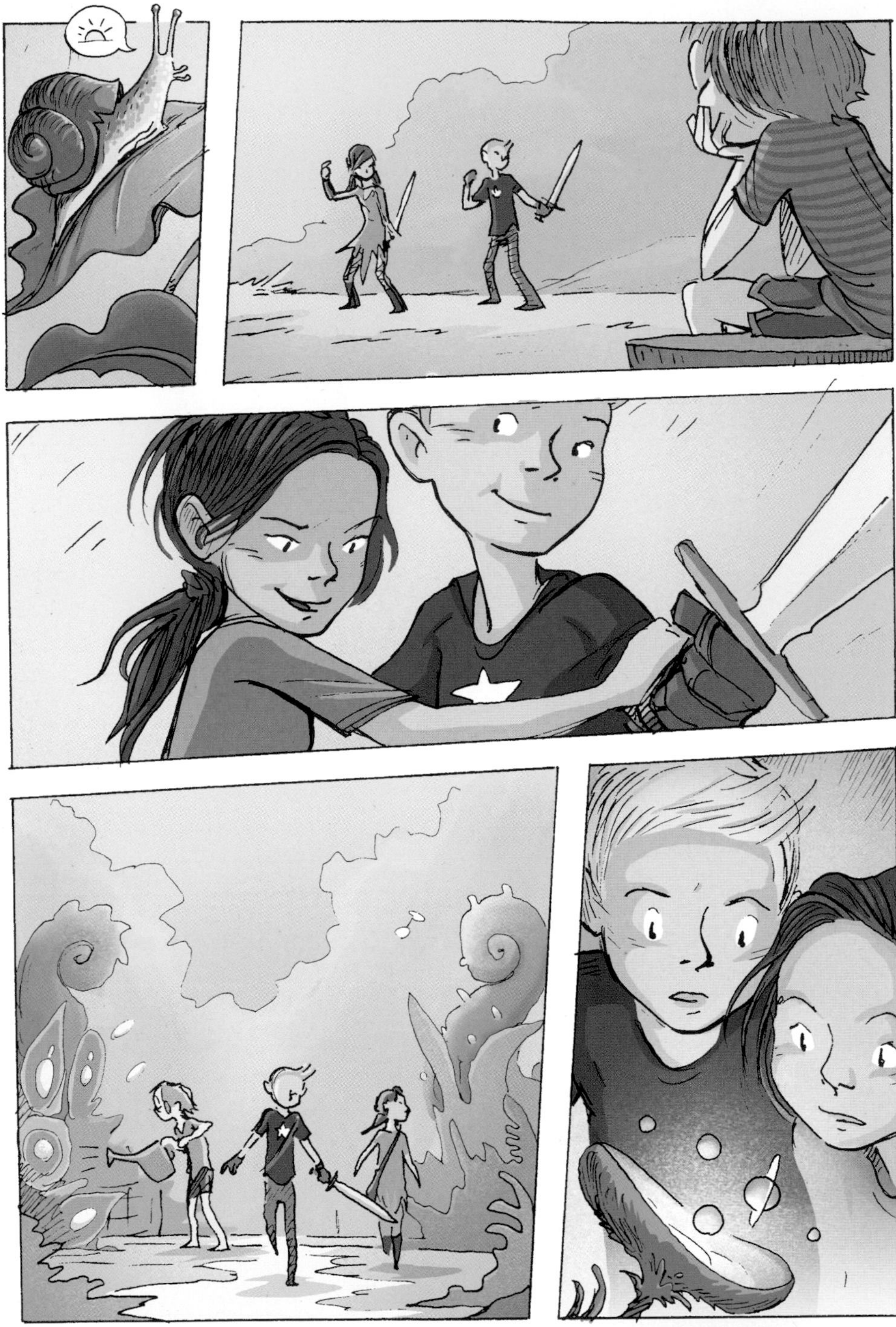

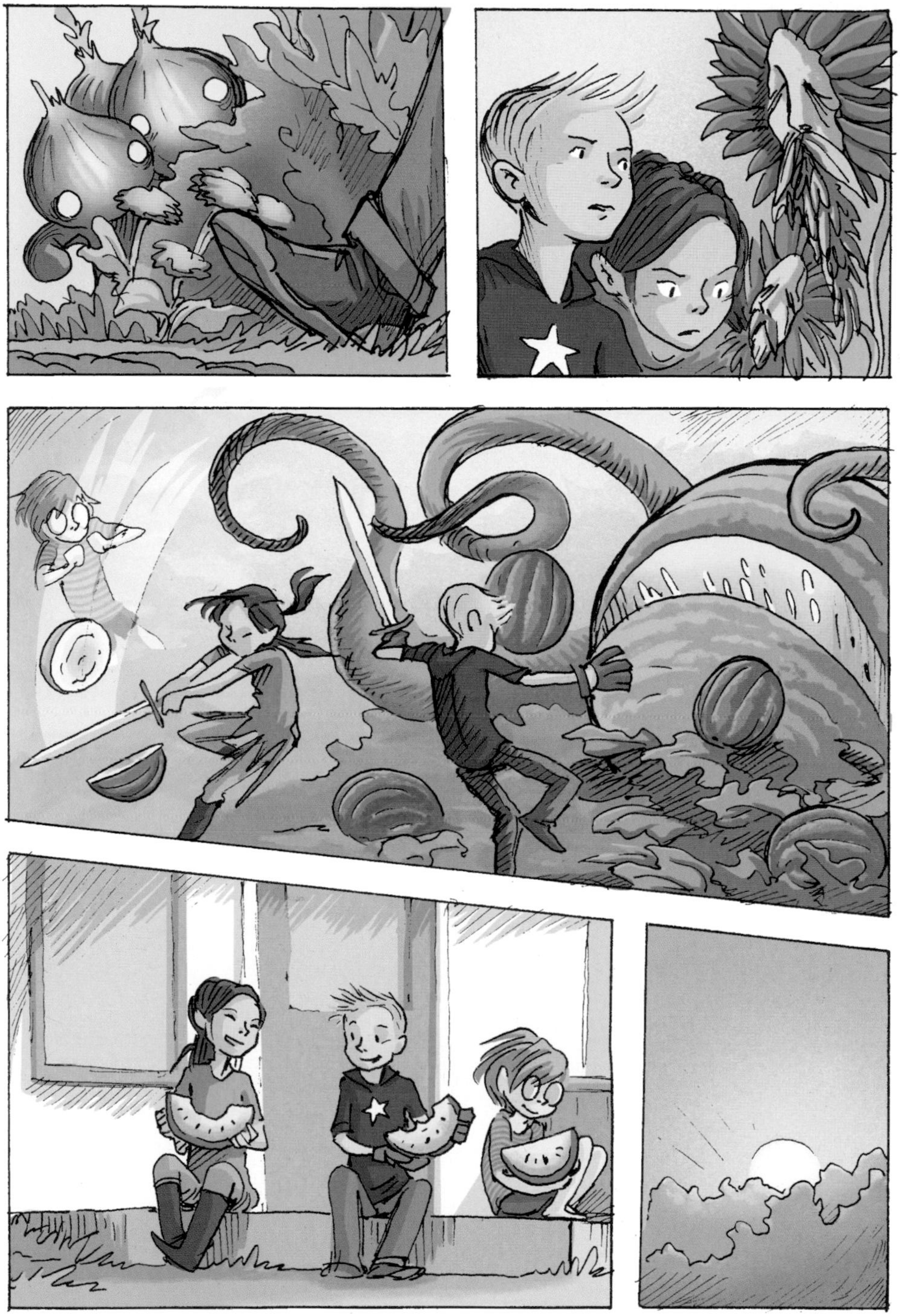

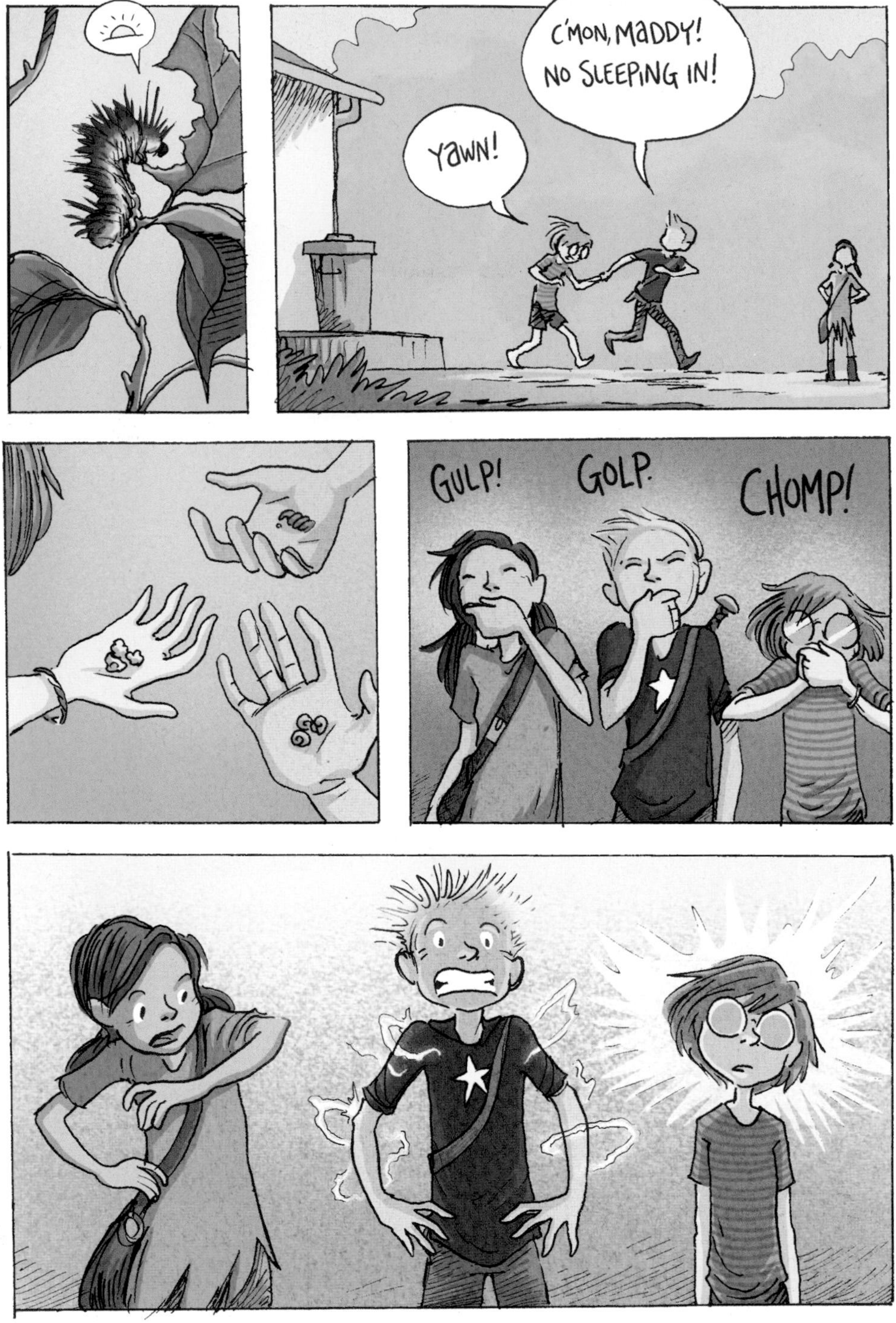
C'MON, MADDY! NO SLEEPING IN!
YAWN!
GULP!
GOLP.
CHOMP!

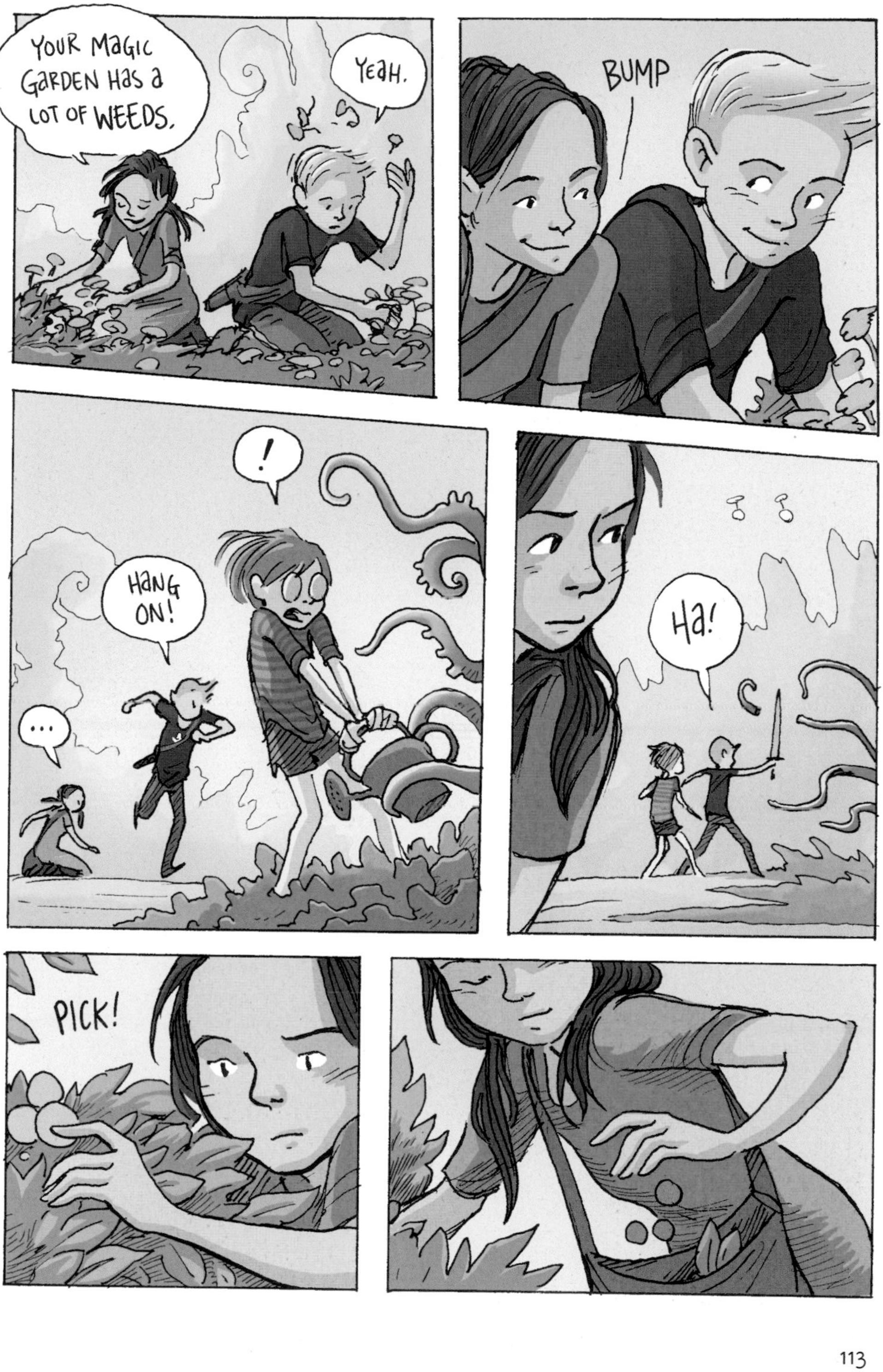

YOUR MAGIC GARDEN HAS A LOT OF WEEDS.
YEAH.
BUMP
!
HANG ON!
...
HA!
PICK!

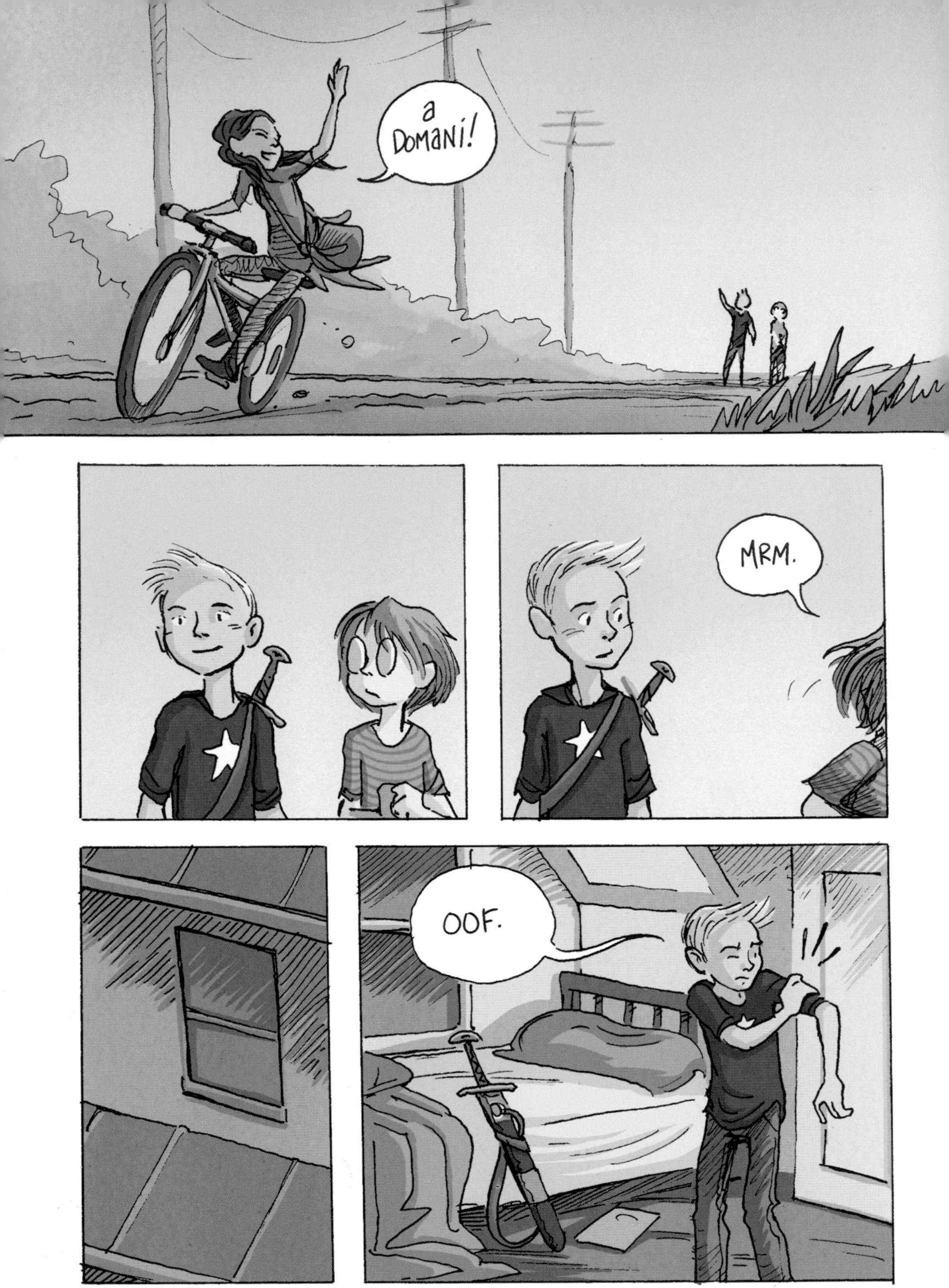
a DOMANI!
MRM.
OOF.

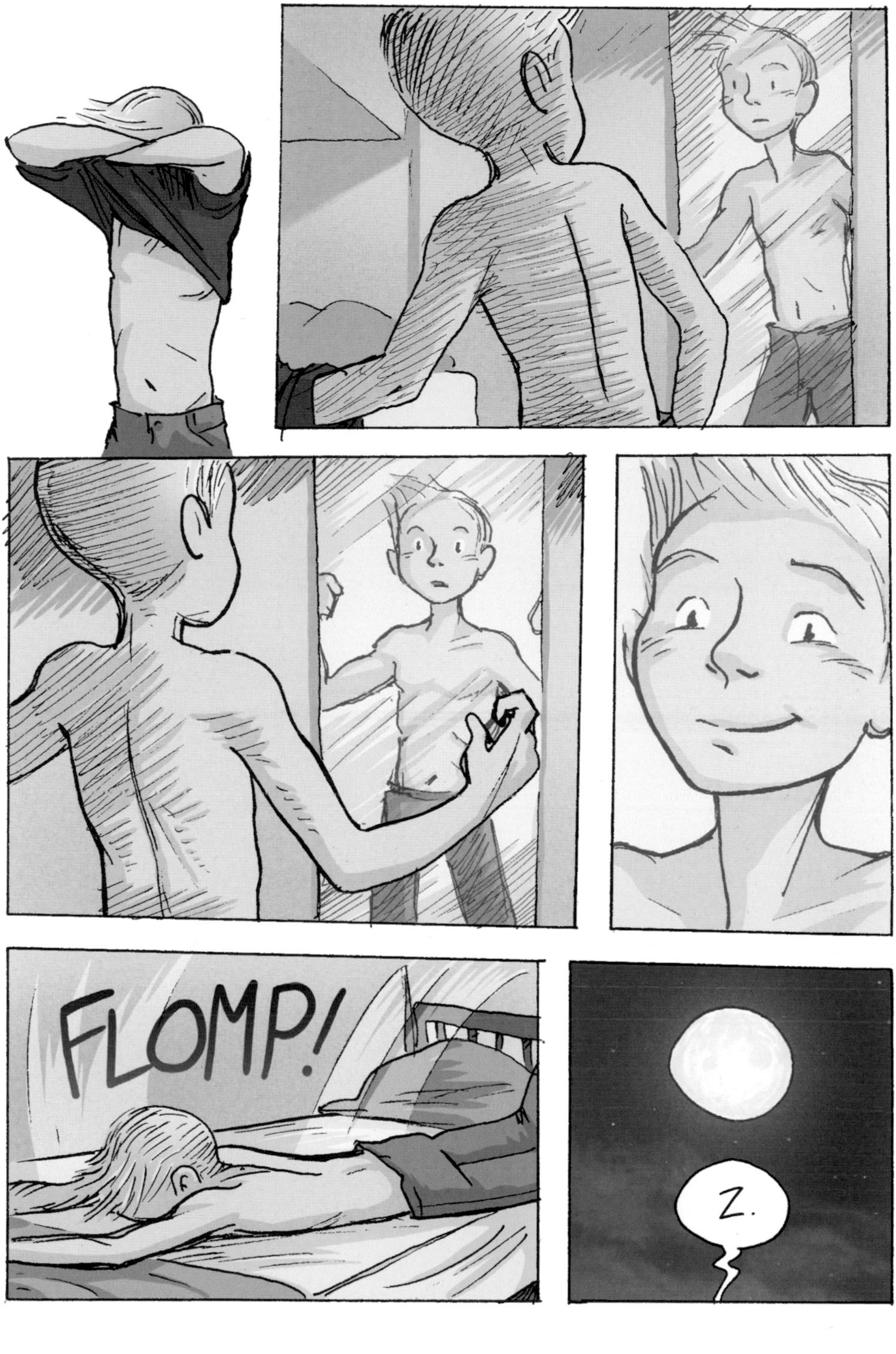
FLOMP!
Z.

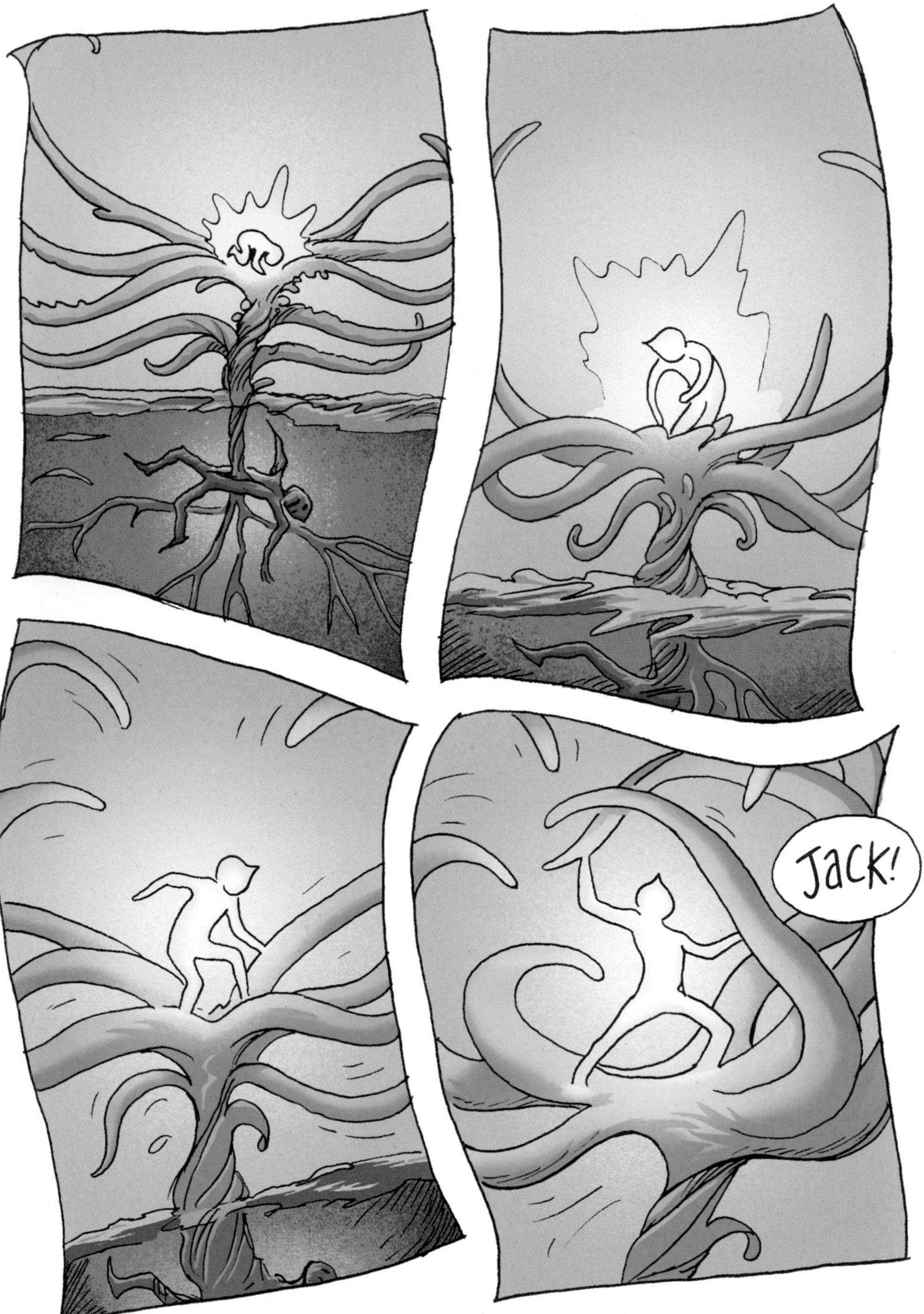
JACK!

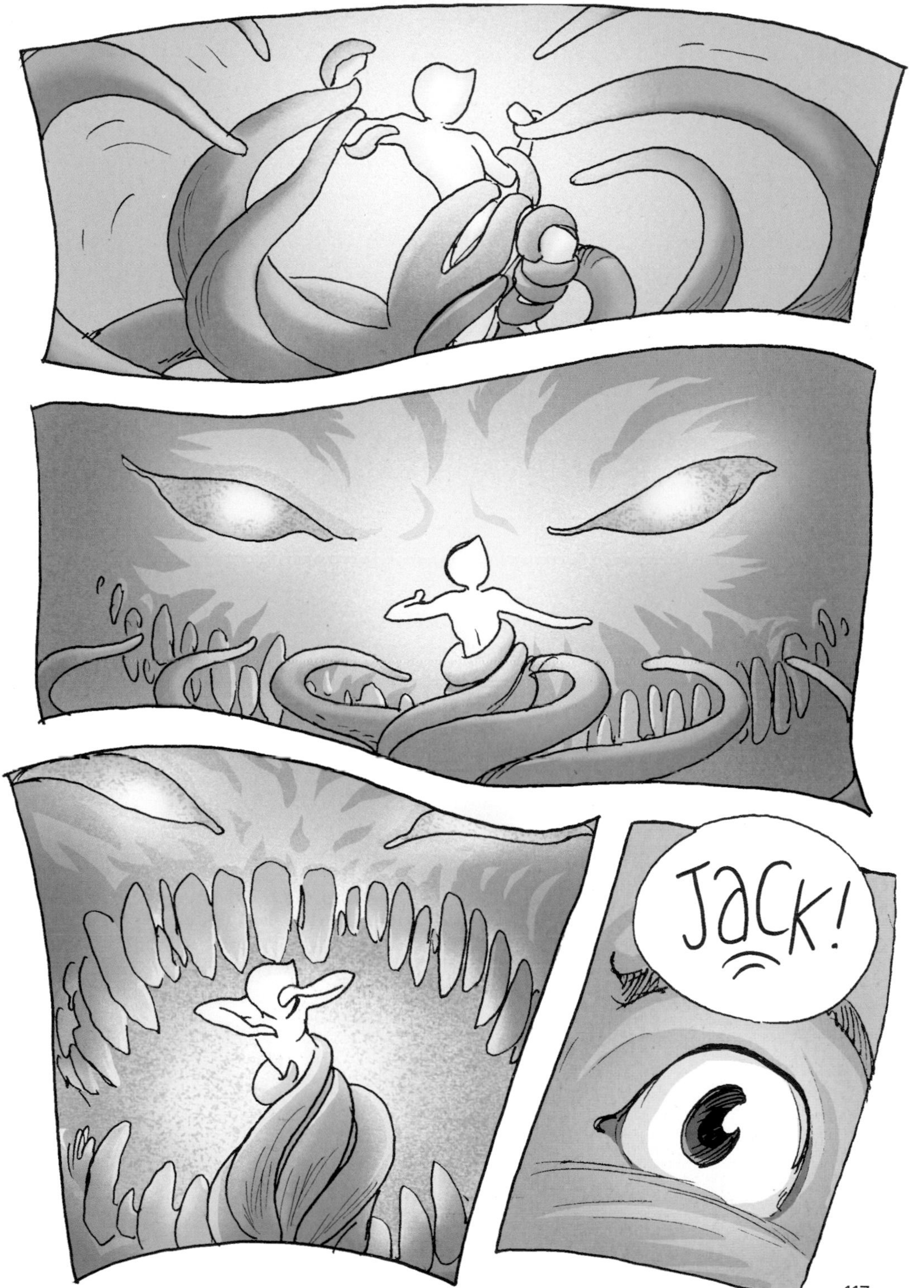
JACK!

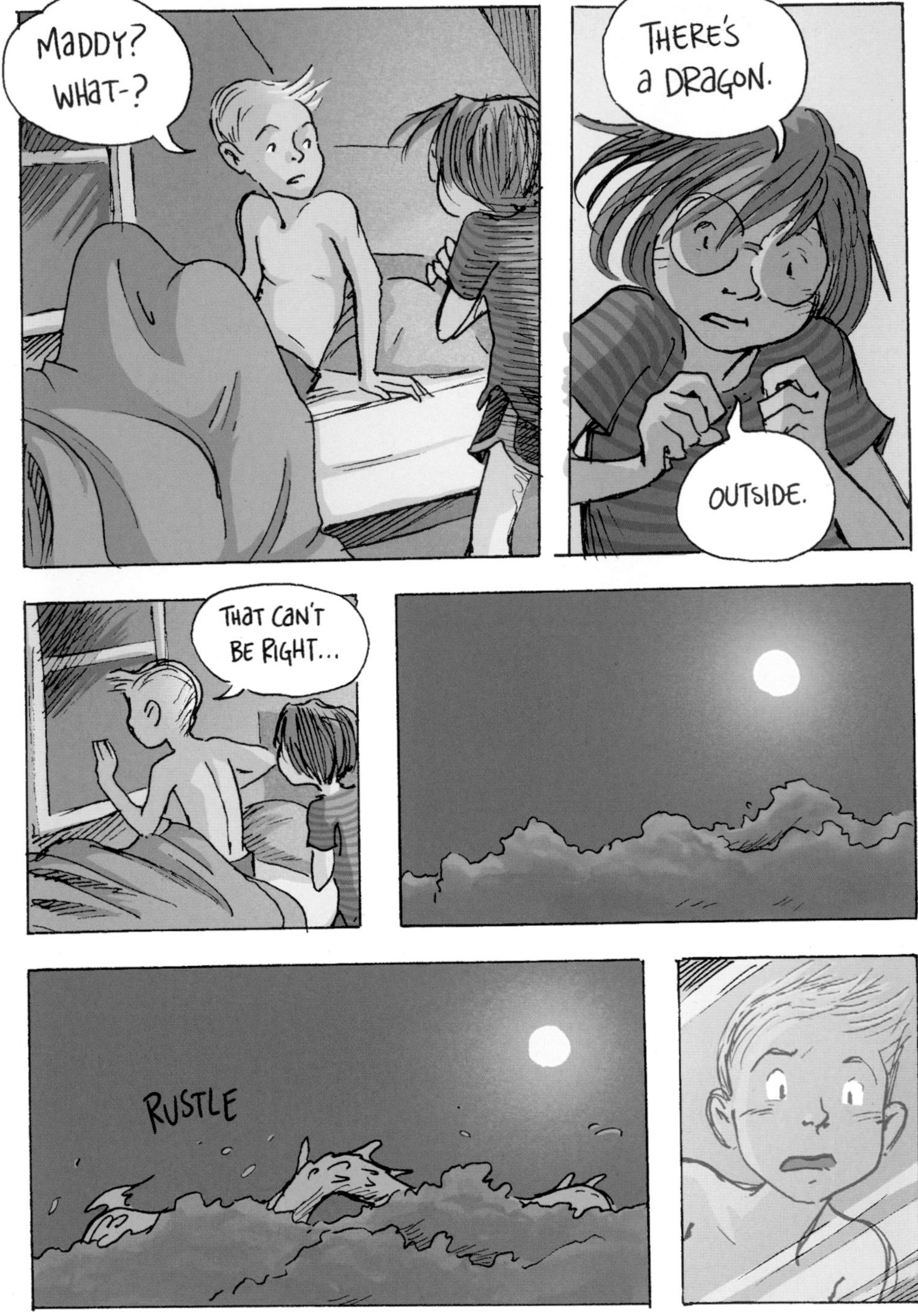
MADDY? WHAT-?
THERE'S A DRAGON.
OUTSIDE.
THAT CAN'T BE RIGHT...
RUSTLE

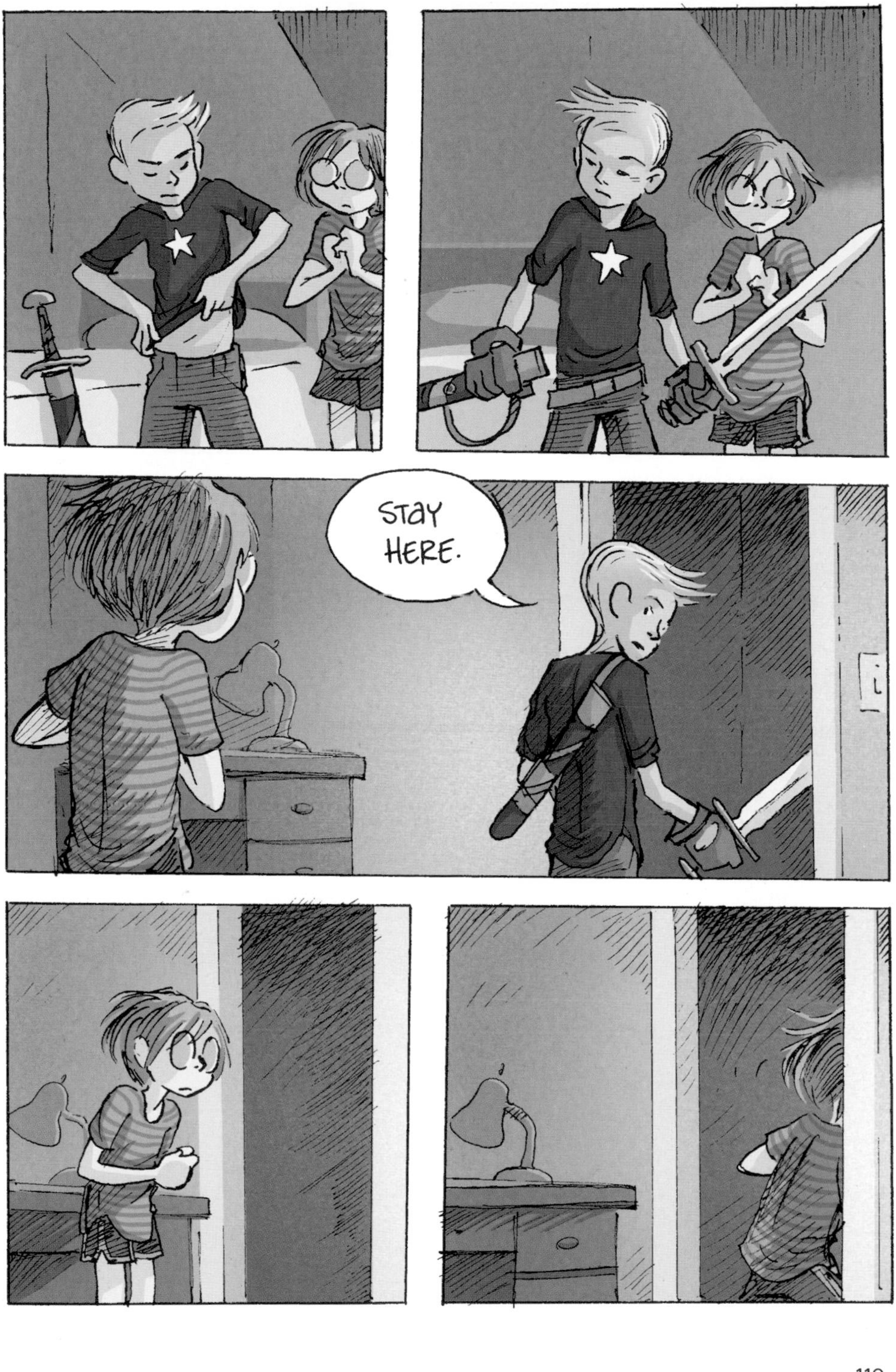
STAY HERE.

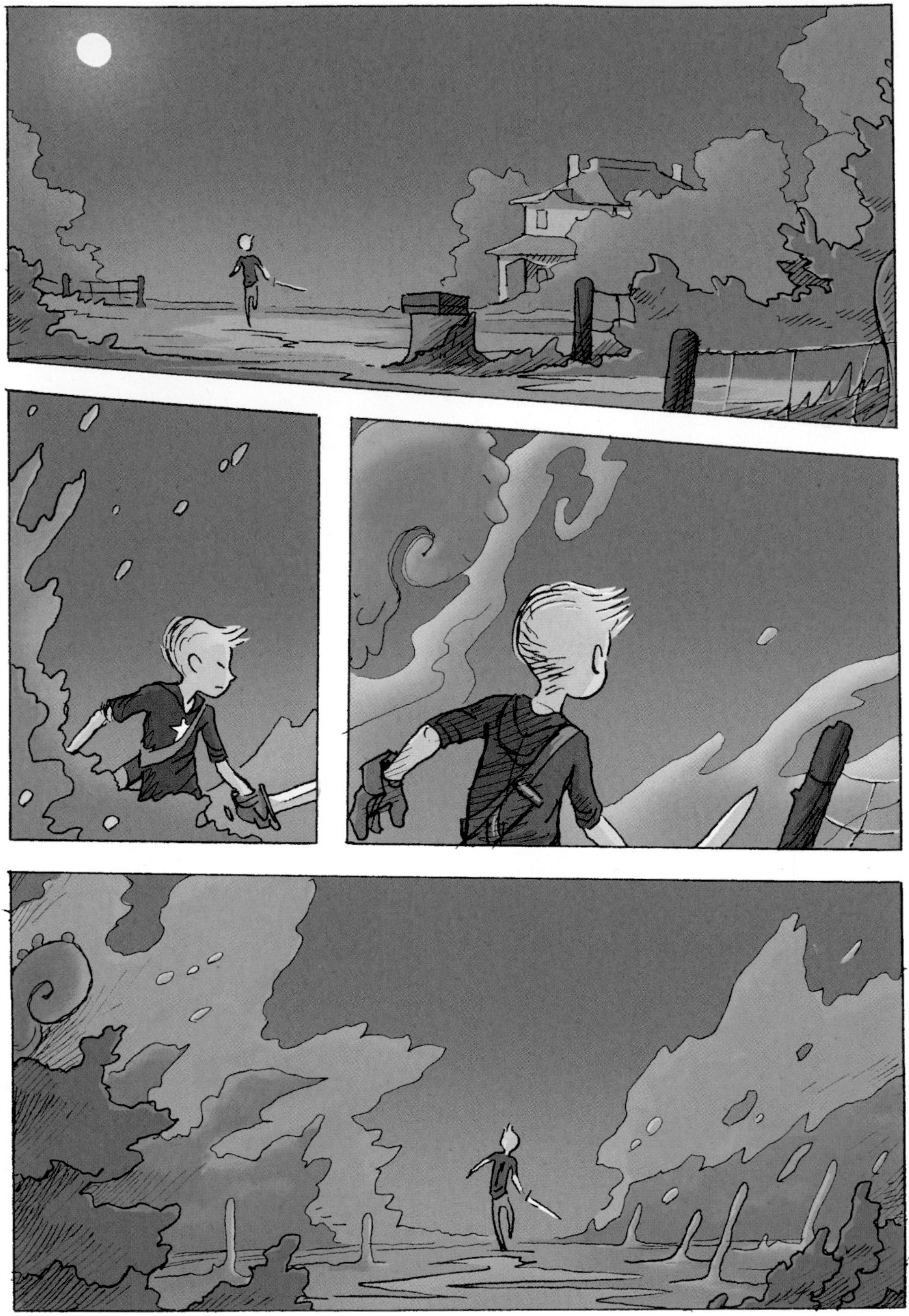

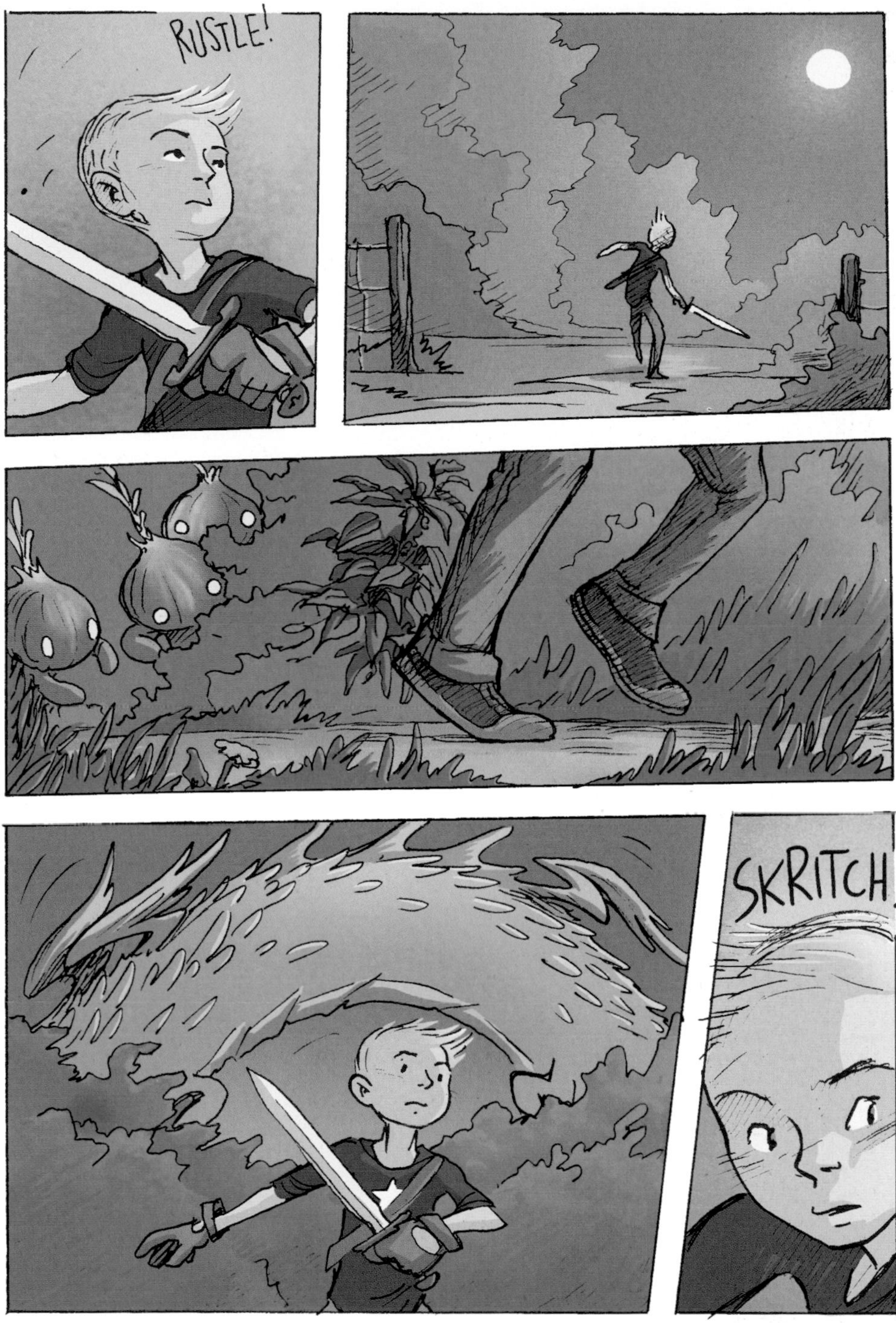
RUSTLE!
SKRITCH!

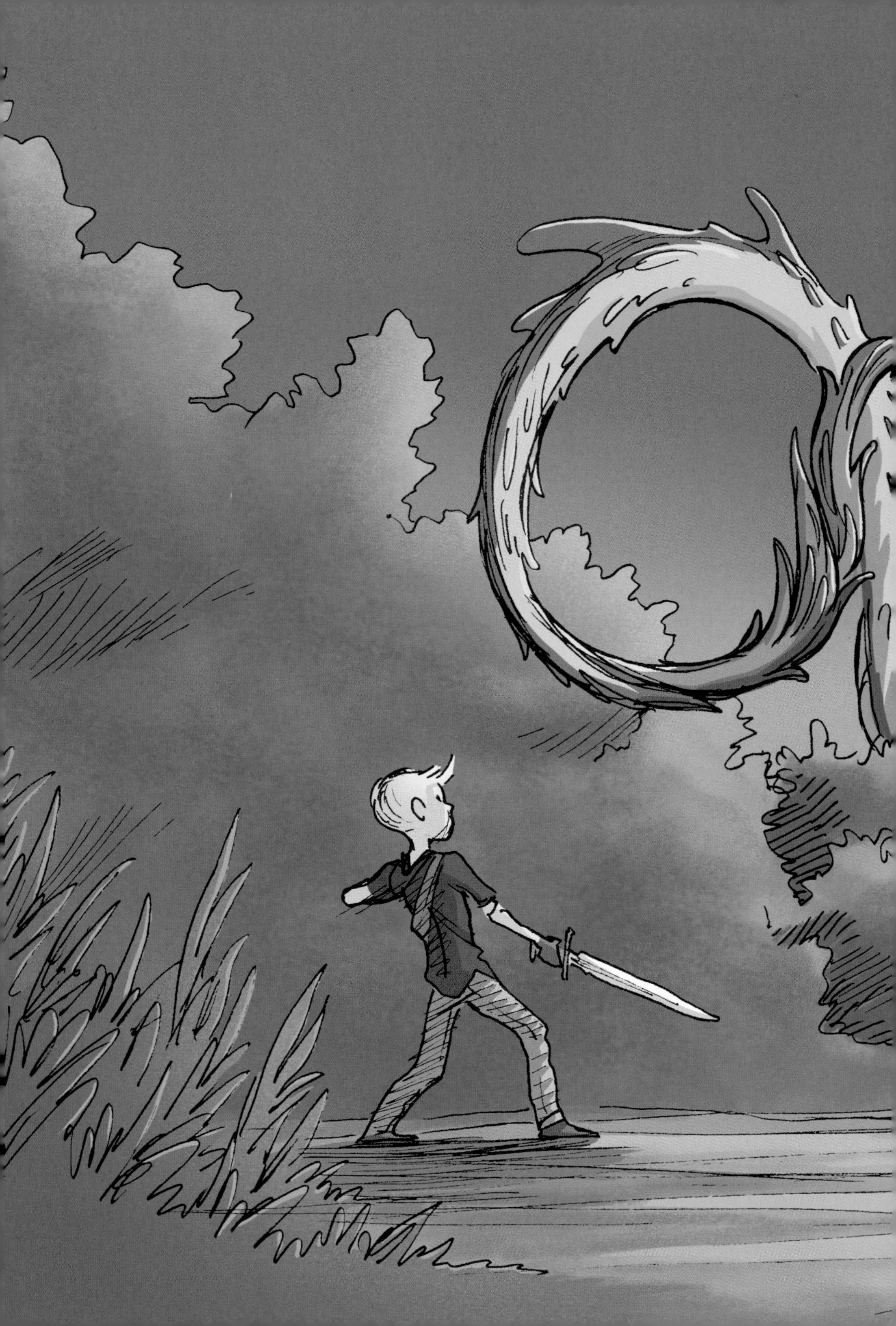

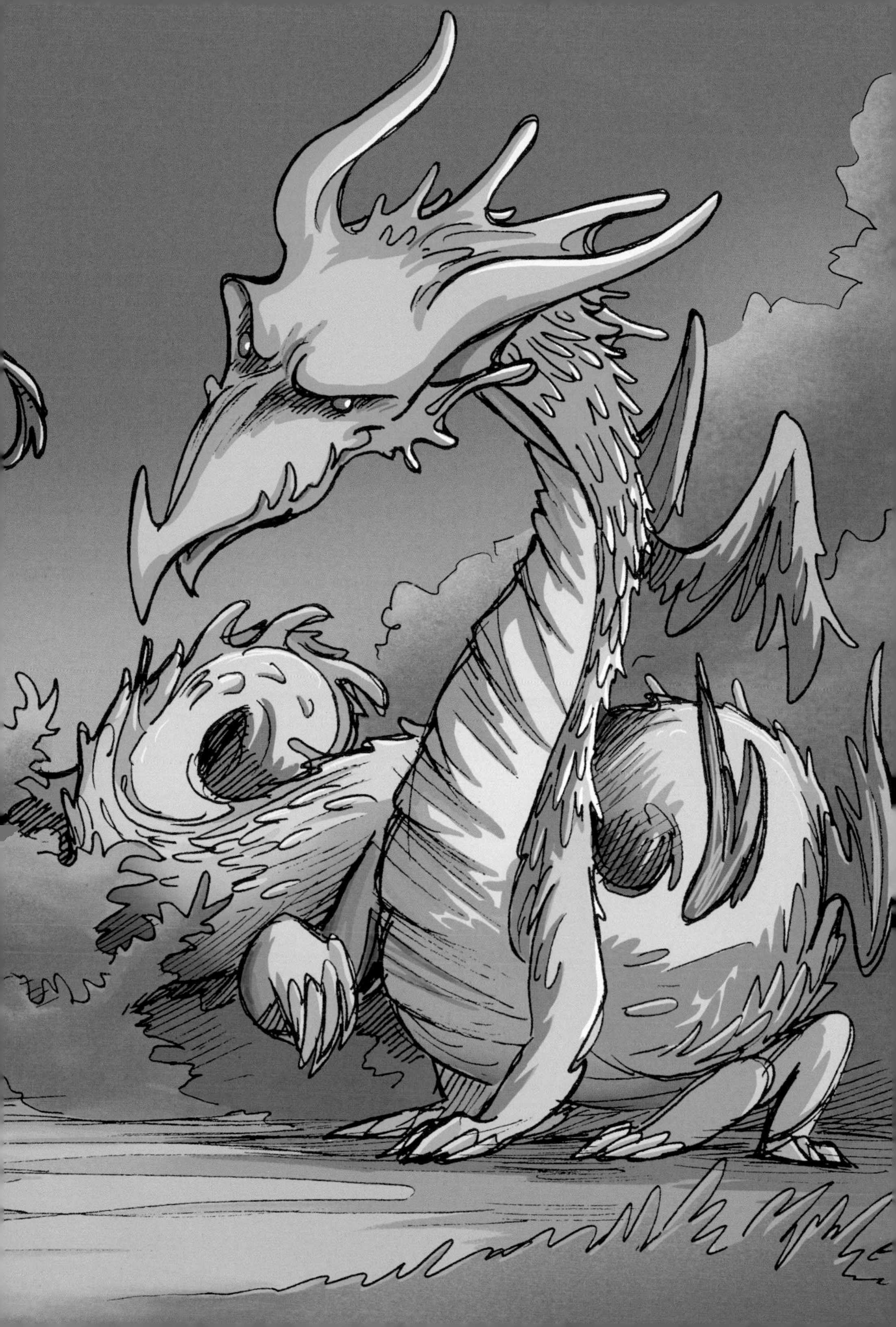

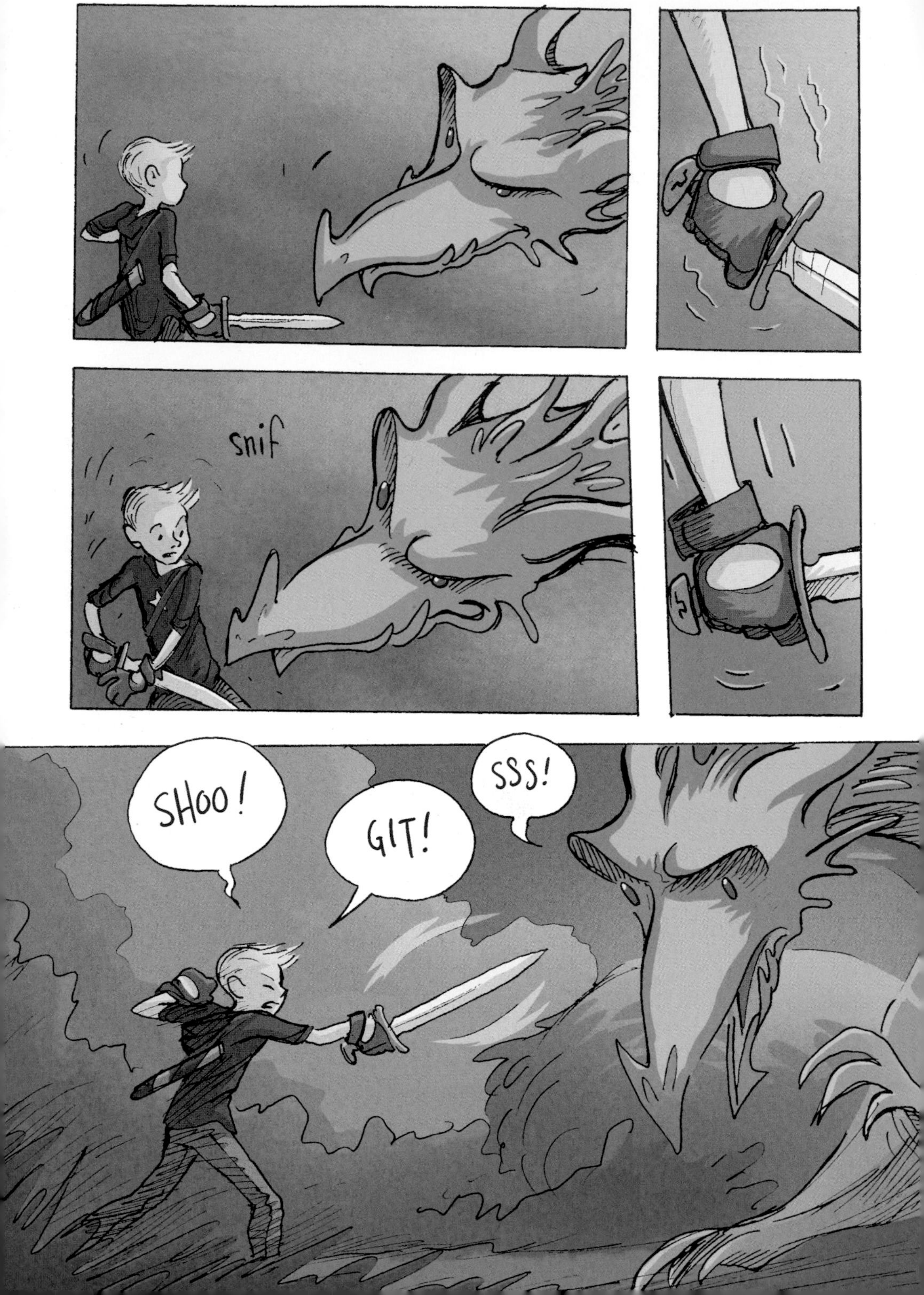
snif
SHOO!
GIT!
SSS!

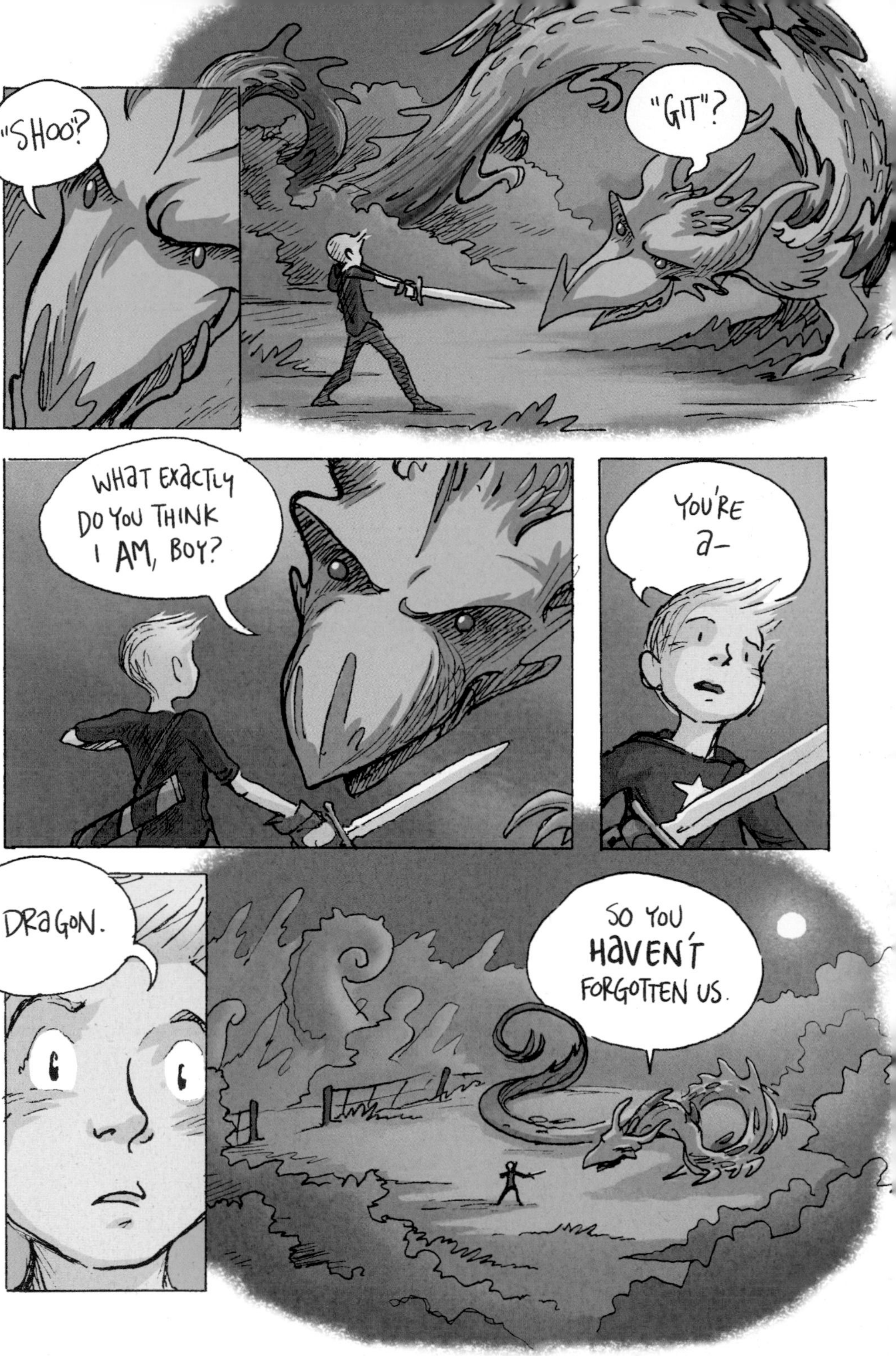
"SHOO"?
"GIT"?
WHAT EXACTLY DO YOU THINK I AM, BOY?
YOU'RE A-
DRAGON.
SO YOU HAVEN'T FORGOTTEN US.

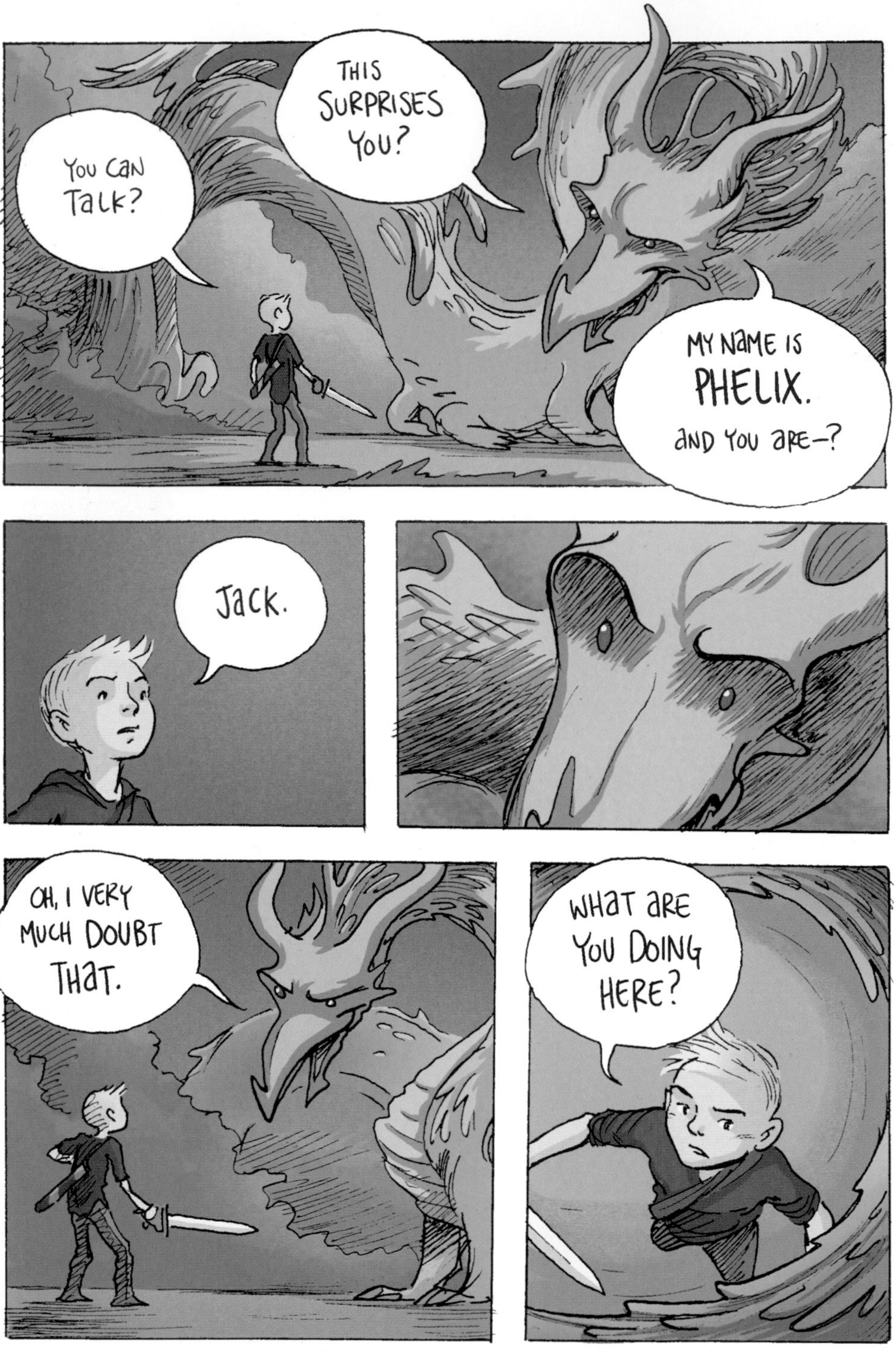
You can Talk?
This surprises you?
My name is PHELIX.
and you are–?
Jack.
Oh, I very much doubt that.
What are you doing here?

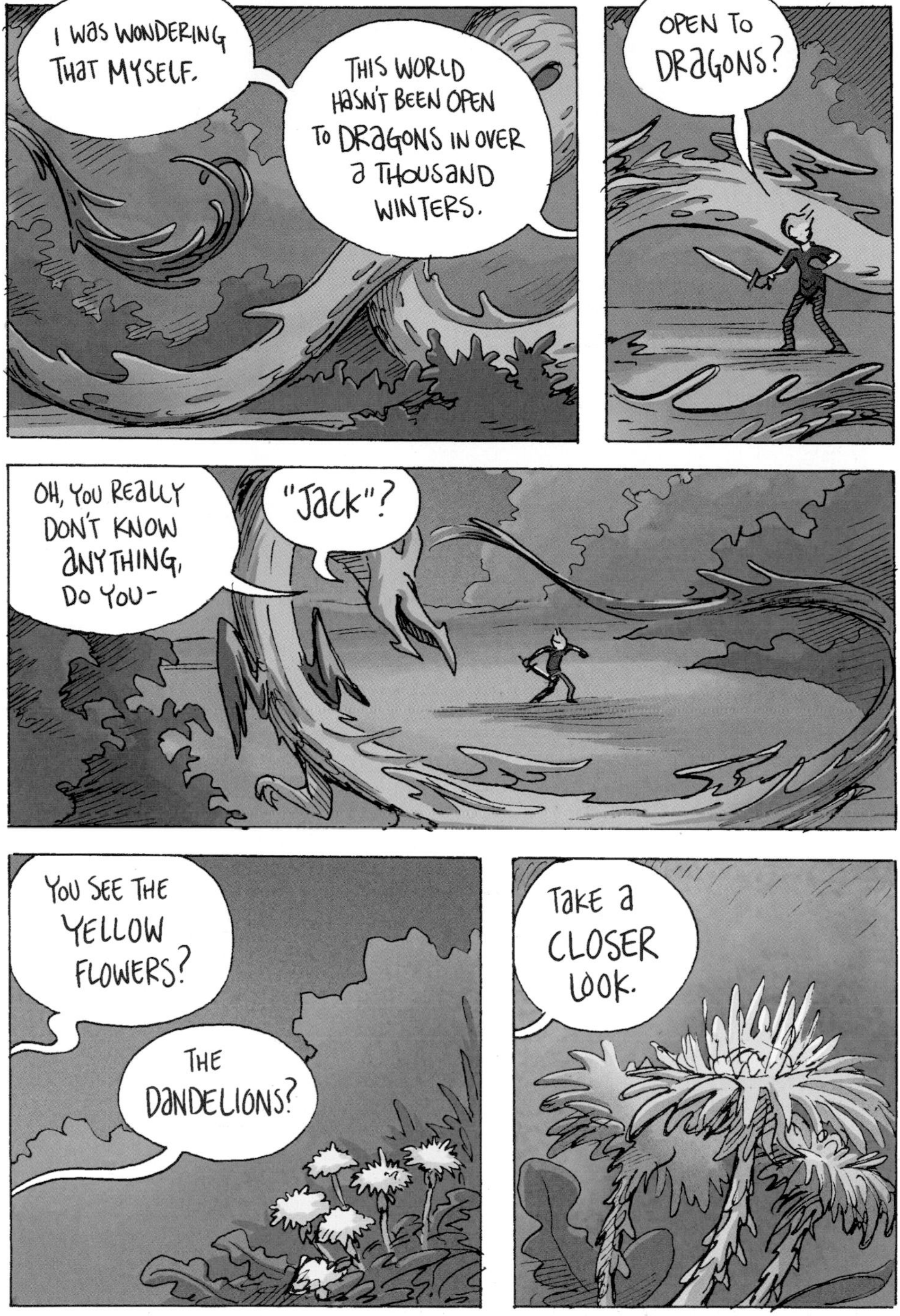
I WAS WONDERING THAT MYSELF.
THIS WORLD HASN'T BEEN OPEN TO DRAGONS IN OVER A THOUSAND WINTERS.
OPEN TO DRAGONS?
OH, YOU REALLY DON'T KNOW ANYTHING, DO YOU-
"JACK"?
YOU SEE THE YELLOW FLOWERS?
THE DANDELIONS?
TAKE A CLOSER LOOK.

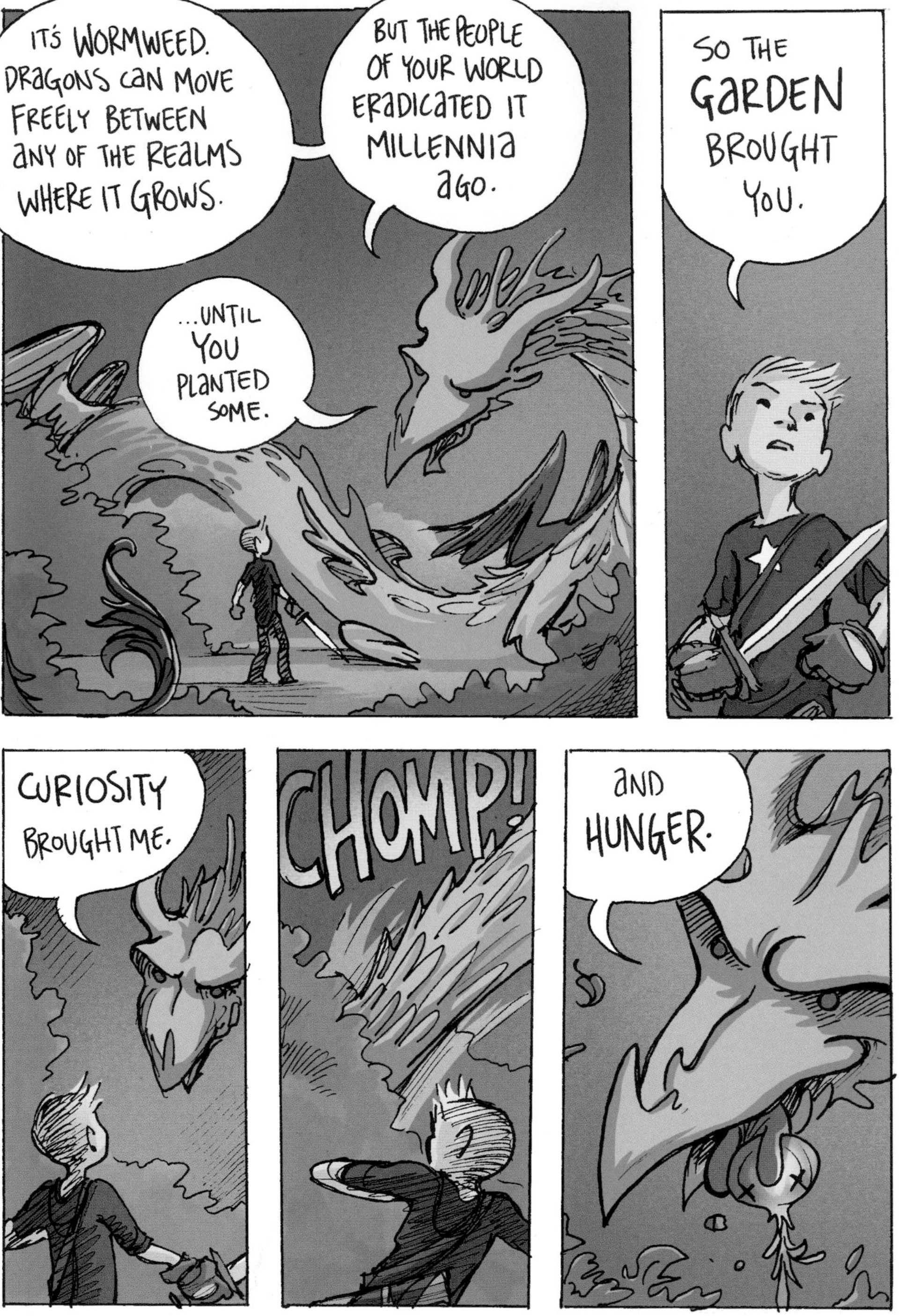
IT'S WORMWEED. DRAGONS CAN MOVE FREELY BETWEEN ANY OF THE REALMS WHERE IT GROWS.
BUT THE PEOPLE OF YOUR WORLD ERADICATED IT MILLENNIA AGO.
...UNTIL YOU PLANTED SOME.
SO THE GARDEN BROUGHT YOU.
CURIOSITY BROUGHT ME.
CHOMP!
AND HUNGER.

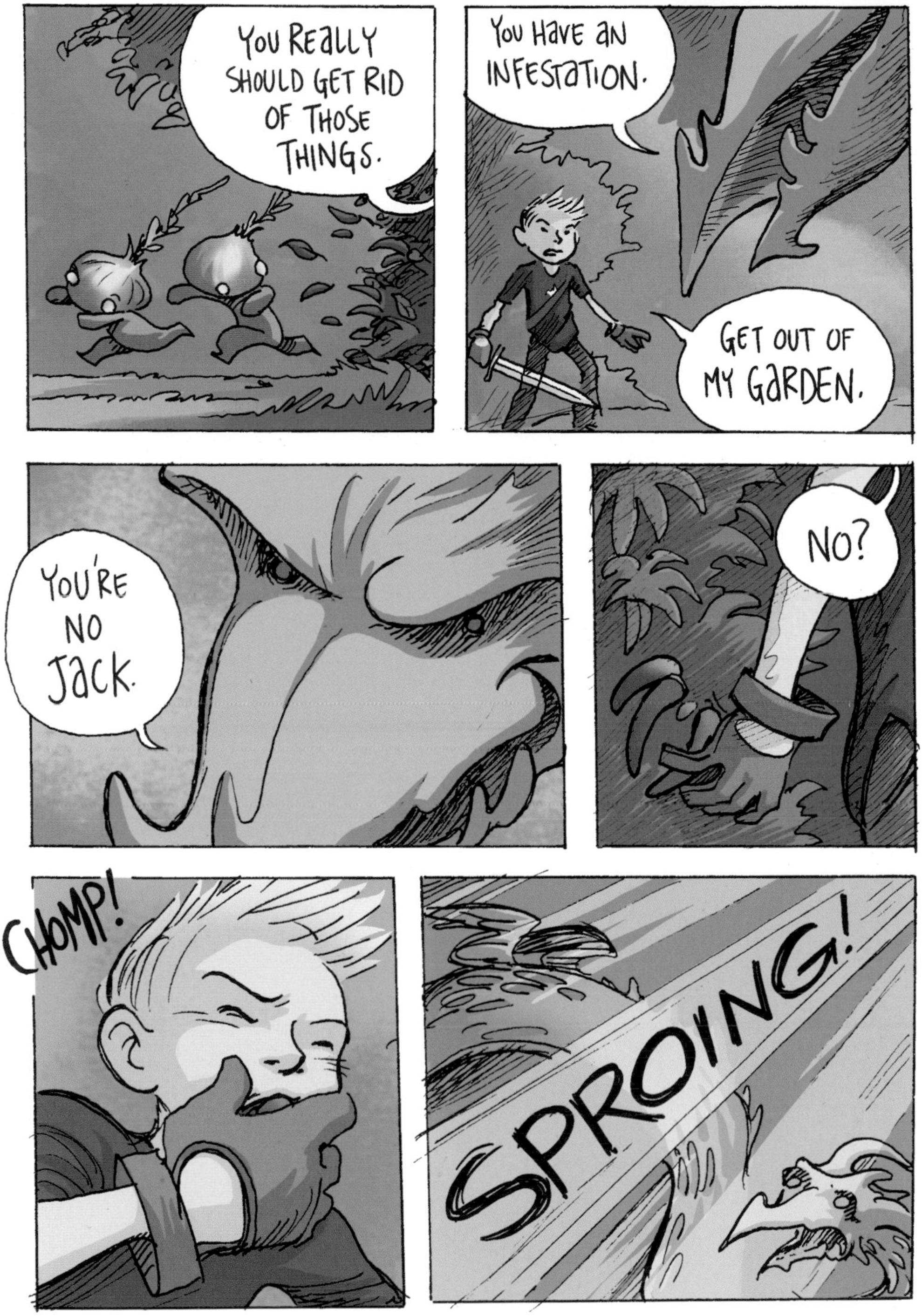
YOU REALLY SHOULD GET RID OF THOSE THINGS.
YOU HAVE AN INFESTATION.
GET OUT OF MY GARDEN.
YOU'RE NO JACK.
NO?
CHOMP!
SPROING!

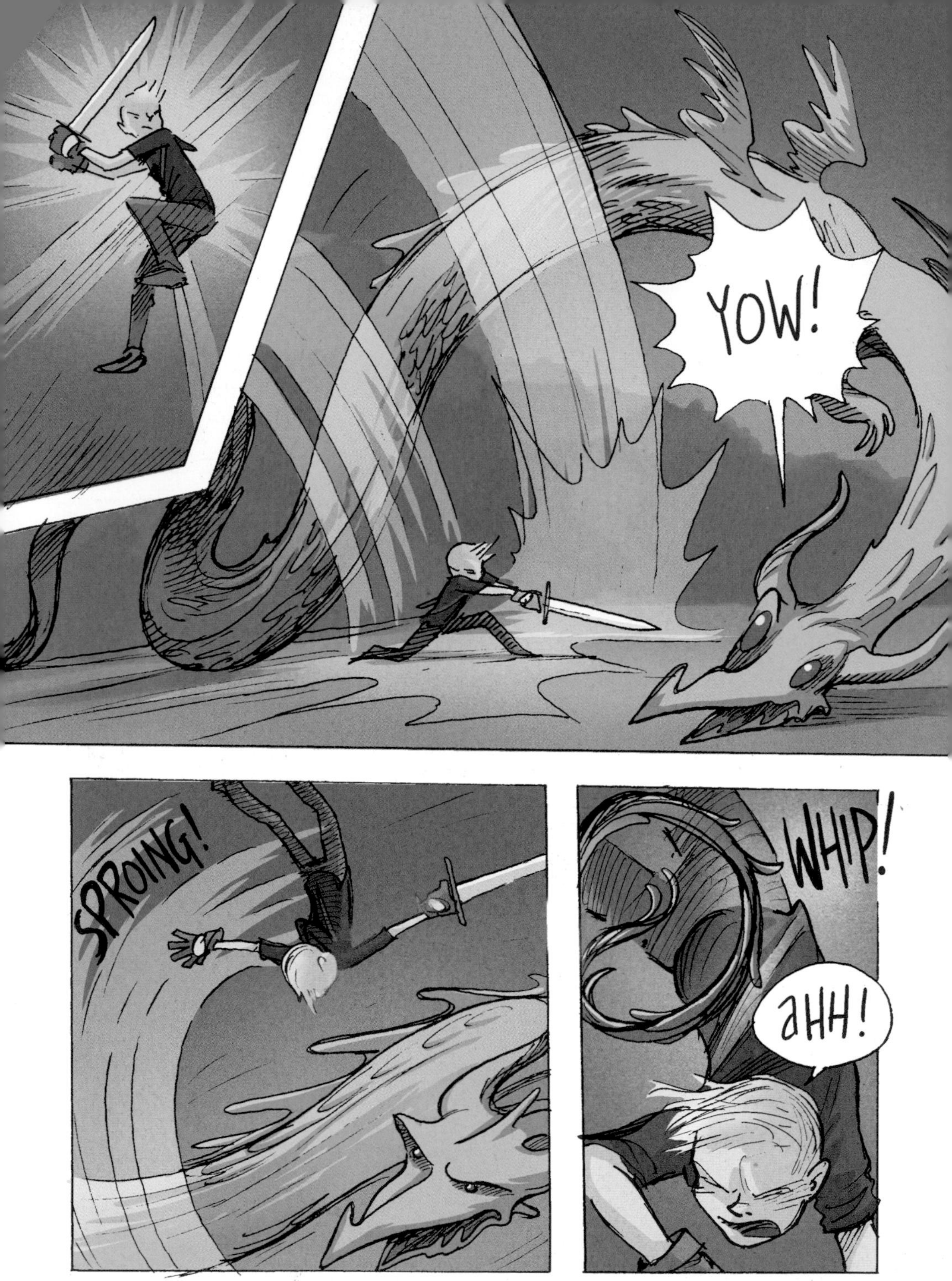
YOW!
SPROING!
WHIP!
aHH!

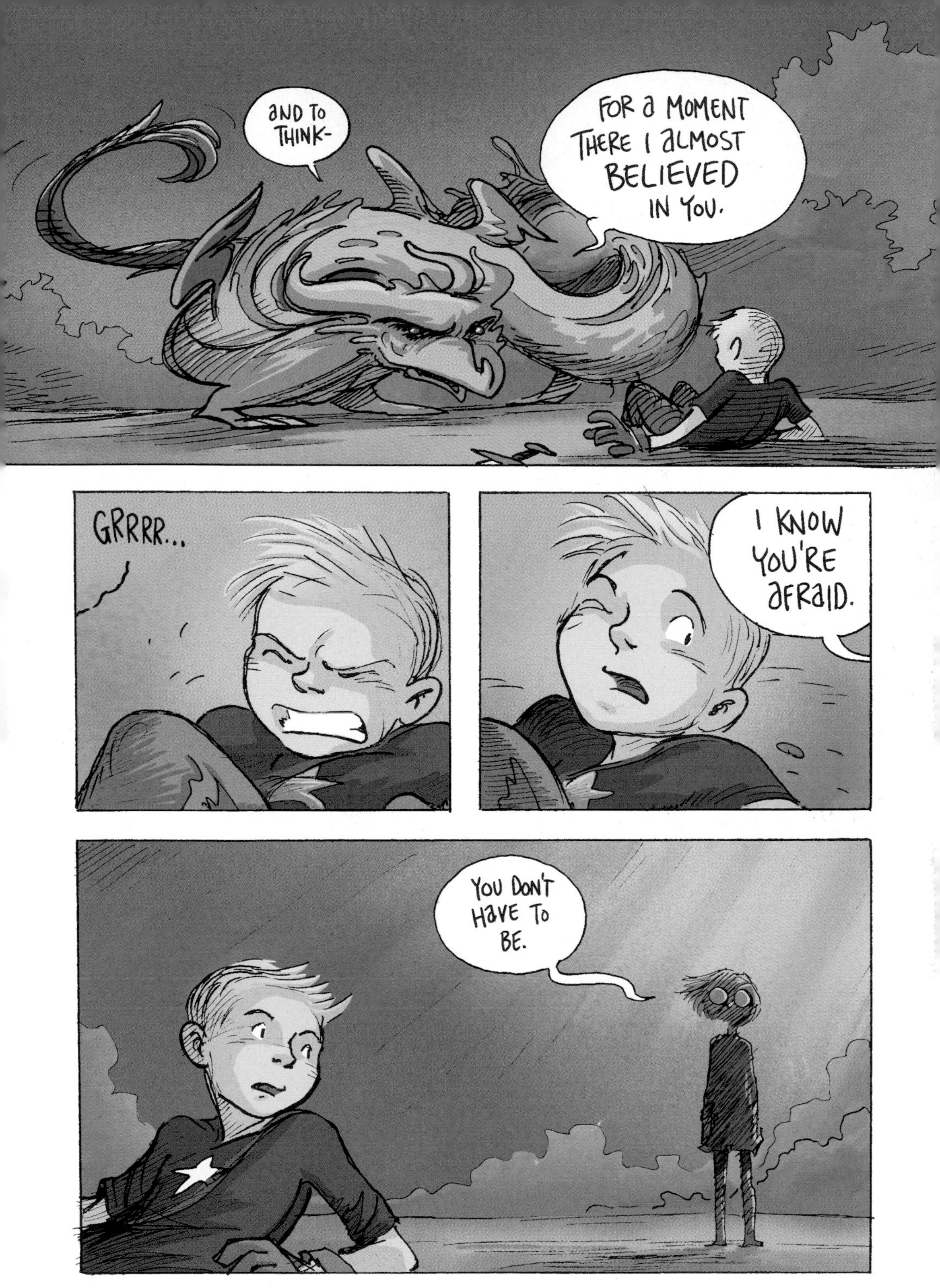
AND TO THINK-
FOR A MOMENT THERE I ALMOST BELIEVED IN YOU.
GRRRR...
I KNOW YOU'RE AFRAID.
YOU DON'T HAVE TO BE.

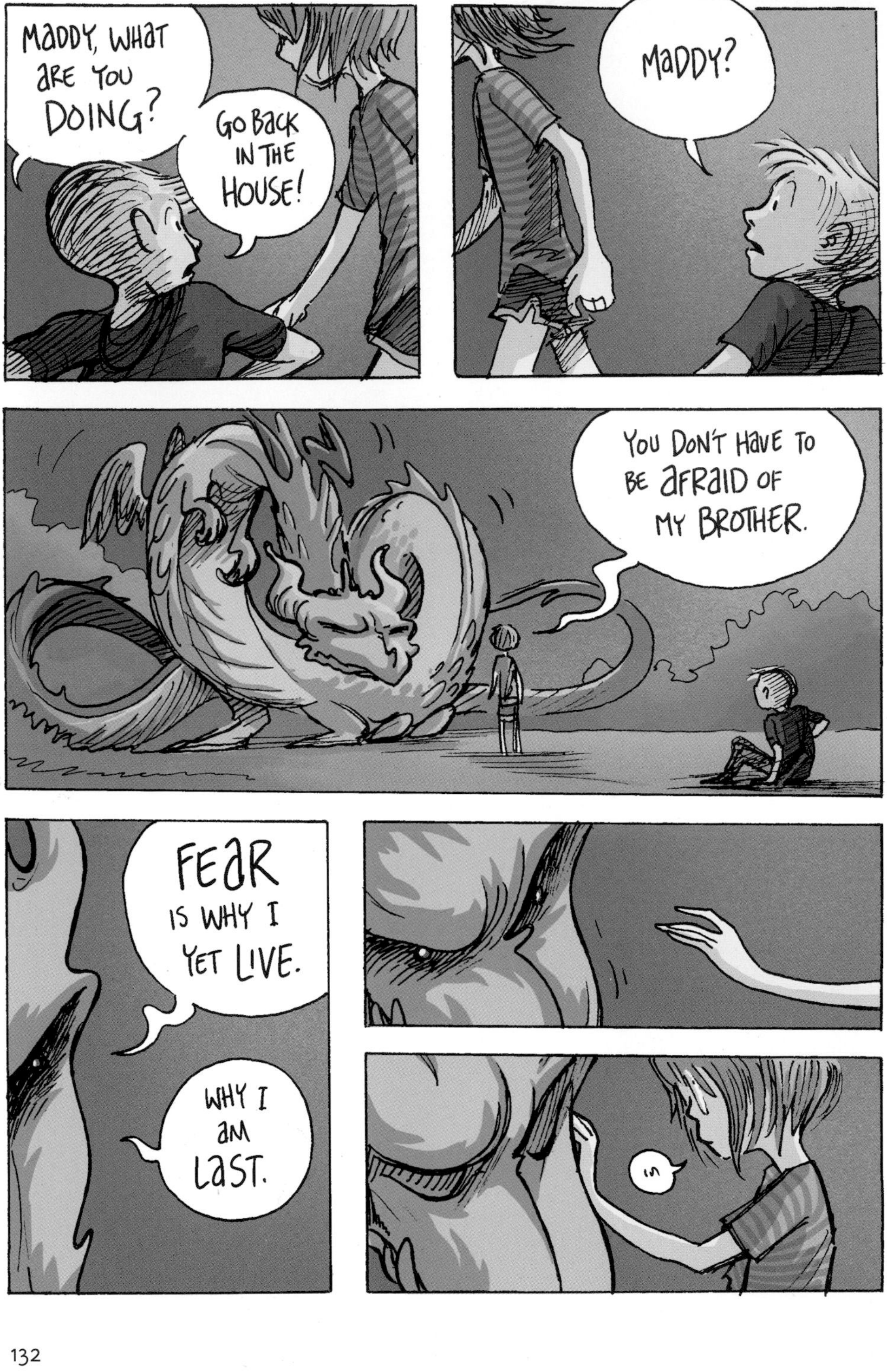
MADDY, WHAT ARE YOU DOING?
GO BACK IN THE HOUSE!
MADDY?
YOU DON'T HAVE TO BE AFRAID OF MY BROTHER.
FEAR IS WHY I YET LIVE.
WHY I AM LAST.

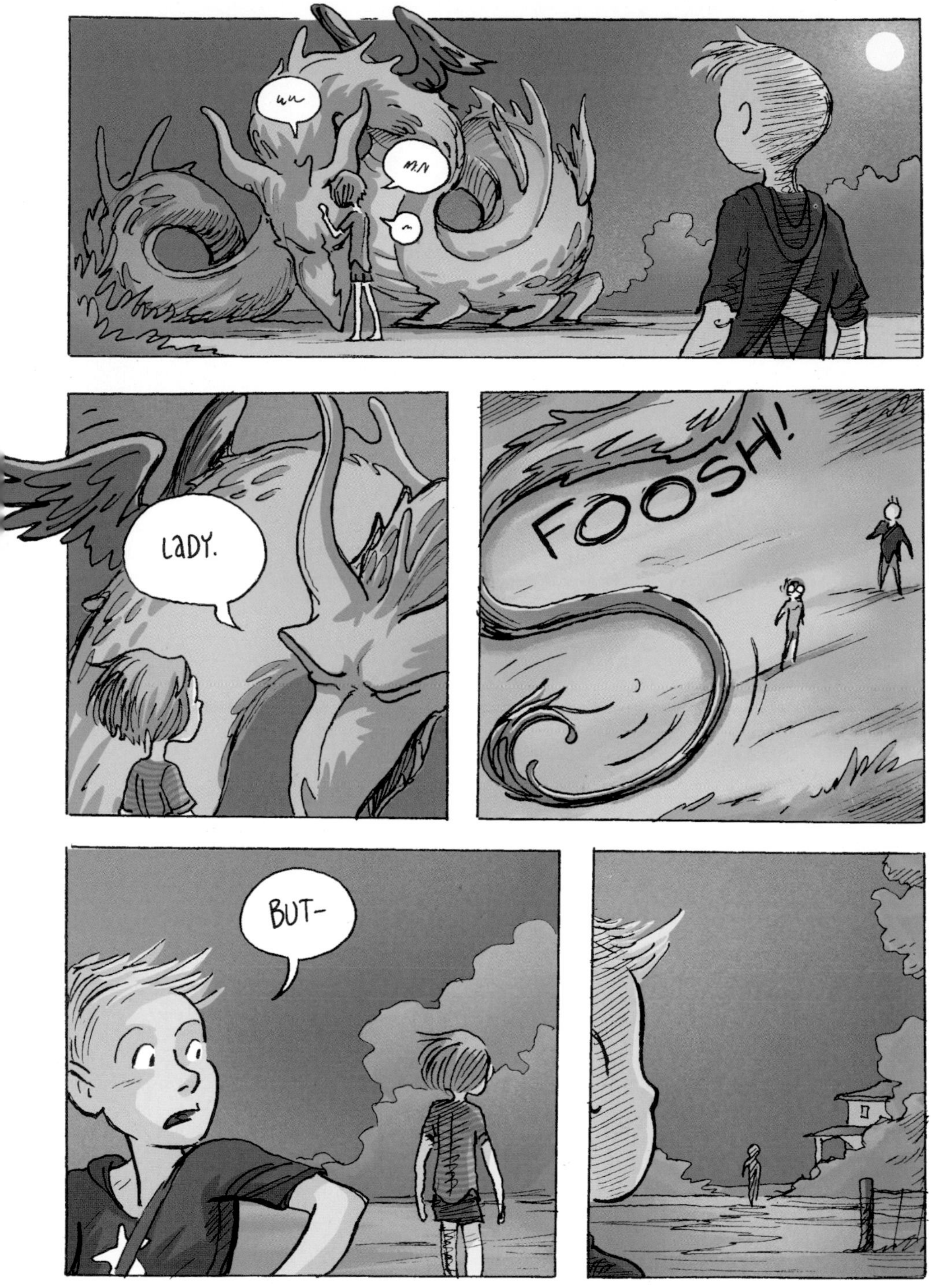
LADY.
FOOSH!
BUT-

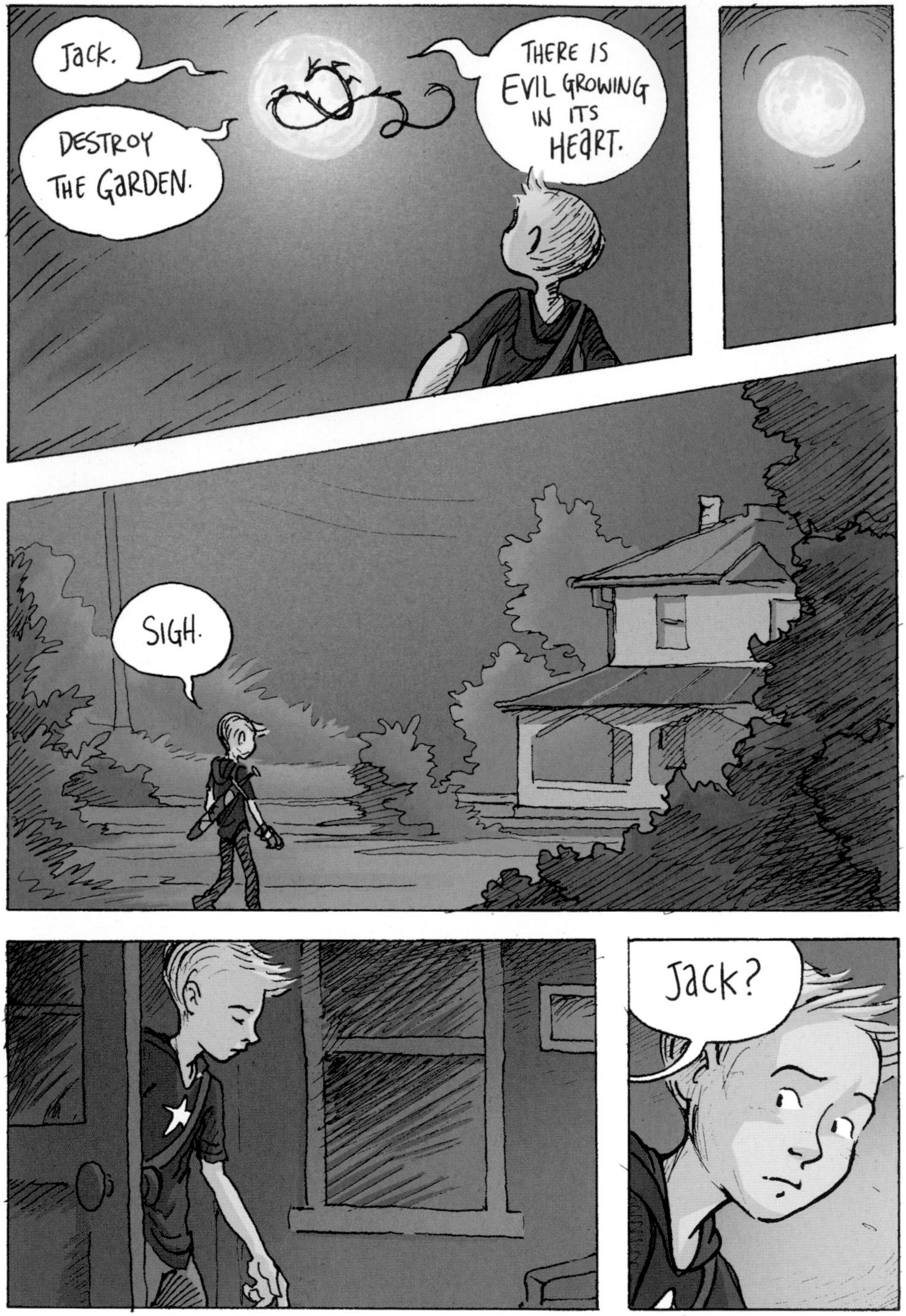
JACK.
DESTROY THE GARDEN.
THERE IS EVIL GROWING IN ITS HEART.
SIGH.
JACK?

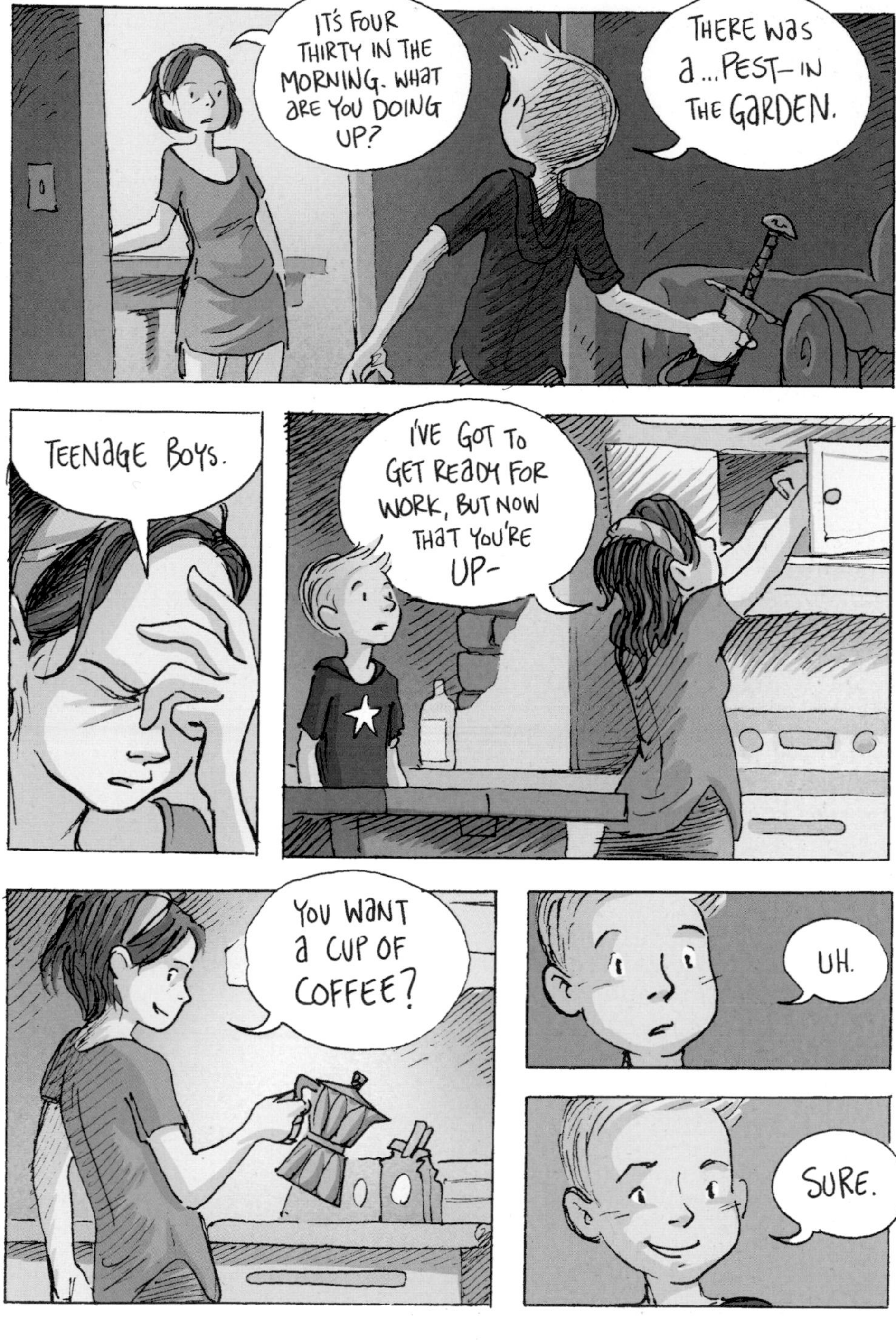
IT'S FOUR THIRTY IN THE MORNING. WHAT ARE YOU DOING UP?
THERE WAS A... PEST- IN THE GARDEN.
TEENAGE BOYS.
I'VE GOT TO GET READY FOR WORK, BUT NOW THAT YOU'RE UP-
YOU WANT A CUP OF COFFEE?
UH.
SURE.

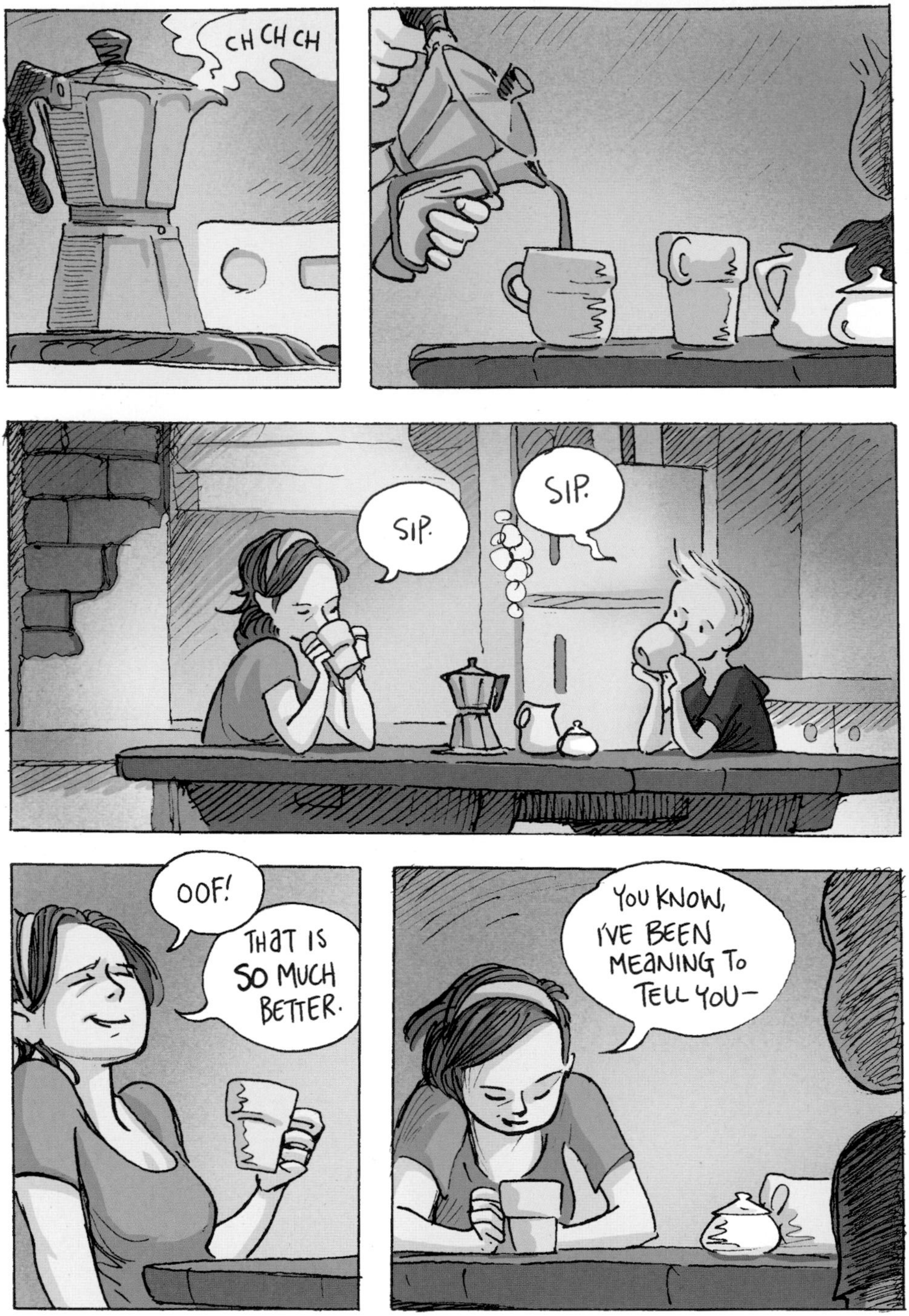
CH CH CH
SIP.
SIP.
OOF!
THAT IS SO MUCH BETTER.
YOU KNOW, I'VE BEEN MEANING TO TELL YOU—

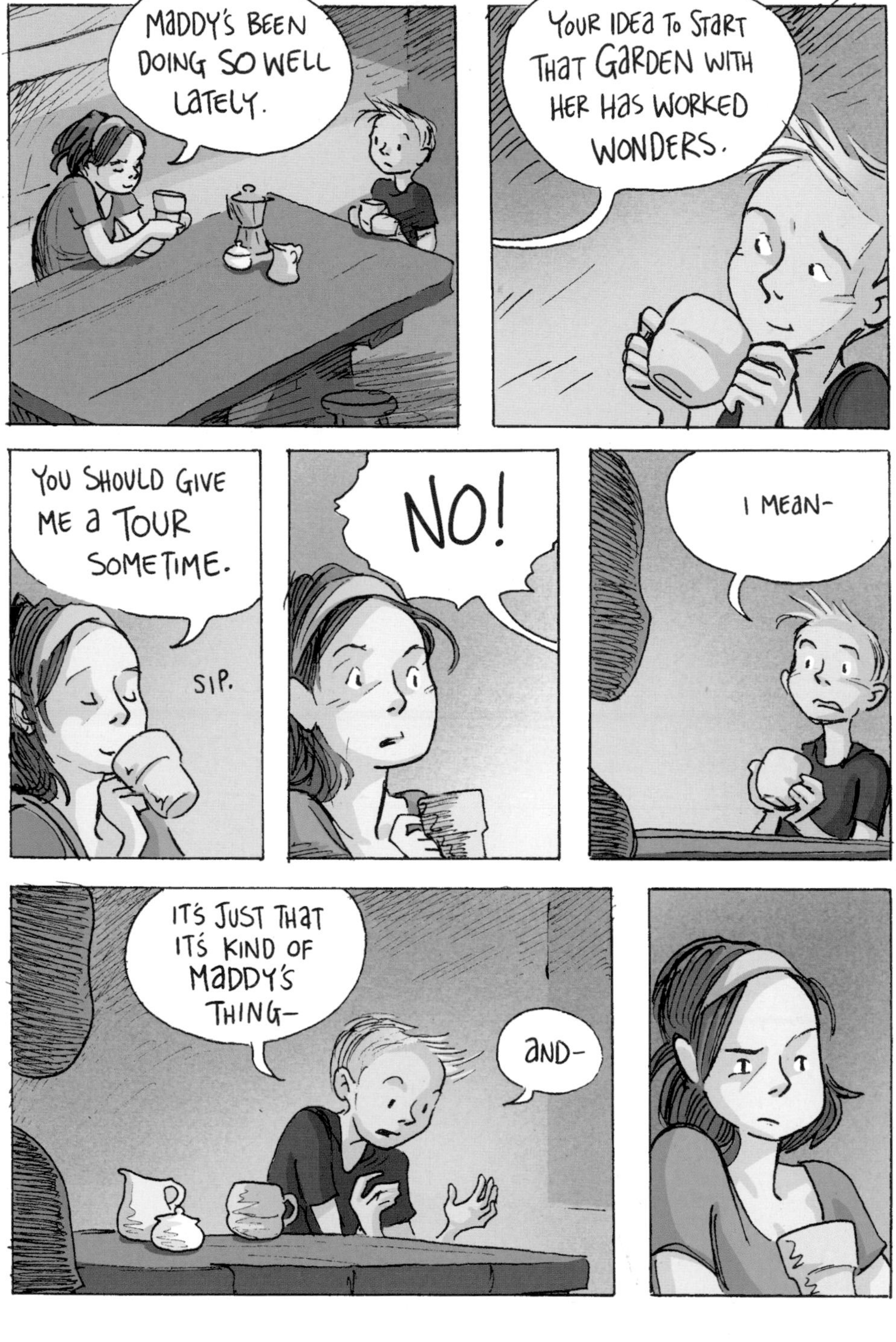
MADDY'S BEEN DOING SO WELL LATELY.
YOUR IDEA TO START THAT GARDEN WITH HER HAS WORKED WONDERS.
YOU SHOULD GIVE ME A TOUR SOMETIME.
SIP.
NO!
I MEAN-
IT'S JUST THAT IT'S KIND OF MADDY'S THING-
AND-

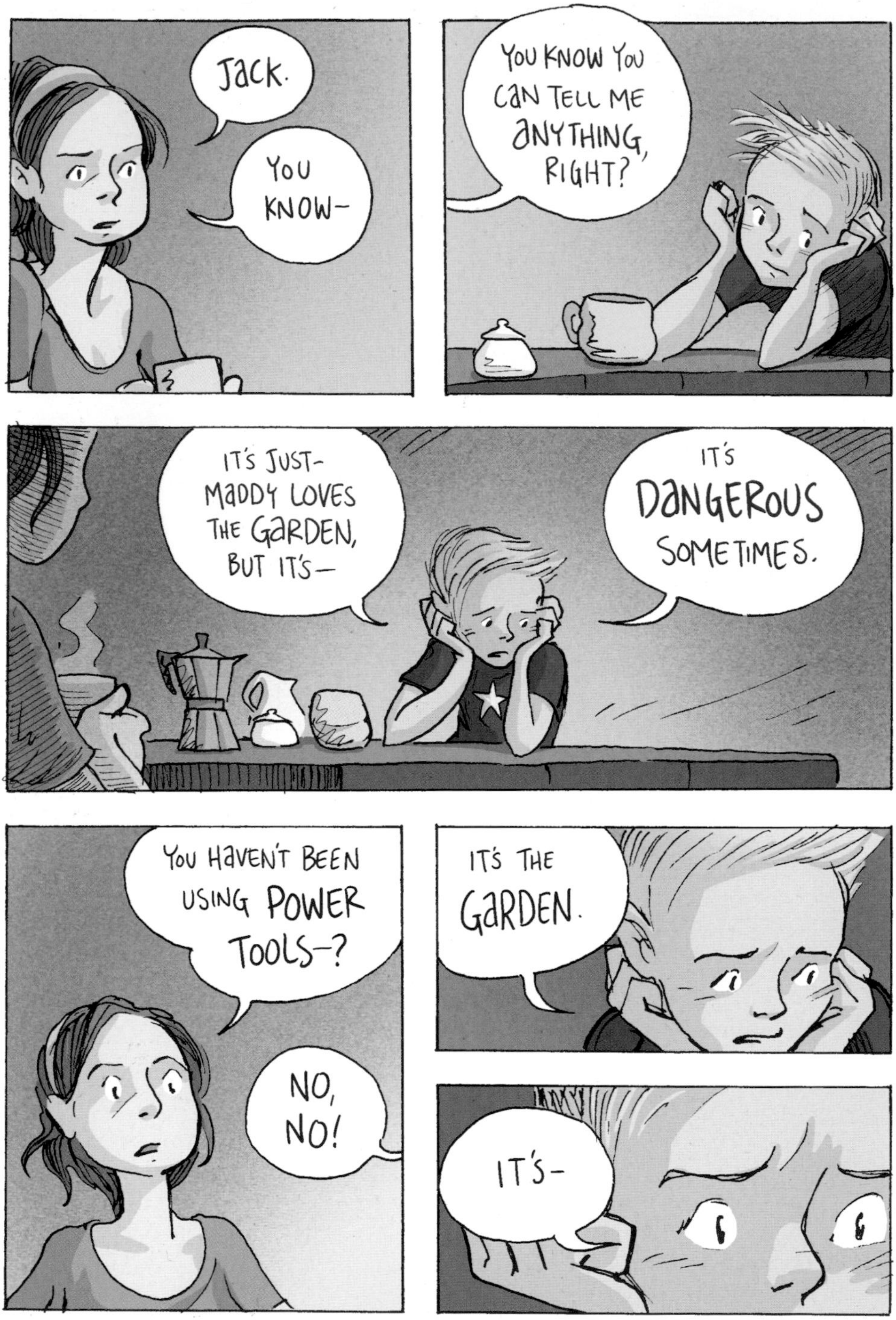
JACK.
YOU KNOW-
YOU KNOW YOU CAN TELL ME ANYTHING, RIGHT?
IT'S JUST- MADDY LOVES THE GARDEN, BUT IT'S—
IT'S DANGEROUS SOMETIMES.
YOU HAVEN'T BEEN USING POWER TOOLS-?
NO, NO!
IT'S THE GARDEN.
IT'S-

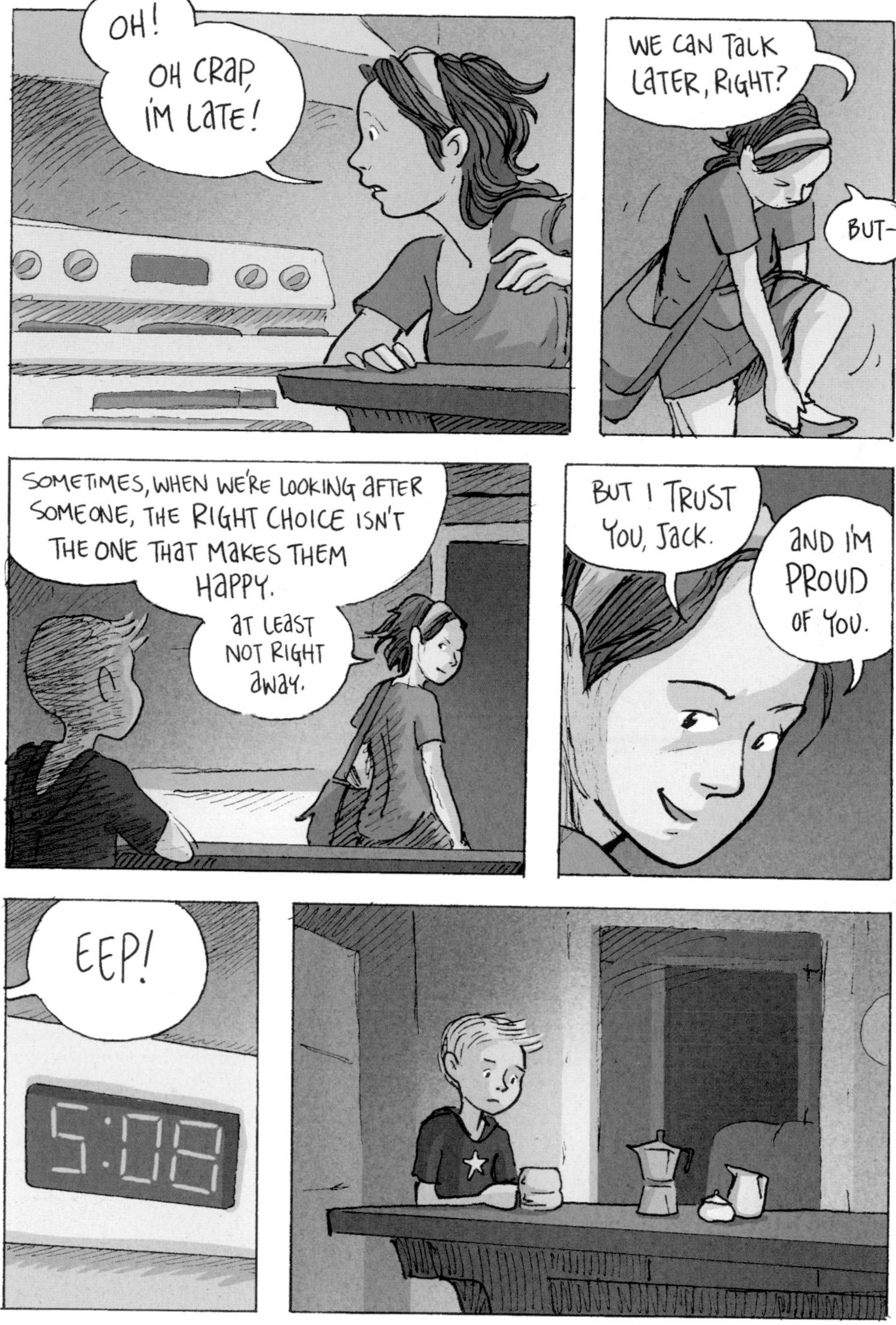
OH!
OH CRAP, I'M LATE!
WE CAN TALK LATER, RIGHT?
BUT-
SOMETIMES, WHEN WE'RE LOOKING AFTER SOMEONE, THE RIGHT CHOICE ISN'T THE ONE THAT MAKES THEM HAPPY.
AT LEAST NOT RIGHT AWAY.
BUT I TRUST YOU, JACK.
AND I'M PROUD OF YOU.
EEP!
5:08

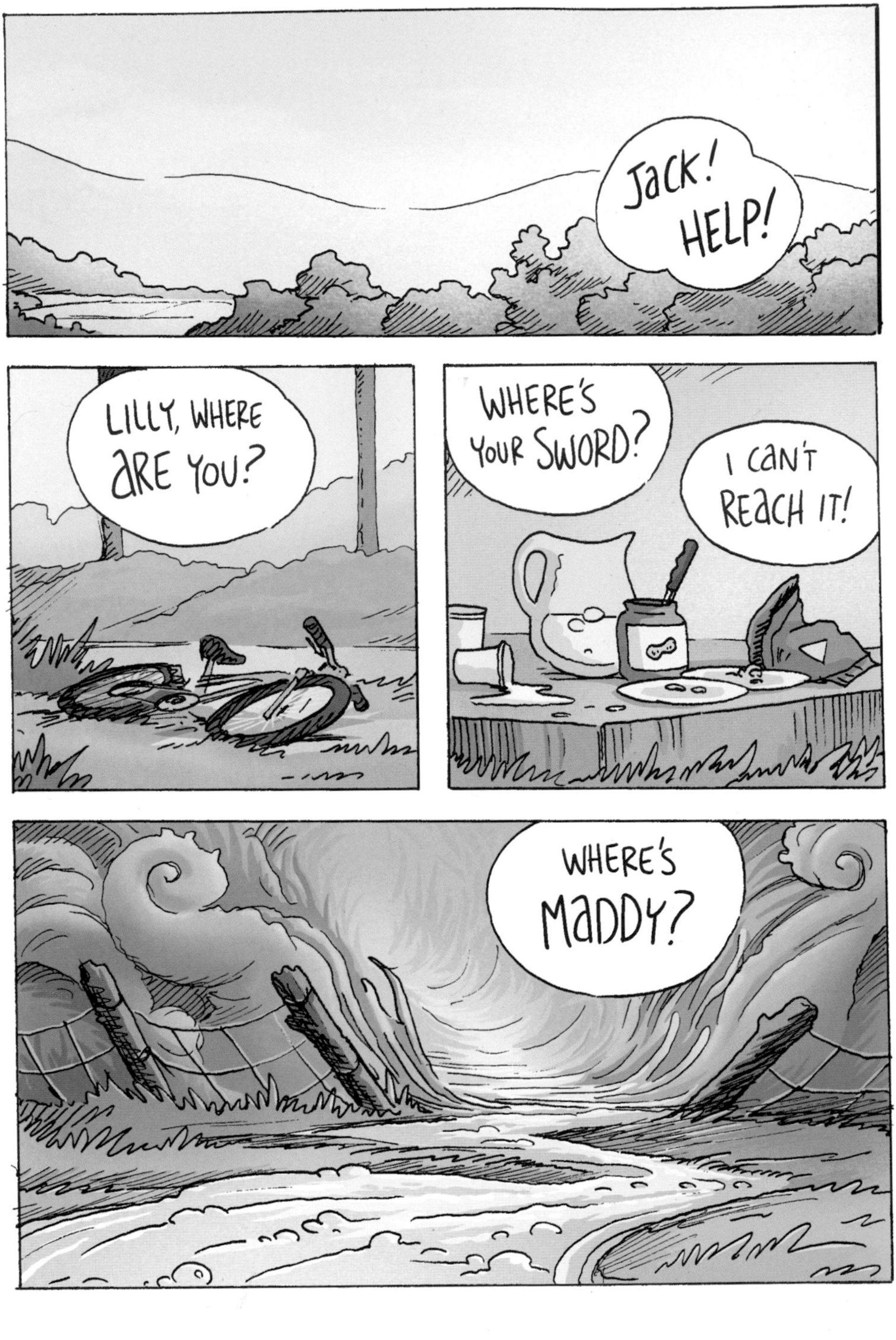
JACK! HELP!
LILLY, WHERE ARE YOU?
WHERE'S YOUR SWORD?
I CAN'T REACH IT!
WHERE'S MADDY?

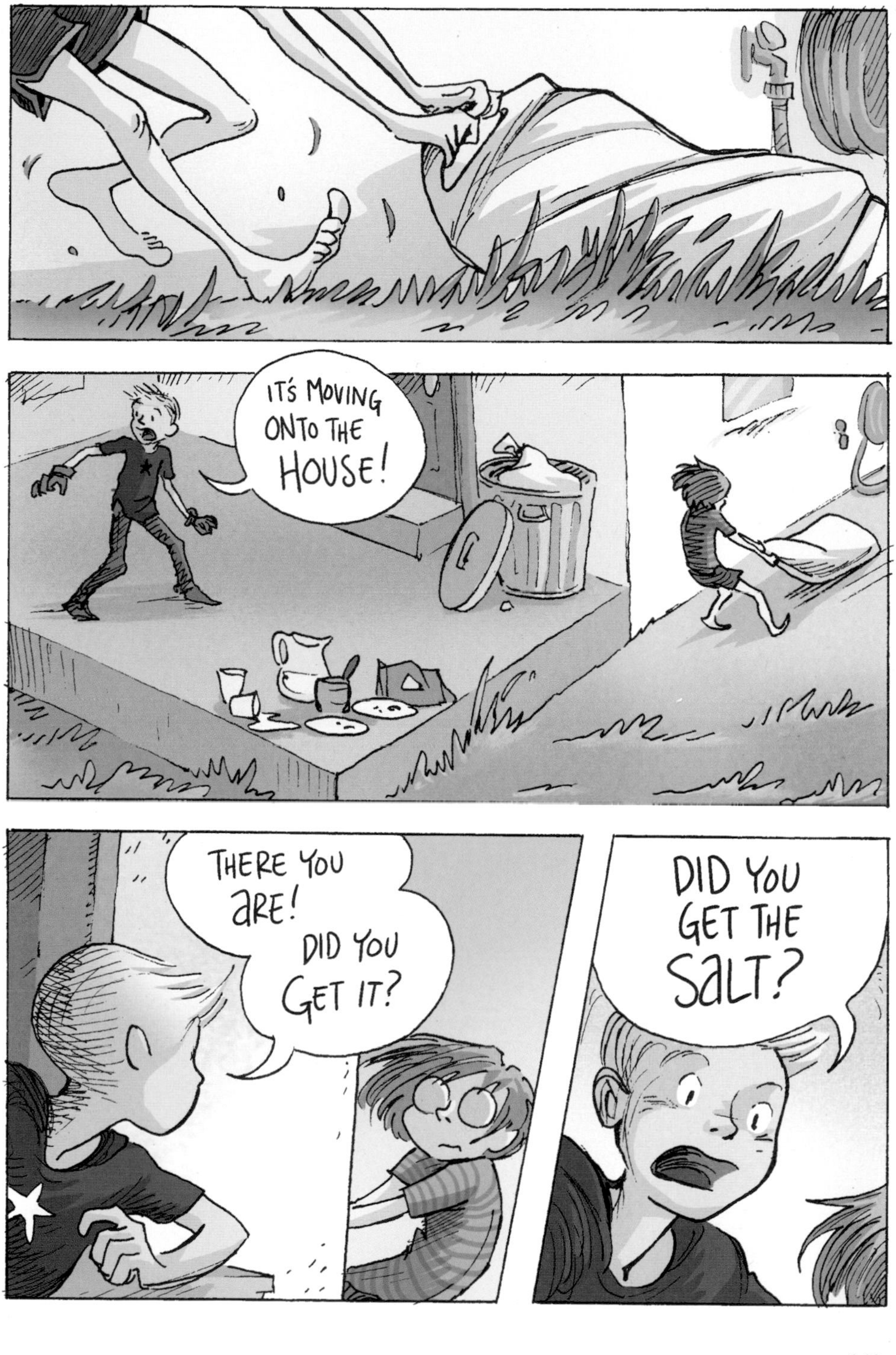
IT'S MOVING ONTO THE HOUSE!
THERE YOU ARE! DID YOU GET IT?
DID YOU GET THE SALT?

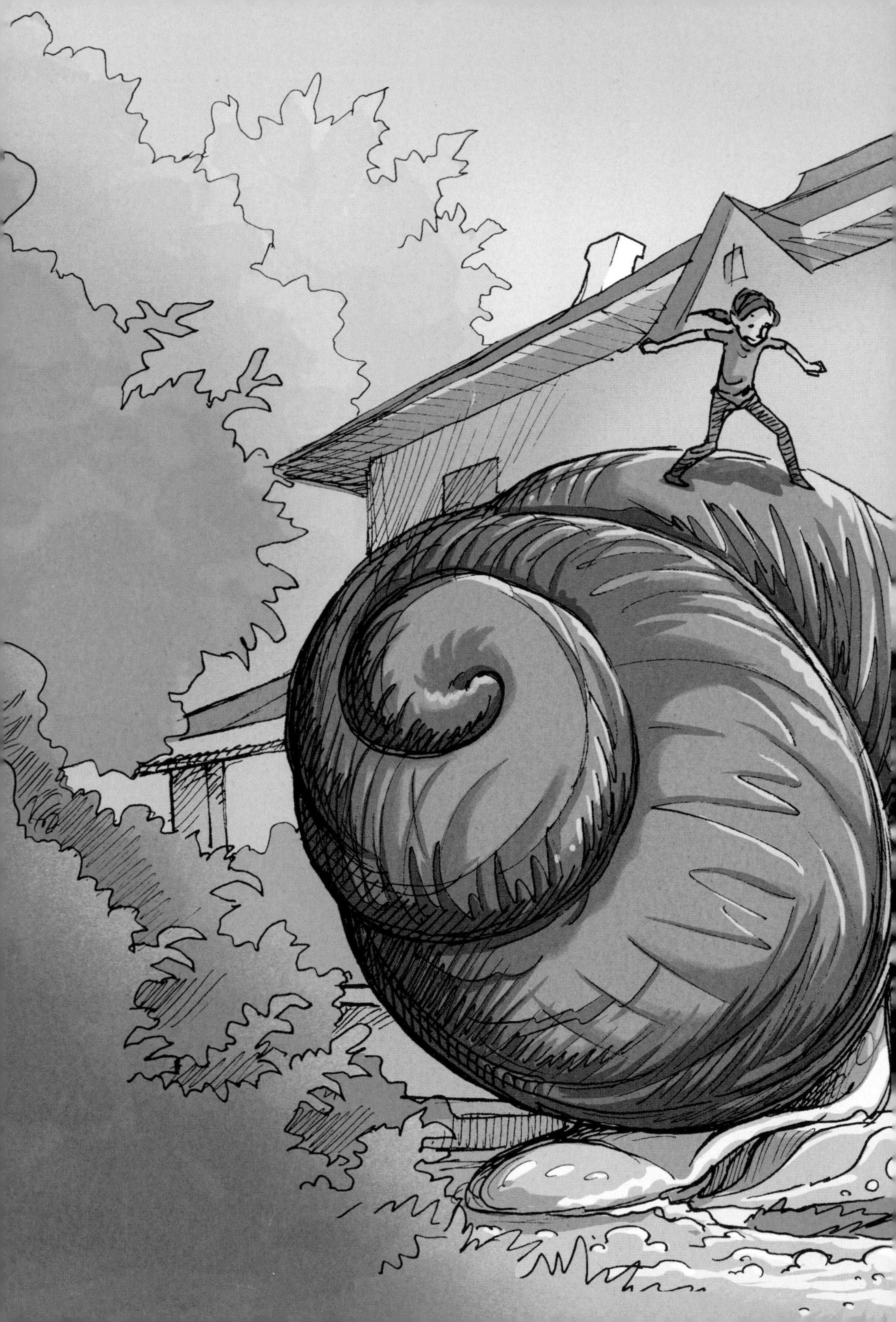

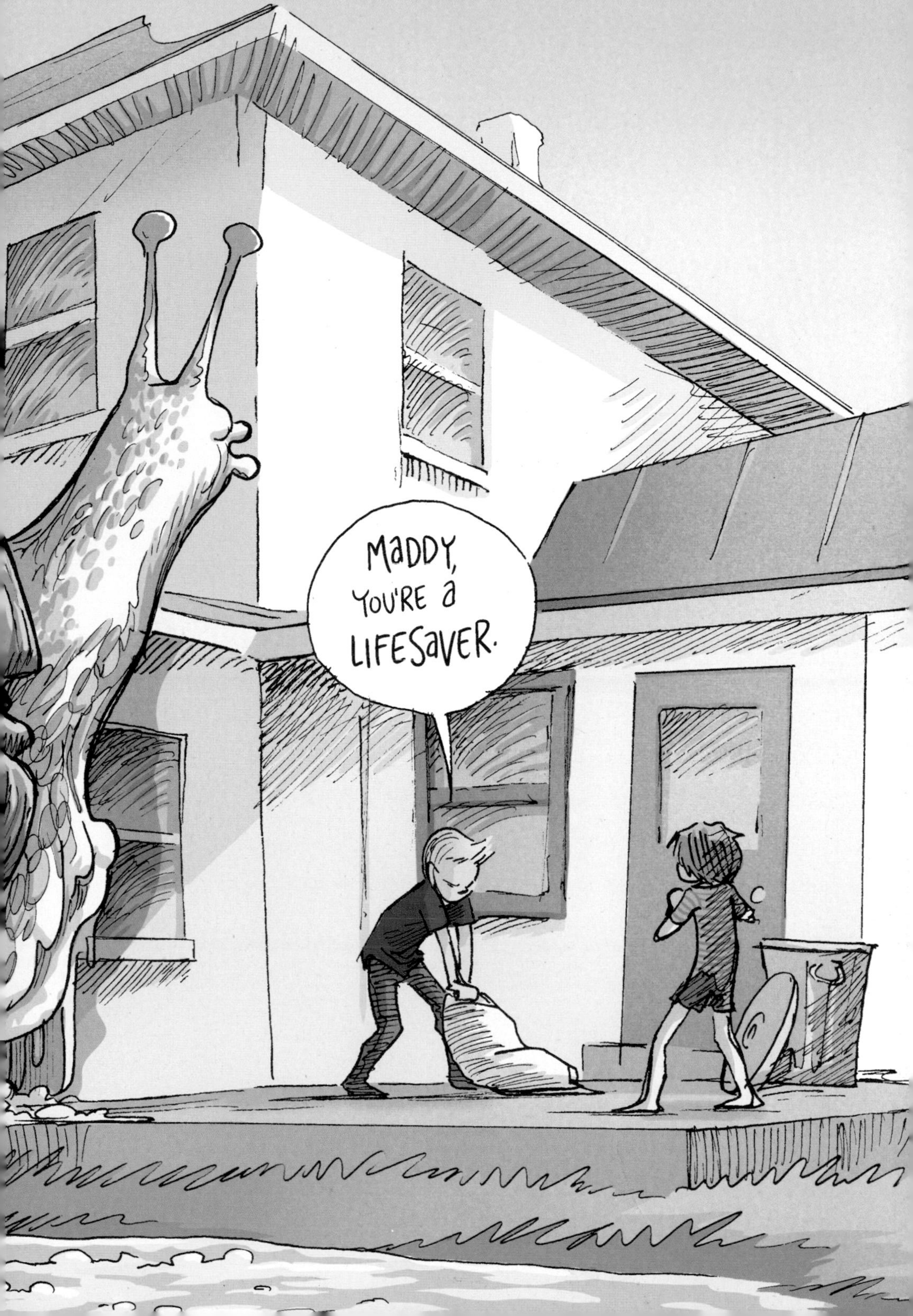
MADDY, YOU'RE A LIFESAVER.

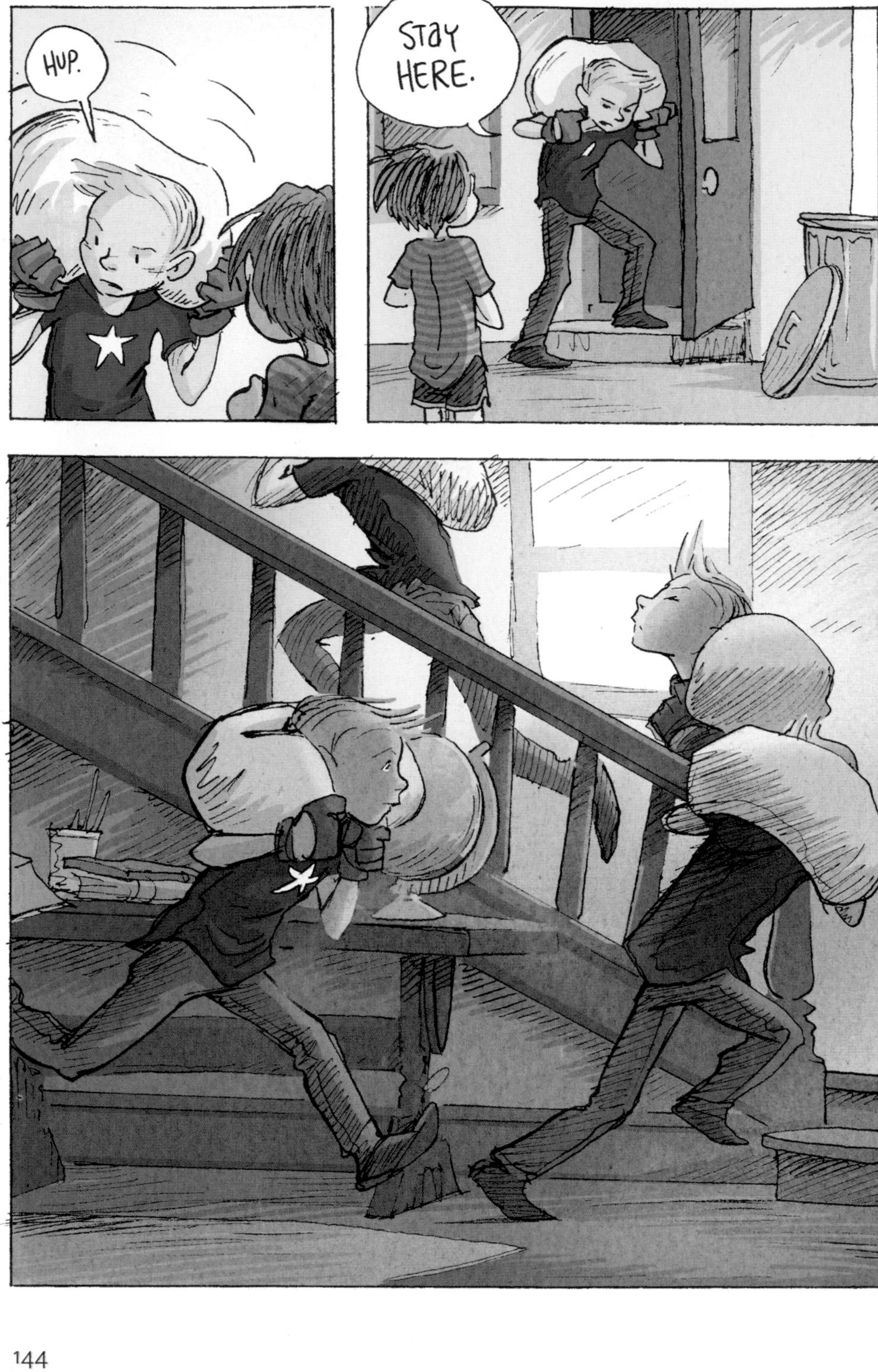
HUP.
STAY HERE.

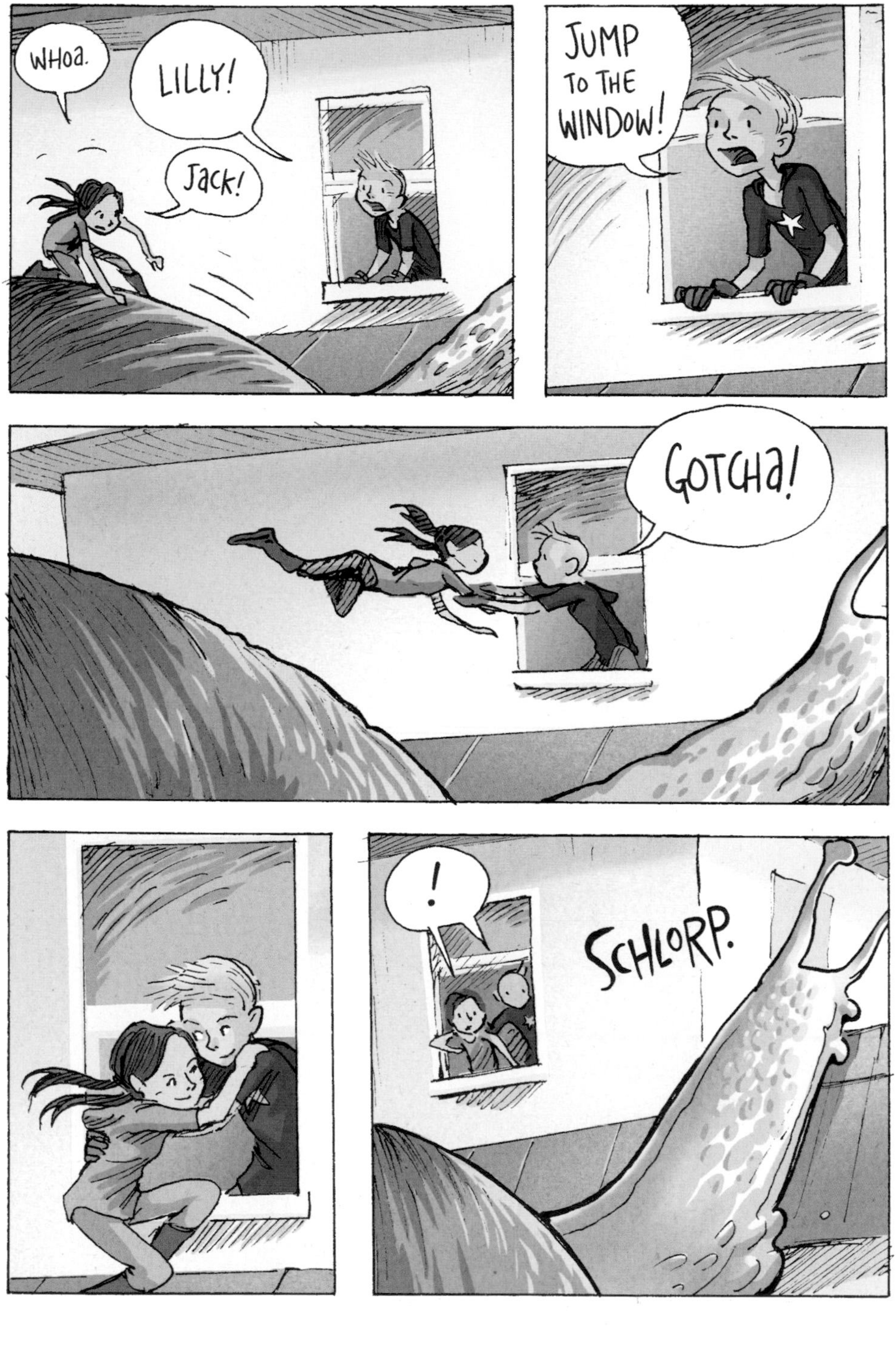
WHOA.
LILLY!
JACK!
JUMP TO THE WINDOW!
GOTCHA!
!
SCHLORP.

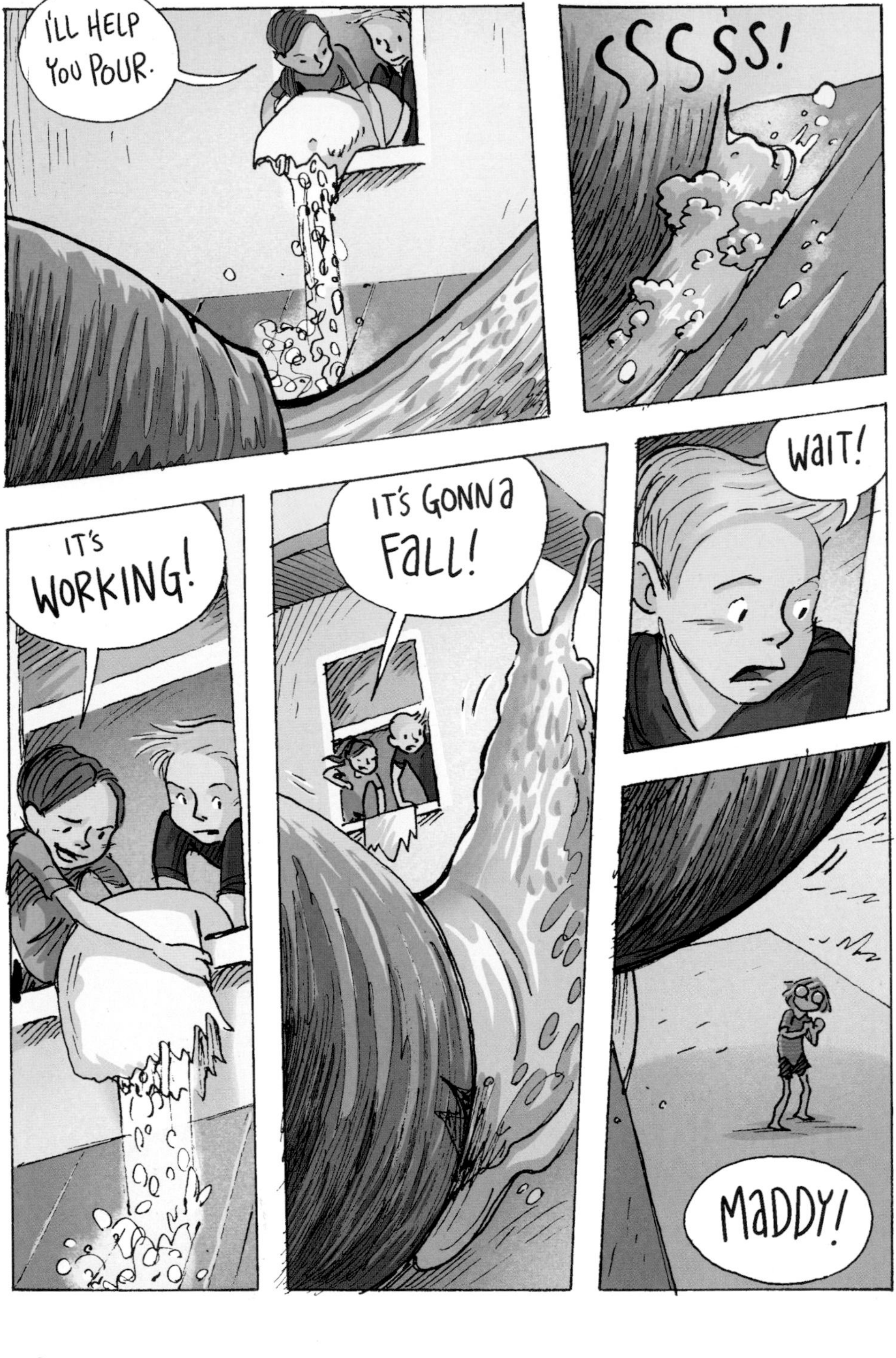
I'LL HELP YOU POUR.
SSSSS!
IT'S WORKING!
IT'S GONNA FALL!
WAIT!
MADDY!

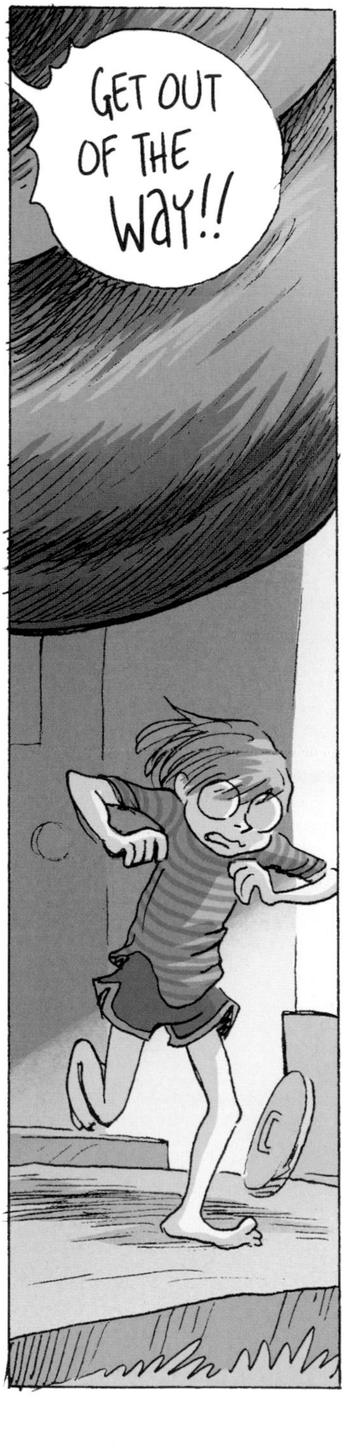
GET OUT OF THE WAY!!

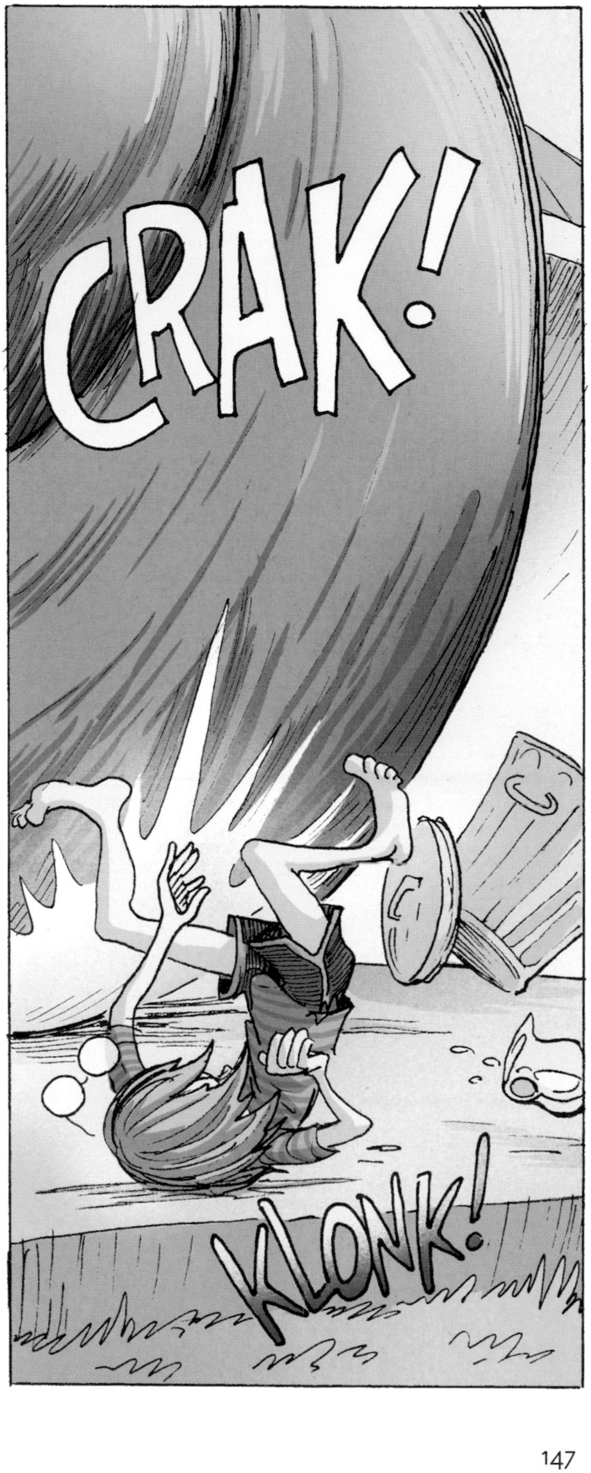
CRAK!
KLONK!

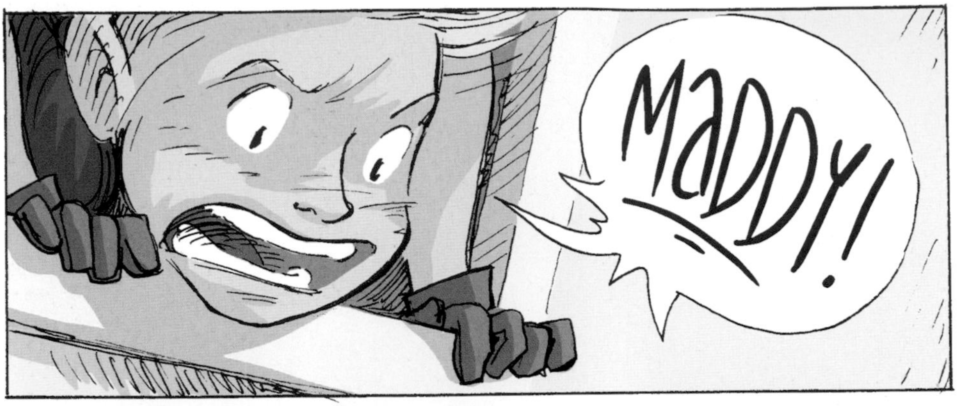
MADDY!

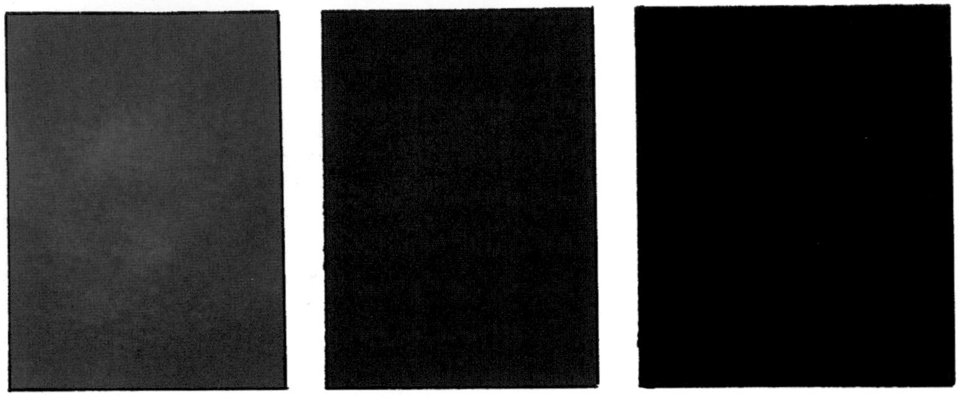

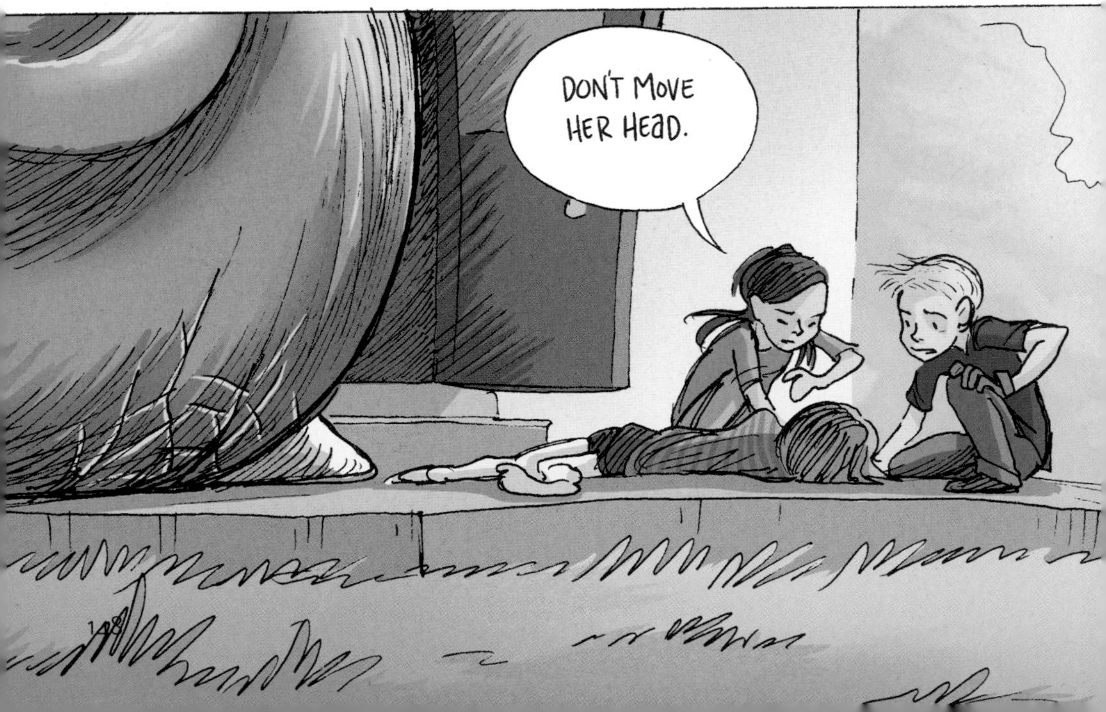
DON'T MOVE HER HEAD.

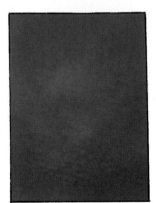

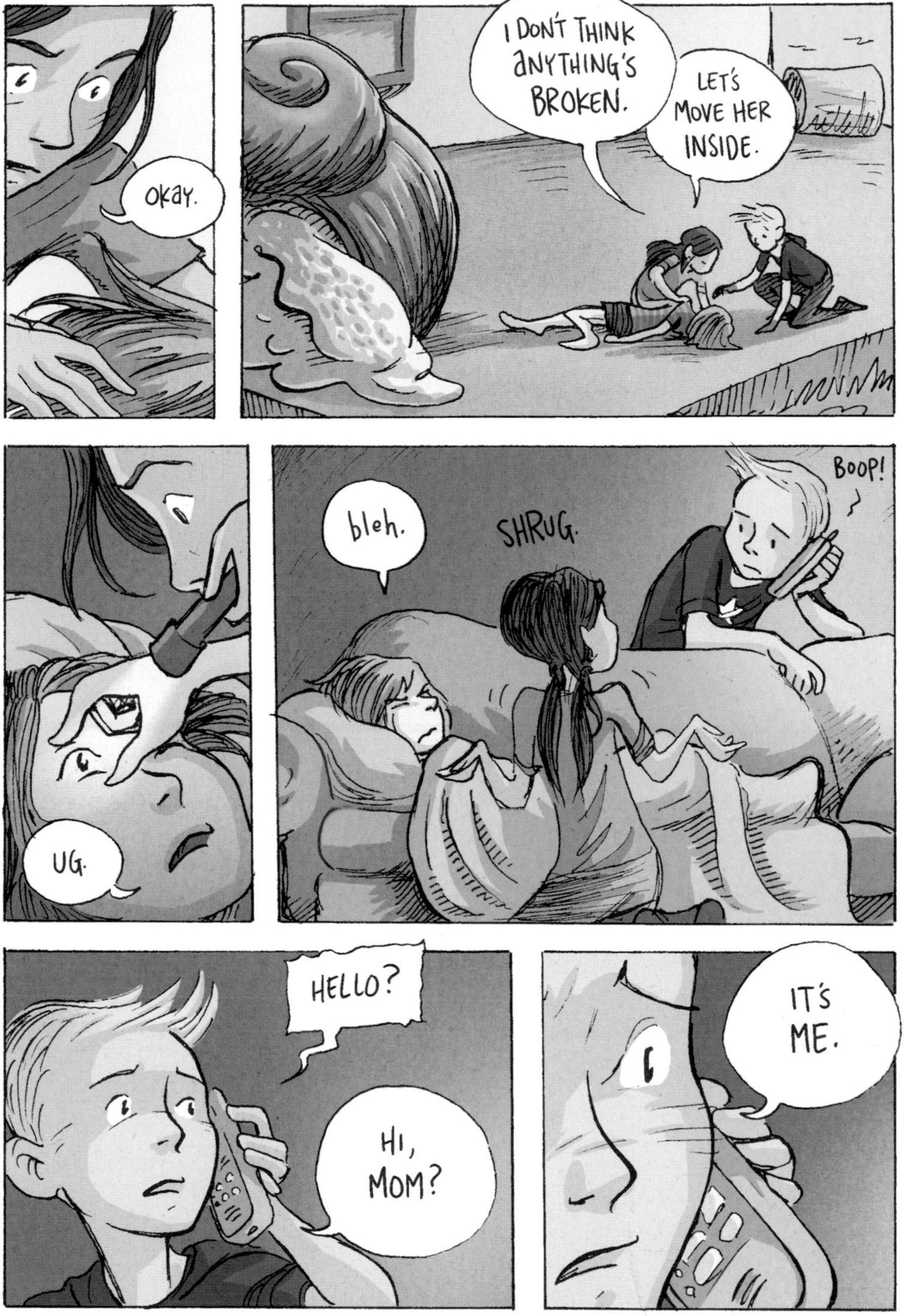
OKAY.
I DON'T THINK ANYTHING'S BROKEN.
LET'S MOVE HER INSIDE.
UG.
bleh.
SHRUG.
BOOP!
HELLO?
HI, MOM?
IT'S ME.

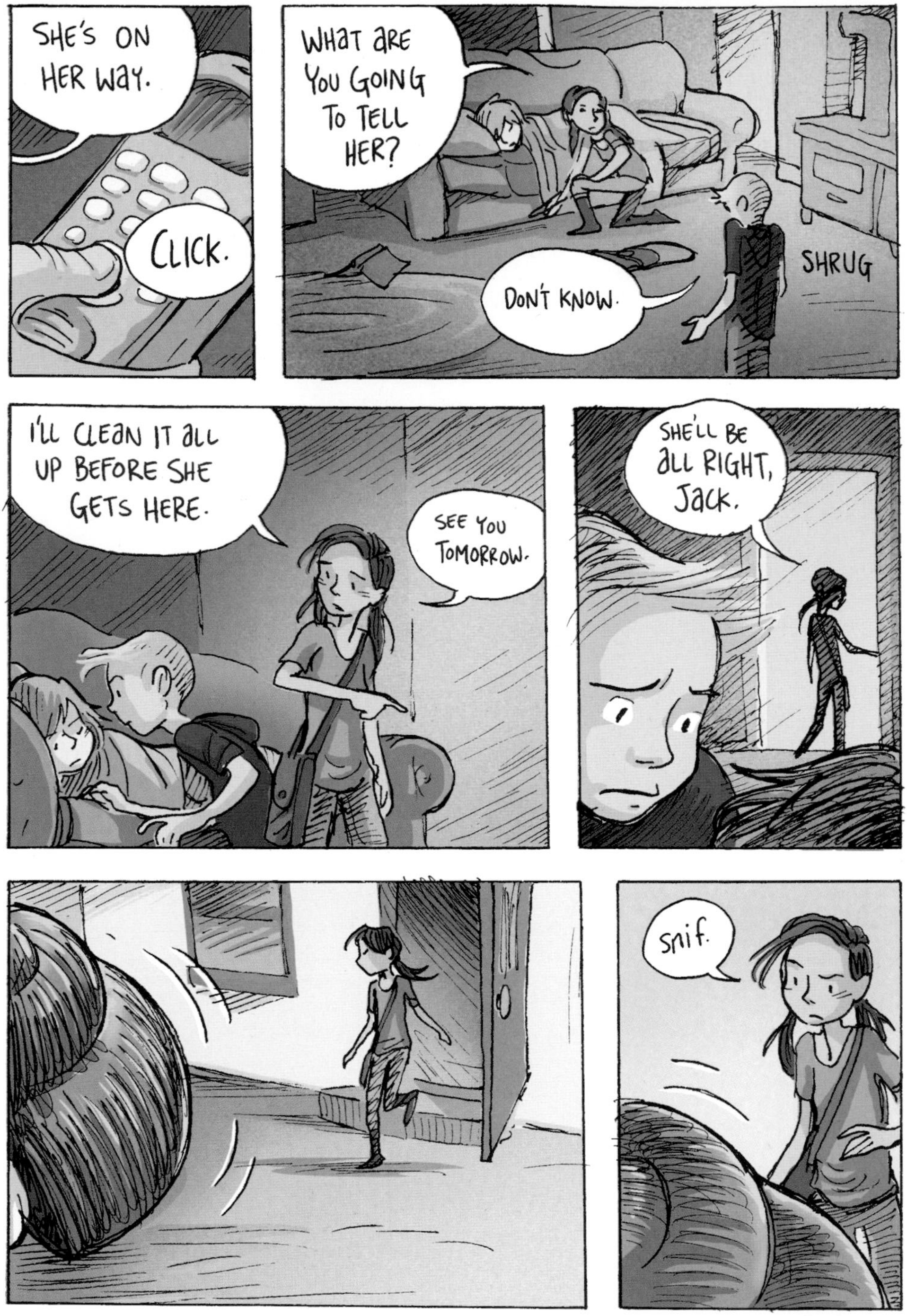
SHE'S ON HER WAY.
CLICK.
WHAT ARE YOU GOING TO TELL HER?
DON'T KNOW.
SHRUG
I'LL CLEAN IT ALL UP BEFORE SHE GETS HERE.
SEE YOU TOMORROW.
SHE'LL BE ALL RIGHT, JACK.
snif.

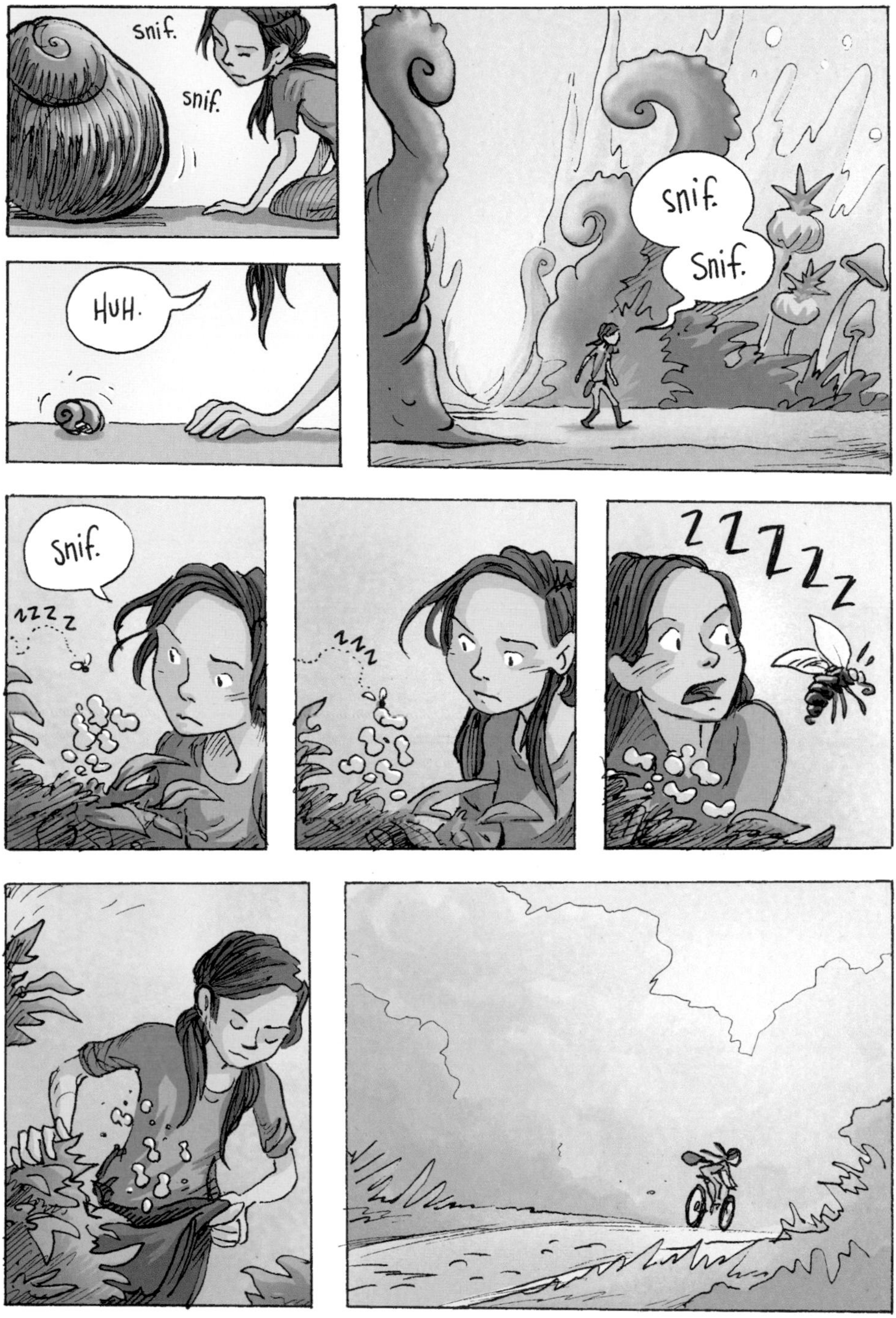
snif.
snif.
HUH.
snif.
Snif.
snif.
zzzz
zzz
ZZZZZ

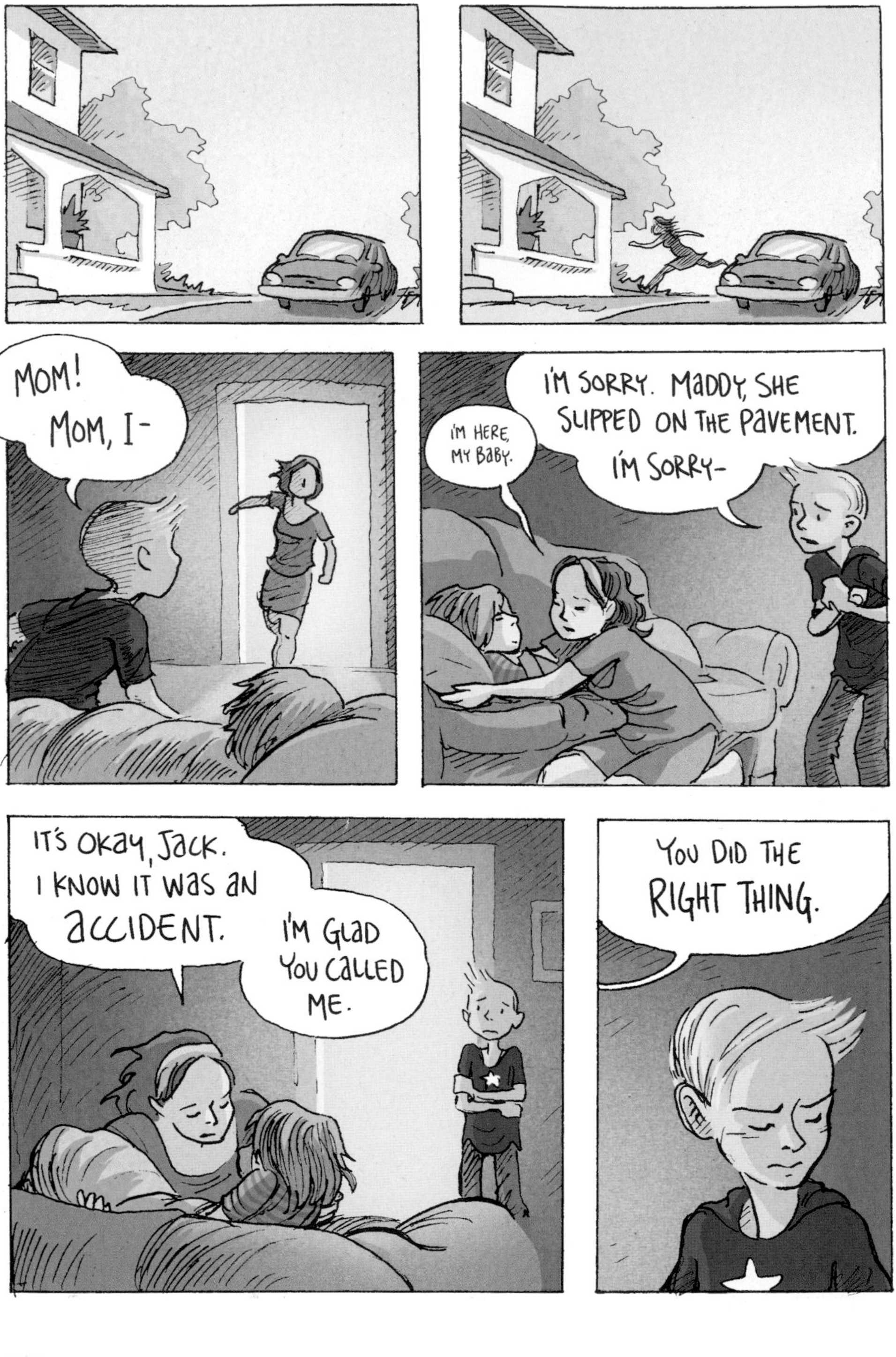
MOM!
MOM, I-
I'M SORRY. MADDY, SHE SLIPPED ON THE PAVEMENT.
I'M SORRY-
I'M HERE, MY BABY.
IT'S OKAY, JACK. I KNOW IT WAS AN ACCIDENT.
I'M GLAD YOU CALLED ME.
YOU DID THE RIGHT THING.

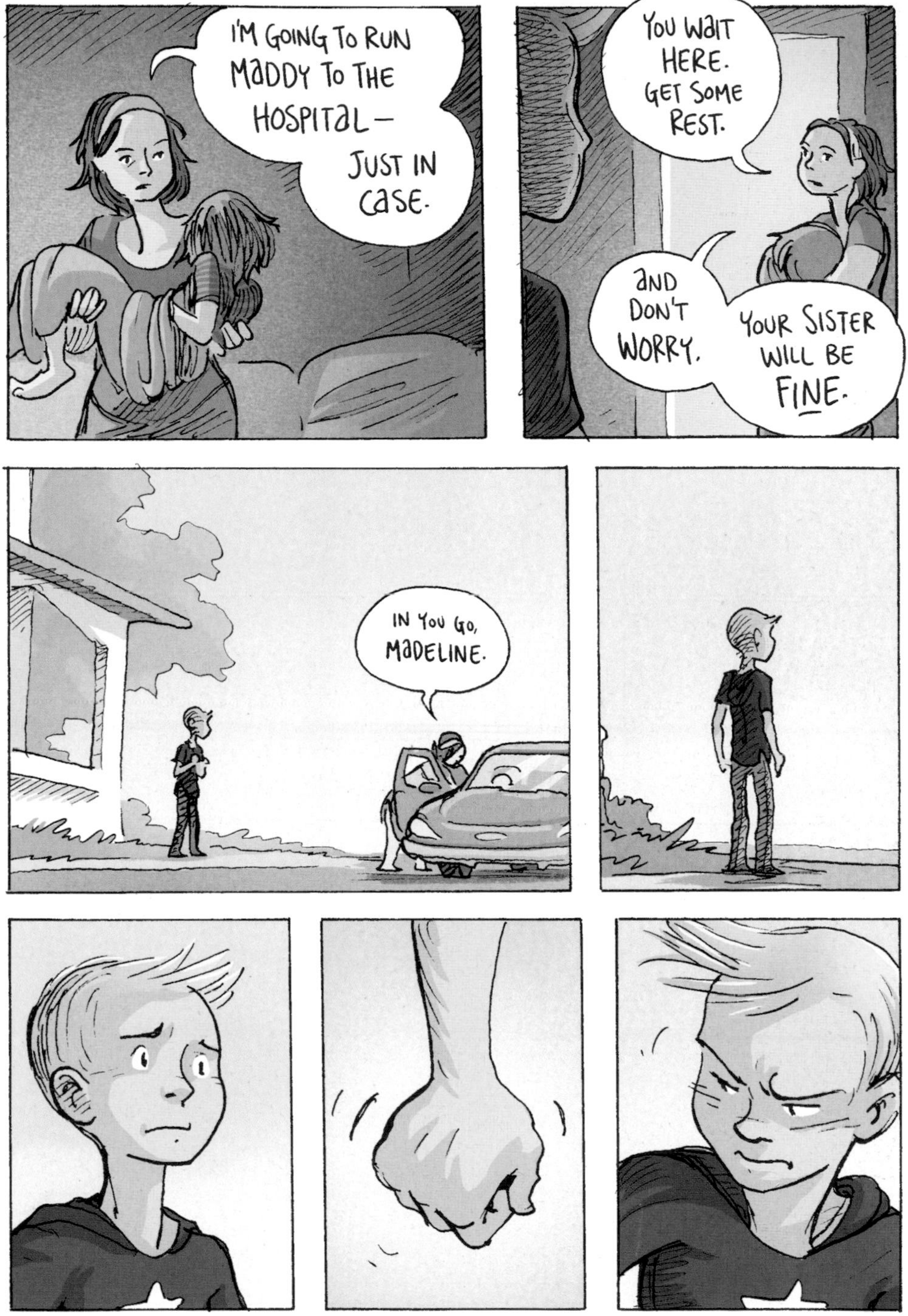
I'M GOING TO RUN MADDY TO THE HOSPITAL—
JUST IN CASE.
YOU WAIT HERE. GET SOME REST.
AND DON'T WORRY.
YOUR SISTER WILL BE FINE.
IN YOU GO, MADELINE.

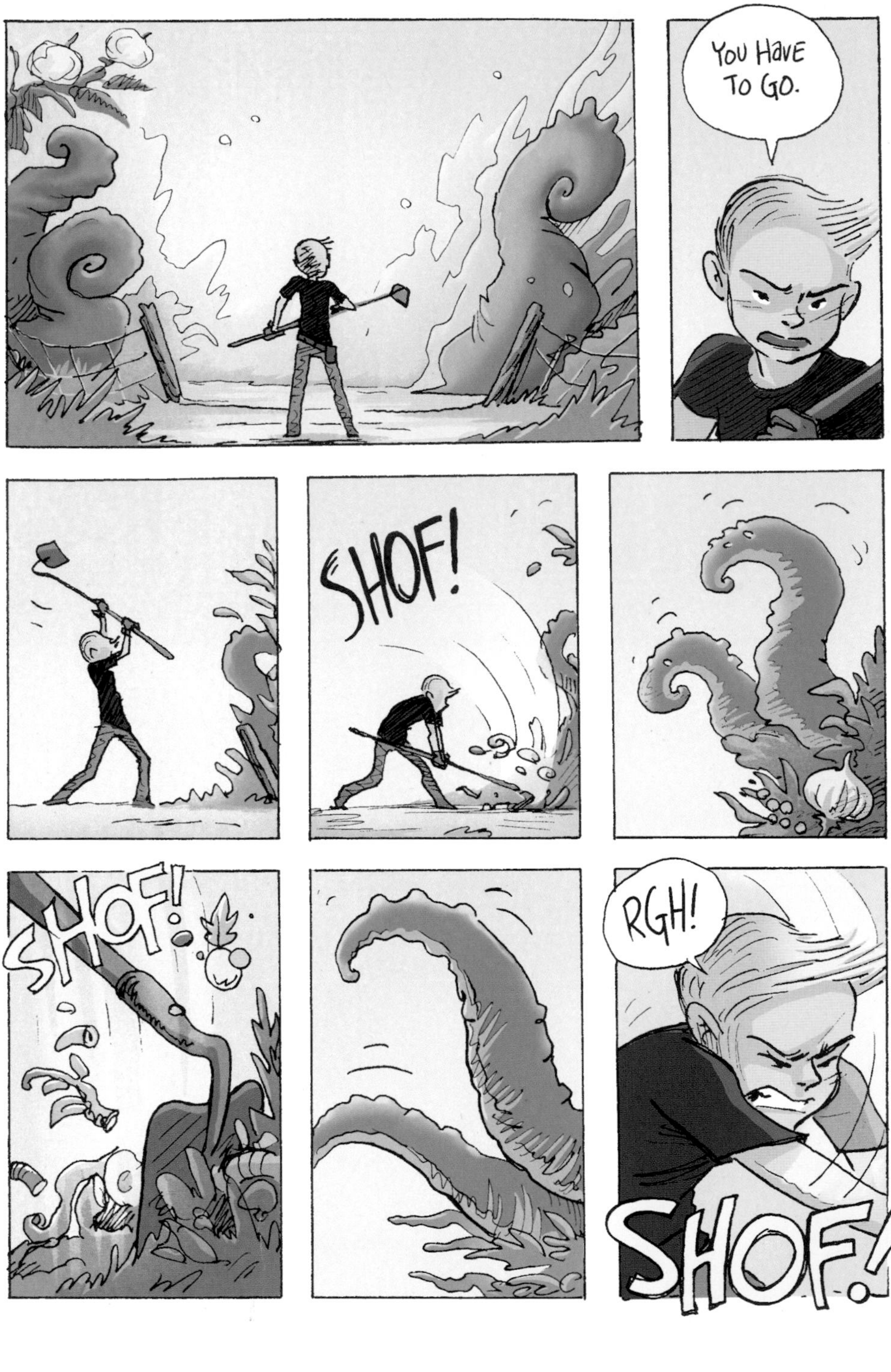
YOU HAVE TO GO.
SHOF!
SHOF!
RGH!
SHOF!

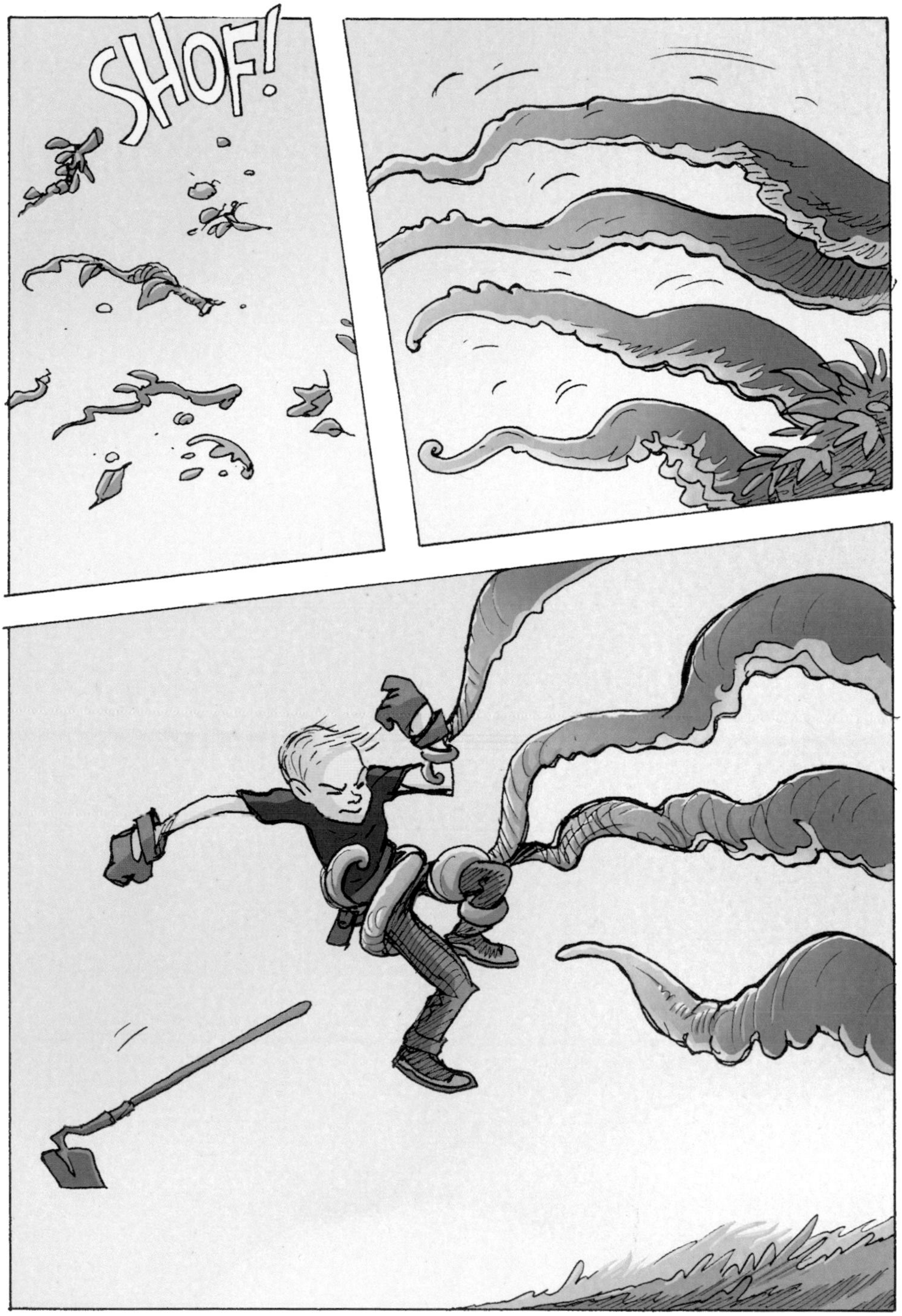
SHOF!

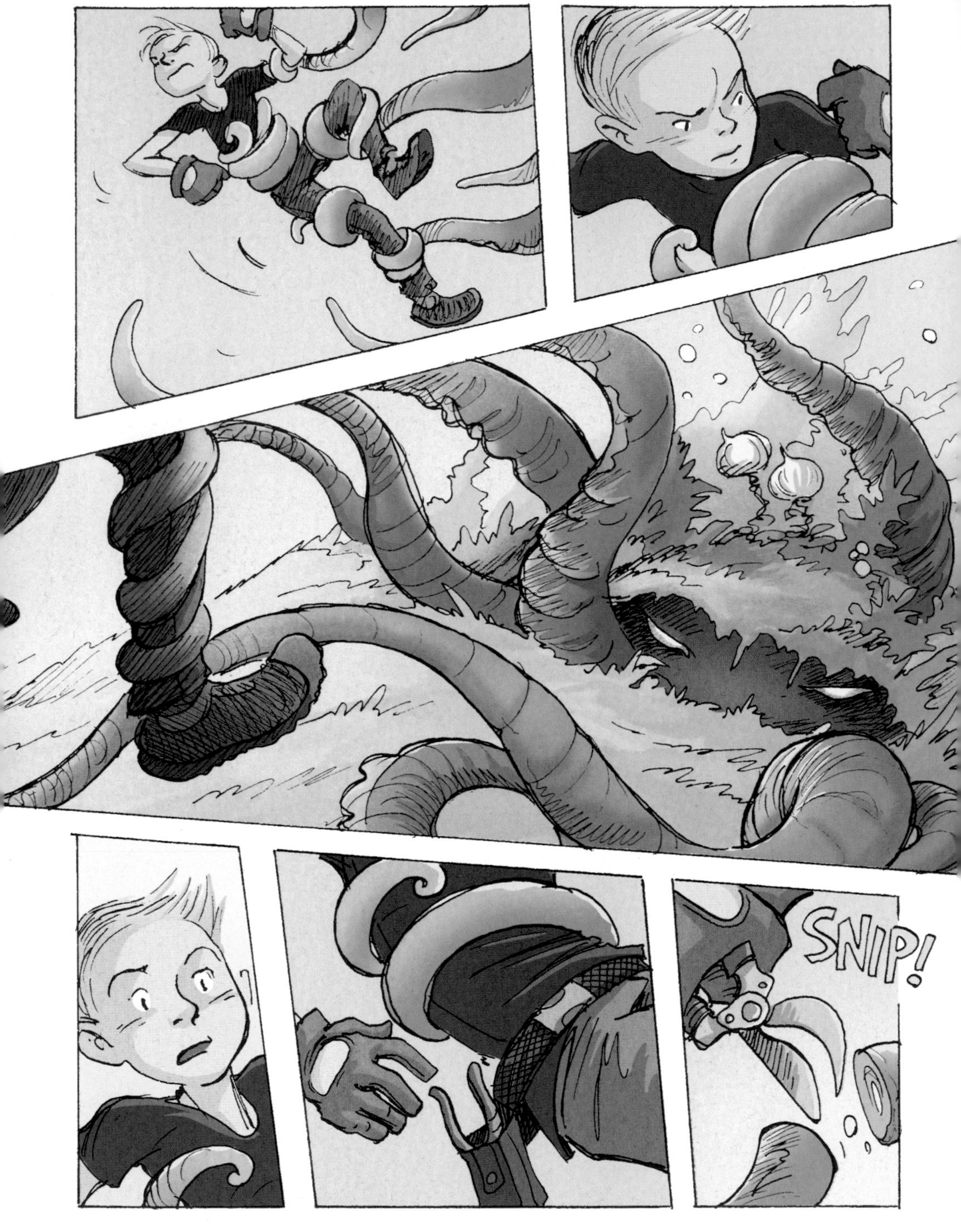
SNIP!

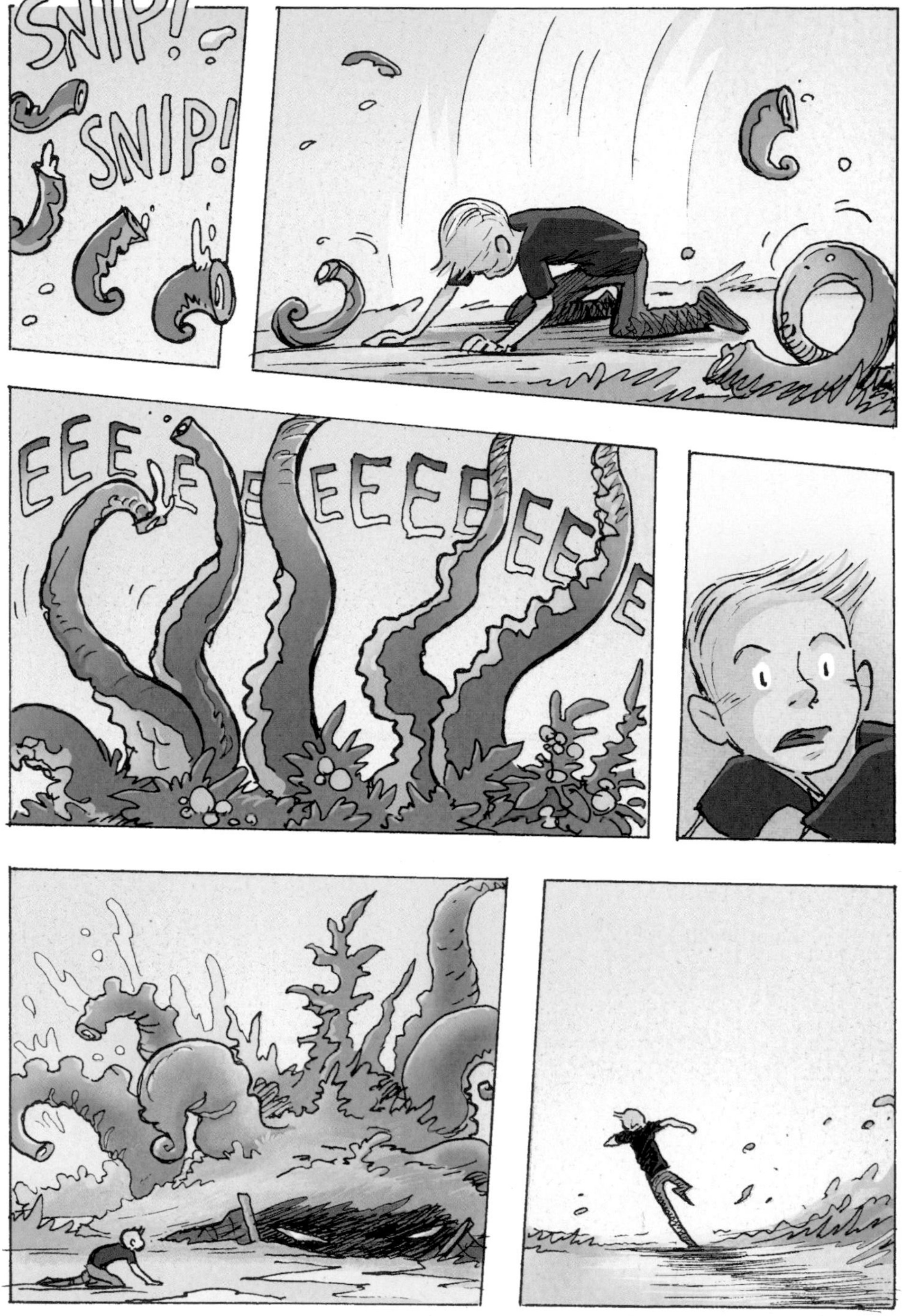
SNIP!
SNIP!
EEEEEEEEEEEEE

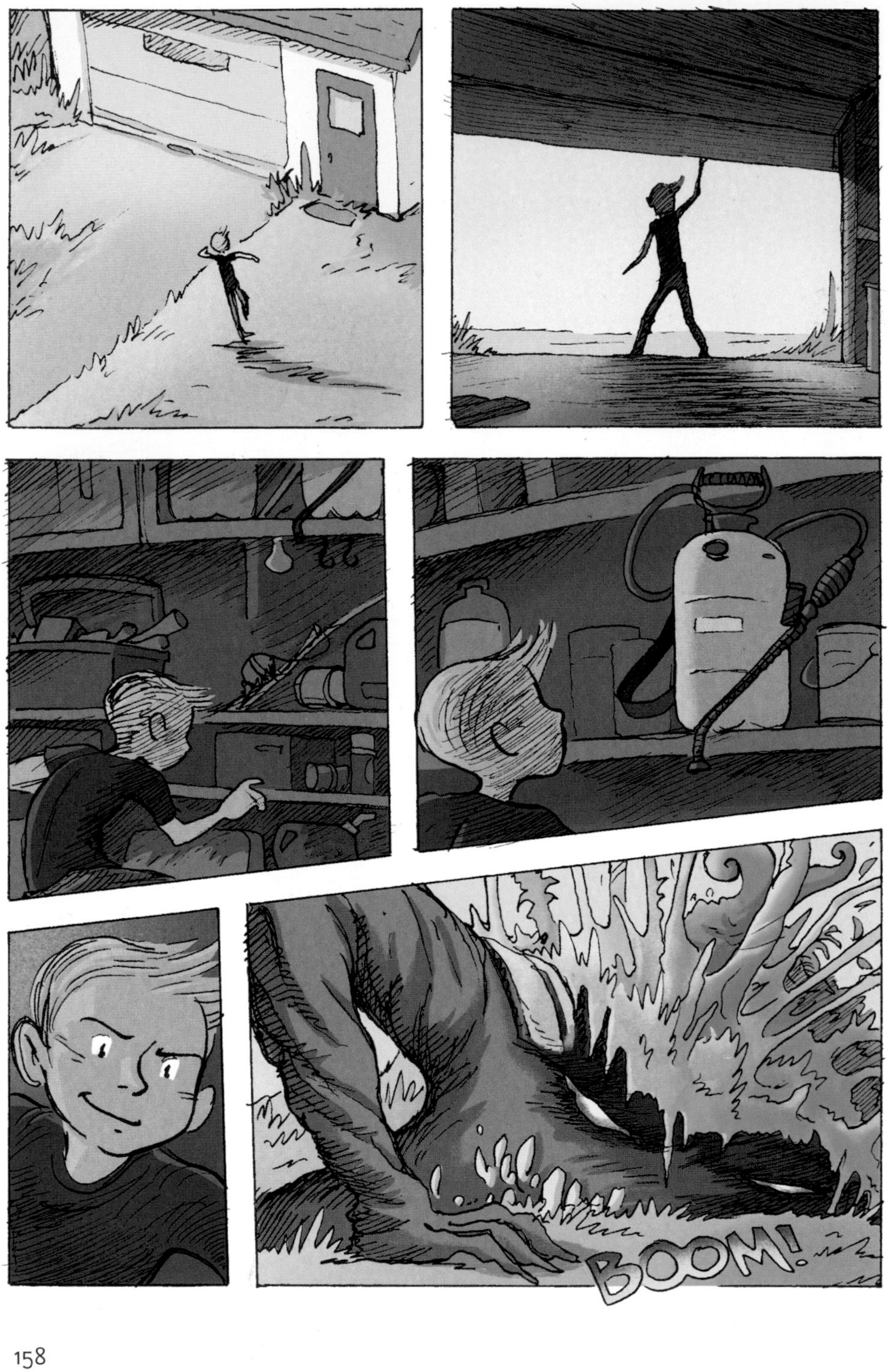
BOOM!

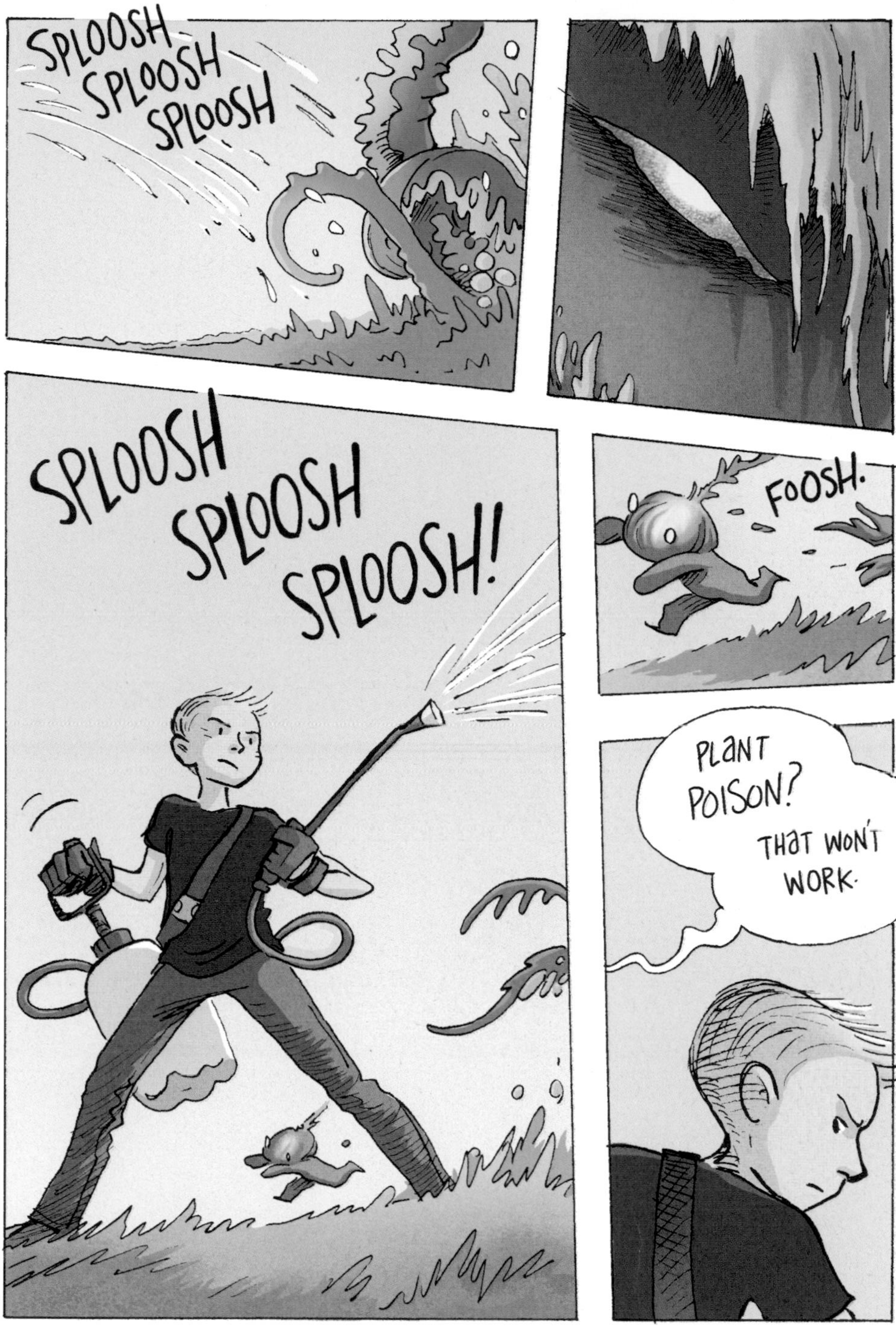
SPLOOSH
SPLOOSH
SPLOOSH
SPLOOSH
SPLOOSH
SPLOOSH!
FOOSH.
PLANT POISON? THAT WON'T WORK.

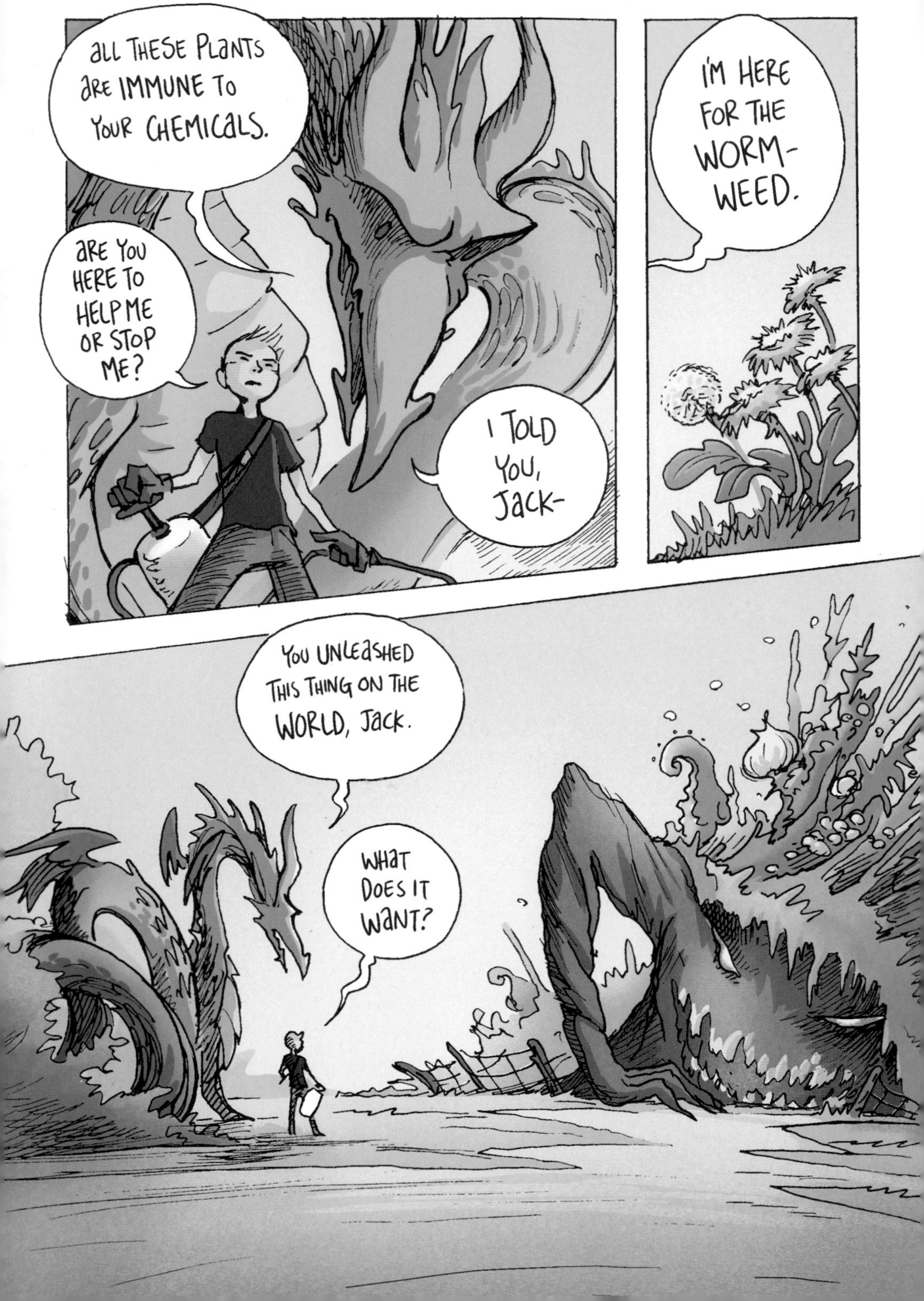

ALL THESE PLANTS ARE IMMUNE TO YOUR CHEMICALS.
ARE YOU HERE TO HELP ME OR STOP ME?
I TOLD YOU, JACK-
I'M HERE FOR THE WORM-WEED.
YOU UNLEASHED THIS THING ON THE WORLD, JACK.
WHAT DOES IT WANT?

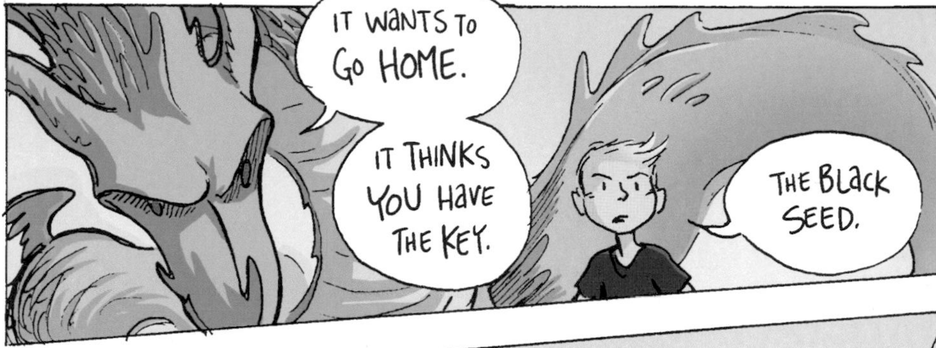

IT WANTS TO GO HOME.
IT THINKS YOU HAVE THE KEY.
THE BLACK SEED.

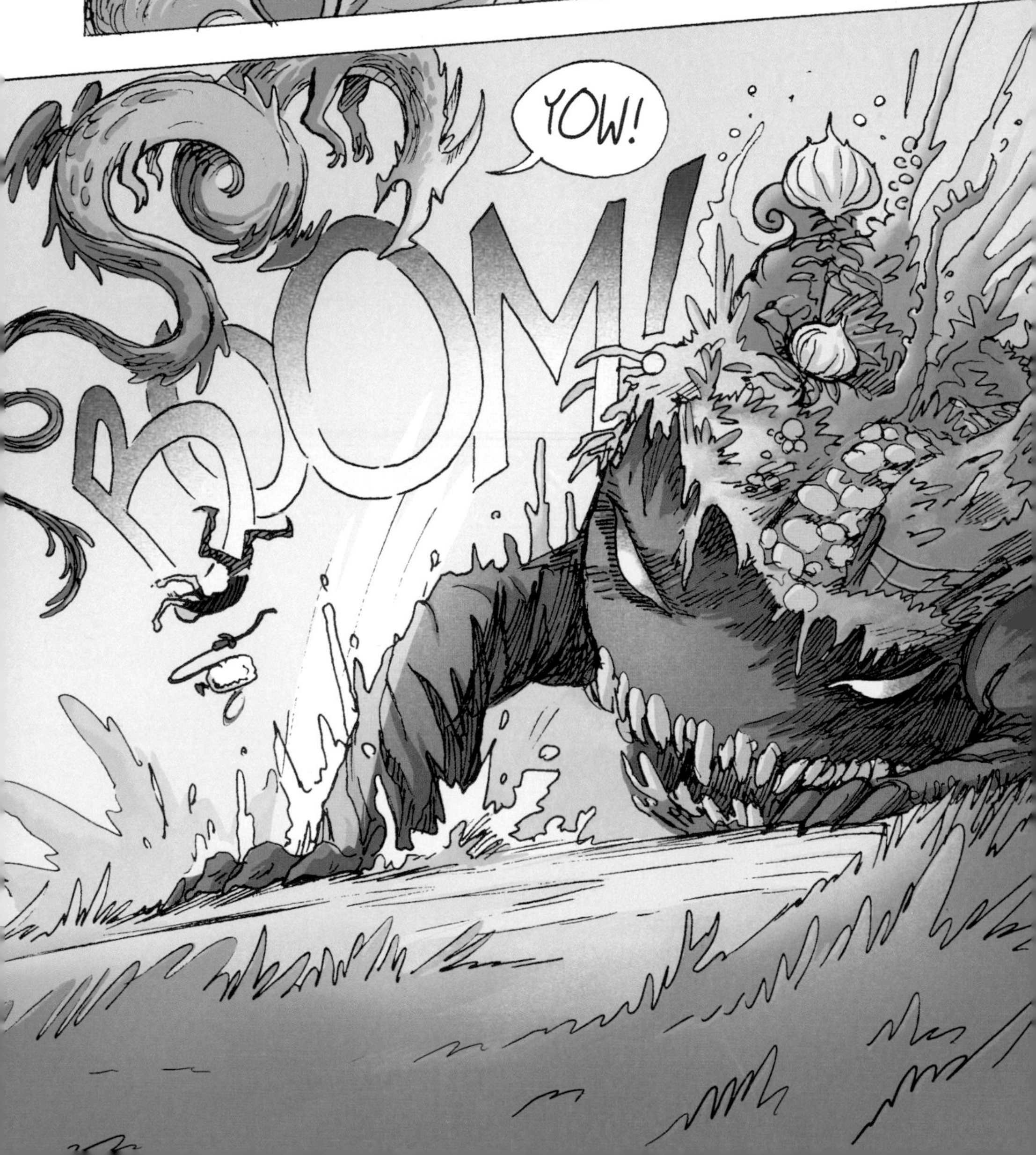

YOW!
BOOM!

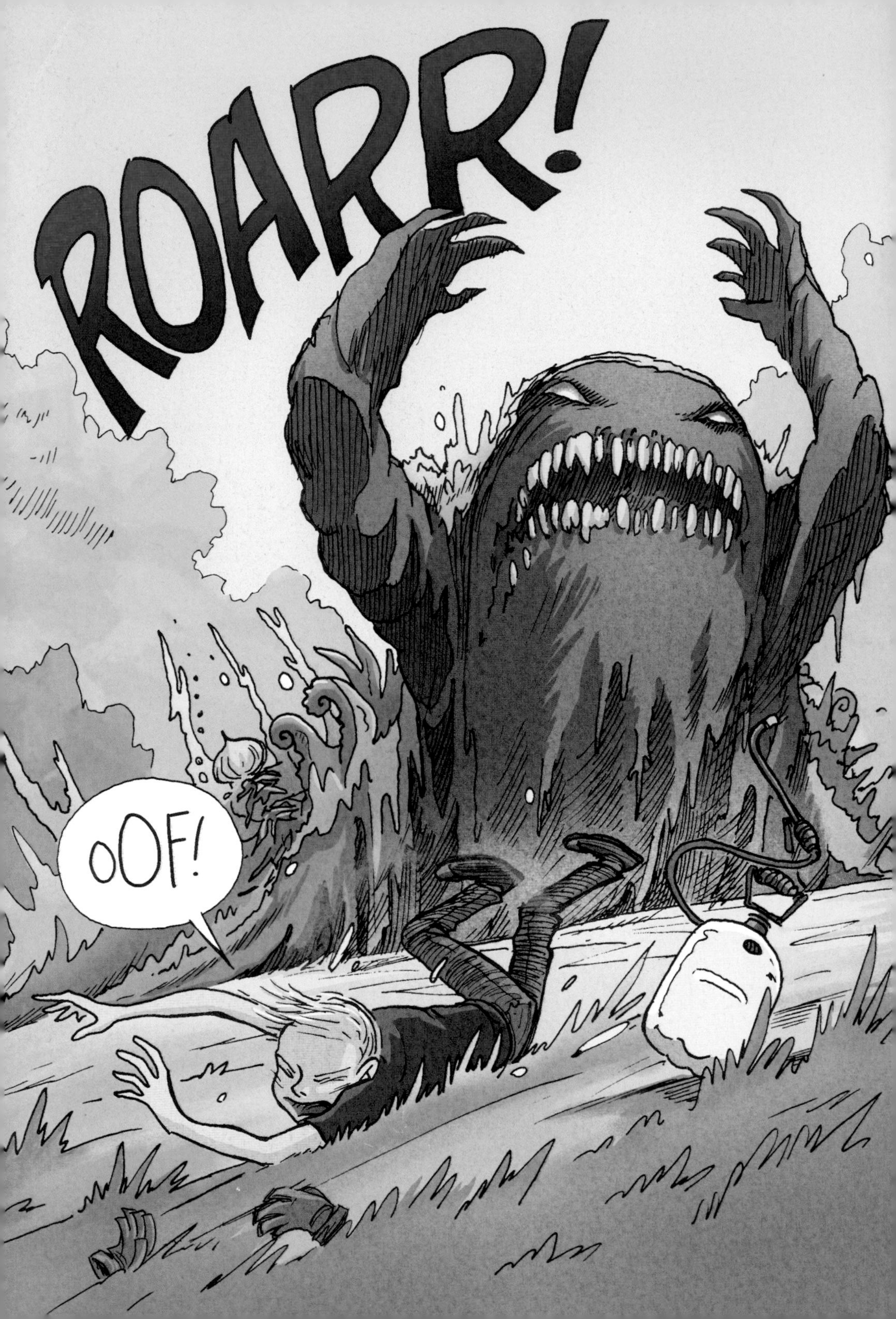
ROARR!
OOF!

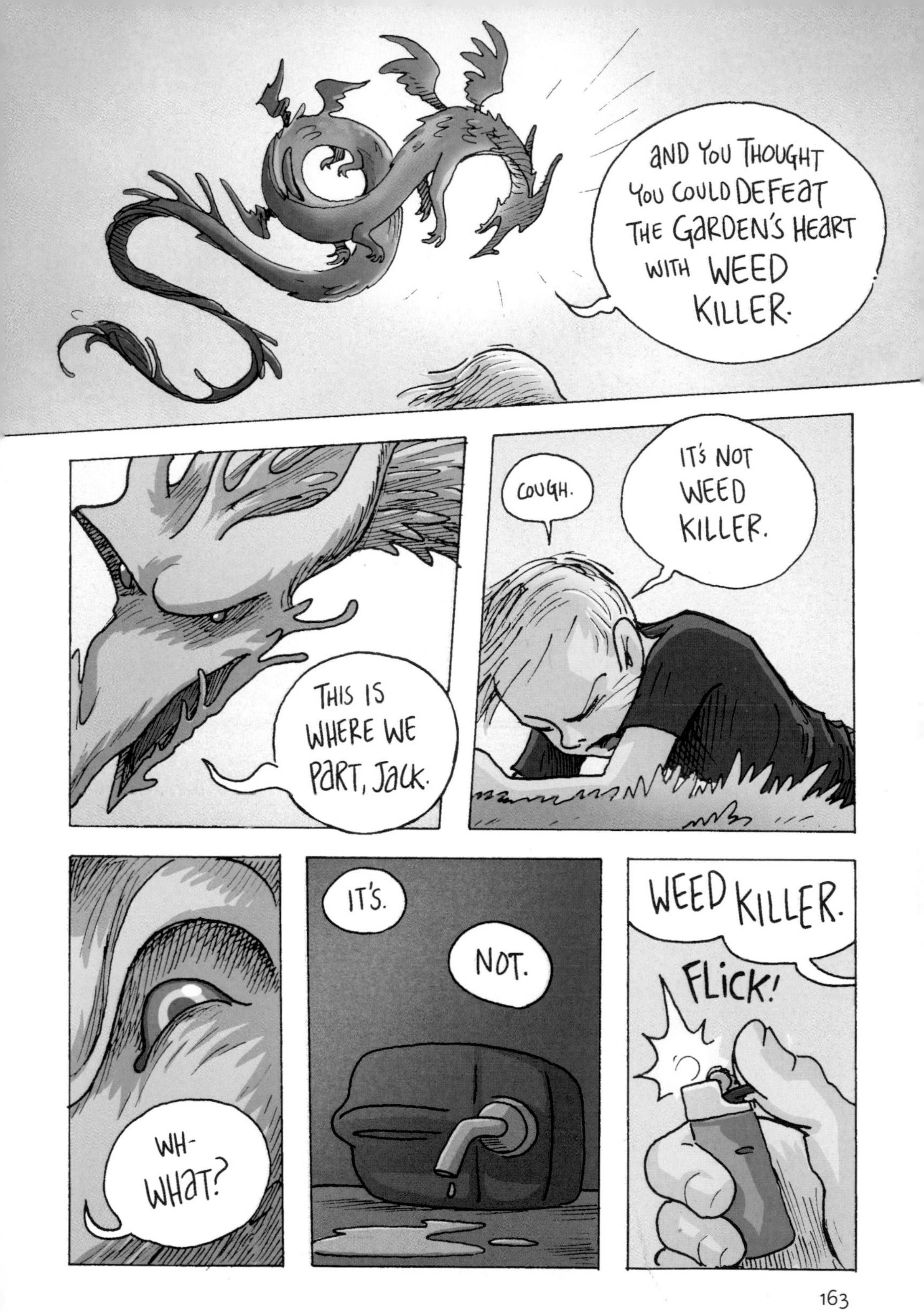
AND YOU THOUGHT YOU COULD DEFEAT THE GARDEN'S HEART WITH WEED KILLER.
THIS IS WHERE WE PART, JACK.
COUGH.
IT'S NOT WEED KILLER.
WH- WHAT?
IT'S.
NOT.
WEED KILLER.
FLICK!

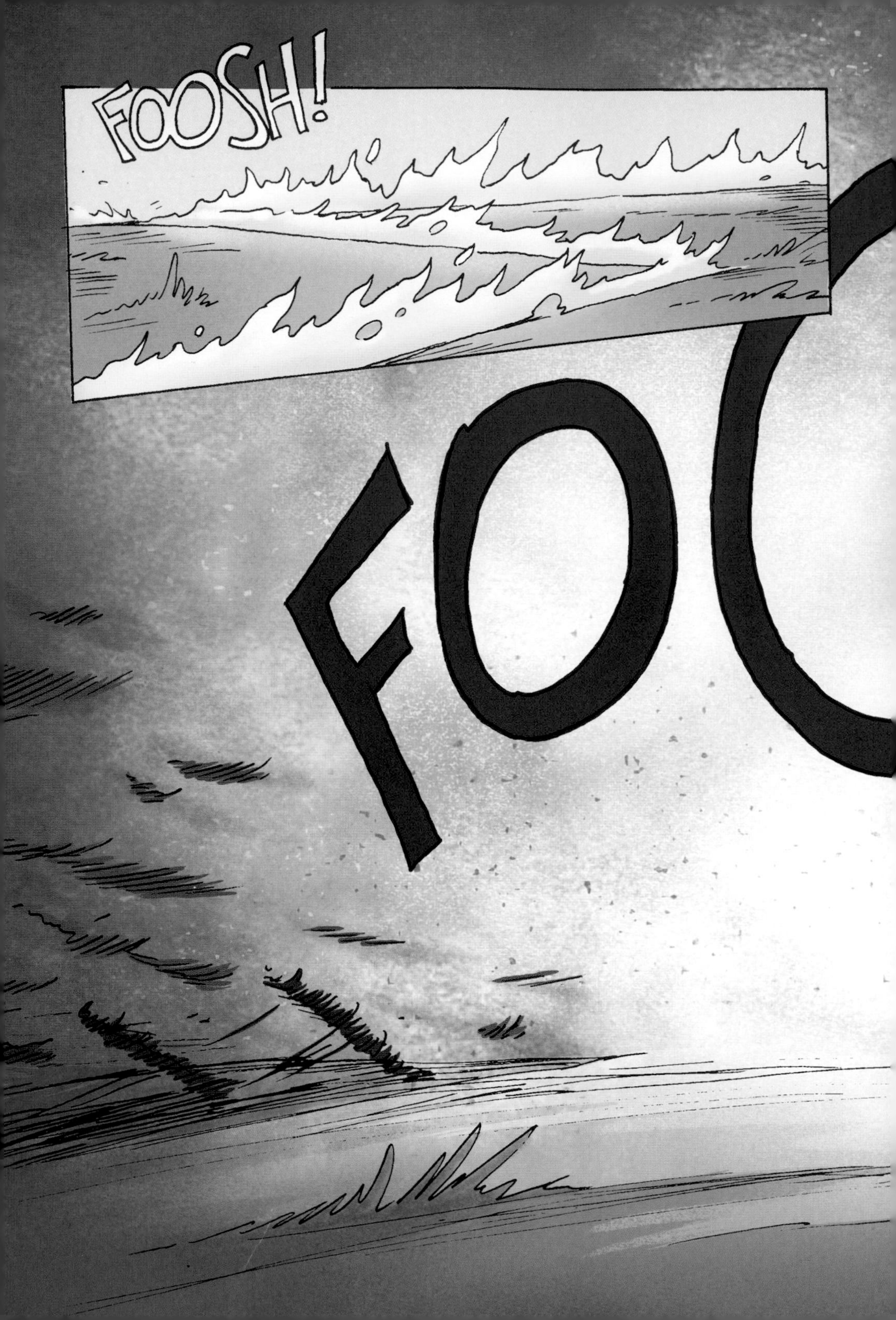
FOOSH!
FOO

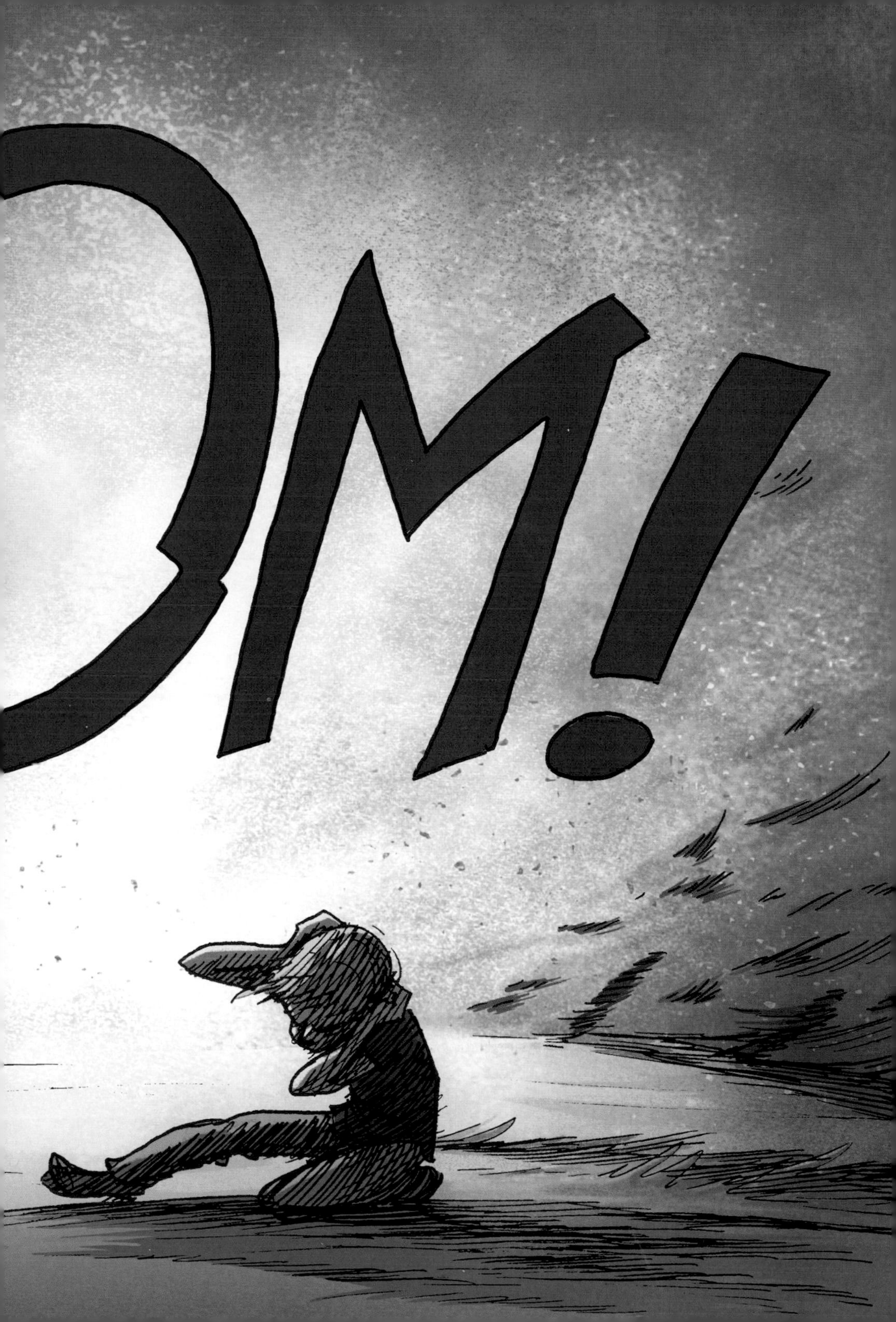
OM!

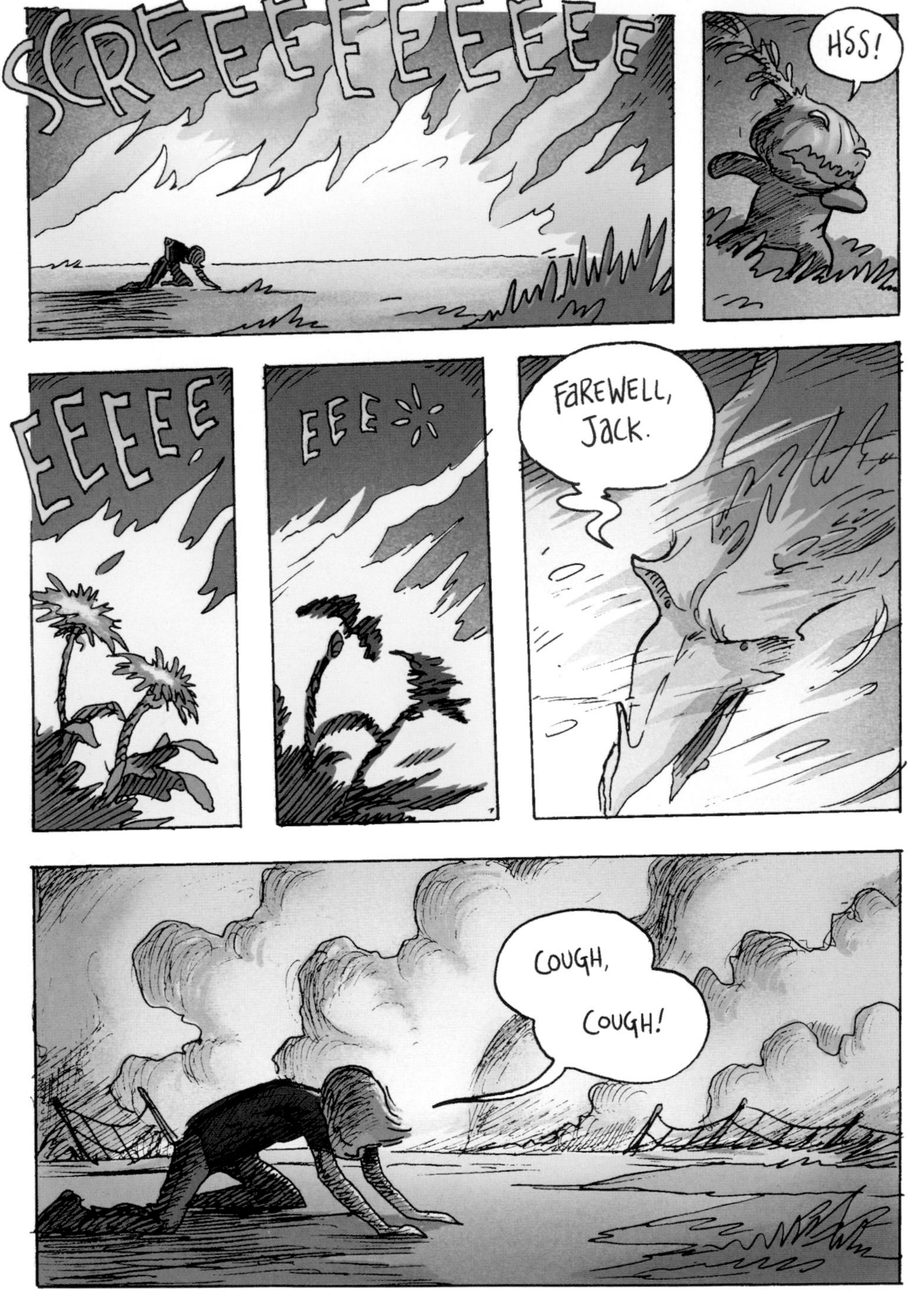
SCREEEEEEEEEE
HSS!
EEEEE
EEE
FAREWELL, JACK.
COUGH,
COUGH!

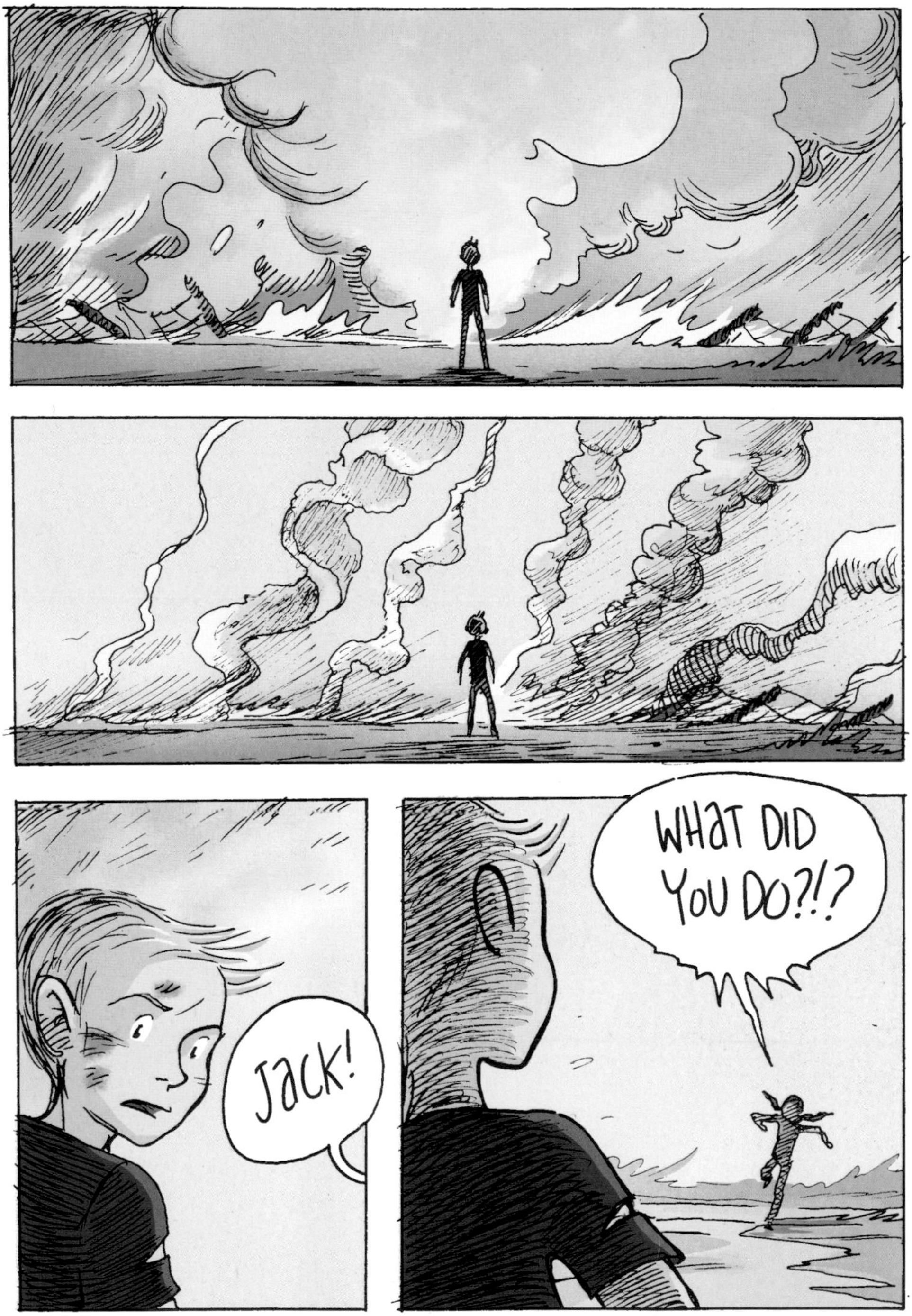
Jack!
WHAT DID YOU DO?!?

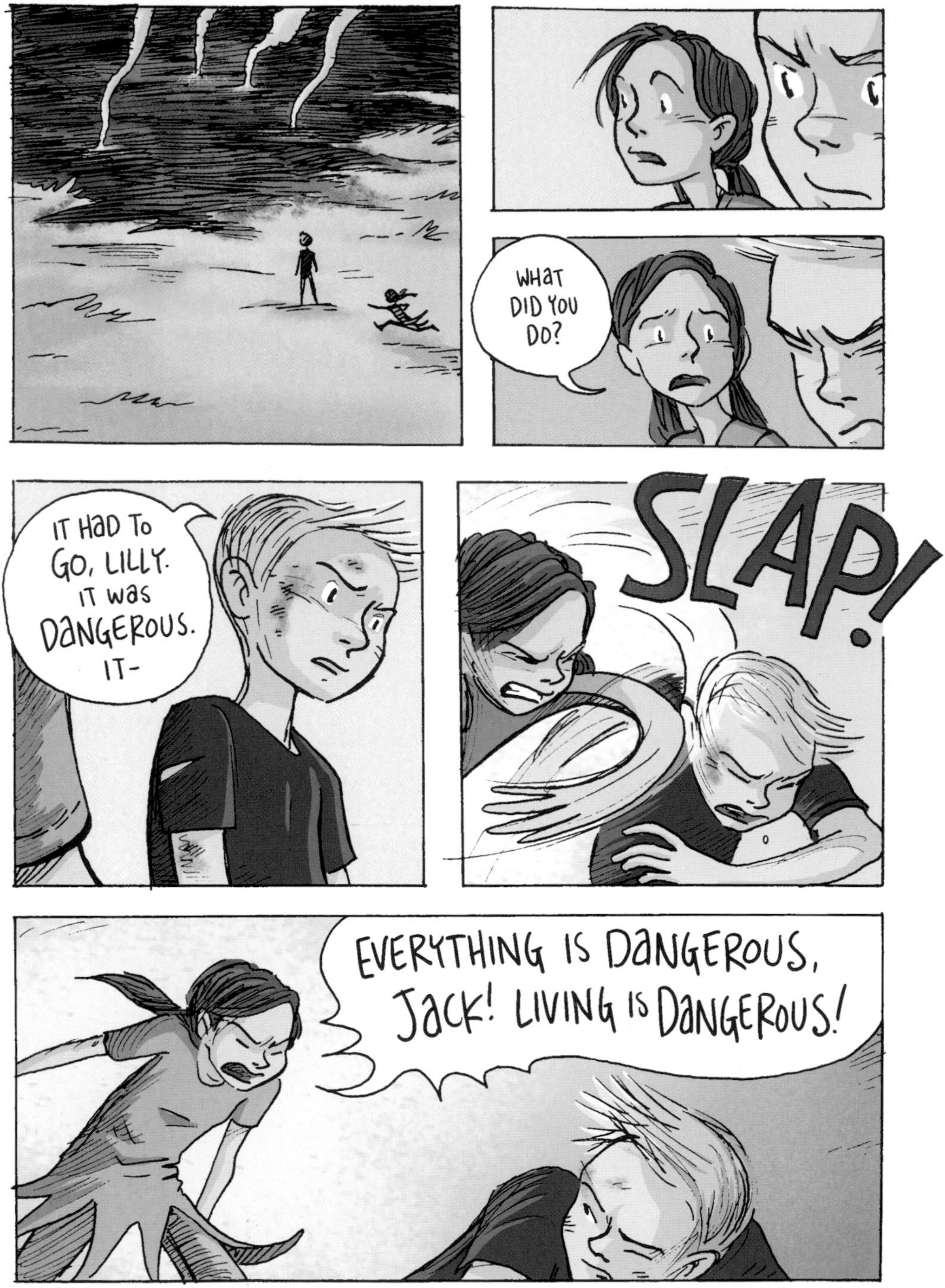
WHAT DID YOU DO?
IT HAD TO GO, LILLY. IT WAS DANGEROUS. IT-
SLAP!
EVERYTHING IS DANGEROUS, JACK! LIVING IS DANGEROUS!

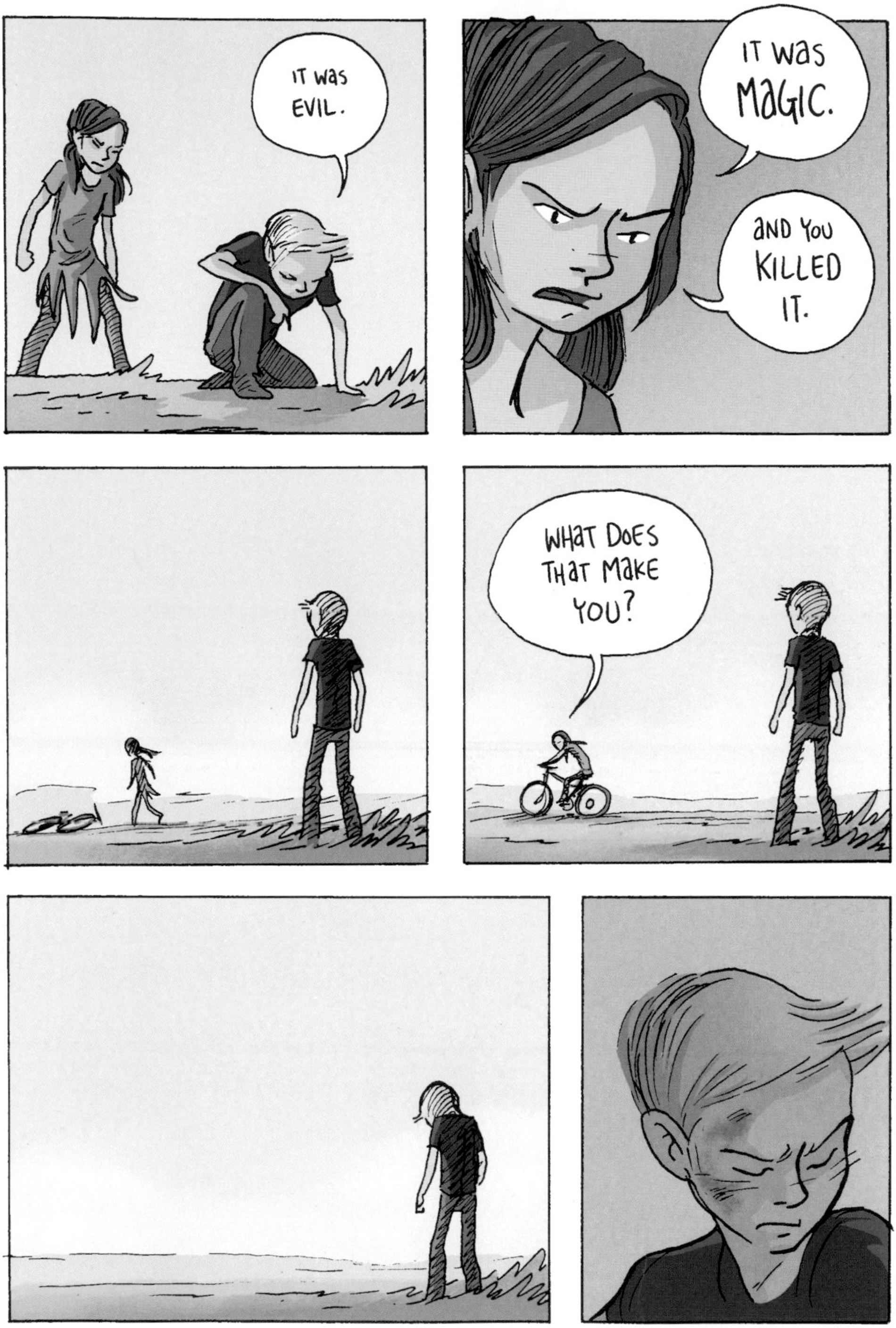
IT WAS EVIL.
IT WAS MAGIC.
AND YOU KILLED IT.
WHAT DOES THAT MAKE YOU?

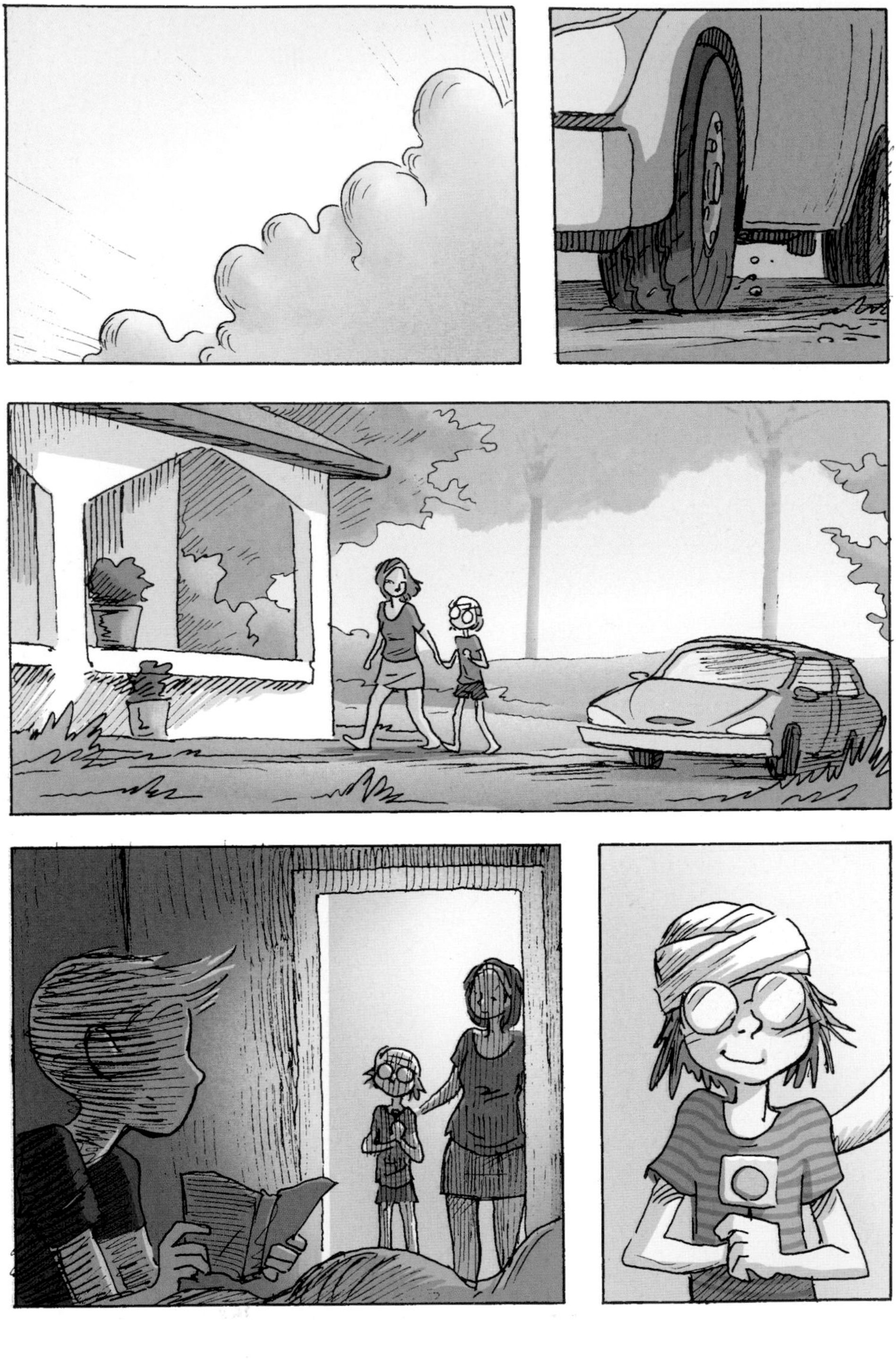

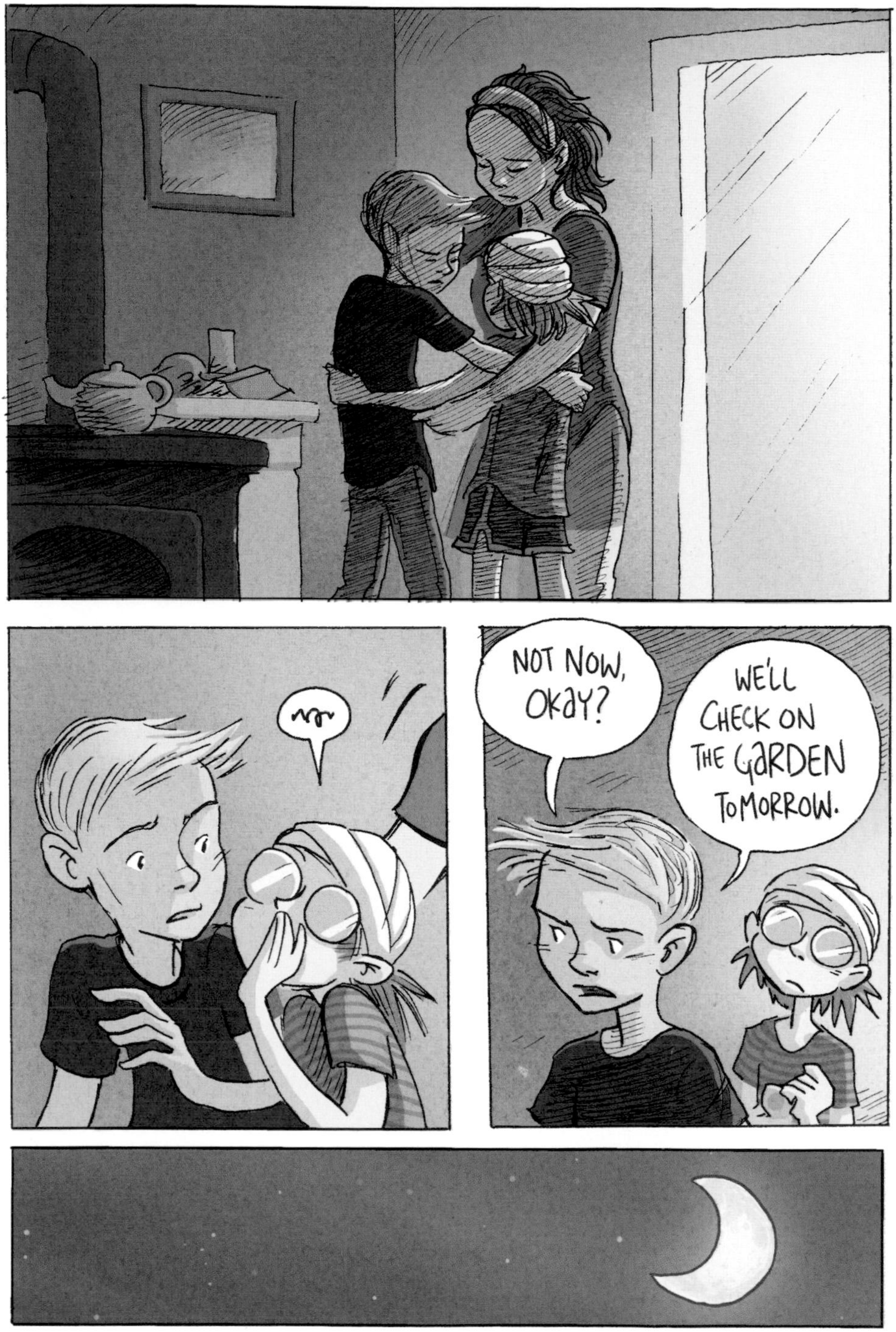
NOT NOW, OKAY?
WE'LL CHECK ON THE GARDEN TOMORROW.

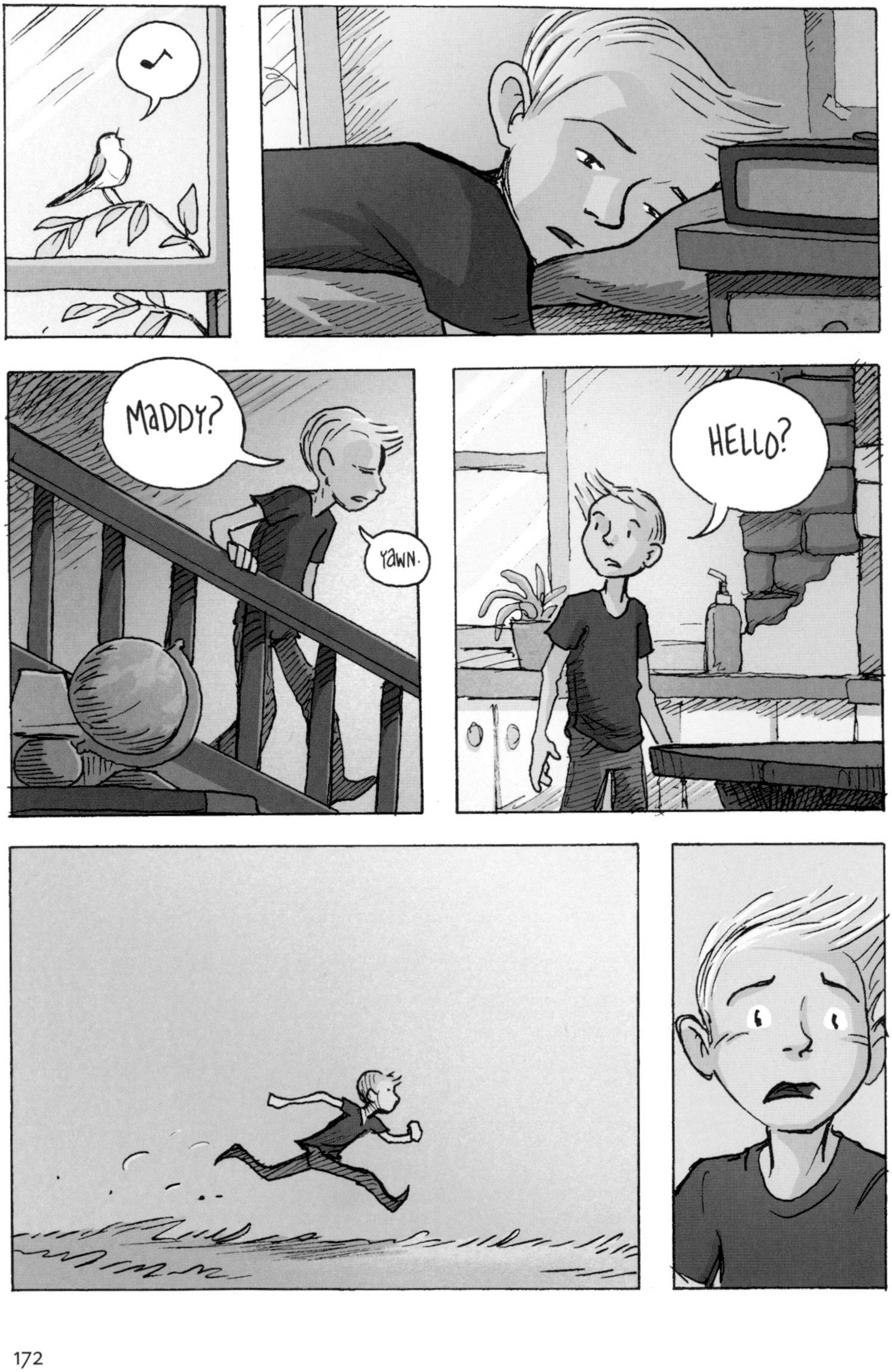
♪
MADDY?
YAWN.
HELLO?

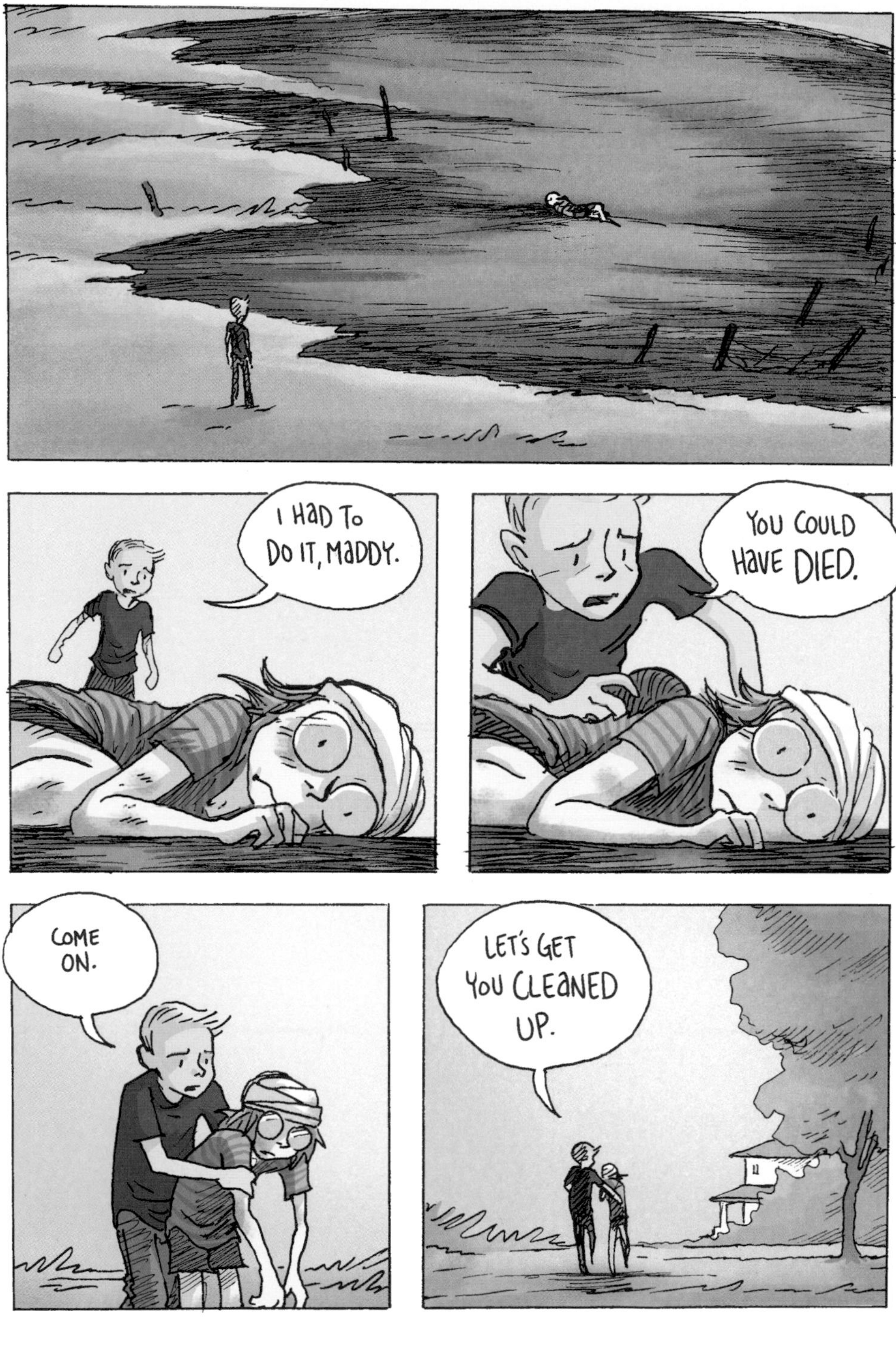
I HAD TO DO IT, MADDY.
YOU COULD HAVE DIED.
COME ON.
LET'S GET YOU CLEANED UP.

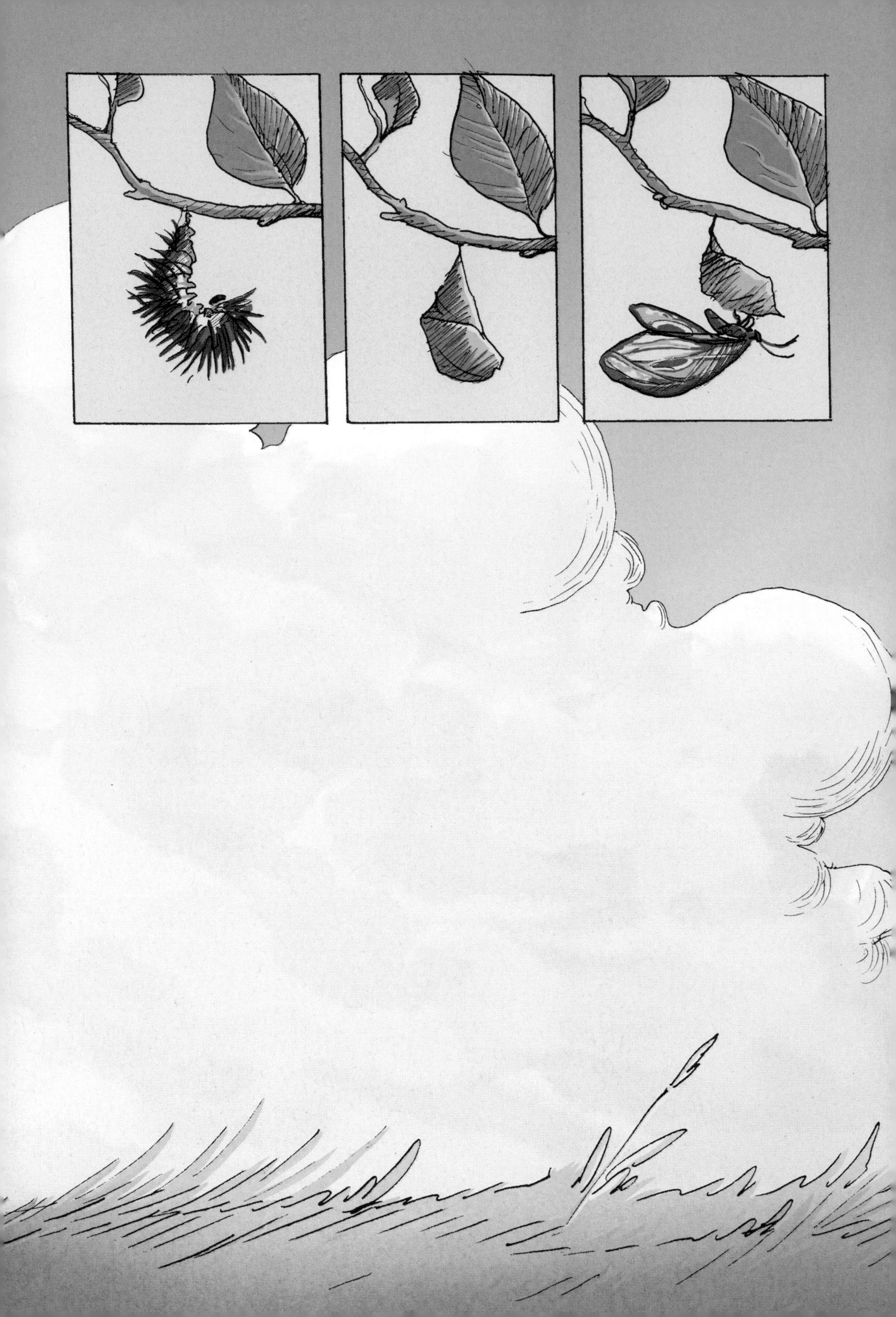

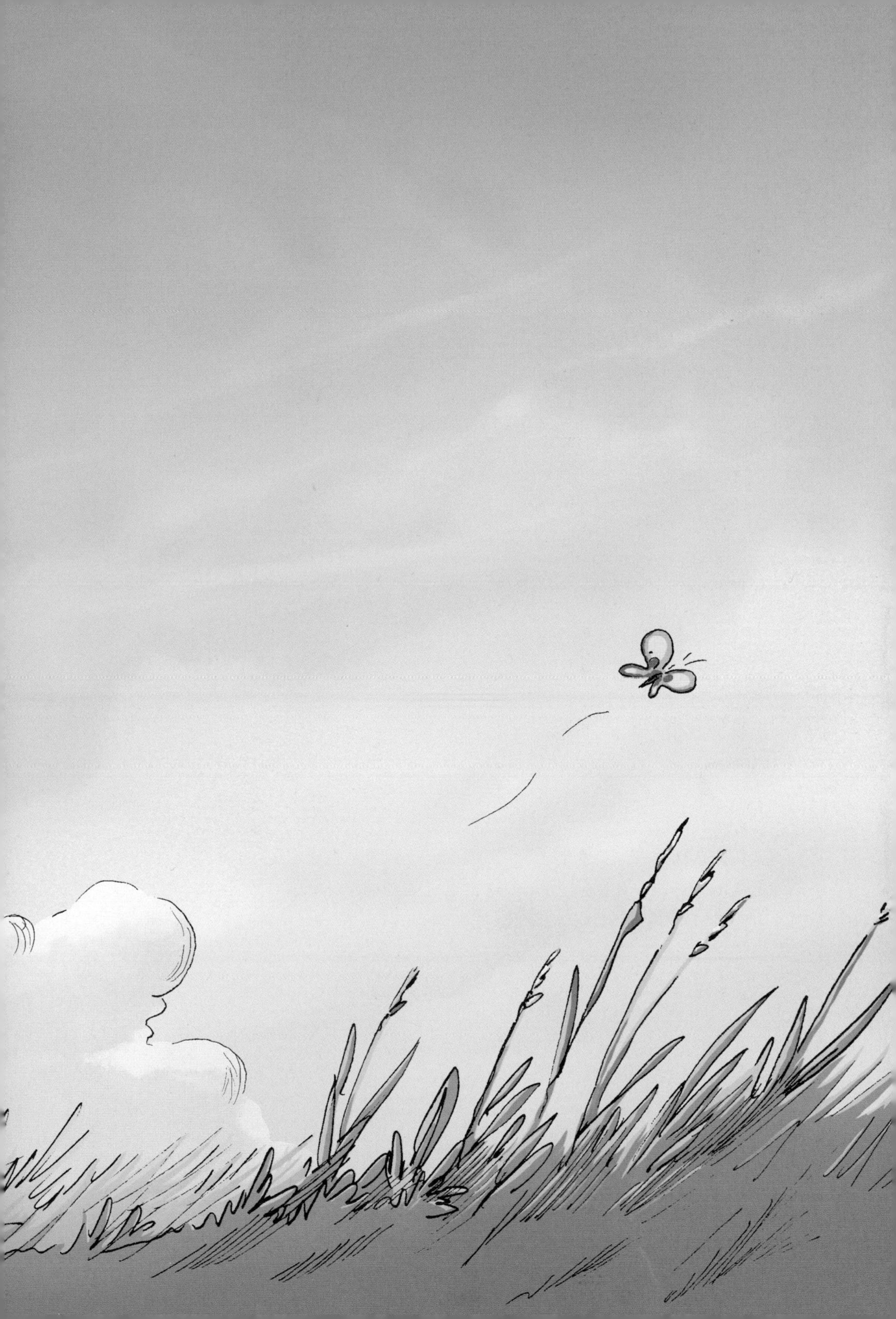

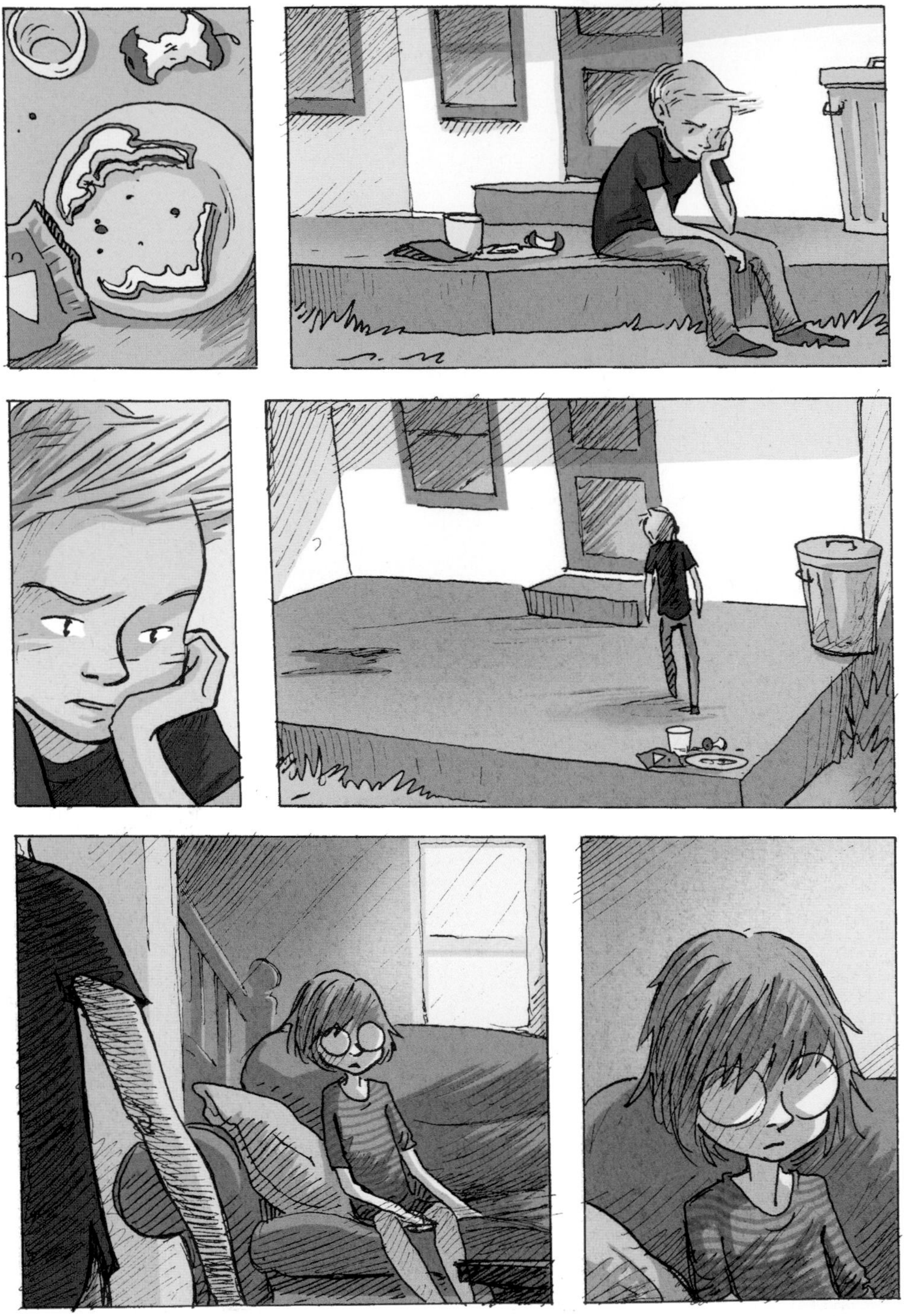

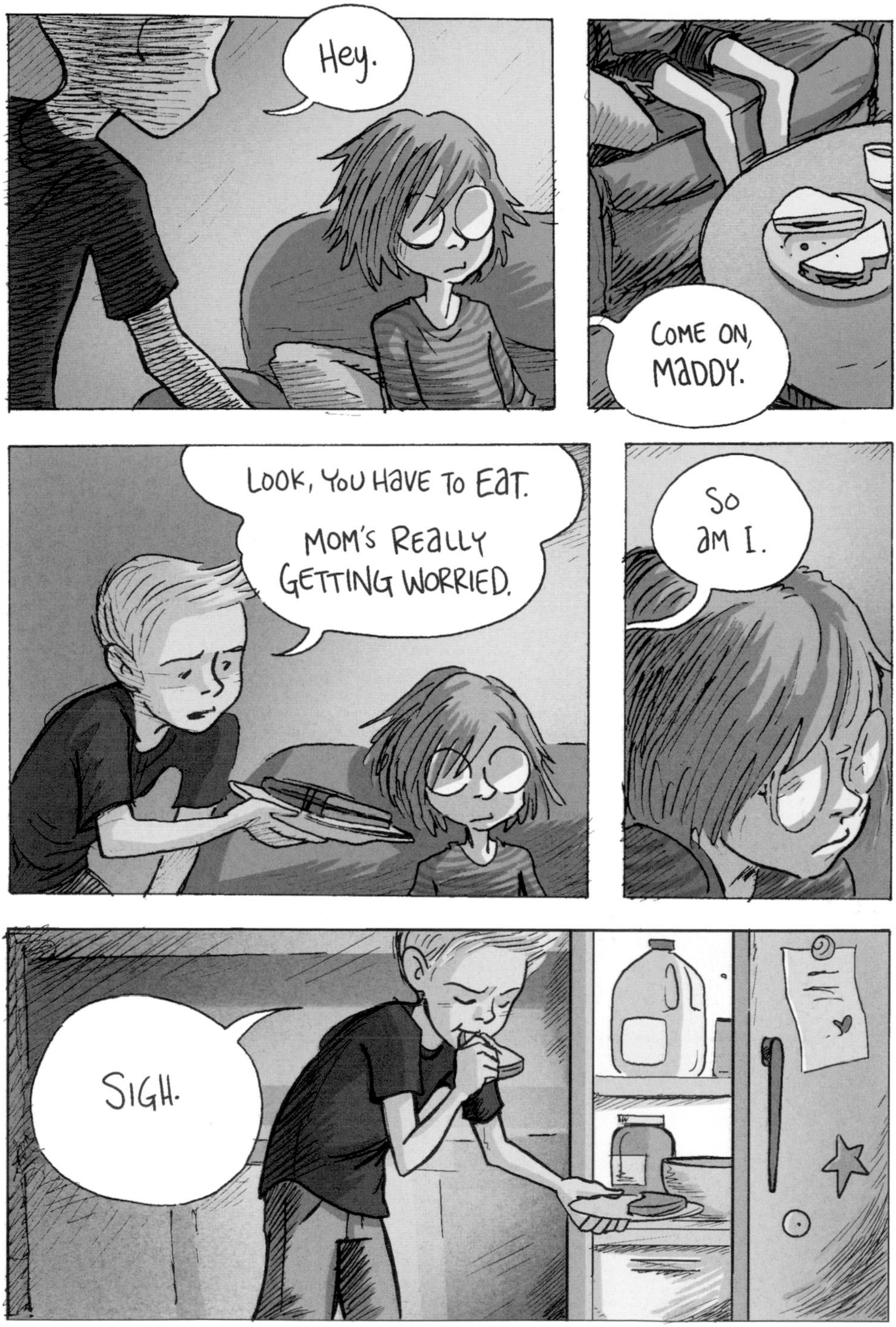
Hey.
COME ON, MADDY.
LOOK, YOU HAVE TO EAT.
MOM'S REALLY GETTING WORRIED.
SO AM I.
SIGH.

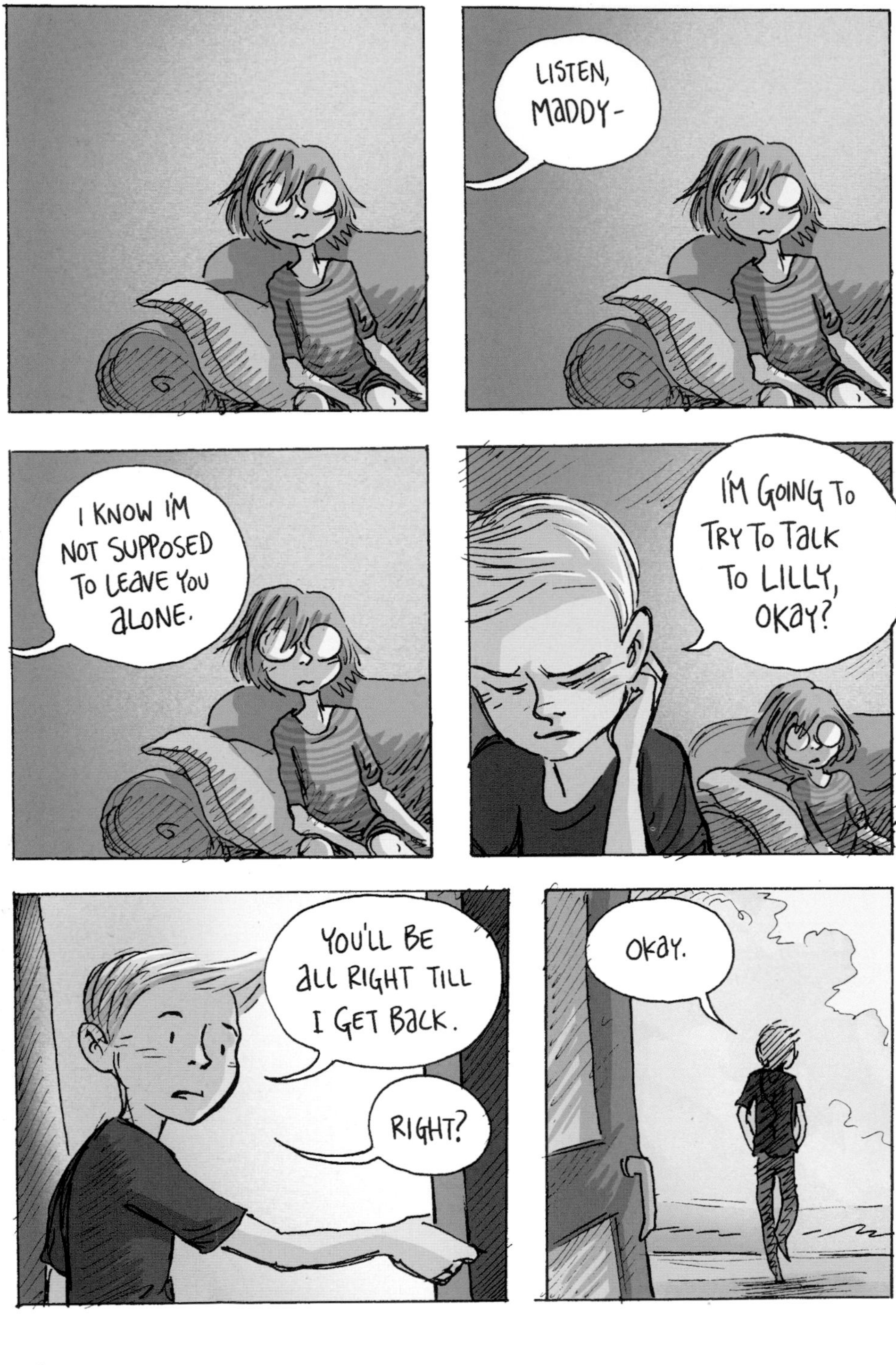
LISTEN, MADDY-
I KNOW I'M NOT SUPPOSED TO LEAVE YOU ALONE.
I'M GOING TO TRY TO TALK TO LILLY, OKAY?
YOU'LL BE ALL RIGHT TILL I GET BACK.
RIGHT?
OKAY.

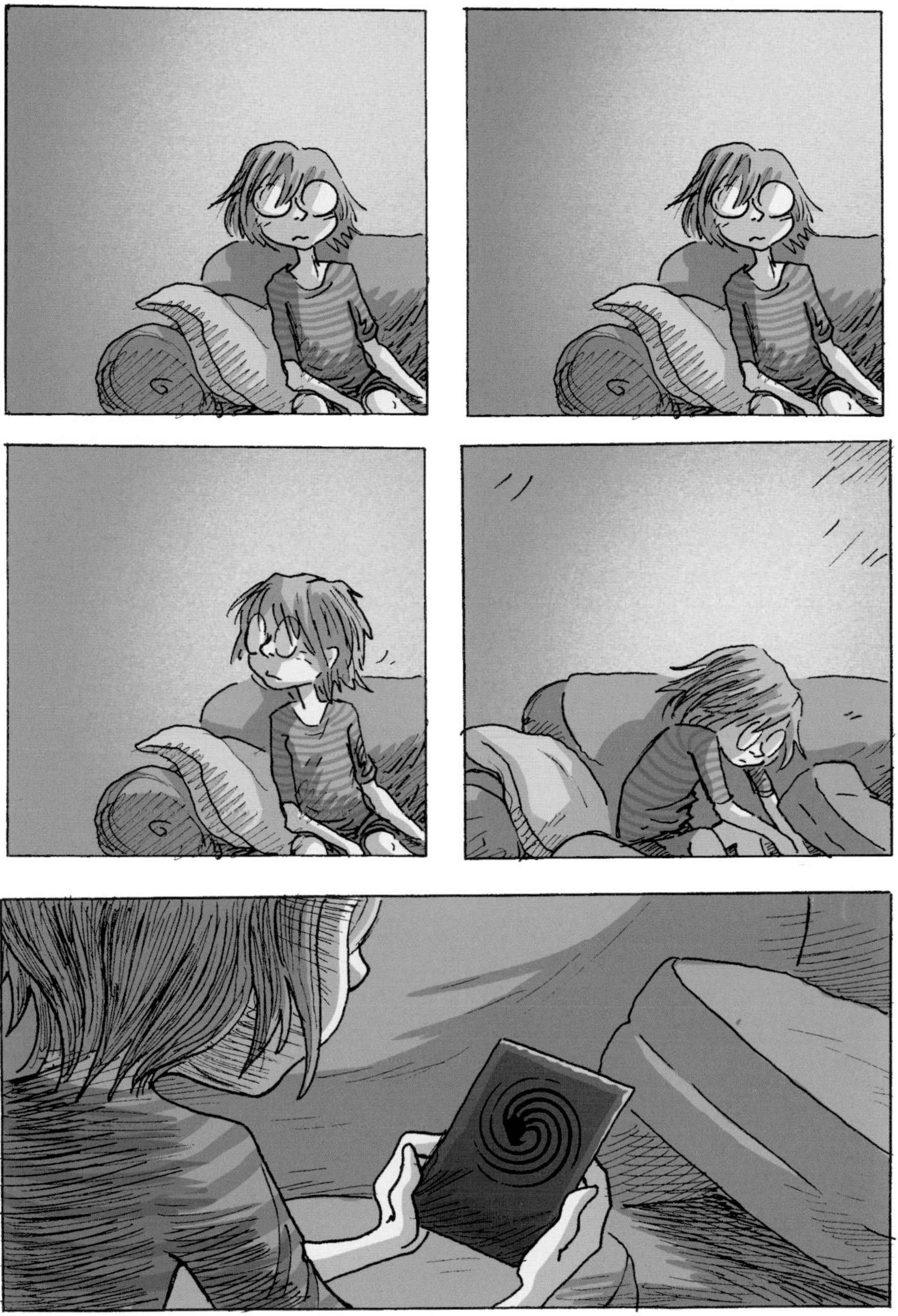

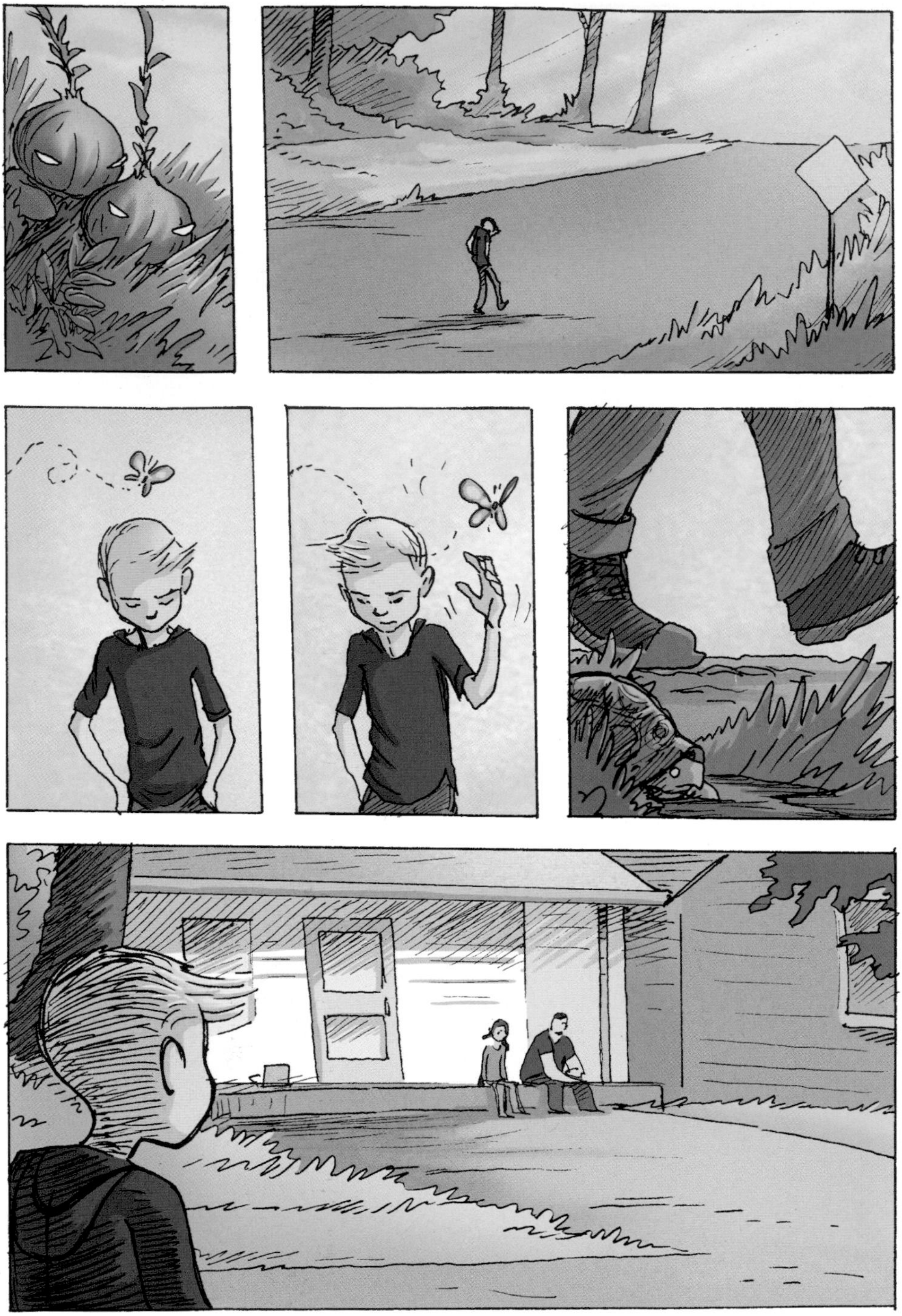

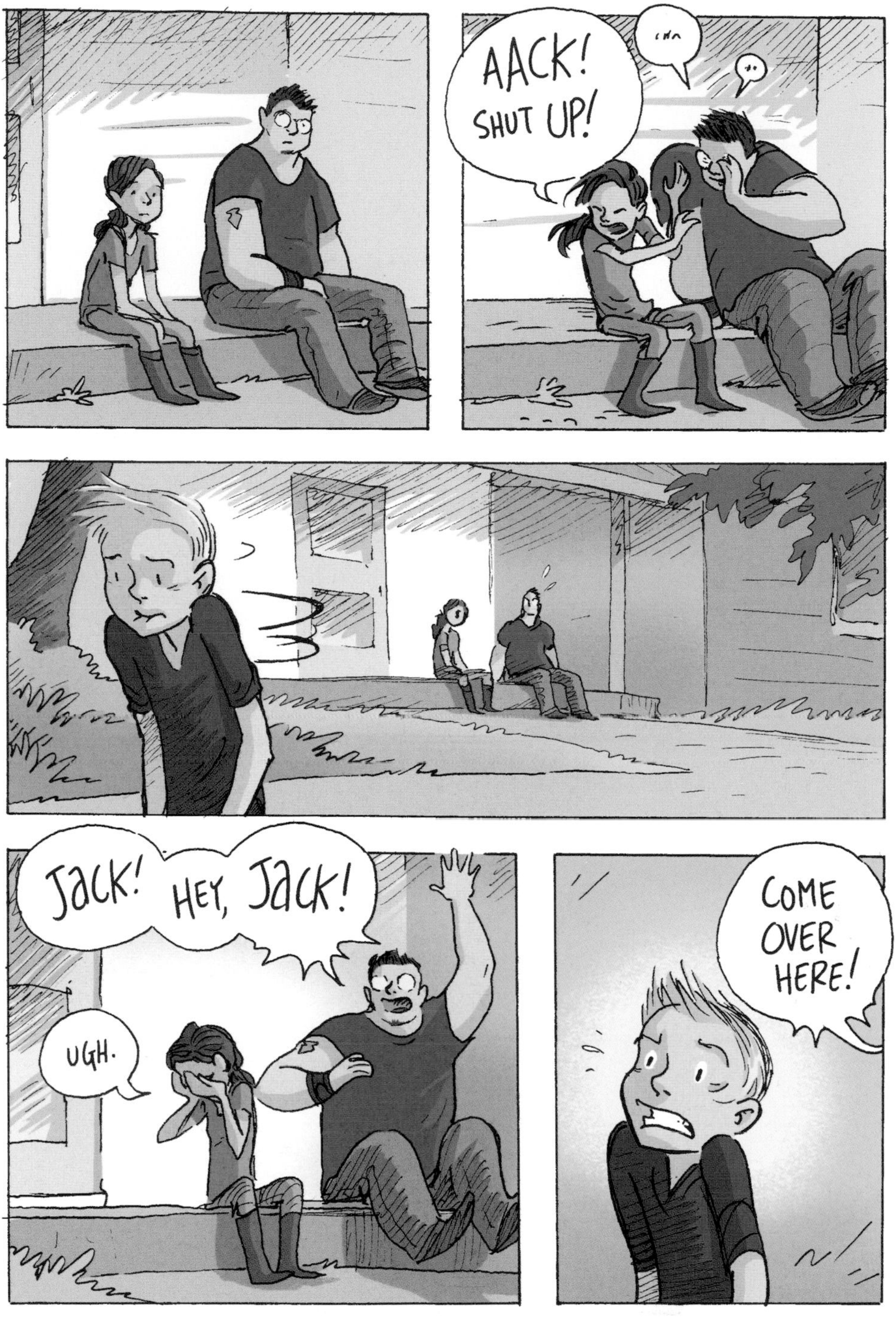
AACK! SHUT UP!
JACK!
HEY, JACK!
UGH.
COME OVER HERE!

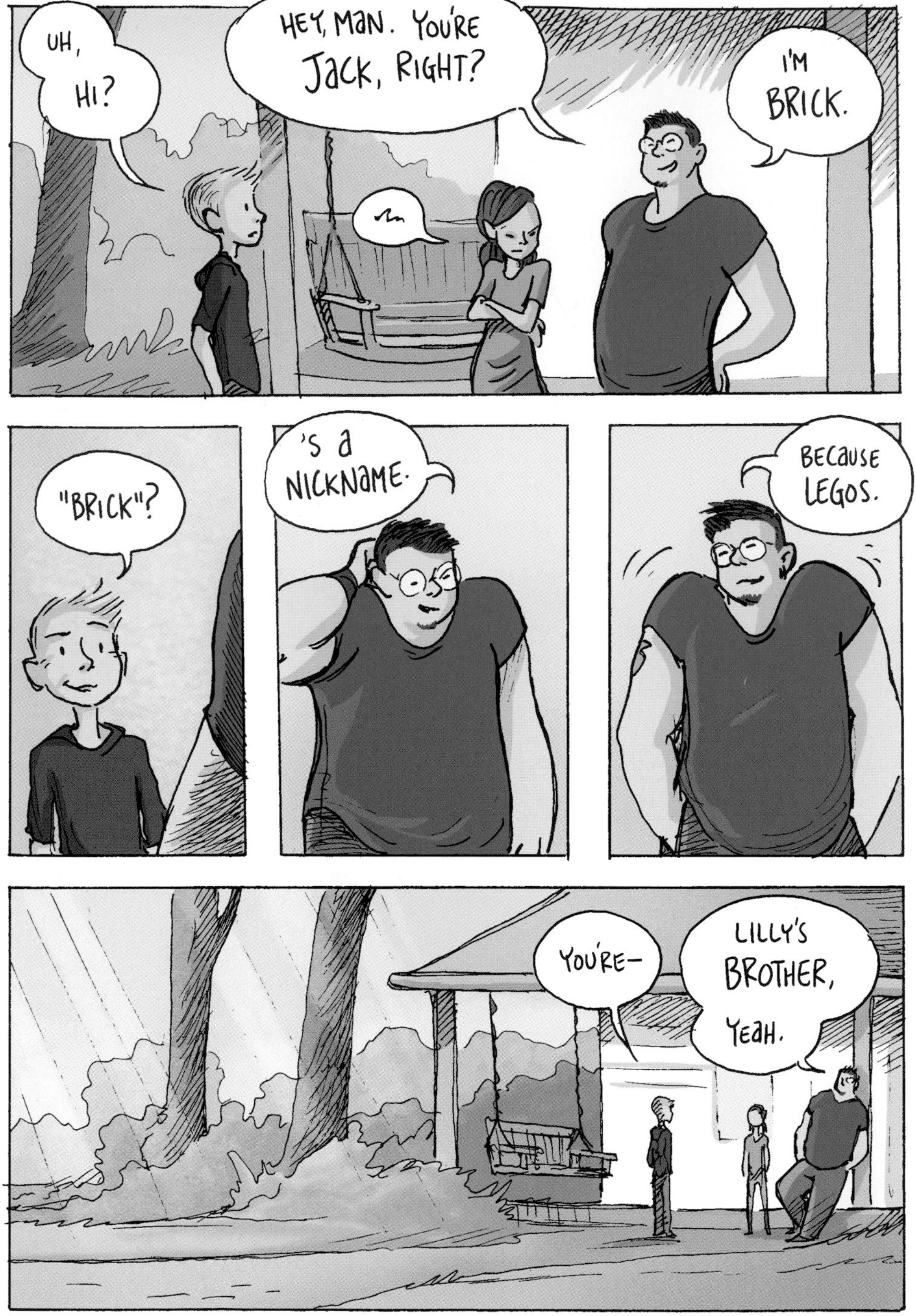
UH,
HI?
HEY, MAN. YOU'RE JACK, RIGHT?
I'M BRICK.
"BRICK"?
'S A NICKNAME.
BECAUSE LEGOS.
YOU'RE–
LILLY'S BROTHER, YEAH.

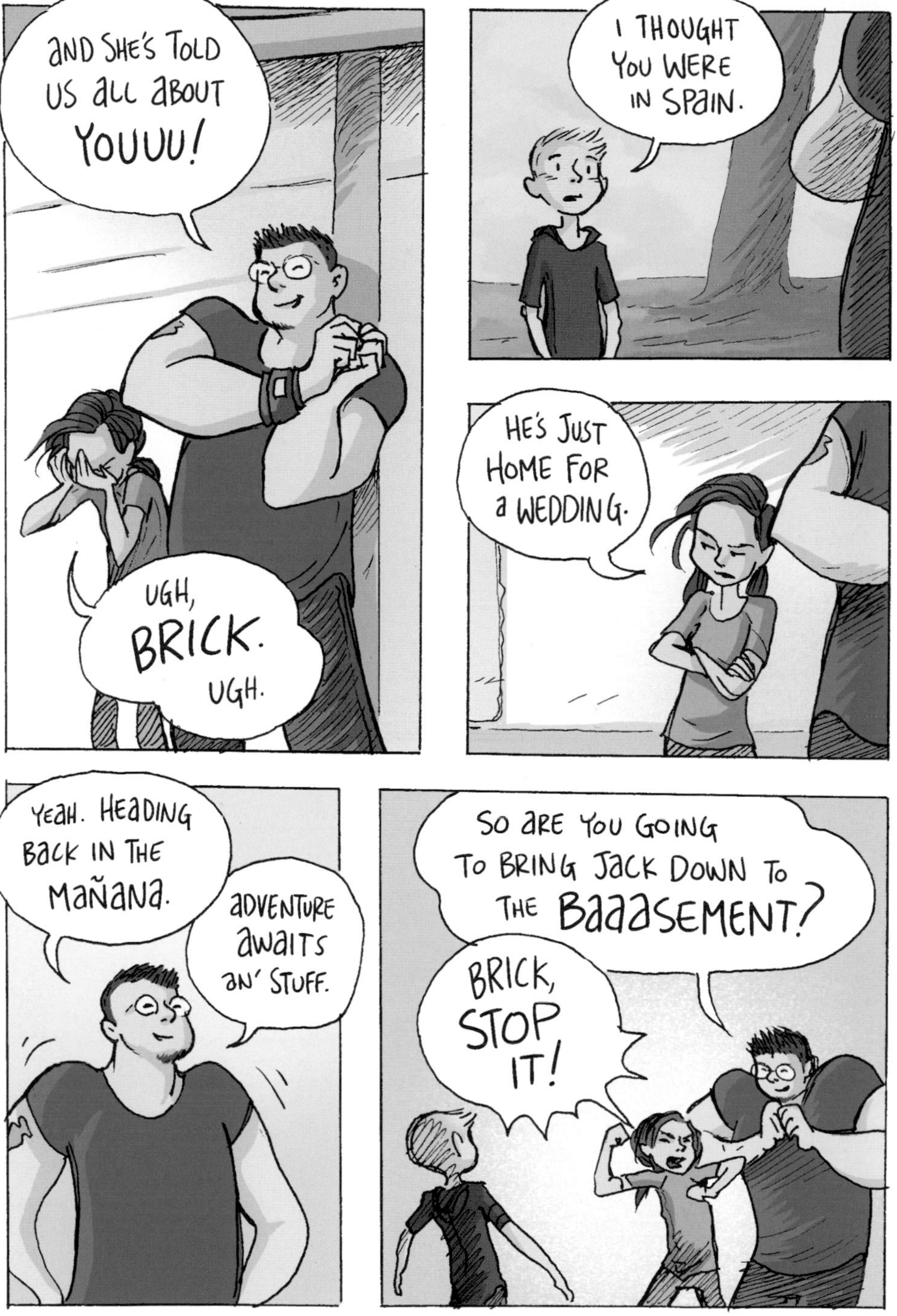
AND SHE'S TOLD US ALL ABOUT YOUUU!
UGH, BRICK. UGH.
I THOUGHT YOU WERE IN SPAIN.
HE'S JUST HOME FOR A WEDDING.
YEAH. HEADING BACK IN THE MAÑANA.
ADVENTURE AWAITS AN' STUFF.
SO ARE YOU GOING TO BRING JACK DOWN TO THE BAAASEMENT?
BRICK, STOP IT!

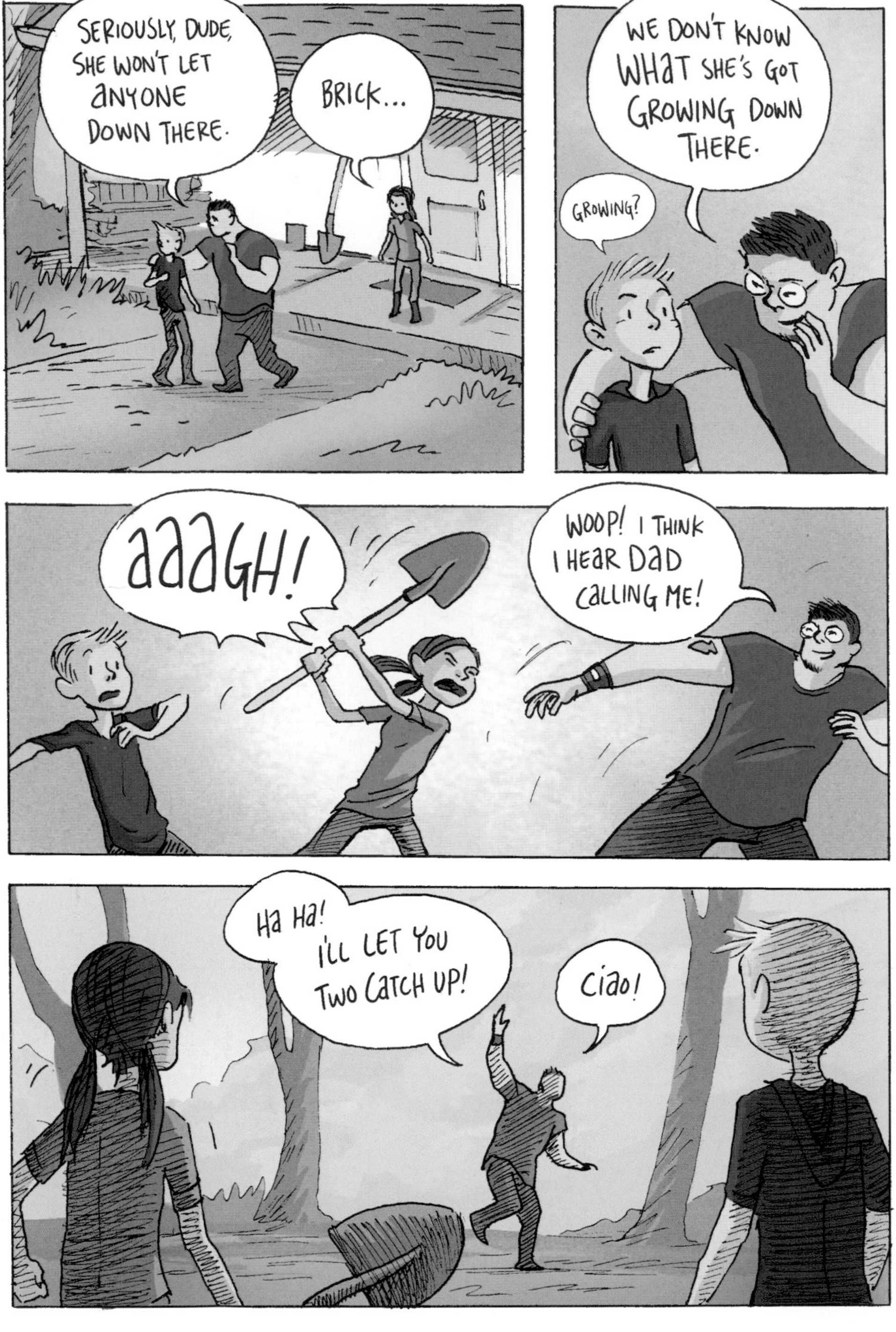
SERIOUSLY, DUDE, SHE WON'T LET ANYONE DOWN THERE.
BRICK...
WE DON'T KNOW WHAT SHE'S GOT GROWING DOWN THERE.
GROWING?
AAAGH!
WOOP! I THINK I HEAR DAD CALLING ME!
HA HA! I'LL LET YOU TWO CATCH UP!
CIAO!

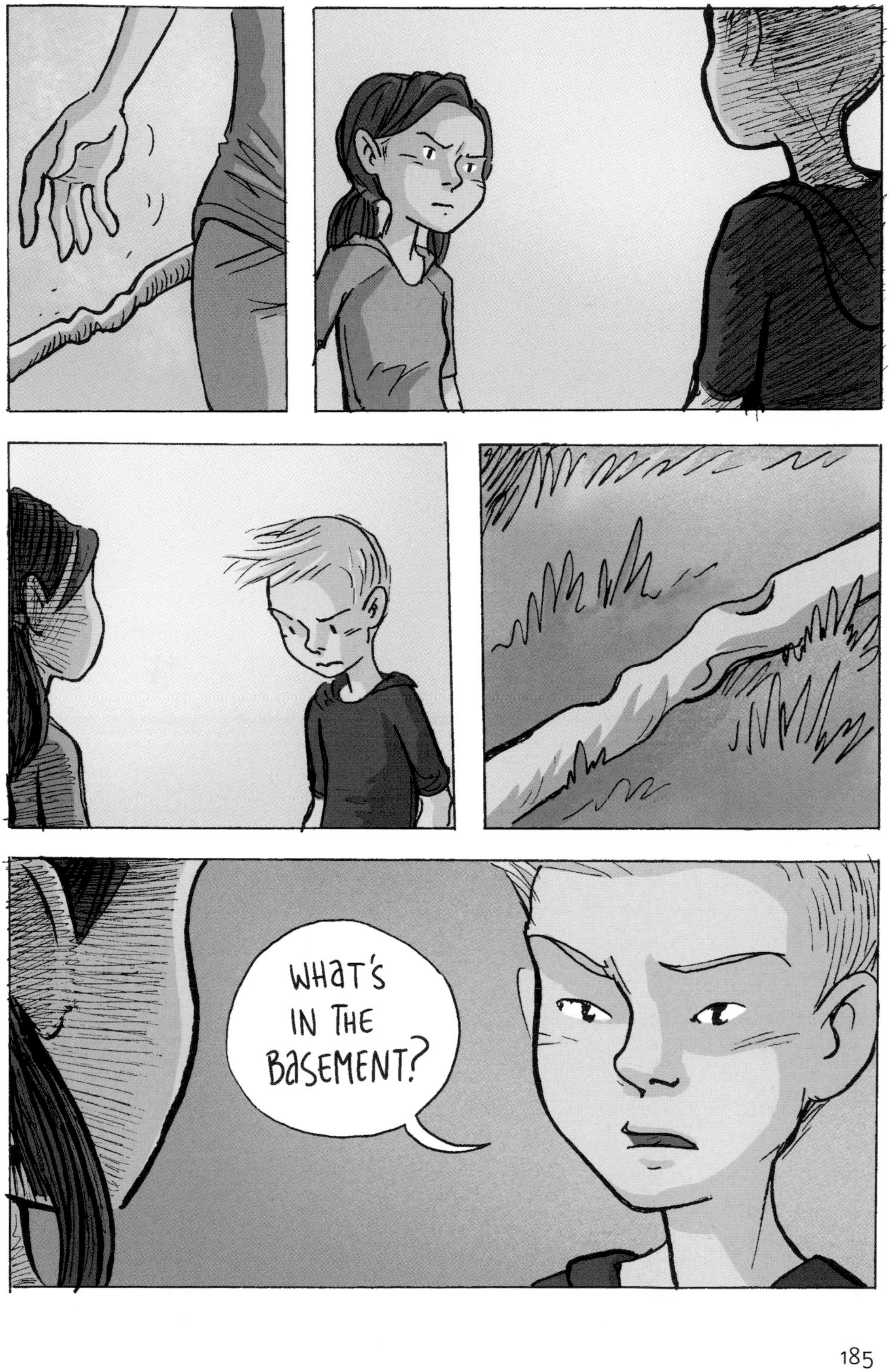
WHAT'S IN THE BASEMENT?

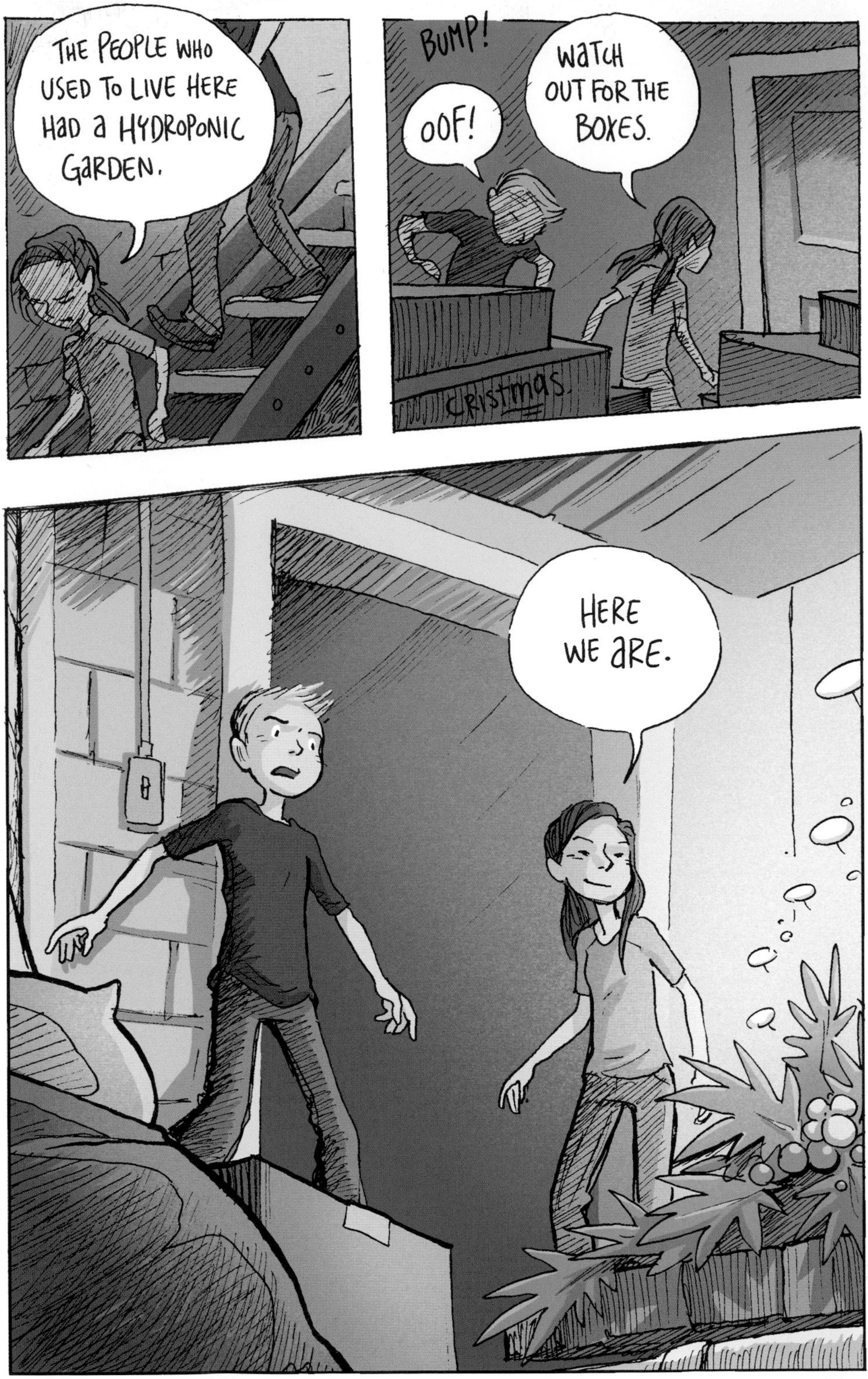
THE PEOPLE WHO USED TO LIVE HERE HAD A HYDROPONIC GARDEN.
BUMP!
WATCH OUT FOR THE BOXES.
OOF!
CRISTMAS.
HERE WE ARE.

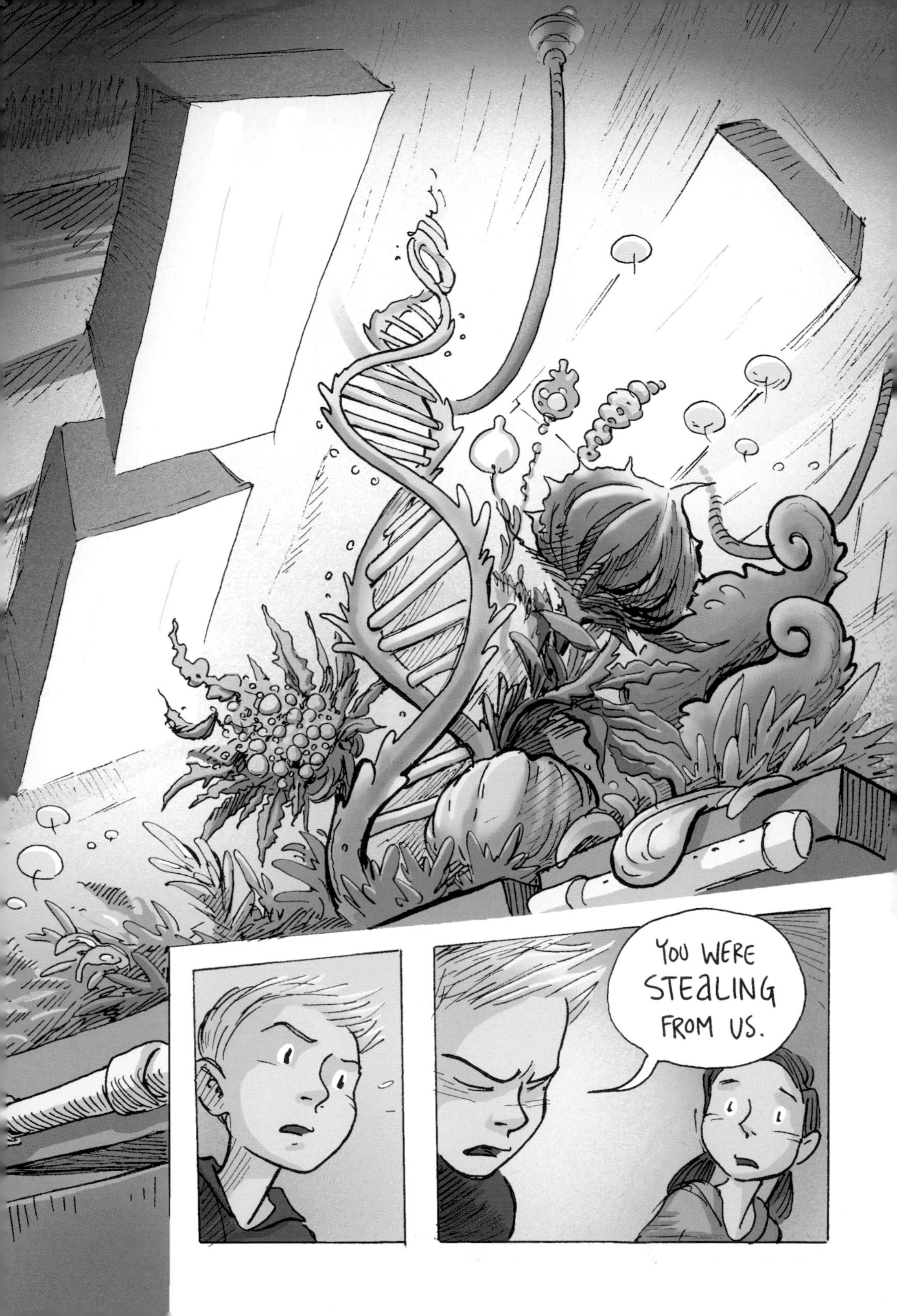
YOU WERE STEALING FROM US.

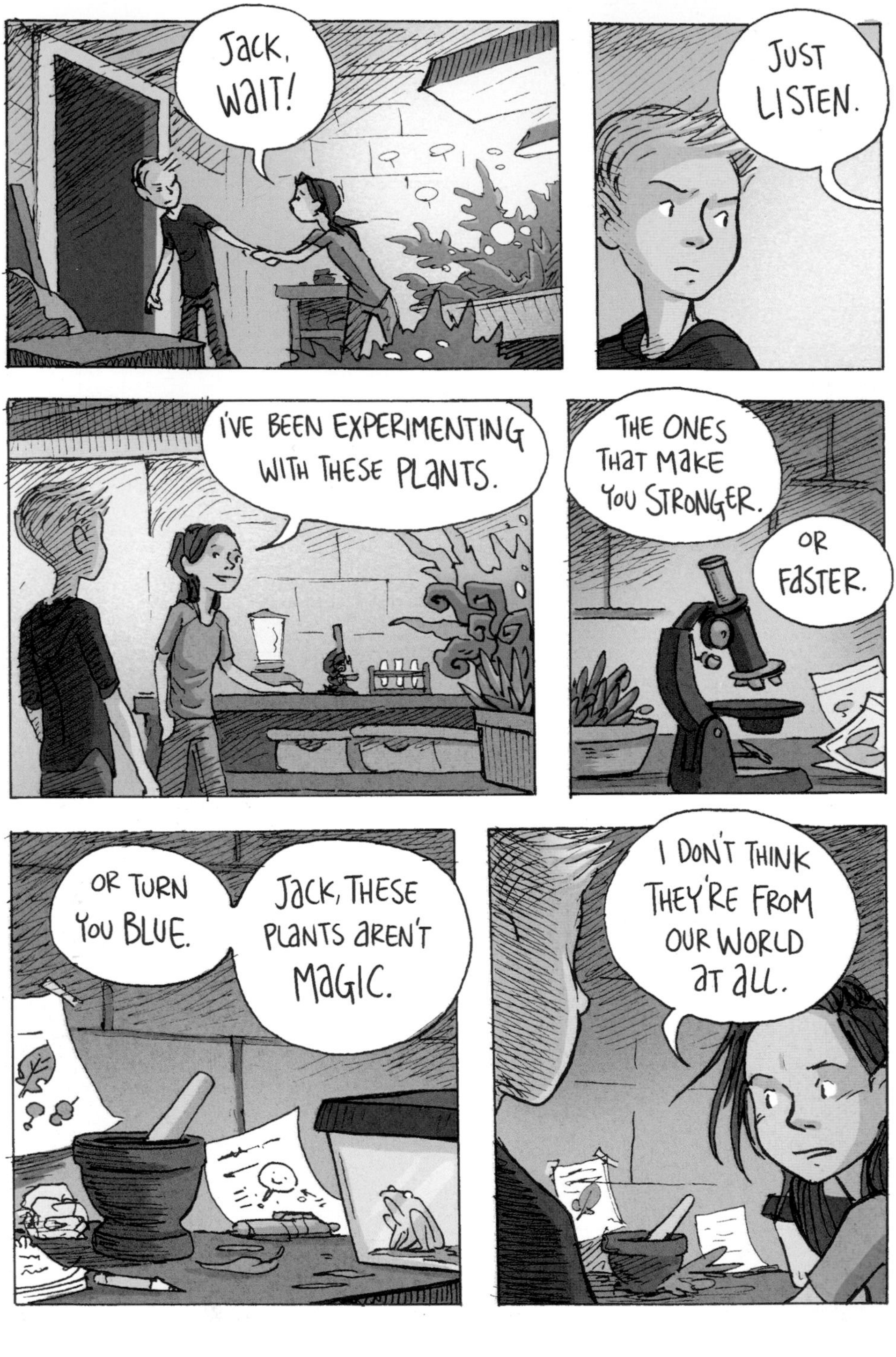
JACK, WAIT!
JUST LISTEN.
I'VE BEEN EXPERIMENTING WITH THESE PLANTS.
THE ONES THAT MAKE YOU STRONGER.
OR FASTER.
OR TURN YOU BLUE.
JACK, THESE PLANTS AREN'T MAGIC.
I DON'T THINK THEY'RE FROM OUR WORLD AT ALL.

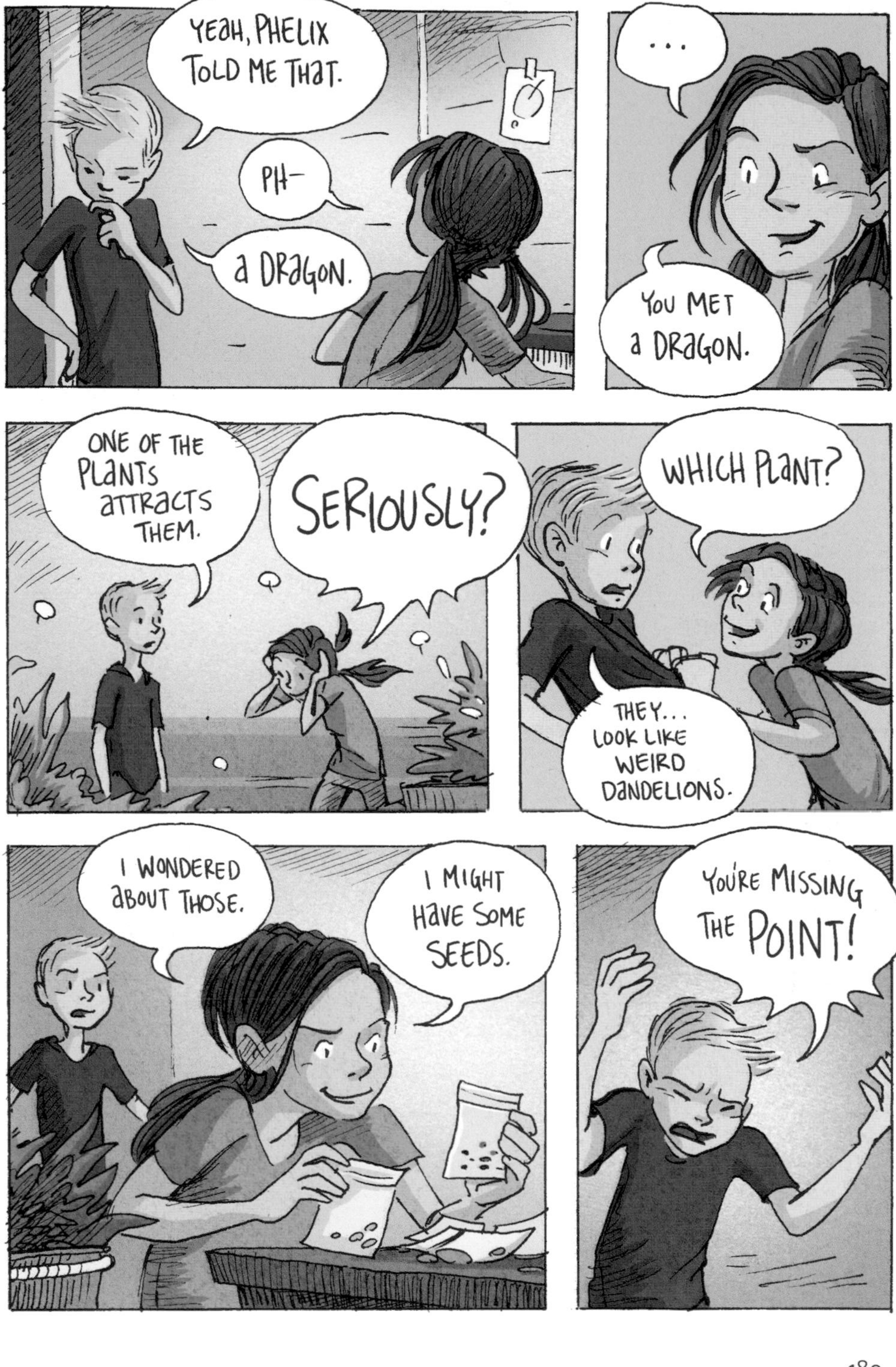
YEAH, PHELIX TOLD ME THAT.
PH—
A DRAGON.
...
YOU MET A DRAGON.
ONE OF THE PLANTS ATTRACTS THEM.
SERIOUSLY?
WHICH PLANT?
THEY... LOOK LIKE WEIRD DANDELIONS.
I WONDERED ABOUT THOSE.
I MIGHT HAVE SOME SEEDS.
YOU'RE MISSING THE POINT!

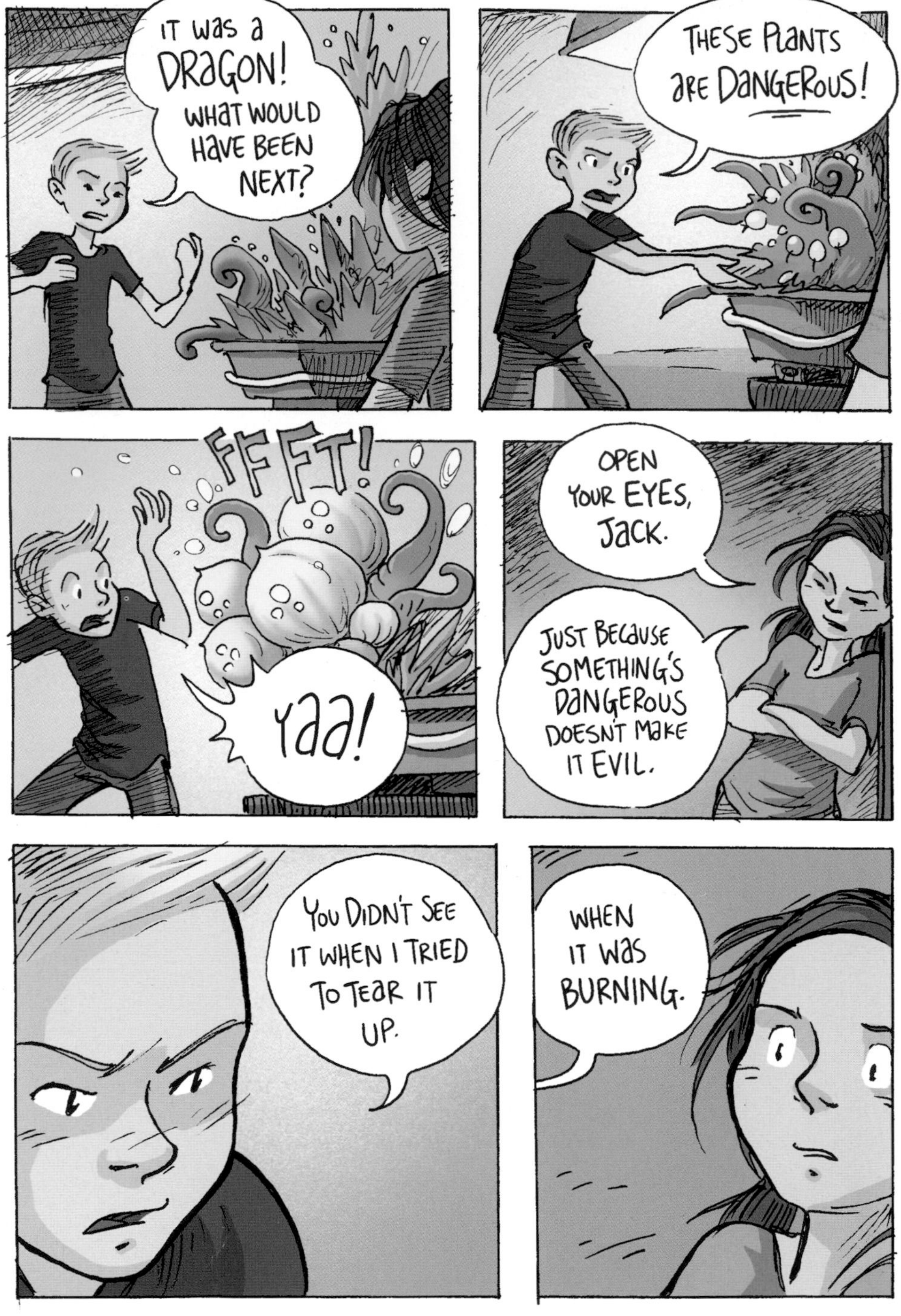
IT WAS A DRAGON! WHAT WOULD HAVE BEEN NEXT?
THESE PLANTS ARE DANGEROUS!
FFFT!
YAA!
OPEN YOUR EYES, JACK.
JUST BECAUSE SOMETHING'S DANGEROUS DOESN'T MAKE IT EVIL.
YOU DIDN'T SEE IT WHEN I TRIED TO TEAR IT UP.
WHEN IT WAS BURNING.

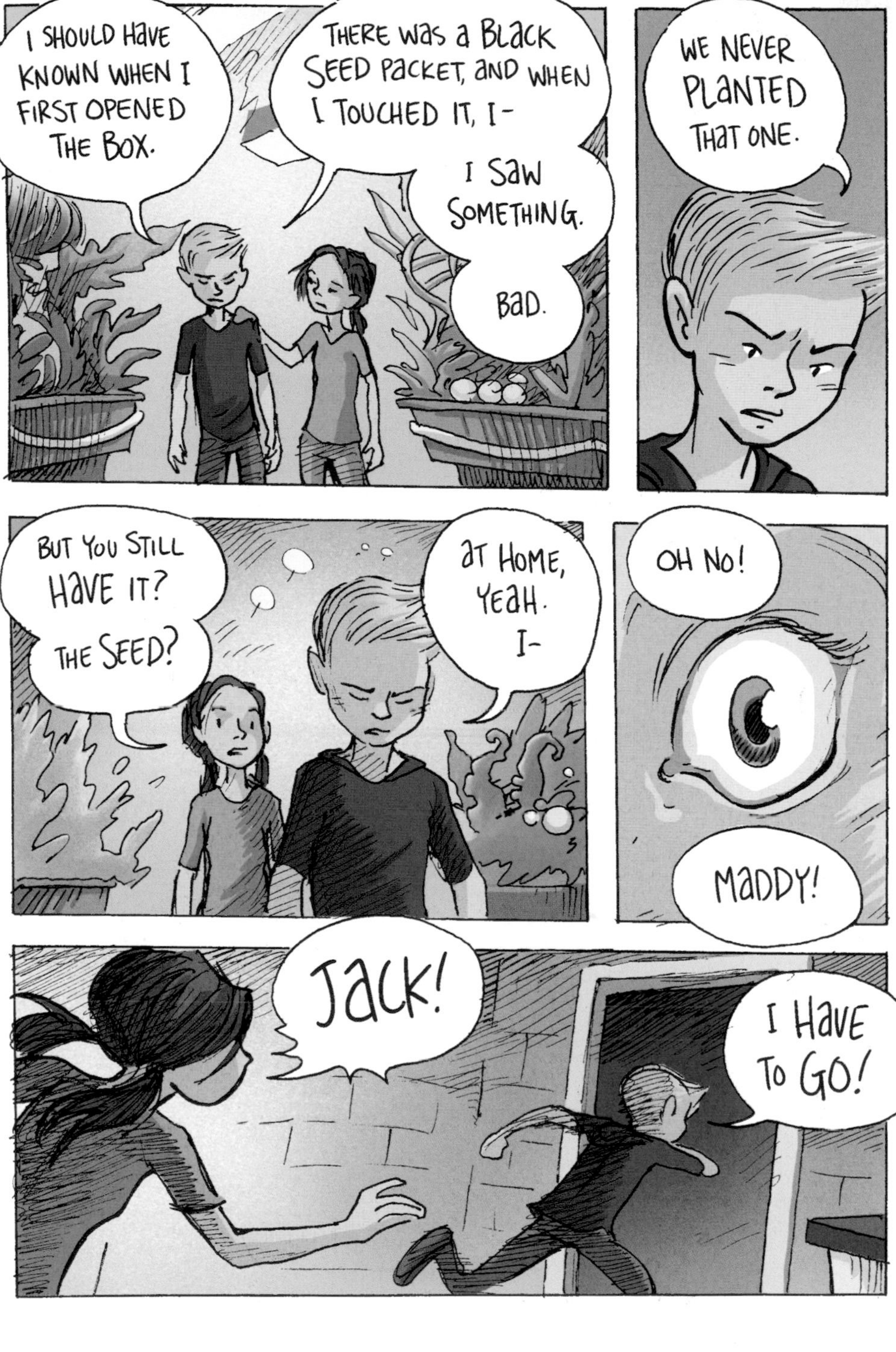
I SHOULD HAVE KNOWN WHEN I FIRST OPENED THE BOX.
THERE WAS A BLACK SEED PACKET, AND WHEN I TOUCHED IT, I-
I SAW SOMETHING.
BAD.
WE NEVER PLANTED THAT ONE.
BUT YOU STILL HAVE IT?
THE SEED?
AT HOME, YEAH.
I-
OH NO!
MADDY!
JACK!
I HAVE TO GO!

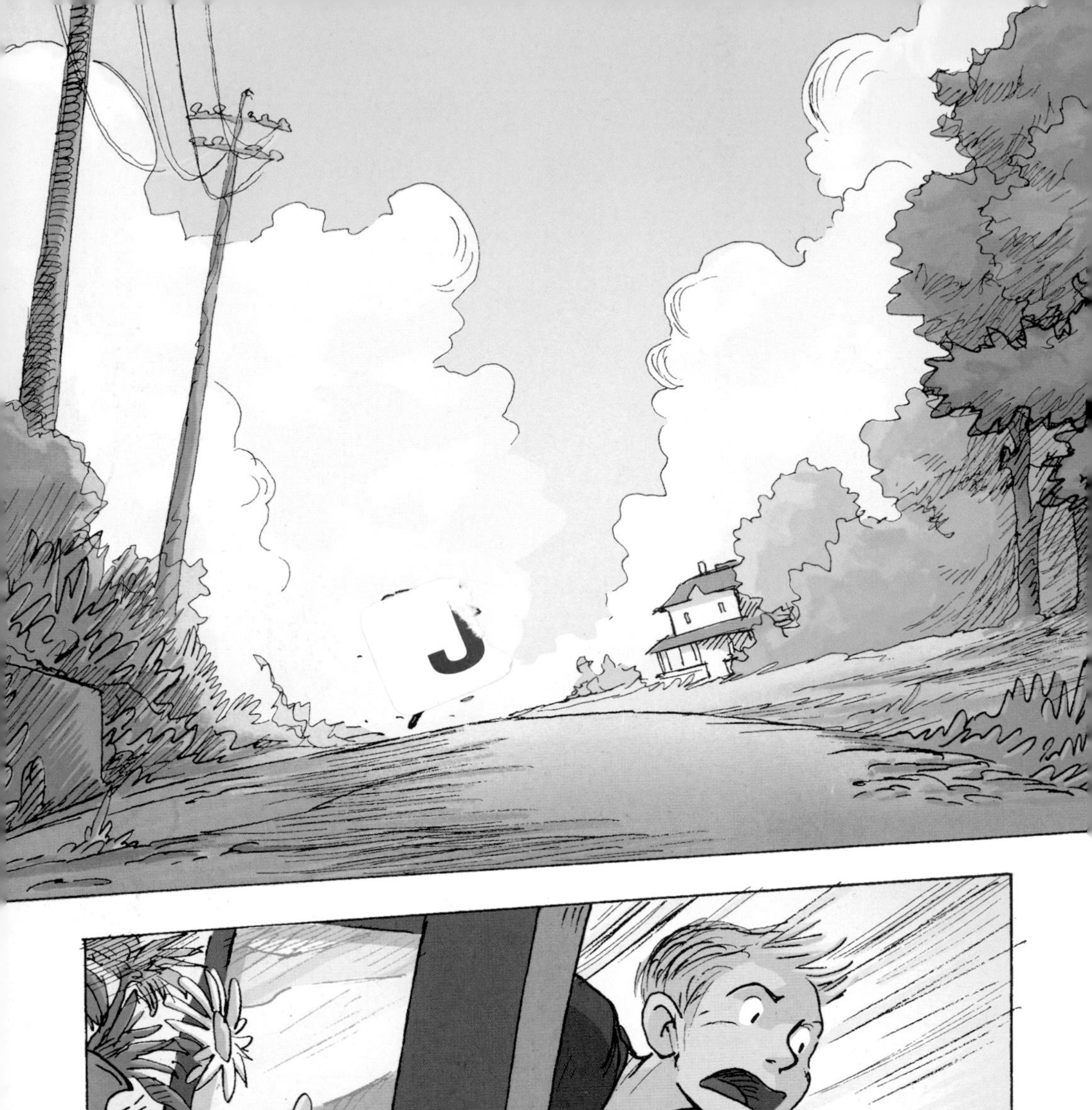
J

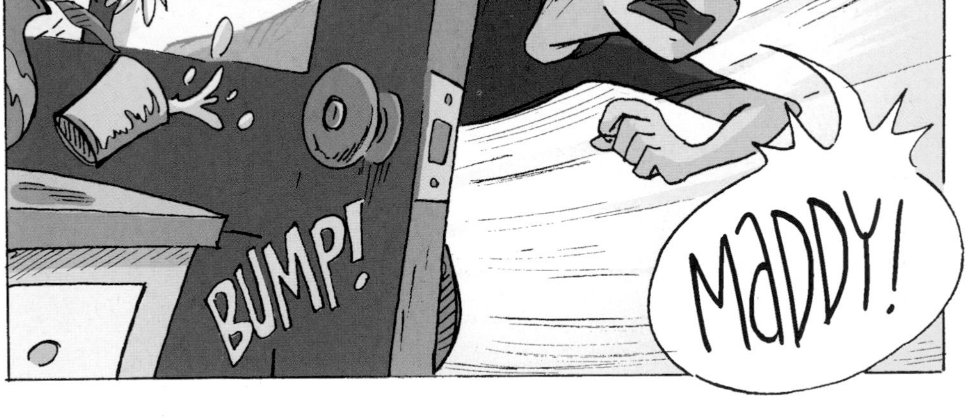
BUMP!
MADDY!

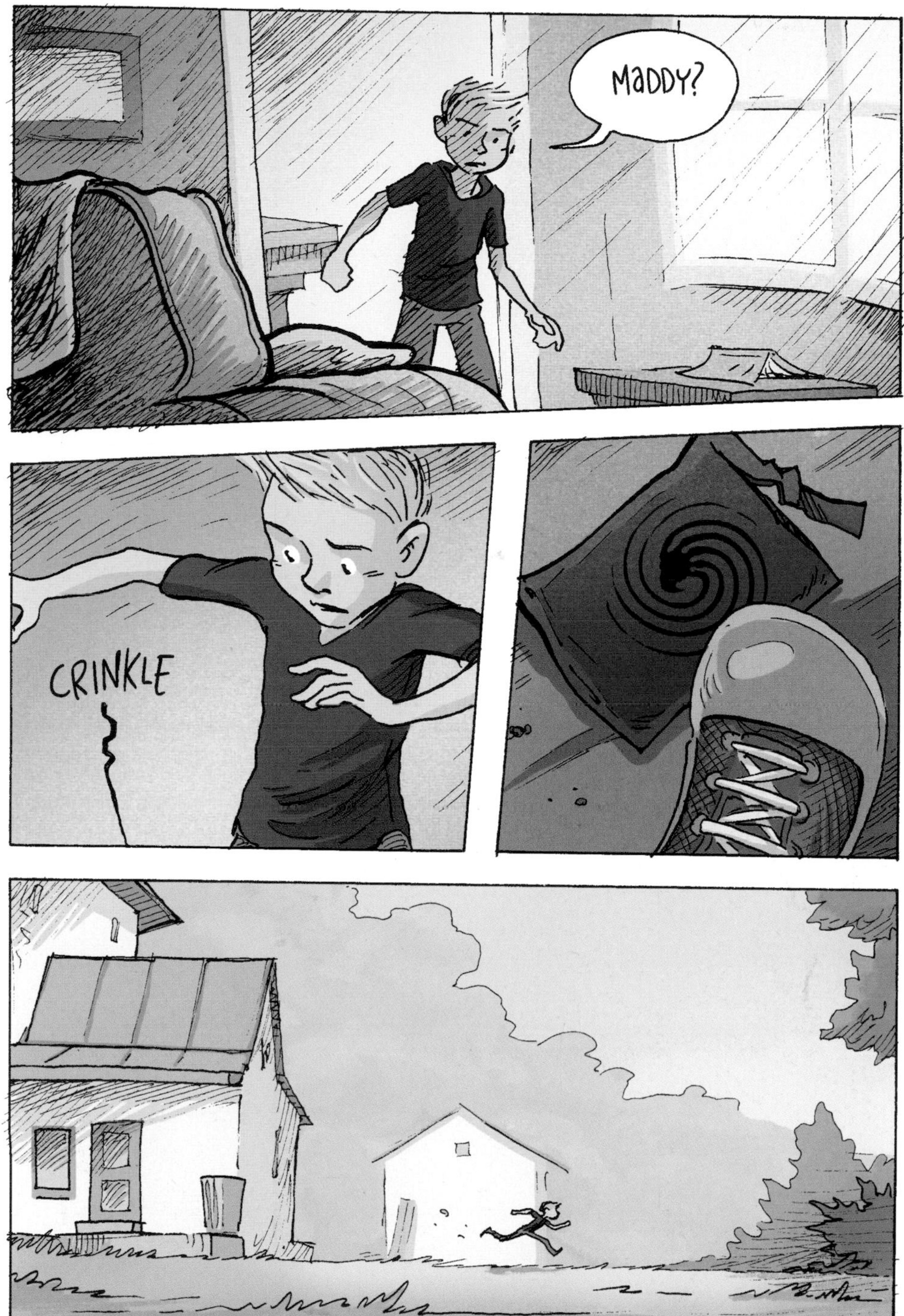
MADDY?
CRINKLE

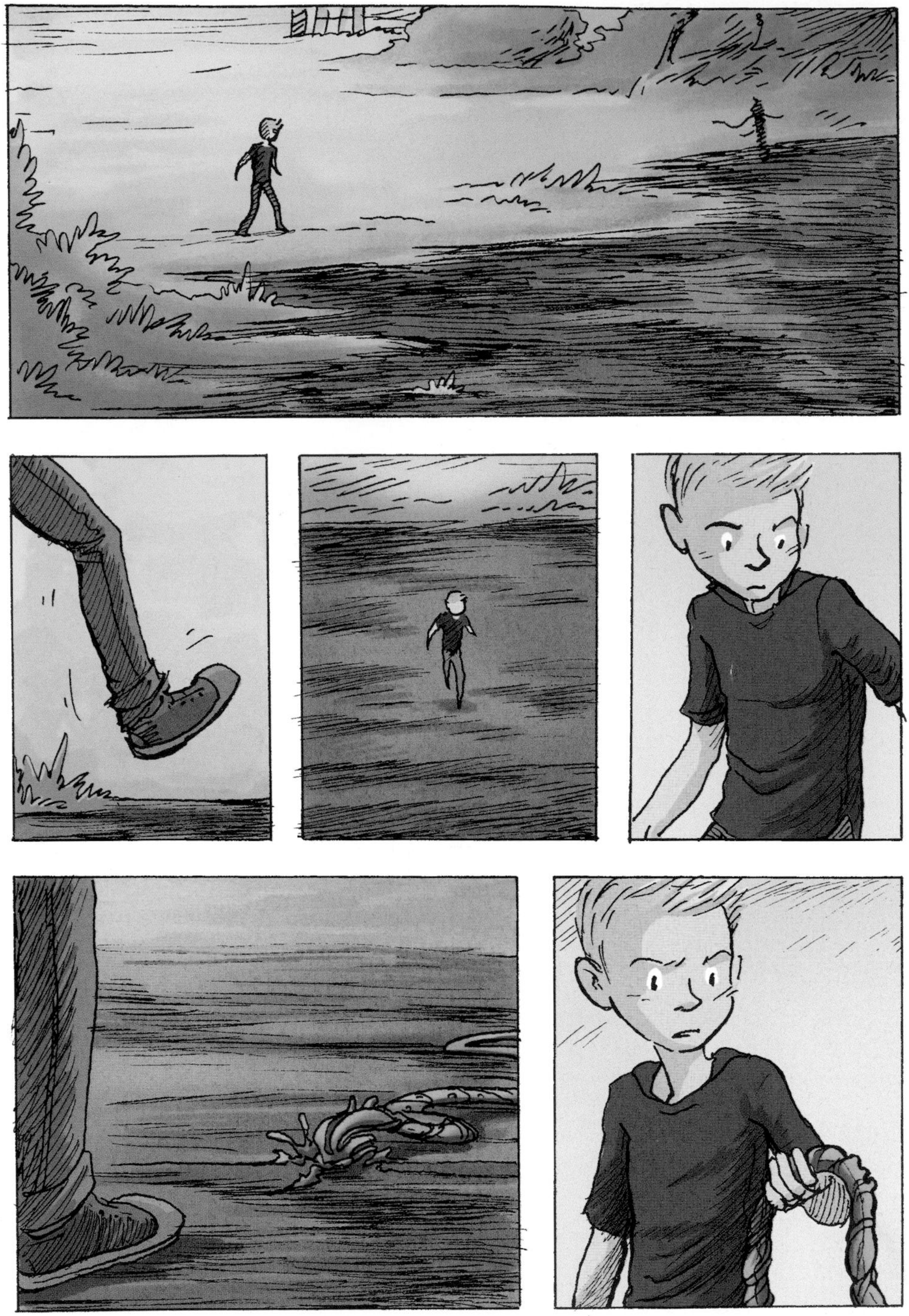

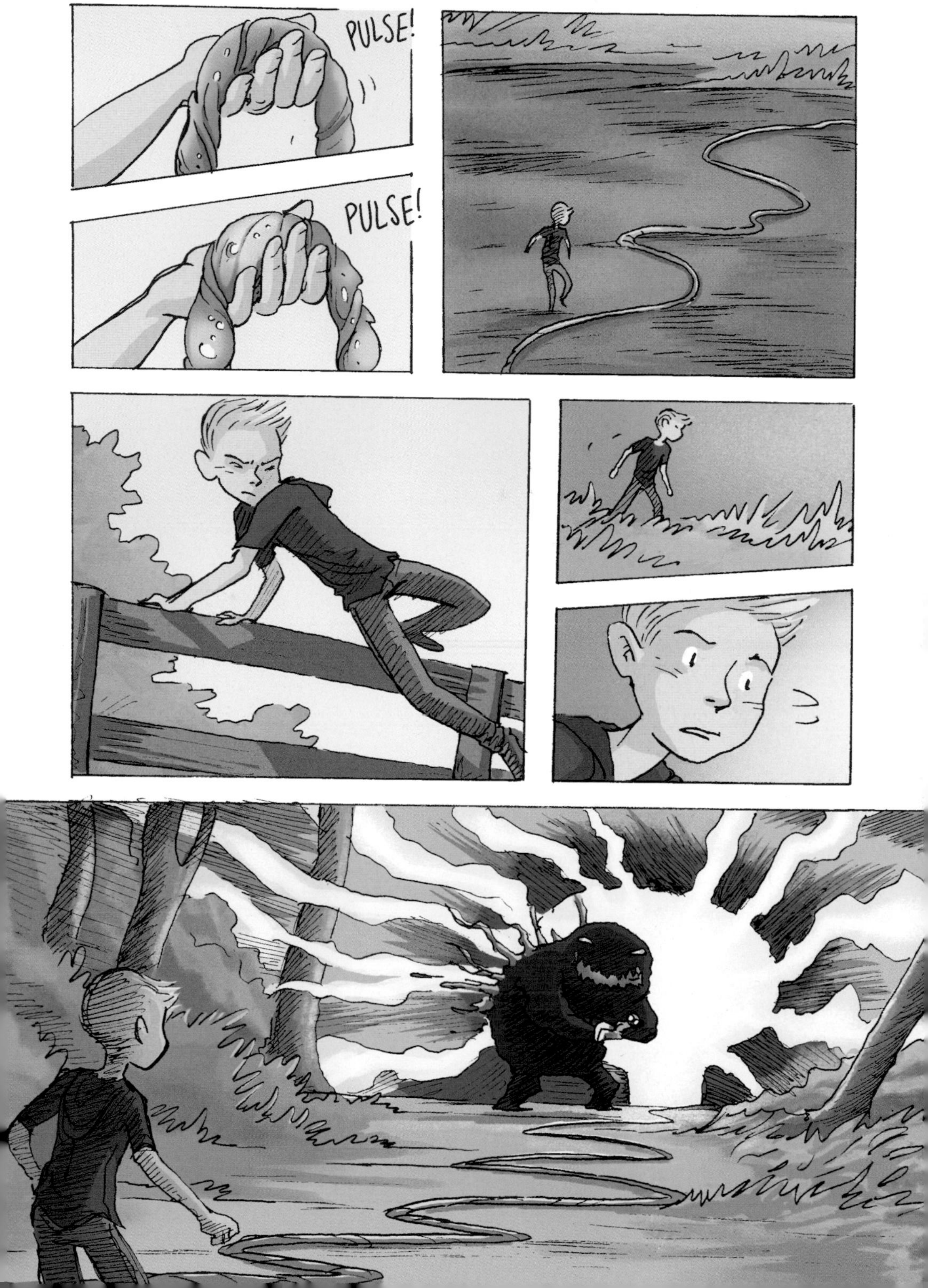
PULSE!
PULSE!

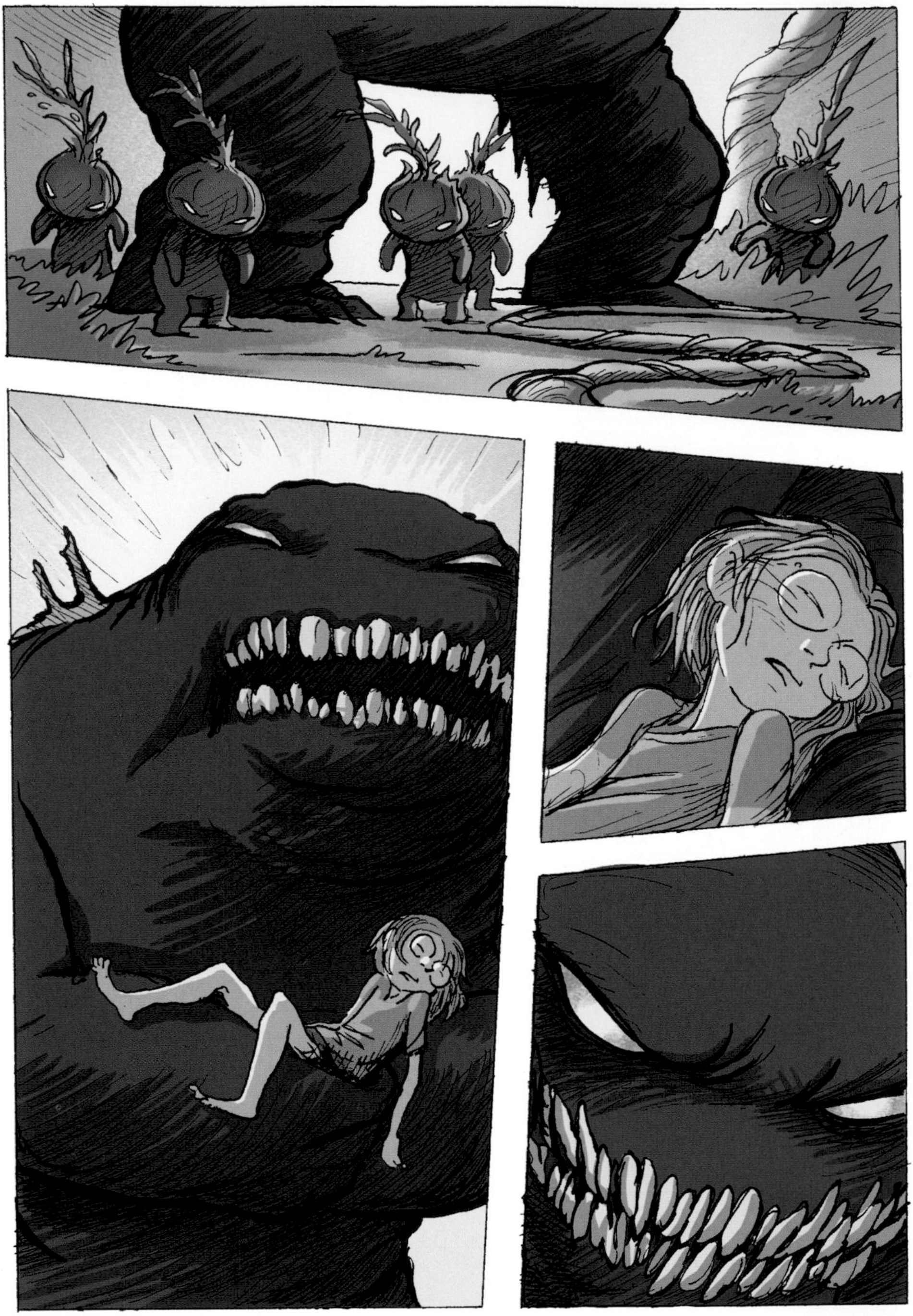

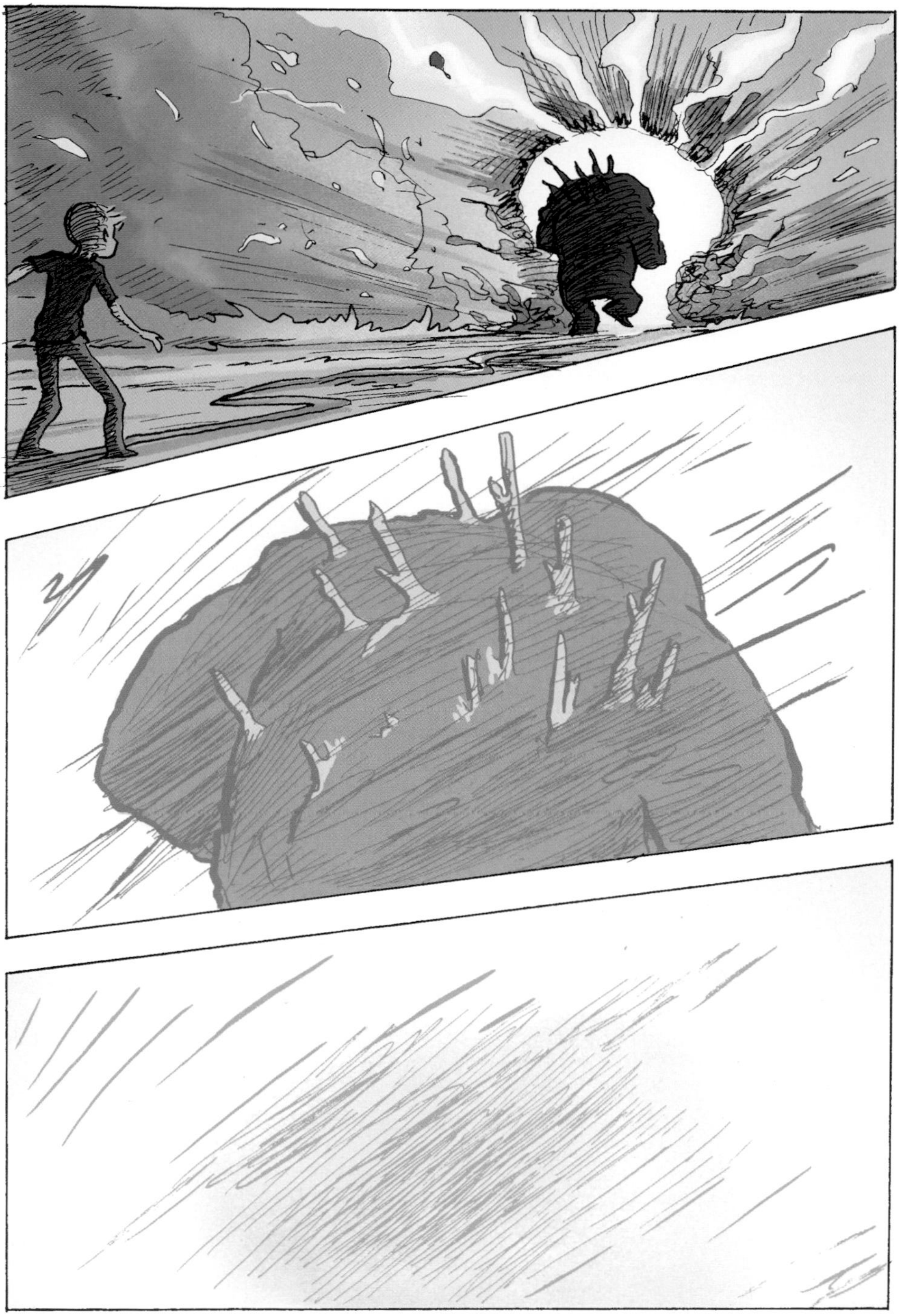

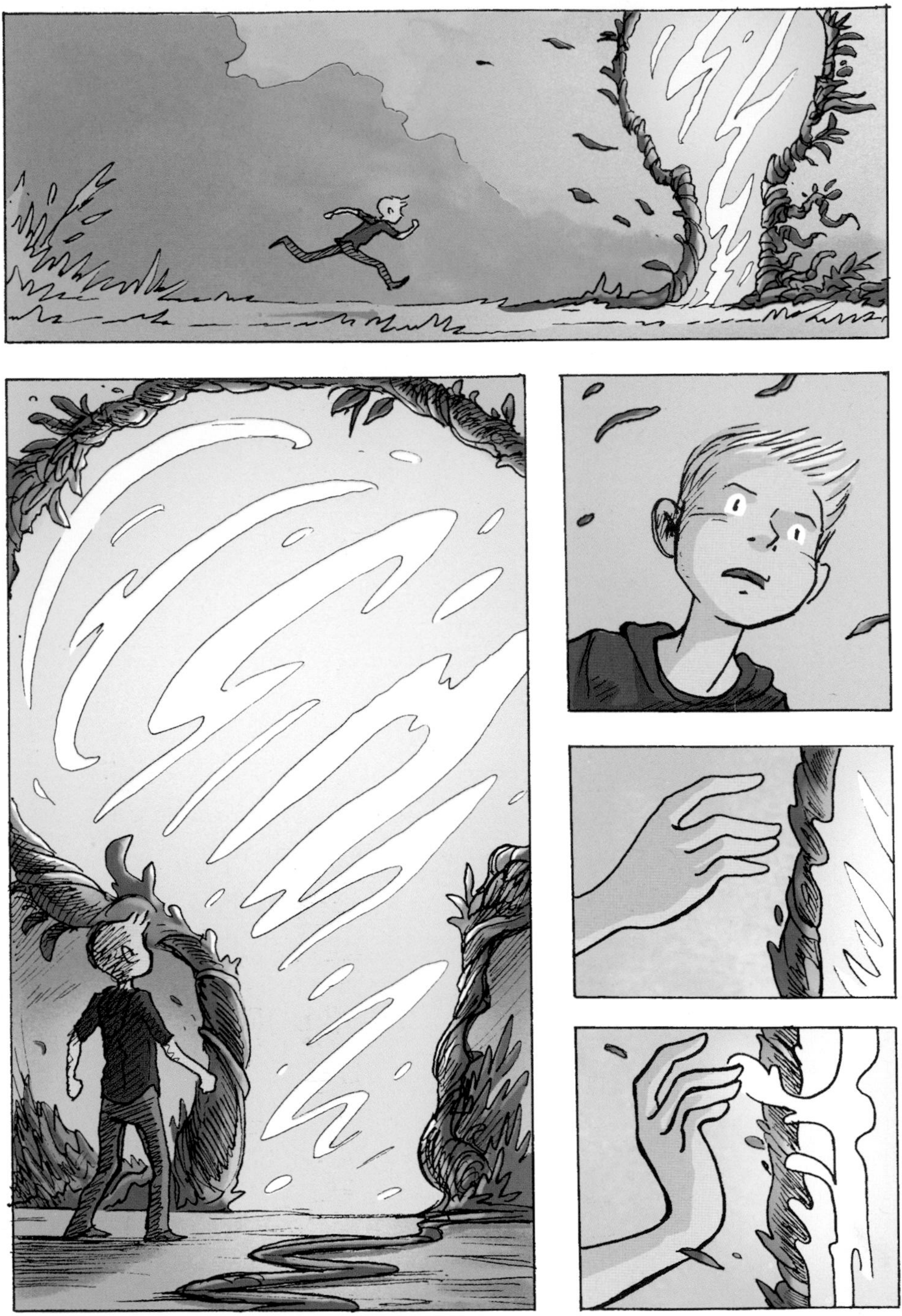

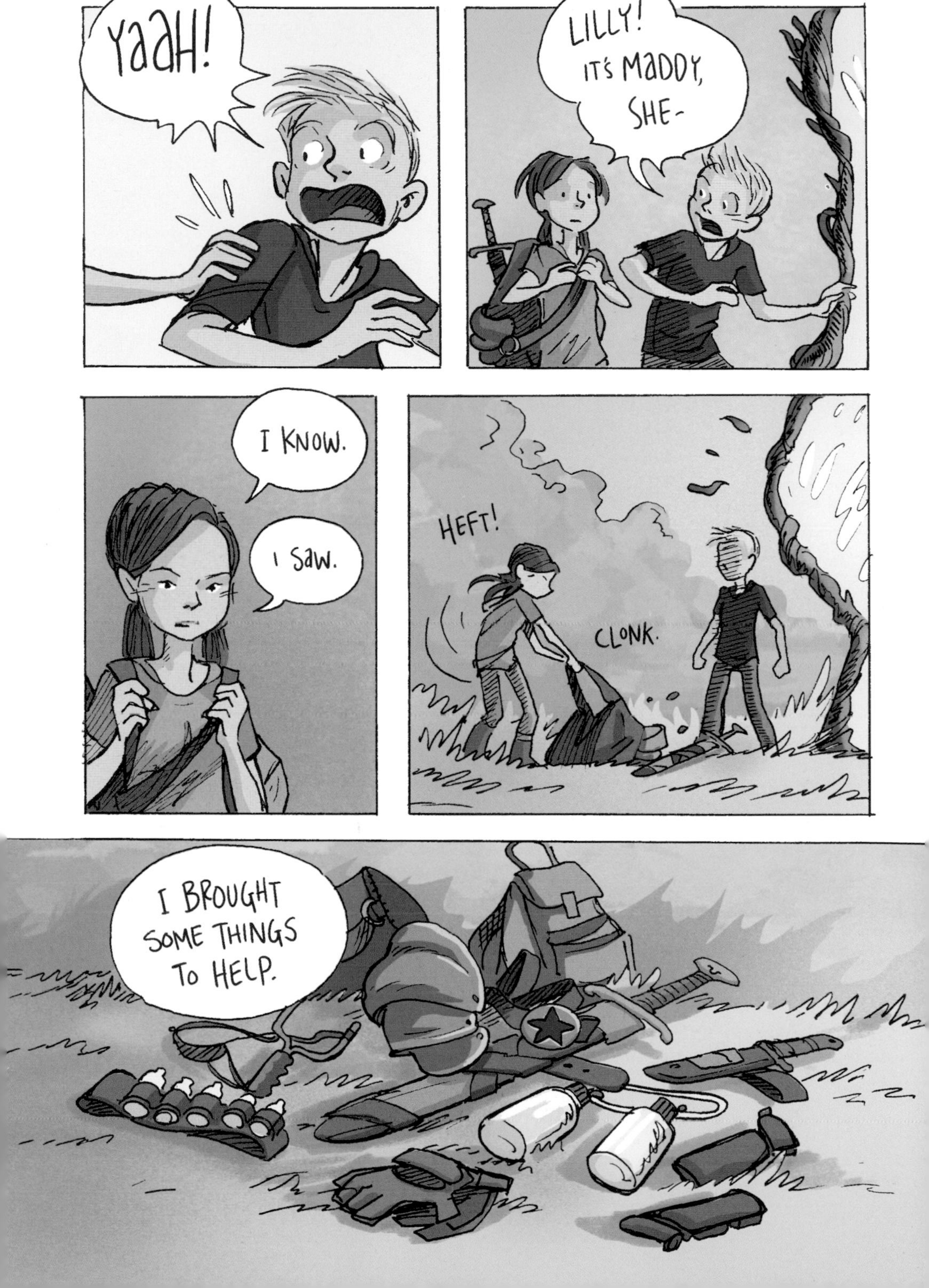

YAAH!
LILLY! IT'S MADDY, SHE-
I KNOW.
I SAW.
HEFT!
CLONK.
I BROUGHT SOME THINGS TO HELP.

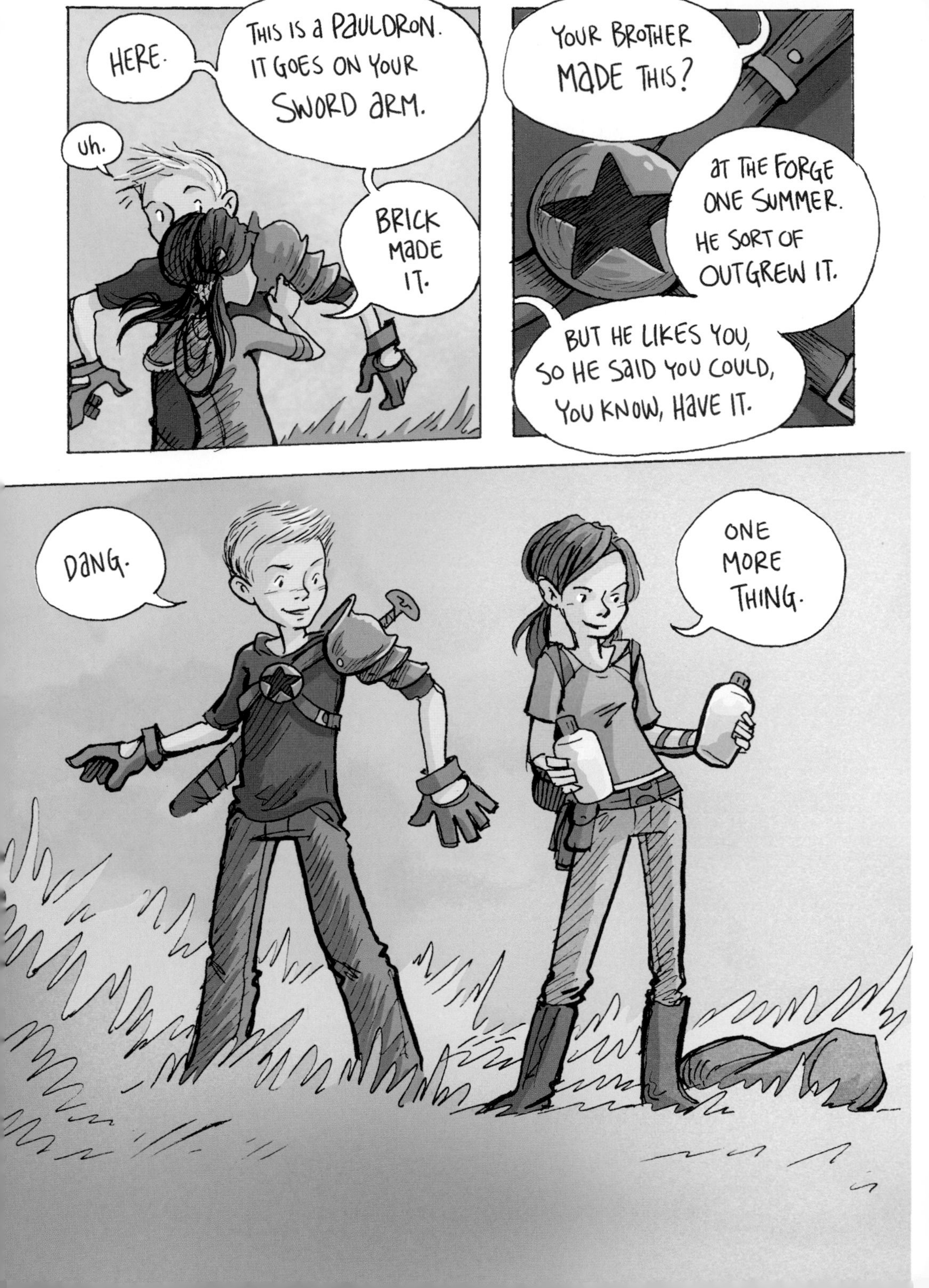
HERE.
THIS IS A PAULDRON. IT GOES ON YOUR SWORD ARM.
UH.
BRICK MADE IT.
YOUR BROTHER MADE THIS?
AT THE FORGE ONE SUMMER. HE SORT OF OUTGREW IT.
BUT HE LIKES YOU, SO HE SAID YOU COULD, YOU KNOW, HAVE IT.
DANG.
ONE MORE THING.

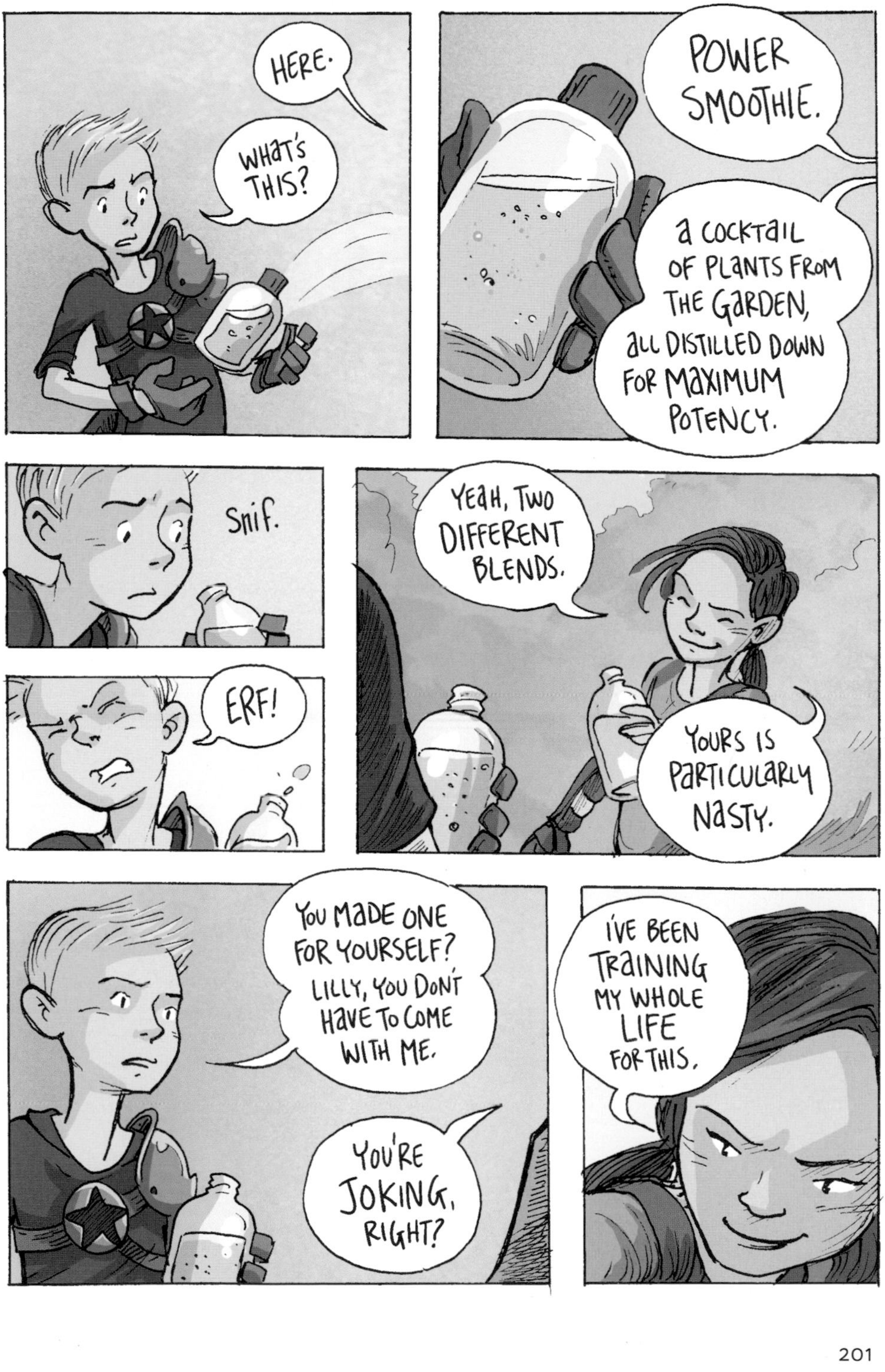
HERE.
WHAT'S THIS?
POWER SMOOTHIE.
a COCKTail OF PLANTS FROM THE GaRDEN, aLL DISTILLED DOWN FOR MaXIMUM POTENCY.
SniF.
ERF!
YeaH, TWO DIFFERENT BLENDS.
YOURS IS PaRTICULaRLY NaSTY.
YOU MaDE ONE FOR YOURSELF? LILLY, YOU DON'T HaVE TO COME WITH ME.
YOU'RE JOKING, RIGHT?
I'VE BEEN TRaINING MY WHOLE LIFE FOR THIS.

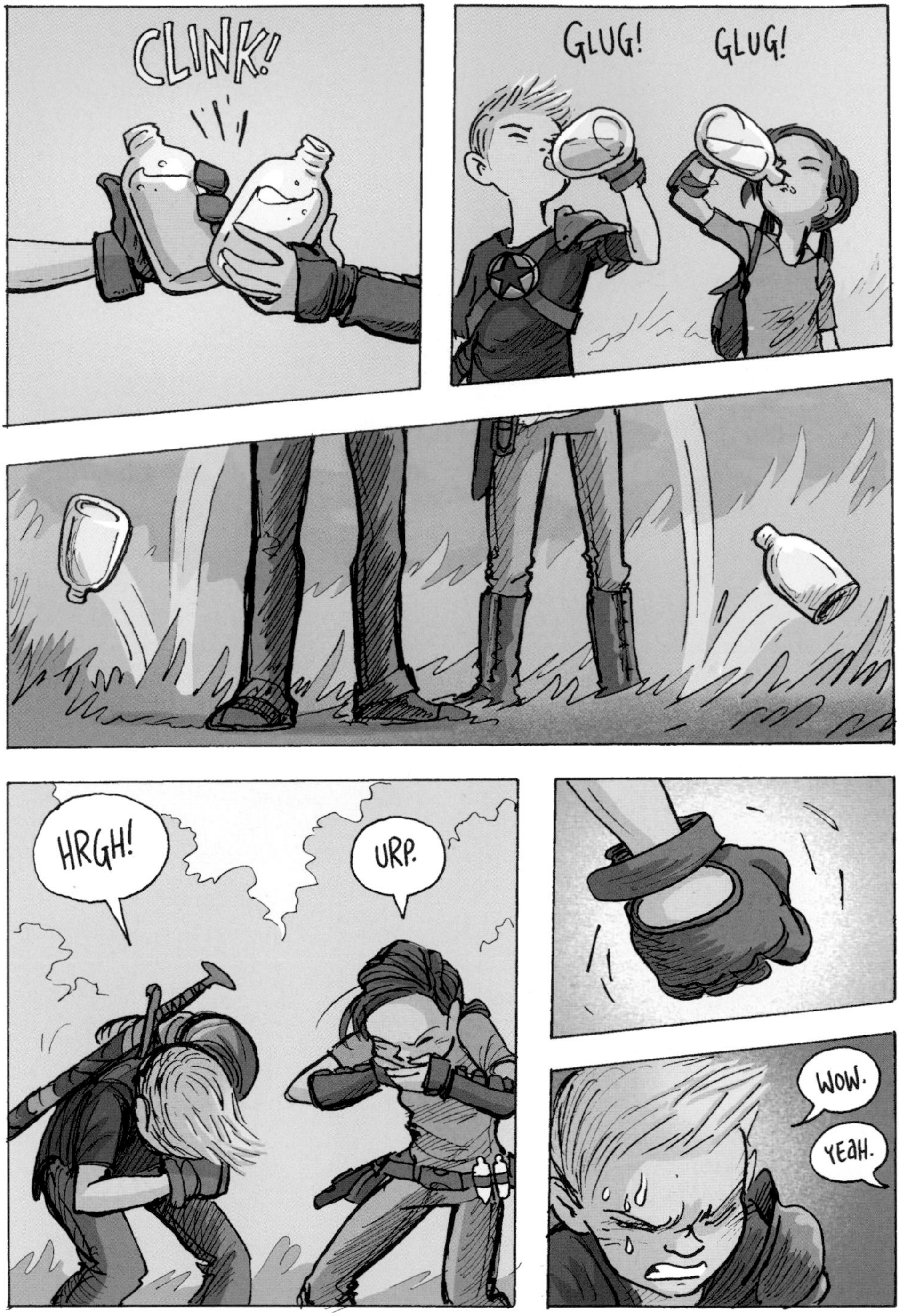
CLINK!
GLUG!
GLUG!
HRGH!
URP.
WOW.
YEAH.

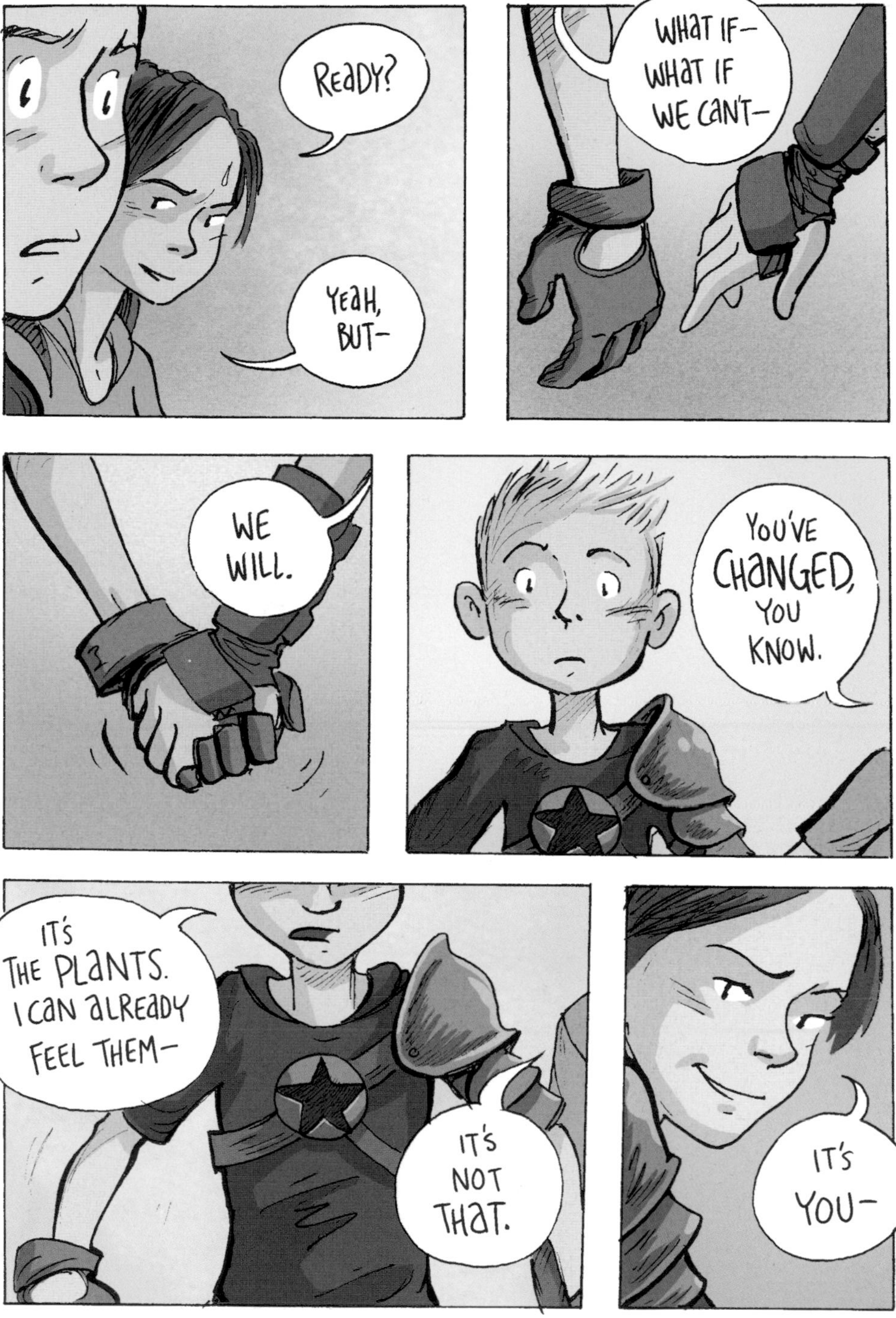
READY?
YEAH, BUT–
WHAT IF– WHAT IF WE CAN'T–
WE WILL.
YOU'VE CHANGED, YOU KNOW.
IT'S THE PLANTS. I CAN ALREADY FEEL THEM–
IT'S NOT THAT.
IT'S YOU–

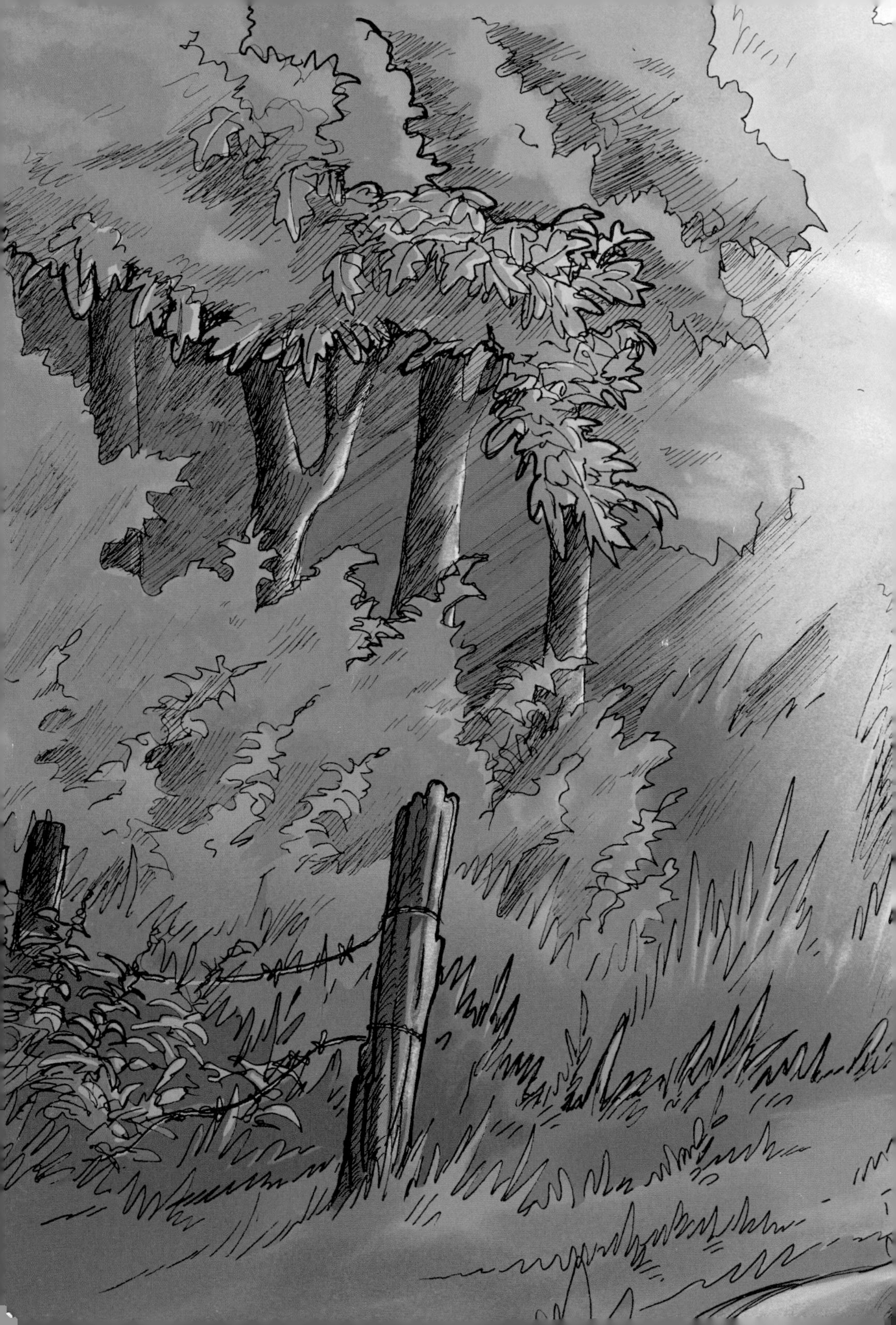